Praise for

*Rockstarlet*

"If ROCKSTARLET were a reality show it would be GAY ROCK STAR SURVIVOR. Instead, with its detail, dialogue and drama, it's a great read."

—Kate Clinton, humorist; author of *What the L?*

"Stewart Lewis's ROCKSTARLET is a sexy, dishy tale of finding oneself amidst the moral wasteland of the music industry. Though Lewis's novel is undeniably fiction, it could easily have been taken from the lives of some of today's leading closeted pop stars. In this fast-paced story of scandal and corruption, Lewis has a sharp eye for the nuances of the glitterati and a sensitivity to the pressures of hiding one's sexuality in a straight world. For anyone who's ever dreamed of being famous, ROCKSTARLET is the ultimate fantasy read."

—Tom Dolby, author of *The Trouble Boy*

"Rollicking good read...a deliciously fun-filled, true-to-life tour of today's rock stardom...this book rocks!"

—Melissa de la Cruz, author of *The Fashionista Files*

# Rockstarlet

a novel

by

Stewart Lewis

 alyson books
NEW YORK

ALL CHARACTERS IN THIS BOOK ARE FICTITIOUS. ANY RESEMBLENCE TO REAL INDI-VIDUALS-EITHER LIVING OR DEAD-IS STRICTLY COINCIDENTAL.
© 2006 BY STEWART LEWIS. ALL RIGHTS RESERVED.

MANUFACTURED IN THE UNITED STATES OF AMERICA.

THIS TRADE PAPERBACK ORIGINAL IS PUBLISHED BY ALYSON BOOKS,
P.O. BOX 1253, OLD CHELSEA STATION, NEW YORK, NEW YORK 10113-1251.
DISTRIBUTION IN THE UNITED KINGDOM BY TURNAROUND PUBLISHER SERVICES LTD.,
UNIT 3, OLYMPIA TRADING ESTATE, COBURG ROAD, WOOD GREEN,
LONDON N22 6TZ ENGLAND.

FIRST EDITION: MARCH 2006

06 05 04 03 02 a 10 9 8 7 6 5 4 3 2 1

ISBN 1-55583-909-6
ISBN-13 978-1-55583-909-3

LYRICS FROM "COMING UP FOR AIR" BY PATTY LARKIN ARE REPRINTED COURTESY OF THE ARTIST..

LIBRARY OF CONGRESS CATALOGING-IN-PUBLICATION DATA
HAS BEEN APPLIED FOR.

CREDITS
COVER PHOTOGRAPH © LAWRENCE MANNING/CORBIS.
AUTHOR PHOTOGRAPH BY RUSSELL DUCHAND.
COVER DESIGN BY MATT SAMS.

For my dad

# ACKNOWLEDGMENTS

I'd like to thank: my family for always being there; Angela Brown for believing; Tiffany Watson for her discerning eye; Christopher Schelling for his graciousness and sharp wit; Neil Fieneman, Michael Braverman, and Eric Diamond for reading drafts and sharing wisdom.

Nick, Hilary, Michelle, Vicka, Bruce, Manon, Paul, Manuela, Kat, Simon, Mark, Reed, Ryan, K Starr, Greg, Mike, Bradford, Amos, Motha, Ken, Joy, GSD—there are pieces of you all between these covers.

Russell Swanson for giving me a life-size map of the world; Michael Aisner for loyalty, love, and thinking outside the box; John Rechy for being the most inspiring teacher I ever had; Michael Dichand for his generous support of my music career; Mia Sole for reading me the Raymond Carver stories that first encouraged me to write.

Kate Gibson for being the most passionate, dedicated editor I could've ever dreamed of.

And especially Tom Dolby, whose insight, inspiration, and contribution have been priceless.

"Distrust any enterprise that requires new clothes."
—*Henry David Thoreau*

My life began and ended on the day I signed my first record deal.

As I waited in the spacious, streamlined entrance of Virgin Records, my trendy, hungover manager, Aden, kept nudging me to uncross my legs. I wanted to scream.

"Think aloof, think heroin addict," he whispered.

Even though I was about to sign a major recording contract, part of me was still an excitable boy who liked to giggle and amuse. Aden was squinting his eyes in a methodical, controlled way—sliding the rim of his glasses repeatedly up the slope of his perfect nose. He insisted I appear heterosexual at all times. "I'm not sure you understand how imperative the situation is. We're talking about making or breaking your career."

I changed sofas to get away from Aden and did a small pirouette just to push it. He gave me a look of sheer terror even though the black-bobbed receptionist hadn't noticed.

Aden's boyfriend, the legendary songwriter and co-manager of my career, Derek Jacobs, tried to disguise his laugh as a cough. Even under Aden's meticulous eye, Derek appreciated my antics.

Ten years Aden's senior, and adorable in that aging, Jewish kind of way, Derek was charming, quick, and easy on the eyes. He, too, was an artist, having written three smash singles for pop stars, in the process cultivating a core group of Hollywood A-listers in his court.

Aden's category was that of the highly neurotic, alcoholic Hollywood wife. Though quite articulate and convincing, he fancied himself "CEO" of the management company that was purely based on Derek's money and contacts. Derek and Aden had been together for years, though no one had ever seen them touch each other. The only proof they ever had was a picture in their hallway where Derek's arm rested tentatively over Aden's shoulder. Their smiles looked drugged, faces shiny. If you looked closely, in the background you could just make out Sting and his wife, Trudy.

When we'd first arrived in New York for the meeting, there was a faint snow swirling over Madison Avenue. With our tanned skin and wide eyes, the three of us were clearly LA transplants. Virgin Records had flown us out and put us up in a boutique hotel whose elevator showed esoteric images on a tiny flat screen and contained furniture that looked like a high-end version of IKEA.

"This place was very in last year," Aden said. "During the boutique hotel craze. The lighting is far too subdued."

Aden could find a flaw in everything and was the guru of hip. Though slightly worried and apprehensive about my impending life change, I was delighted with the chicness of our surroundings and felt a wonderful sense of beginning: the start of my glamorous foray into inevitable rock stardom. At least that was the plan.

While styling my hair in our suite before the meeting, Aden reiterated that I must emanate all things "hetero." He had a habit of using pop-culture icons to describe things, as if celebrities were the obvious standard by which to judge everything.

"Very Pete Yorn," he said, while perfectly messing up my spiky, dirty-blonde hair. "You look twenty-eight, definitely."

To Aden and the cruel world of the image-obsessed entertainment business, thirty was over the hill. I had just turned thirty-three, and he was obsessively opposed to letting anyone in on my real age. Aden's constant diatribes resulted in a mantra that floated in and out of my head: *I'm straight, I'm twenty-eight, and my hair is very Pete Yorn.*

Aden described my sound as contemporary emo-pop with a slight edge. Heartfelt lyrics about break-ups and get-back-togethers, but not syrupy—more poetic, all infused with drum loops, a raw acoustic guitar sound, computer bleeps, and an occasional fuzzy guitar or melodic keyboard line.

"Just remember in the meeting that you need to have an edge," he said, "but still be soft. You've got to appeal to soccer moms and teenagers alike. Emotional, yet icy." I often wondered if he even listened to his own circular logic. Most of the time it was probably the chardonnay talking.

"John Mayer meets Michael Stipe."

"Michael Stipe's gay!" I retorted.

"Bi, but he didn't come out until well after he became established. I mean look at Elton..."

Aden constantly had to remind everyone that he was a friend of Elton John's, when in reality Elton probably only knew Aden as that mousy friend of Derek Jacobs.

"By the way, Elton *loved* your demo," Aden told me, as if he had just enjoyed a long breakfast with him. "His interest is clearly piqued, and you know he helps out young artists all the time..."

"Yeah, the ones who give him blow jobs," I said.

"Please Jackson, must you always turn everything into fellatio?"

This was the only time I had ever referenced a blow job in Aden's presence, but who knows what prescription drugs were kicking around in his brain at that moment. Between him and Derek, their master bathroom could have passed for a pharmacy.

As Aden was putting the finishing touches on my hair, I got a call on my cell phone from Neil, my best friend and the real engine behind Clean Slate Management. Even Neil, whom I knew was just as connected to his inner Bette Davis as I was, was now telling me to tone it down for the meeting.

"You mean I can't wear a cropped T-shirt and short shorts?" I said.

"Only for me, darling."

I wished. Neil was an immaculately dressed bargain shopper who'd never had a pimple. He was, as Aden would say, "very Martha Stewart" and spent a lot of time gardening and cooking in his Los Feliz home. He was cute, Italian, had teeth white as snow, and always gave great advice. With a big smile and a giant heart, there wasn't anything he wouldn't do for me. Naturally, I'd had a crush on him from the moment I'd met him. But I felt it would never actualize since we worked so closely together. There were moments when we had come close to kissing, but it never happened.

"I know you'll be great," he said. "Just try to relax, and ignore Aden as much as possible."

At that moment, Aden was picking imaginary lint off my shirt in a fit of anxiousness. I laughed. "Trust me, I'm trying. Listen, we have to go now, but I'll call you when it's over."

An underling in a chic black suit came out and greeted us in the Virgin reception area. She led us into Clyde Anson's high-windowed office, where Clyde shook my hand warmly and asked us all to sit down. While he and Derek made small talk, I tried to unobtrusively look around the room. Gold and platinum albums and framed promotional posters lined the walls. I looked at the artists' faces, their confident eyes seeming on top of the world—was I going to be one of them? Was I going to fit into a marketing box that would become a machine to replenish the outrageous sums of money Virgin would invest in me? Or would I be one of the 12,000 artists a year who make records that never hit the stores, or get dropped because I wore the wrong clothes?

I glanced at Aden, who was trying to act like he was part of Derek and Clyde's conversation. He caught my eye and looked me up and down for any offending signs of gayness. I pointedly turned away from him. Like I wasn't nervous enough already!

To Aden and many people in the music industry, there was a difference between being a glam rocker and a pop star. Eyeliner and scarves were okay if you were Robert Smith or Steven Tyler, but when you were trying to be a folk-pop-rocker type that look was simply uncool, not to mention too "gay." Apparently gay doesn't sell to teenage girls, a demographic gold mine for label execs like Clyde Anson, who know that when it comes down to it, it's a business. I was paranoid that Clyde would catch something in my eye or my body language that would give me away. He was known for his unpredictability, though he seemed perfectly nice right now. I had flashes in my mind of him yanking the contract out of my hands.

After the small talk was over, it was time to sign. Derek's lawyer had gone over the contract earlier, so all I had to do was write my name. I had been waiting ten years for this. My pinkie twitched as I picked up the silver pen and reached to sign. Dampness formed on my inner palm, and I felt a drop of sweat trickle from my armpit down my side. Derek smiled like a proud father, and Aden tried to look cool and collected, but thumbed his glasses and let out a thin, nervous smile.

I handed the signed contract back to Clyde, who offered me a cigar. I couldn't think of anything more repulsive at that moment, but I coolly obliged. Aloof, disconnected rock star, I told myself. Keep calm. We stank up the entire office while Clyde played my song, "Got Even" on the surround-sound stereo. As always, the pronouns in the song were not gender specific. It was all about "you."

While blowing the thick, rank smoke out of my mouth, I had a quiet smile on my face over the fact that the particular "you" in that song referred to a male professor of mine whom I'd dated in college.

> *I hated to see you go*
> *with baited breath my heart slowed*
> *and the back of you looked so beautiful in that light*
> *that I will always remember that night*

We put out our expensive cigars and I shook hands again with Clyde, remembering to keep my grip firm. I noticed that he had sexy wrists and shunned the thought. Back in the reception area, Miss Black-Bob arranged a limo back to our hotel. It smelled of cleanliness, leather, and promise.

"Hey, kiddo, get used to this," Derek told me as the limo navigated the crowded streets.

I looked out at the New Yorkers flooding the sidewalks, rushing through the cold, determined and alive. This is what I've always wanted, I thought. I've finally signed a record deal. And after my first record hits, I'll get a boyfriend and a dog, not necessarily in that order.

"You need to keep your hair long," Aden said out of the blue, "not Adam Duritz long, more like Rob Thomas long."

I tried to ignore him. There were times, and this was one of them, when you simply had to turn Aden off. Open the ear channel and let it pass right through.

I called my mother from my cell phone and told her it was official. She started crying.

"Can you believe it?" I asked.

"You did it, angel!"

I heard my father in the background saying, "Yay, Jackson!"

My parents were always in the front row of my high school talent shows, and I never doubted their unconditional love and support. I spoke to my mom on a regular basis, and her motherly role had morphed into more of a friendship.

"I had to be totally butch. Dad would have been proud."

Mom laughed. Dad was the bad cop regarding the sexuality issue, and though he had accepted it, he tended to side with Aden, having dabbled in music law and become savvy about music industry no-no's.

"Well, I don't care how you got there, just show me the money."

Mom fantasized about being flown around the world by her rock-star son. I felt proud knowing this could actually become a reality if I was lucky.

"After my record goes platinum, I'll set up an IV of cash flow directly into your accessories."

"Fabulous. There's always room for more jewelry in my box."

I could hear Dad let out a groan in the background. He didn't like when Mom and I talked about hair or shoes and couldn't fathom how I used to spend entire days with her at the mall. He only shopped catalogues.

"Okay, well, some celebration is in order here," I said. "I'll call you again later."

I hung up and looked at Derek's warm eyes and smiled.

When you wish for something so much you begin to believe it's not real. So when it actually comes true, you feel like you're inside a dream.

# 2

Until I'd come up against Aden and Dad's strong feelings about the need to act hetero, it had honestly never occurred to me that my sexuality would be an issue in my music career. I'd had a similar kind of blind confidence going into my first same-sex experience back in high school.

I was fifteen and my best friend, Chris, was eighteen. We did just about everything together—first hit of acid, finding girls, driving around in his father's Peugeot smoking but not inhaling cigarettes while listening to Dire Straits on ten, getting in a car accident, acting opposite each other in a school play, being caught with stolen Budweiser on the side of the road by bored, small-town police.

One night after a long party, we were driven home by a crazy townie named Rusty, in his Trans Am. Chris and I were in the back and I started to get sleepy, so I lay down on the seat with my head in his lap. The streetlights gave the inside of the car a slow heartbeat, flashes of gentle light. As he put his hand on my head, I felt completely safe for the first time—even with Rusty the drunken landscaper speeding us through the streets.

When we reached my house, the field behind it was frosted and steaming. It had to have been one in the morning, with not even the sounds of distant cars. Just stillness, and our soft footsteps walking down the driveway. We shivered as we entered the house, chilled by the crisp air.

There were two beds in my room, and I always slept on the one by the window. Chris always slept on the one along the wall, just as at his house I always slept on the top bunk. That day my mother had stacked heaps of things on the spare bed. For several years, I would think about the results of that simple act. What if she hadn't been cleaning out the closets on that particular Friday?

Without thinking or speaking, Chris and I stripped down and

got into my bed, then held each other closely through the whole night, like angels. We were innocence defined, unaware of circumstances or hidden agendas, simply basking in a beautiful experience. Not needing to actually have sex. It was a newfound freedom. A wonderful risk.

I don't remember much of the morning after, but I do remember this: One night shortly afterward I stole my mother's car (she had gone away with Dad for the weekend), and we went to a concert. We were in a part of the city underneath train tracks—dimly lit warehouses, bits of paper scurrying in the wind. It was the sort of place that breeds a mysterious excitement, too quiet not to have something looming in the shadows. I took a turn too sharply and ran over the median, giving both tires on the left flats.

I could hear my heart beating wildly, but Chris was the perfect person to be with. He was my best friend. I was so scared, yet I also felt that somehow it would be okay. In the cab on the way home I watched him sleep. When we said goodnight, there was a moment of silence as we stood face to face, not touching. A moment of nothing that meant everything. We were falling in love.

The next morning we got Rusty to drive us from our Boston suburb to Providence to get the car fixed before my parents came home. I drove back alone, Chris in the other car. He kept looking back through the rear window, checking on me. Since my parents were still away that night we drank cheap beer and cranked Van Halen. At the end of the night we got into my parents' king-size bed. After a frenzied pillow fight, we collapsed and lay still for what seemed an hour. Suddenly he jumped on top of me. I touched his rock-hard penis as if it were some magical thing, surging and warm and perfectly shaped. We just rubbed against each other with startled eyes until sounds emerged from our throats, high-pitched cries that were uncharacteristic of our normal voices. After we simultaneously came, he dropped his mouth onto mine as if it was his long-awaited reward, the prize at the bottom of the cereal box. His lips were like pieces of a cloud.

After that evening, it only happened once more. I was in his bedroom on the top bunk and he gently pushed on the bottom of my mattress. I came down to his bed. Halfway through he stopped—told me he was "feeling heterosexual." I was angry and didn't understand what he was going through—he looked different after we actually did it, like he knew it couldn't go on. I wanted it to, but after that moment he became emotionally unavailable. We never were that close again.

The strange thing was that I went to college and had a girlfriend my freshman year, not even looking at or thinking about another man. It wasn't until my handsome professor called me in at the end of second semester to go over my sophomore courses that I again thought of a male in a sexual way. I looked at his hand resting on the desk, turning an unlit cigarette through his slightly tanned, slender fingers. The masculinity and beauty of it struck me—equal amounts of grace and strength.

That was it. Though I wouldn't really act on it till months later, that was it. I knew.

# 3

When we got back to the hotel lobby, Aden booked our victory dinner at the latest über-hip Lower East Side restaurant, confirming on the phone with the hostess that the décor was "industrial chic." He told her, "A corner table preferably, we've got a rising star in our party." I noticed the concierge roll his eyes.

I excused myself and smoked a victory joint in my room. I drew a bath and called Neil in Los Angeles.

"For the cover of my first album, I want a shot of me naked, preferably taken by Bruce Weber, and I shall be emerging out of a giant white lily—like a birth."

"Right, honey, Aden will really go for that. So it went well, I take it?"

"You should have seen Aden watching my every move like a hawk. Although I did sneak in a pirouette."

"Oh Lord, don't even tell me."

Like almost everyone that came in contact with the pair, Neil had a warm spot for Derek and an icy chill for Aden. He had been putting up with their dysfunctional world for almost four years and it was wearing him thin. He told me once that part of the reason he hadn't left Clean Slate was that he felt in his heart I would take the company to new ground.

As it was, Derek's ground was starting to get a little shaky. He was considered old school and lately had mostly been writing cheesy music for TNT movies starring washed-up celebrities trying to hurl themselves back from obscurity. Neil had told me he suspected Derek's main reason for taking that kind of work was that it kept Aden in all the little luxuries he had come to expect. Neil was the one who picked my demo out of the haystack and made them listen. Of course, if you asked Aden, he would say only he was responsible for discovering me. But we knew the real truth.

"Neil, we did it."

"I know, sweetheart. I'm proud that you put up with the A-word and let us take you there."

"It's unbelievable. I feel like I should trash this hotel room or something."

"That is so Eighties, dear. Now you have to adopt an African child or paint 'make trade fair' on your forehead. It's about using your power in humanitarian ways."

"Well," I took a hit and slid into the warm, peach-scented water, "right now I'm supporting a fabulous New York City delivery service, titled, 'Weed Deliver.'"

"Whitney, are you stoned already?" Neil asked.

He had called me that ever since Whitney Houston got arrested with marijuana at an airport.

"Of course, darling, and I'm about to pop open some Moët."

"From the room?" This was Neil's practical, motherly side coming through, even though it was clearly time for celebration. "You know they'll charge an arm and a—"

"I just signed a record deal! Besides, it's on Virgin. Moët from the mini!!"

Neil laughed his endearing, boyish laugh. "Not incidentals, princess, those are on us. But you do deserve it. All I can say is, what's going to happen when you're *really* famous?"

"Then this bath I'll be taking will be in Moët."

"I'm so proud of you," he said, his voice a little thin. Neil, along with Derek, had worked so hard to get me to this moment. Aden had done his part, too, but I knew that Derek let Aden take a lot of undeserved credit just because he was a good guy. He didn't need the credit himself, so he was happy to have Aden soak up the spotlight.

"I couldn't have done it without you guys."

"Listen, you're doing *Interview*'s top ten new artists to watch tomorrow, and Ingrid, the journalist, seems highly unimpressed, like she'd rather be writing for the *Times*. But if Timothy Meyer is there, be sure to make a connection with him."

"Why, can he get good pot?"

Neil made a *yeah, right* noise.

"He's the senior editor, dear. Runs the show. And Whitney, put down the crack pipe."

Smoking pot and taking baths were two of my favorite recreational activities. Neil, although known to suck down a few cocktails, didn't smoke and felt it was a bit passé.

There was a knock at the door. It was Derek. I told him to come in. He cracked the door open.

"Hey, darling, meet us in the lobby soon, okay?"

"I'll be right down, sweetie," I called out from the bath. If the record executives knew we called each other sweetie and darling, they'd probably shit their Prada. I made one more call on the hotel phone, to my friend Brian, massage therapist to the stars.

"I did it, honey, I'm going to be a rock star."

"Don't you know you always were? This is just the planets aligning for you."

Brian was bald and bohemian, tattooed and very into the spiritual side of things. My spirituality ended with finding the perfect outfit.

"Well, now I may actually see a paycheck," I said.

"Right. But remember, mo' money, mo' problems."

Brian frequently pretended he was ghetto fabulous, despite being a white boy with a passion for aromatherapy and herbal detoxifiers. Once you'd been around him for a while, the contrast didn't seem so jarring.

"I'd rather that than no money, mo' problems. You should have seen me, Bri, I was very butch."

"Yeah right, until you opened your mouth and Judy Garland's purse fell out."

"Actually, I didn't say much."

"Well, I hope Derek did most of the talking and not the A-word."

I splashed a little while reaching for more champagne, and he said, "Oh, you're in the bath, something new and different."

"Yes, but now I'm employed by Virgin records. And by the way, I'm thinking of writing you into the budget because clearly massage is essential to my well-being."

"Fo' sho, honey," he said. "Listen, gotta scram. I need to work some knots out of another Hollywood power lesbian. Congrats, baby!!"

"Thanks."

"Keep it real," he said.

Somehow, a white bald guy saying "keep it real" just didn't work. I laughed anyway.

After some rapid exfoliation and moisturizing, I put on an oversized tee and baggy jeans (this was all part of my new "straight" wardrobe) but snuck in a faux-fur belt just for a little flair. I headed down to the sleek, understated lobby. Aden was on his second martini and chatting up a sexy WAM (waiter/actor/model) in the lounge. Derek was oblivious to Aden's slutty behavior, reading the *New Yorker* and nursing a Campari. He had a slight smile on his face, as if he knew he was about to get a present of some kind.

He expertly folded a page of the magazine back and said, "I just read the cartoons—they're so brilliant."

"Hey, sport," Aden said, turning away from the WAM, "all clean?"

"Yes."

Aden snorted in his irritated, impatient way. "Jackson, did you just get high?"

"Yes. Why? Are we taping *Oprah* tonight?" At the mention of Oprah, the WAM quickly turned his attention from Aden to me.

Derek looked up from the magazine and deadpanned, "No, *Total Request Live.*"

As Aden let out one of his how-do-I-put-up-with-you sighs, the WAM said, "Cool!"

This was yet another issue Aden harped on, my pot smoking. Although clearly it was okay for him to down four martinis, a couple of bumps of coke, and a bottle of white every night.

Derek came to my rescue. "Aden, it's fine, he's a rock star now;

he can get high."

"I know. It's just a slippery slope."

Derek looked at him as if to say, *You mean the slope you've been on for five years?*

Aden glared at Derek, whose body language deflated. Derek's resistance to Aden was rarely verbalized, but I could read it in his eyes. I didn't understand his attraction to Aden, but I'd always loved Derek from the minute I met him. Derek was a disarming, lovable, witty, pushover on pills.

The entire cab ride was filled with the sound of Aden's voice talking about how hip the restaurant was, how hip the area was becoming, how hip his new French-cuffed Parisian shirt was, and how hip my first record was going to be. (I did listen carefully to that part.)

Derek was busy trying to pronounce the cab driver's name. Though the oldest of us all by far, Derek was the most connected to his inner child. He was like a flighty, somewhat disheveled, middle-aged boy. There was something in the way his eyes rested on me that made me feel peaceful. In a way, he grounded Aden's chaos, so maybe they were right for each other.

On the street, I told Aden, "When I go on tour, I want Neil to be my tour manager."

Aden laughed. "Neil is not qualified for that sort of thing. He's our assistant, Jackson, remember that. He's in his place."

I didn't bother to contradict his cold words this time because I'd heard them all before. Aden was jealous of Neil, partly because Neil was younger and cuter, and partly because Neil and I had become such close friends. More important, on some level he had to know that Neil was the backbone of the company, which threatened his delusion that Clean Slate existed solely because of his efforts.

When we got to the restaurant, it was, in fact, industrial chic, complete with aluminum walls, steel tables, and brushed cement floors. It resided on a Lower East Side street that used to be junkie land, now overflowing with dressed-down models and sexy career girls with expensive hair, ordering fifteen-dollar martinis to accompany their Dover sole.

At the end of the meal we toasted to Clean Slate Management and Virgin records, and the promising future of new recording artist Jackson Poole. Yours truly.

"I knew from the moment I heard your voice you were destined for greatness," Derek said with watery eyes.

"Thanks, you guys, for everything."

"You're more than welcome, Jackson," Aden said, then lifted up my shirt, "but please, lose the belt. It's too *Will & Grace*."

Silence at the table. Aden went on.

"You can repay the favor by being as heterosexual as possible at the *Interview* shoot tomorrow. Oh! And I need you to help me come up with a more detailed bio for the press, preferably with lots of previous girlfriends."

I downed the rest of my drink and took a deep breath.

"Jackson, please. You realize the media coverage Virgin has planned for you? You could be doing as many as ten, twenty interviews a day—they don't sink several million dollars into an artist who won't be press worthy, who won't eventually pay back the debt you have created for them. It's a huge risk, and I know I've told you this before, but if an inkling of your sexuality is revealed you could be dropped as fast as you can say—"

"Size queen?"

Derek laughed. Aden went to the bathroom in a huff. Was it really as bad as he said? Would I have to spend hours talking about my previous girlfriends and who I thought would win the Super Bowl? I could just see the look on my dad's face if during an interview, when asked about the Super Bowl, I said something like, "Is that baseball?"

Reminder to Jackson: Inflate and exploit hetero past.

# 4

That night as I lay in bed I wondered what would come next. Was I going to be recognized everywhere? No longer be an anonymous civilian? Check into hotels under assumed names?

It had not always been easy. I remember being booked at a sports bar where the stage was actually a cage suspended above the bar. They kept the TVs on during my performance, and I almost cried. And that wasn't the only place that wasn't exactly what musicians refer to as "listening rooms." At times it had felt just so humiliating—especially driving in a beat-up Honda eight hours from one shitty gig to the next.

But if I looked hard enough, I could always find some ray of hope—a smile from a counter cappuccino girl pausing to connect with a line from one of my songs or a fascinated kid who abandoned his parents to stand nearby and watch me sing.

In trying to dredge up my hetero past for Aden, I immediately thought of Autumn. There were fans that followed me from gig to gig, and among the groupies in the early years, none stuck in my mind as much as her. Aside from our brush with the law, Aden would have thought she was perfect to name drop at *Teen People*.

I was playing for tips in a small club in the Northwest on a slightly raised corner stage—a big improvement over the cage at the sports bar. There were flies hovering in the single, lonely spotlight, as if the previous musician had a voice of nectar. It was the sort of small town where residents talk about two things: how small it is and when they are going to move somewhere else. Some actually did move, but the ones who didn't wore their envy like a wound.

Three songs into my set I noticed an older woman straining to watch me over the cowboy hat of the man in front of her. She had a look of relief on her hardened, ruddy face. After my first set the lady smiled at me and slipped a twenty-dollar bill into the warmth of my pocket.

"I feel like listening to your music took me to another place."

"Wow, thanks." One of the reasons I loved performing. To *move* people.

"No, thank you, young man. That was just what I needed." She slid her hand onto the small of my back and said, "Now, let me introduce you to my granddaughter, Autumn. I think you kids will get along."

I thought, oh no, a small-town girl, but quickly obliged.

She led me over to a girl who was resting her head on the bar, using her forearms as a pillow. I was pleasantly surprised by her raspberry shoulder-length wig and knowing smirk.

"C'mere," she sat up, grabbing me, "you and I need to go to my place, put on rubber boots and play Twister."

Her purse was a miniature lunchbox with a picture of a woman flexing her biceps on it, circa the 1950s.

"Cool," I said.

"You can look inside."

I indulged and found lavender nail polish, a severed extension cord, a grape lollipop, and eleven dollars.

"What's this for?" I pointed to the cord.

"Oh! It's for the pickle trick. Here, hang on." She motioned for the waitress. "Honey, can you get me a pickle spear?" Several people nearby gave me looks that read, *You have no idea who you're getting acquainted with.*

"Can I get a plug-in?" She asked brashly and to no one in particular.

"Over there, Autumn," the bartender said reluctantly, pointing to the end of the bar.

"Okay, c'mere." A few people gathered around as Autumn stuck the severed end of the cord into the pickle flesh and plugged it in. The seeds and the pulp started to bubble and spark, and a slow flame built, bursting out the pickle's insides.

When it was over, a few people laughed and clapped. We sat

back down and she asked me what I thought.

"Astounding," I said, mock serious. "Better than *Cats*."

"I know. I gotta get a new gig; I'm thinking maybe jalapeños."

She broke the silence that followed with, "I wish my cousin Duane was here, he always has a pile of cocaine and a *great* attitude."

"Hey, you fancy a joint?" I asked.

"Does Dolly Parton sleep on her back?"

I had to think for a second.

We stepped out the side door into the alley and took turns on the joint. At that point I wasn't thinking about record deals or where my next gig was or the fact that Autumn was a girl, I was just aware of the cool air and the soft light in the alley and the smoke lingering in silent wisps above our heads. I was not thinking that this was the start of anything or that Autumn would enter my life sharply and quickly, working to heat and expose the insides, like the cord in the pickle, and then disappear.

And I was not thinking that within the next few hours, the two of us would be cuffed and in the back of a police car, sharing a charged and impulsive first kiss, our hands behind our backs.

We ended up getting beers and drinking them in the alley, singing cheesy songs from our childhood. A cop came and told us someone who lived nearby had complained about our loud voices. We mouthed off a little and he ended up cuffing us, saying he was taking us in for being drunk and disorderly. After we kissed, I heard Autumn's grandmother calling the cop by name, telling him to release us into her care or she would tell his wife about his extracurricular activities at the strip club she did the books for. It worked and we giggled as he took our cuffs off.

For the next couple of weeks, Autumn came on tour and sold my CDs for me. After the shows we would make out in the dingy hotel rooms and talk about life. Though fleeting, it felt right, as if both of us were gathering a piece of a puzzle that would eventually make us whole. She went off to art school at the end of the summer, and although we wrote each other off and on, she eventually found a steady boyfriend who was, funny enough, in a rock band. Our correspondence faded out, although according to Aden, I should milk that experience as being more than just a summer fling. But clearly the public would see a gap in my heterosexual history, as they did with other stars that were not "out" but whose oscillations were common knowledge. Whatever, it was about the music anyway, right?

# 5

When I woke up my mouth was dry and the sheets were ruffled, and I had to orient myself to where I was: hotel, New York, becoming a rock star. I was immediately consumed by overwhelming happiness. I'd gotten a record deal!

I'd dreamed I was the It-Boy. Neil was explaining to a promoter that they must put only orange M&M's in my dressing room, and I was being chased by groupies everywhere I went. I was caught in flashes by sleazy paparazzi. It was fabulous.

I got out of bed and swilled a bottle of Evian.

It seemed fitting that my first big-time interview would be with *Interview* magazine—a publication I used to gape wide-eyed at as a kid. They shot me in an old car with a baseball hat on, in an alley covered in snow near their offices. The snow on the car was artificial and somehow kept getting in my eyes. By that time my hangover had kicked in.

Out of respect for Aden—or was it fear?—I waited until he went to get espressos to talk shoes with Sergio, who was doing my hair. We agreed that the new Gucci collection ruled and that Miu Miu was overrated.

After the shoot we went into the offices, and the interview was pretty painless. I explained that I grew up in a musical household, that my parents were in fact part of a country and western band, that I'd started out playing drums, and at the mere age of five I was thrown onstage with a tambourine.

"Very Partridge Family, but more hip of course, more rootsy," Aden said.

Ingrid, the pale, fifty-something interviewer, seemed to like that almost as much as the latte she was lapping up. Neil was right; she looked like she should be at the *Times*—less artsy and more pedantic. Not amused to say the least. Thank god somebody brought her the latte.

Mr. Senior Editor, Timothy Meyer, showed up and I told him how much I'd always admired his magazine, how I used to cut out all the pictures when I was little. He was in a suit (can you say weakening knees?) and extremely attractive. He looked like an even more approachable Richard Gere, circa *Pretty Woman.* Salt and pepper at the temples. Essential for any meal.

Aden was chatting up the assistants, telling them how huge I was about to become. Little did he know I was literally huge on account of Timothy Meyer and his Armani suit. The bulge in my pants grew after Timothy loosened his tie and undid two buttons on his shirt, and I decided to excuse myself for a quick release.

When I returned, Derek was busy picking over the refreshment table, smelling a brownie before eating a bite and putting it back. He was pudgy and counting, but it was all part of his charm. Derek could simply do no wrong. Except of course, in choosing the A-word.

But who was I to complain? I was getting a full spread in *Interview.* And later I was going to meet Damian Blue, the acclaimed Canadian producer who was slated to helm my Virgin debut. They were doing something right.

After the interview was over, Ingrid told me it was nice to work with an artist who had not yet become jaded. What did that make Miss Morose herself, happy-go-lucky? I thanked her, and she walked me down the hallway. I peeked into Timothy Meyer's office to say good-bye. He was on the phone but slipped me his business card after writing his cell number on the back. He covered the mouthpiece with his big left hand, giving me a faint wink as he said, "Keep in touch."

I turned to leave. Had I imagined the wink? I glanced back for one last look, and he gestured with his hand against his heart, exaggerating the beat, widening his eyes.

As if choreographed, Aden instantly appeared at my side.

"What, pray tell, was that?" he asked, while we walked toward the elevator.

"Nothing, he just wished me luck."

We got to the street and Aden basically stepped in front of a cab to stop it.

I held on to the business card in my pocket the whole way to the producer's place, as if it were a life preserver in the middle of a deserted ocean.

Damian Blue's house was a loft in Soho the size of a football field. (I did see a football game once when I was a kid.) There were long leather couches bookended by old jukeboxes and wiry exotic plants. Damian was drugged-out sexy and smelled of expensive cologne. His leather jacket had the kind of worn look designers strived for, but you could tell his had gotten there over time, naturally. His bushy hair was a shiny brown, and light blue eyes peered out from beneath his large brow.

"I used to live in Alphabet City, but you can't find this kind of space in that part of town. In some ways my heart never left," he said.

"Well, at least your body did."

Aden looked at me hard.

"That's not what I meant," I whispered.

"Arms," he whispered back. He was referring to the fact that my arms were on my hips. God, I even had to worry about where to put my arms?

Clearly, Damian Blue didn't care. He was too busy chopping up a rock of crystal meth. His speech was slow and stilted, which belied the slight British accent Aden had told me he picked up while in London engineering records for U2 and other bands.

"Your demos were spot-on," he said, swiftly forming four short lines with a razor blade. "I especially dug the one tune, what was it, 'Don't Go'?"

"It's called 'Go,'" Aden said.

"Yeah, 'Go,' that has a kickin' drum loop."

I'd done that loop myself, and instantly found myself approving of Damian.

"I want to see if I can get Alanis to do some backup, maybe a duet or something. I think her vibe," he paused to sniff a bump, "her sensibility, would match perfectly with your style."

Was I hearing this correctly? I tried to breathe. *Be aloof.* She was such a huge star!

"I think that would be uncanny," Aden said.

"Certainly," Derek said. The cool indifference thing was rubbing off on Derek and Aden as well—it was how these types of meetings went.

We each snorted our bump and I only did half of mine and secretly wiped the rest away. Aden began going on and on about how he discovered me and how his fingers are on the pulse of what kids are listening to. Damian was semi-ignoring him.

Finally, Derek cut in, "The thing about Jackson is that he appeals to such a broad demographic. I've seen his shows—there are teenagers, hipster moms, minorities, everyone."

"On the Norah Jones tip," Aden shot in.

"Right," Damian said. "What I would like to do is have you down to my studio in the BVI and really flesh out the preproduction, spend about five days down there—on Virgin, of course."

He was losing me now.

"British Virgin Islands," Derek whispered.

Right. Still trying to play cool, I took a sip of Pellegrino and it went down the wrong tube. While almost choking, I kept thinking of Damian, Alanis, and me on an exotic island doing preproduction. Jesus, it was really happening. I was becoming a rock star.

"You okay, mate?"

"He's fine," Aden said, hitting me hard on the back, making it worse. "It's probably the bubbles."

On our way back to the hotel, Aden was unbelievably quiet. Derek and I were thinking up baby names (we had both fantasized, separately, about having a kid).

"I always liked Harry," Derek said, "a solid name. Someone who could fix a stereo, make a casserole."

"Yeah, exactly what I think when I think Harry."

"And for a girl, Esther."

"Esther!? That sounds like the smelly girl in the fourth grade who brings sardines to school. What about something grand, like Gabriella."

"Mexican whore," Derek said.

We were sharing a pretzel we had bought on the street. My half was covered in mustard. He was picking the salt off his half.

"Not even," I said. "Okay, what about George?"

"Too geeky."

"Jeremiah."

"For a farm boy."

"Well, Derek, I'm at a loss."

"You know what I like? Jackson. Your name. It's a great name. It suits you."

I smiled.

When I got back to my room I entered Timothy Meyer's cell number into my Palm and ran another bath, letting it get real hot. I kept seeing Timothy's big hand in my head, tanned and brushing softly against mine as he handed me the card, his long fingers unbuttoning his shirt...

I read the latest issue of *Interview* and tried to picture myself gleaming off the page. It was all too unreal. I had to remind myself it was about the music and remembered what my tenth-grade music teacher had said: "You have a gift, Jackson, never lose it." After I got out of the tub, I strummed a few songs on my guitar and started writing a new song.

> *Is this just an illusion*
> *What I see in front of me*
> *A road unfolding, future holding*
> *My dreams*

# 6

"What you do behind closed doors is irrelevant. I don't care if you fuck sheep, and no one does. But every time you are in the public eye you will be scrutinized, trust me."

Aden and I were at the Royalton having cocktails before my flight back to LA. He was on me for attending a boy party by the Hudson River after my bath last night. Derek and Aden were leaving on a later flight, and since Derek was still sleeping off the three Ambien he took the night before, Aden was seeing me off. I wished it were the other way around.

"So you mean to say I can't go to a fucking gay bar?"

He was sweating, scratching at his temples. "No, you can't. It's as simple as that."

"That's the most ridiculous thing I've heard. What do you expect me to do?"

"Well this is what we have to talk about, Jackson, your change in lifestyle."

"So what, now I'm supposed to attend hockey games and go to tittie bars?"

"No, but seriously, there has to be a considerable alteration."

I had consumed one and a half martinis, so I was leaning toward sassy.

"The only thing I'll be altering is my Diesel jeans, so get over it."

Aden took a breath and sipped his gimlet.

"It's not about your fucking designer jeans, Jackson. It's about your future. You are not Savage Garden. You are not going to end up some tired queen with one cheese-ball, house-dance track hit under your leopard-skin belt."

"What do you mean, like Derek?" I admit, I was getting a little out of line, but it was clearly the Grey Goose talking.

"Jackson, don't start."

"Oh, come on, are we not sensing a little projection here?"

"Listen J, we shall continue this conversation back in LA, in the meantime, please, no more boy parties. And have you been getting your hetero history sorted? We have loads of interviews and you have to get your stories straight."

"Yeah, like the one where I slept with my male professor?"

"Jackson, this is not a joke!"

"I know, I know."

"And we are close to getting penciled in with Lonnie Simpson."

"Cool." I had heard he was the music-in-movies guy.

"Yeah, cool. But with him especially, you have to—"

"Dress in drag? I know."

Aden threw up his hands but actually smiled at that one.

On my way to the airport, I saw a billboard for Britney Spears's new record. She was sporting a ghetto-chic ho-bag dress with come-fuck-me boots.

How come only girls got to dress up?

My cab stopped short at a red light near Soho. I looked out the window and first noticed the black pinstripe Armani suit, the very same suit worn by the sultry senior editor of *Interview* magazine, Timothy Meyer. It was him, face into the wind, those big oval eyes scanning for a cab.

I tried to get his attention through the glass, but to no avail. As we left the light, I caught his profile in the early evening glow of Delancey Street. He was regal, stately. Walked with the ease of a dancer. I pictured the smooth, ripped curves of his body beneath the suit. I located his card in my wallet and stared at the numbers he had written on the back. A curvy sleight of hand, that seemed to dance on the page.

# 7

While waiting for the plane, I thought about my homework assignment from Aden: the hetero past. It seemed mostly every gay guy has dated a girl, at least once. I came out a little late and was actually bisexual for a short time when I first attended college. In the theatre-dance class I took with my first real girlfriend, Rita, the other students seemed to already know each other and were huddled together in the corners. The girls looked like Heidi with rosy cheeks and perfect skin, and the guys looked like they'd just returned from a Tony Robbins seminar, pearly white teeth and big game-show-host smiles.

I was intimidated at first, and the tiny, bubbly instructor, with Liza Minelli eyes and a fixed expression of surprise on her face, sensed my alienation and tried unsuccessfully to integrate me.

There was one girl who, like me, chose to linger in the back of the studio rather than vying for a space near the mirror like the Heidis and the Pat Sajacks, who were exaggerating their movements to outshine each other and impress the instructor. Rita looked like a tough New Yorker (very Rosie O'Donnell, Aden would say) and was slightly tomboyish in her Yankees tank top and backward baseball cap. Her face, although quite youthful, showed a resilience that suggested experience beyond her years. We shared an unspoken acknowledgment of the ludicrousness of our classmates. I knew that when it came down to pairing off, she would be my partner. The two outcasts.

A few weeks into the semester, after learning to waltz, she invited me over to her apartment. We got stoned and she made a fire. After an awkward silence, we started talking enthusiastically, the conversation flowing from subject to subject with a curious ease as if we'd known each other all along.

She showed me her room, which had a shrine to Prince on

the wall. It was one of those giant posters of their favorite band everyone had in high school. Hers was plastered with magazine cutouts—Prince on the cover of *Spin,* Prince with a dog collar, Prince looking mischievous between a pair of breasts, Prince clad in purple velvet—I thought it a bit over the top but reminded myself that I had seen *Purple Rain* three times when it had been in the theaters.

A few days later we went to a pub and did shots of whiskey and danced, for hours and hours. At one point the crowd formed a circle around us, and we milked it, even doing some of our routines from class. Later on, at her apartment, she put on a kettle for tea. As the water began to whistle, we started having a gentle pillow fight on her couch. She leaned into me and kissed me lightly on the neck, just below my ear. The kettle screamed and we stared at each other in slight shock.

"Um...I think I need to take you home," she said.

A simple kiss and everything seemed different. Perhaps her gaydar had been activated. At that point, I didn't even know *what* I was; I just liked being around her.

As she drove me home, snow started to appear from the sky, getting thicker by the second. The world around us was altered, the once-familiar surroundings were lit differently, had moved slightly. Like returning home and, without solid evidence, knowing someone had been there.

I got back to my little dorm room and stared at the ceiling for what seemed like hours but was only minutes. I walked over to the phone, placed my hand on it but didn't pick it up. I tried to choose some music but was distracted. Fuck it, I thought, and called her.

"How's Betty?" Betty was the name she had given her little blue car. It had been making a squeak when she dropped me off.

"She's a survivor," she said.

"Just like you."

"Let's not go that far."

"What are you doing?" I asked.

"Playing golf, you?"

Her solution to nervousness was to crack a joke. The silence that followed was a weighted truce. We both knew what the other was thinking but wouldn't say anything.

"See you in ten." I said.

I put Peter Gabriel's *So* in my Walkman and got on my little red mountain bike. By this time the snow had begun to magically drape everything in a fresh blanket of white. My blood was racing and I was dancing on my bike. The town was deserted; cars were sparse. I swerved through the street, making an impermanent design with the wheels. One that could have been erased at any moment...

The stewardess nudged me out of my memory, and I ordered a coke. I needed to sober up a bit from the preflight drinks with Aden. As the plane effortlessly floated through the thick layer of white clouds, the image of Timothy Meyer permeated my mind, soaking in deeper as the hours passed. I hadn't felt this quixotic about someone since Patrick, my professor in college, the "you" in the song that had turned heads and gotten me signed.

While dating Rita (yes, the girl), I had slowly begun to fall for him. He was distinguished and worldly despite his occasionally tragic clothes (he somehow thought Hawaiian shirts were fashionable). He was our ruddy-faced, red-haired acting teacher, and so serious and passionate about what he did that he often made students cry in class, in order to "break down their walls."

Patrick had a secretary who was the only black person I'd ever seen on campus. She was sassy and smart, and after Patrick and I would quietly have sex in his office with the blinds drawn, she would shoot me knowing glances that read *You go, girl.* She was the only one on the floor who knew, and I couldn't help but crack a thin smile in return.

I couldn't have imagined a more expert tongue. Patrick was the blowjob king, and I was constantly getting serviced. It's not that Rita was lacking in that area, it just wasn't as sexy watching a girl blow me. Patrick couldn't get enough, and who could refuse letting their cock be worshipped incessantly?

Rita and I were equals and had a strong friendship, but Patrick was my mentor, my idol, which made the sex better, crazier. We could hardly wait to get to his place, and we'd sometimes have sex in his office two times in a day, often interrupted by freshmen or TAs. I'd giggle as I buttoned my pants.

In my youthful idealism I thought it would lead to love. If I wasn't going to get married and have kids like the rest of the world, I would get married to a man, or at least live with the romance of forever and believe it.

My transitional bisexual phase went on for about eight months. I found it invigorating, this scandal of having to occasionally sleep with both of them on the same day, even in the same evening. What can I say? I was in my prime. I suppose this overlapping period was inevitable, and that my gayness would eventually emerge.

While on Thanksgiving break that year—home with the heteros—I told Patrick over the phone that I couldn't do it anymore, that I wanted to be with Rita only. So Patrick, knowing that Rita had been attracted to him as well, invited her over, got her drunk, and slept with her just to get back at me. Talk about manipulative.

When I returned home she confessed to me in tears, said she snuck out of his bed at four in the morning feeling gross and so ashamed. That's when I told her I'd been seeing him for eight months, having sex with him not only in that same bed, but also in his office and in his car.

This put her over the edge, understandably so. She started throwing things at me: A plastic cutting board sailed past my head like a Frisbee; a picture frame whizzed past my ear and shattered on the exposed brick wall. She was absolutely livid, and who could blame her? Eventually, to calm her down, I made love to her, our tears turning into moans. It was the last time I had sex with a girl, not counting Autumn.

The day after I returned to LA, I recounted the stories of Rita and Autumn to Aden while sitting on the Astroturf by the pool in his and Derek's Hollywood Hills home.

"How long ago was that?" Aden asked.

"Around ten years ago."

"Okay, well, let's make it that you broke up with Rita last summer, and now you're just playing the field, sleeping with different girls in each town."

"Yeah, with names like Bruce and Kevin."

"I told you, Jackson, what you do behind closed doors is your business, you simply cannot bring it into the public eye."

"But I'm not even on tour yet!"

"Smoke and mirrors, Jackson."

"And I don't think Rita should be my hetero poster girl, seeing as it was so long ago and she knows I'm gay!"

"Well, we shall think about this one. Can she be contacted?"

The thought of Aden contacting Rita made my skin crawl.

"No, I think she lives in Thailand now. Why do I have to tell people about my past anyway? Lots of celebrities hide their private lives."

"There's a certain balance that must be achieved. If you come off as too mysterious, they will try and dredge stuff up on you."

"Great. Good thing I never went to jail or anything."

Derek was downstairs working on music for a movie-of-the-week, and Neil was on his way to pick me up. Since being with Aden was so much easier if you were intoxicated, we were halfway through a bottle of white wine.

The Hollywood Hills were completely silent. The exception was a light snore from Aden and Derek's dog, Blake. Blake was a shorthaired, skinny dog with floppy ears and a constant look of oblivion on its face. The perfect dog for Derek and Aden and the grounds of their home, which Neil and I had appropriately dubbed *Camp Neurosis*.

"It's not like I walk around with a purse or anything," I said, taking an extra-large gulp.

"Yes, but for example, that ring has to go."

The ring Aden was referring to was one given to me by my

then-most-recent boyfriend, Barkley, the millionaire. There was no way I was giving it up.

Although Aden shunned all that was gay in me, I could tell he was intrigued about Barkley. After all, Aden was the quintessential Hollywood wife, and his Botox always got a workout at the prospect of a sugar daddy with more money than Derek. I reveled in my story.

"I met him, and within two weeks, we went on holiday to this super-posh resort in Mexico where the staff stood behind us dressed head to toe in white, spraying Evian spritzers while handing us little chocolates filled with sorbet. It was heaven on earth; I felt like a true princess."

"Prince," Aden said, "and watch the wrist."

"Aden, there are no paparazzi in your bushes."

"But you'll have them soon," he said, "and we must practice. So listen, was this guy a troll or was he cute?"

"Barkley is handsome in a classic, all-American, country club kind of way. He always looked as if he'd walked out of the pages of *The Great Gatsby*. Cream on cream, seersucker, bow ties, vests, and handkerchiefs. All perfectly matched."

"I think I've seen him at the Mayfair...does he wear those hideous Belgian loafers?"

"Yes, he has them in eight different colors. He used to introduce himself as Barkley McFadden the third, and he has a Scottie dog named Archibald who drinks Pellegrino!"

"Does he know about your music?"

"You kidding? He loves it, though he always told me it's impractical. He used to make me give concerts at his dinner parties."

"Great, so you have a millionaire A-list queen who knows you're gay."

"Yes, but they aren't the ones who'll be calling the *Enquirer* with a story."

"You'd be surprised," Aden said while lighting a cigarette. "I'm quitting Sunday," he added.

In the short time I'd known Aden, he had quit about a hundred times. His average relapse time was three days. He was constantly quitting and always had a reason why he couldn't quit until a certain date. "When the demo's finished" was one of them. "When we go to New Zealand" was another.

"Anyway the song 'Everything You Touch' is about Barkley."

"Of course," Aden said, "should've known."

I fiddled with the band on my finger. "So, he got me this ring... it's white gold and aquamarine to match my eyes...he told me that no matter what I must never take it off."

"Well, it's coming off, Jackson. I know I can be a hard-ass, but you'll thank me when you're winning a Grammy."

"As long as I can wear heels."

"Uh, I need another drink."

I never really wore heels, and truthfully, for the most part my "gayness" was undetectable to the eyes of strangers. I just liked to needle Aden. Don't get me wrong, I knew how to turn on the camp, but I took a dark, secret pleasure in the sparring, watching Aden get even more nervous than he constantly was already.

While looking for Mr. Right in LA, I had found it extremely difficult to cultivate a real, wholesome romantic relationship. I could never have imagined a region in which the gay-male population was so utterly self-obsessed. And the ones that weren't were in tightly packaged relationships in which they'd focus almost exclusively on themselves as a couple—a "we" world—seemingly unable to function individually. "We would never do Europe in the summer," or, "we just LOVE the beach house, especially with our new light fixtures—it's *very* Mondrian."

Sure, a gay guy could get sex in Los Angeles, virtually anywhere. From the famous parking lot in West Hollywood known as Vaseline Alley to public parks. Even the 24-hour Home Depot on Sunset turned into a hook-up after the bars let out, for the ones looking for the last-chance booty call, the final shuffle. I used to call it *Home Desperate*. I even saw two guys going at it once in Gardening, though clearly the Power Tool section would have been a hotter choice.

One guy I'd dated, though completely hot, was so mysterious he might as well have just been an anonymous hook-up. He would only see me on Sundays, and all I knew was his first name—Mark. He had small, sexy lips that knew how to kiss, but shortly after we'd finish, he'd get up and start to dress, hinting that I should leave. I wanted to hold him in my arms through the night; his frame was just the right amount size smaller than mine. But that was it. After orgasm he just changed modes. I started to refer to him as "Mr. Cuddle."

Yes, I could get laid. But I was a romantic, always had been. I wanted to be barefoot and pregnant. Well, figuratively. But in the current scenario, I was beginning to wonder if a boyfriend would even be possible.

After Aden returned with another bottle, I knew it could get ugly, so I made an excuse to leave.

"Okay, but wait," Aden said, "I want to brief you on tomorrow. And Neil's not here yet."

This was Aden's favorite thing, to "brief" me, as if Derek's contacts and inside knowledge were his. I grabbed one of his cigarettes, wishing it were a joint.

"Lonnie Simpson is a fanatical, Sixties throwback who is in charge of all the music for Warner Brothers films. He is one of those high-powered executives who is constantly scattered and has the attention span of a six-year-old." Sounds familiar, I thought.

"Nevertheless," Aden said, "he is in love with your song 'When I Grow Up' and wants to use it as the title song in his new movie with Tom Cruise. He is even considering giving you a cameo."

I couldn't believe what I was hearing. I was going to be in the movies now?

"However," Aden said sternly, "if he even sniffs a whiff of gaydar you're finished. You need to wear something baggy and NO belts. I forbid you to accessorize in any way."

Was Aden losing his mind? Did this hippie film executive really care if I wore a bracelet or a silver belt?

"Fine, Aden, I don't care."

Neil appeared on the patio and said hello. We both had the code for the gate, and free rein to come into the house as long as the DO NOT DISTURB sign by the front door wasn't flipped over. I gathered my things quickly to spare Neil having to talk to Aden. My car was in the shop and Neil had been carting me around in his Saab convertible.

We sat in easy silence and let the wind blow over us as he navigated the curves down the hill. When we got down to Sunset, Neil turned to me and said, "So I see Aden had a buzz on already, shocker."

"Yes, and me too. It's the only way I can deal."

"Just chant 'Burundi' in your head."

During one evening at his little place in the Los Feliz hills, Neil and I had shared a bottle of wine and sat on his porch smoking cigarettes, lamenting about the ridiculousness of dating in LA. It was then and there that we made a pact: if we didn't have boyfriends by the time we were forty, we would pack it up and move to Burundi together. The thing was, neither of us really knew where Burundi was. Just that it was far away from the fake-tanned, Gucci sunglass–wearing LA fags. Whenever something harrowing was taking place, which was quite often, one of us would bring up Burundi.

"But don't you worry, honey, as I always tell you, this is what great things are made of."

Was it? I was definitely thankful that I wasn't waiting tables, but something inside me was apprehensive. I craved the attention of success, but I didn't want to feel like an imposter.

"He briefed me on the Lonnie Simpson meeting tomorrow and told me I can't accessorize. I'm like, how can someone who is supposedly so brilliant constantly talk out of his ass?"

"I've been asking myself that same question for three years."

"Well I guess it's a small price to pay, as long as I don't have to wait tables."

I suddenly remembered one of my meals with Aden and Derek in New York—we'd been eating at some chic bistro and Aden had sent his drink back three times, jumped down Derek's throat for no reason, and then excused himself. I couldn't help it—I'd turned to Derek and asked, "What do you see in him?"

Derek paused and all of sudden looked his age, lost his boyish charm.

"Well," he was searching for what to say. "He's brilliant. So smart. And he's the most eccentric person I know."

Although he was right, I wasn't satisfied with that answer, but I'd decided to let it go.

I told Neil about the exchange.

"He's a pushover," Neil said, referring to Derek. "He's insecure and they have something that works, something that feeds each other's weaknesses. It's dysfunction central."

"Aren't all relationships?" I said. Neil and I were ones to talk.

"Well, of course," Neil replied with his cute smile, "but theirs is, on a scale of one to ten, about a fifty."

# 8

The next morning I woke up with my heart racing, covered in sweat. I'd had another waiter dream, which were the worst kind of nightmares possible. After waiting tables on and off for ten years, I had several recurring nightmares. I could still feel the reality of the one I'd just experienced. It was the worst of them, in which I was assigned a VIP table of ten, except the table was two blocks away from the restaurant, sitting there in an alley, white tablecloth and all. The guests were beyond high maintenance: they wanted everything on the side, medium well but a little pink, cooked through but not dry, water without ice, extra lemon, and do you bake the croutons here?

During most of the dream I was running, six arugula and pear salads balanced on one arm, a tray of Perriers and martinis in the other. A woman dressed head to toe in peach and sporting a horrendous wind tunnel facelift asked me for coffee.

I ran back, sweating and breathless, and returned again with the coffee. "I wanted decaf," the evil peach-woman said. I started to cry. When I got back with the decaf, she not only wanted cream, but wanted me fired as well. That's when I always wake up.

I got out of bed and took a shower to clear my head and get ready for my meeting with Lonnie Simpson.

The Warner Brothers lot was swimming with eager interns sporting thirty-dollar haircuts, carrying frappuccinos and laptops. Out of the corner of my eye I saw Cameron Diaz outside a trailer talking on her lime-green cell phone. Her T-shirt read "Team Cameron."

"Look!" I said to Aden.

"She's so last year," Aden said, "and it looks like she's gained a few pounds."

We were in Derek's old Mercedes, and Aden was driving. Derek was in the back eating a pop-up Popsicle and straining to see Miss Diaz.

"I love her," he said, "she's my favorite Angel."

"No way, Drew rocks," I said, messing up my hair a little more in the pop-down mirror. After the accessory comment, I would not let Aden touch my hair.

"Don't spike it, just wave it. The effect should be just-out-of-bed, very *Trainspotting*. Heroin chic."

I watched his serious expression. Despite his annoying ways, Aden was my biggest fan. He truly believed in the potential of my music to reach the masses. I was just wondering if it was worth all the stress when I saw Robert Downey Jr. come out of a white Lexus SUV. He looked sexy in a charcoal sweatshirt and Adidas sweats. Someone handed him a smoothie, while another person held a parasol over his head. *Definitely worth it,* I thought.

We got to Lonnie's office and they made us wait for almost a half hour. Apparently this was record time—he'd been known to make people wait hours.

Just before we were escorted in, while Aden was in the smoking lounge, Derek turned to me and said, "Just be yourself."

Although I was touched by Derek's sentiment, I said, "You can't really mean that."

"Well, I don't want you pretending to be somebody else. Unfortunately the devil is in the details."

"What do you mean?"

"Well, Jackson, listen. If you can lose the occasional hand flip, then great. But I don't want you to force anything. Obviously Aden takes it a little too far."

I was shocked to hear him acknowledge Aden's craziness out loud, even if it was only mildly. I felt a slight lessening of the tension that had been building in me at the thought of having to "pass" yet again.

We finally got in to see Lonnie, and Derek reminisced with him while Aden and I sat on a black leather couch. Aden was sitting straight and business-like, while I, naturally, was trying to be very *Trainspotting.*

Derek lamented with Lonnie about the death of a famous photographer they had both known, and how Sting's performance at the funeral was "chilling" and "although subdued, beautiful."

Lonnie finally turned right past Aden to me and reached out a big, hairy hand.

"I'm Lonnie, pleased to meet you."

"You, too," I said. Normally I would have said something like, "the pleasure is mine," but I was now relegating myself to hetero-heroin talk. *See Spot run.*

"I have to tell you I haven't been so excited by a song in a long time. I'm not sure if these guys told you but I was *jumping* around the office the first time I heard it. Now these references may be before your time, but your stuff reminds me of a modern-day Cat Stevens or even Don Henley, but you sing better!"

I was red in the face but trying to remain cool.

"I'm glad you like it," I said. *See Jane cook.*

"I have a call in to the director I'm working with, and I sent him a copy. We'd love to use it for title and credits on our new film with Tom and Angelina."

I had thought it was starring Tom and Gwyneth, but Angelina was more of an It-Chick anyway, with the whole adopt-the-world thing.

Just then, someone brought a guitar in, and it seemed as if the entire floor of the building paraded in. Secretaries, marketing people, all looking like they stepped onto Sunset Plaza out of their BMWs. Apparently Lonnie had planned a little on-site market research. I looked at Aden and Derek as if to say, what's this?

I noticed my hands slightly shaking as I took the guitar. People were beaming at me, and in such close proximity, it was unnerving. I tried to use my nervousness, however, and played the song with sincerity. I made sure to look everyone in the eye at least once. By some miracle, I'd always felt comfortable in the spotlight. A few of the secretary ladies seemed choked up, and one looked at another as if to say *He's really what everyone says he is.*

A couple of the "suits" looked like they were trying to hide some new emotion I had stirred in them. Lonnie sat behind his desk beaming, chewing on an unlit cigar.

This was the thing. If all I had to do was perform, there would never have been a problem. Because when I performed, I was no longer categorized as being straight or gay. It wasn't a drag show or a comedy act. These were my songs, my truth, my life, and I could step into it as easily as a warm bath.

> *You say your life has no velocity*
> *We all settle for mediocrity*
> *Walking around like wounded soldiers*
> *Waiting just to get*
> *Older and older well,*
> *This is not*
> *What I wanna be when I grow up*

After I finished, the room filled with applause. While shaking hands, I tried not to smile too much. Somehow, moving all these jaded industry people made me feel like I really could make it. I tried to remain aloof, but I couldn't—I was too overwhelmed with joy. After so long, my music was being recognized, and I was so excited I could've screamed. Aden kept secretly motioning with his hand as if to say *Bring it down,* while Derek shook his head and rolled his eyes as if to say, *Do whatever the fuck you want because you just completely won them over.*

"Now let me ask you," Lonnie said after everyone was gone, "Aden said you were single, and I just so happen to know a very pretty girl who is also 'on the market' as we say. She's my lawyer's daughter, you may have seen her on *The Young and the Restless.*"

"He doesn't watch soap operas," Aden blurted out.

Lonnie Simpson laughed, turned to Derek and said, "He does now."

# 9

That night consisted of me sitting in my little Laurel Canyon house calling everyone I knew.

My mom didn't know who Alanis was, but the movie thing got her.

"It's too much, angel! I'm going hoopy over here!"

Brian yowled in his hip-hop voice.

"Now that's what I'm talkin' bout!"

My gym buddy Jed freaked.

"Oh my god. You are so going to be the It boy."

Neil knew all along about the movie thing and played it real cool.

"Don't let it get to your head now. I gotta go—I'm making risotto."

And so on, and so on. I did my tri-weekly 400-sit-up routine and took a long shower, during which I reminded myself that Neil was right—I was going into the studio! Right now I needed to concentrate on my songs. Especially since so much was riding on them—the average cost to produce an "indie" CD was around $15K, and my budget was $300K and that didn't include publicity/marketing. I had once heard that they had dumped six million on promotion for Macy Gray. *She was everywhere.* Would that be me? The buzz seemed to be gaining momentum. Some key radio stations had already been playing my demo produced by Derek, and I knew my single would be released in Europe before the new record even hit the U.S. Aden was getting an electronic press kit together to blitz major media and publicists worldwide.

I got out of the shower and practiced the songs we had chosen for the record, trying to find guitar hooks and harmonies. I fell asleep with the guitar still on the bed, and while dreaming about Timothy Meyer's naked curves next to me, I tried to spoon it. It gave me a low E in response.

The next morning I met Jed at the gym.

"This place is crawling with NECs," he said. Jed always spoke with acronyms. In this particular case he meant *not even celebrities*.

"They walk around like they're Nicole or Brad, but they've never had more than two lines in a B movie, or even worse, they're extras on soap operas. They've got their Prada and their Range Rovers, but they live in tiny studios in the valley."

This was funny coming from Jed, who last I heard, worked at a smoothie shop.

Jed insisted I resign from American Fitness (American Princess) and join this particular Crunch, where working out consisted of walking around like it was so hard being beautiful. In LA there was no cell-phone etiquette. "The champagne was WARM!" I heard a woman in the latest chic sportswear say while mildly exercising on her treadmill. Another guy was clearly fielding calls from so-called agents and publicists, and kept saying, "If De Niro's not in the picture, there's no green light." Then there were the young, sexy, thirty-something wives of the REAL green lighters, who would gladly spend $300 on a herbal body wrap at some modish spa and naturally follow it up by gulping Stoli vanilla martinis and lifting bumps of cocaine to their "altered" noses with perfectly painted pinkie nails.

I deliberately picked a Stairmaster without a mirror in front of it. I find it repulsive to stare at oneself while perspiring. Who wants to watch themselves pant and drip like an animal? It's like those sex hotels with mirrors above the bed. The point of sex is to enjoy yourself, become lost in the moment, not wonder if that really is a zit forming on your forehead or if your ear has noticeable hair in it.

Jed took the treadmill next to me. When I was starting out in the small clubs, Jed never came to my shows, but if you mentioned the word gym, he'd drop everything, including his towel in the sauna.

This particular day he was sporting black Adidas sweatpants and a shiny red retro baseball top. Even though he looked like he stepped off the set of an NSYNC video, somehow he could pull it off. Jed was beautiful. Too beautiful, in fact, to be called Jed.

Jed spent most of his time trying to move up the LA social ladder, believing when he got to the top everything would make sense. Like true happiness was getting flown to a circuit party in David Geffen's Lear jet while flirting with male supermodels. He seemed wary of my impending success and we didn't talk about it.

I was never sure why I even liked Jed, other than the fact that his face was so pleasant to look at. He had huge ice-blue eyes that glimmered behind his long dark lashes—even more so when he was hung over. I slept with him once, when I first met him. He had mirrors in his bedroom, and I kept getting distracted by a birthmark on his lower back. After we were done, we ate bad Chinese food and watched *The Hand That Rocks the Cradle*. He was so earnestly intrigued by the movie that I found him irresistible. I just stared at him, soy sauce coating his lovely lips and a stray piece of rice on his tanned cheek. I had decided to become his friend, which is more than I could say for most of my other one-night stands. (Why do they call it that anyway? Shouldn't it be a one-night sleep? Or a one-night fuck?)

On the treadmill Jed kept sucking on his water bottle as if it were a grape Popsicle. He had a high metabolism and natural hair color that people in LA would kill for. He was always eating cheeseburgers and ice cream but never gained weight and remained blemish-free. He was skinny even when he sat down, like Mr. Cuddle. It's not that I was fat, or even chubby, but when you're constantly around people with flawless appearances it starts to grate on you. I began to notice a centimeter of fat here or there.

I knew I could not live in LA forever. It was all too much.

After cardio we moved on to free-weights. While spotting Jed, I studied his teeth and noticed their symmetry. This had always been an obsession of mine, studying people's physical assets, noticing their perfections and flaws. Flaws that are perfections and vice versa. Like Derek's scar just below his eye or the curl of Neil's upper lip—both so sexy. In LA most people saw the goal as one big perfection—magazines as life.

In the steam room Jed kept eyeing me as if to say *look, look.* In the corner, through the fog, I noticed what he was so overtly referring to. It was Ben Stiller. The only other big celebrity I'd seen so close was Macy Gray, in a little stationary store on La Brea. She told me she liked my belt—a blue plastic one that Aden would have adamantly vetoed. She'd touched my shoulder as she walked by. She smelled of cinnamon. I melted.

Jed flashed Mr. Stiller a smile. I wondered if he was naked under his towel. He left in a hurry, probably because Jed was trying to pick him up. Jed sees stars all the time. It's almost comical. He literally bumped into Jodie Foster at Trader Joe's, spilling her can of Spirutein. And he got stuck on an elevator with k. d. lang in Larchmont. Meanwhile, I once followed a guy all the way from Culver City to Santa Monica, only to discover it wasn't Seal. His face was scarless and he was short. I was an inept starfucker compared to Jed, but apparently I was about to become a starfuckee.

I worked on my songs for the next few days, and met with Aden in preparation for the upcoming phone interviews. My mom was calling a lot, asking all these questions, but I was distracted by practicing. She couldn't believe I was flying to an exotic location to record part of my album.

"What, do they give you a personal masseur and manicures too?"

"I hope so."

The truth was, only the big stars got treated like kings and queens. Even some of the finest venues in the country still had crappy dressing rooms. But it was the stage that mattered, right?

The stage at the KXPC Music Fest that Aden booked me for—last minute, as the previously booked performer got a bigger gig—was tiny compared to the parking lot full of concertgoers. The dressing room consisted of two poles holding up some white canvas behind which was a table and an empty ice bucket. Glamour!

The show was great though—aside from the stage manager being bitter that the original artist didn't show up. Even I knew that the music business was not about loyalty—if you got a better gig you had to ride with it, simple decisions could make or break you.

It was nice to play in front of a crowd again. Ironically, after I had signed with Clean Slate, I cut back on performances as they wanted to keep the buzz and not oversaturate. But I wanted to try out the changes to my songs in front of an audience before going in to record. I got an encore, and though most of the crowd seemed to be hearing me for the first time, there was a group of girls in the front who knew most of my lyrics!

As I was leaving, I felt a hand on my shoulder.

"Well, you've come a long way from slinging hummus!"

It was Kane, a woman I'd worked with years before in a little Turkish restaurant in the gay ghetto.

"Hey!"

"Hey, sexy. You sounded great—tough crowd, but you made it through!"

"What are you doing now?"

"I'm a P.I."

"No way."

I remembered how observant she always was.

"Way. Here's my card sweetie, call me sometime."

I felt pride at her seeing I had moved on from waiting tables. I noticed the address on her card. She certainly had come a long way as well.

On the way home I took a mental note of the songs that pulled the crowd in. It was a crapshoot—you never knew what would fly, so you had to keep tabs on what worked. I was determined to hone the perfect set of music that would take me (and the crowd) where we needed to go.

The sky was the limit.

# 10

That next Tuesday I was on a plane to the British Virgin Islands, to Damian Blue's studio. Neil had booked me in first class, and over warm shrimp salad the gentleman next to me started bragging about his kids, but in a charming way. I told him I was going to our exotic destination to begin recording my major-label debut. He was beside himself.

"Wow, a real star," he said with widened green eyes. "I have to tell my daughter."

Did he know I was gay? I couldn't tell, but I tried to press my forearm slightly into his, especially after our first mini-bottle of red wine. Something about flirting in the sky had always appealed to me—I was alone and so was he, and for that time suspended above the earth, it seemed as if anything could happen.

From the genuine way he was talking about his kids, I could tell he was a great dad—a sensitive and nurturing one, as opposed to one who simply paid the bills. He seemed so involved in his children's lives, and so proud, that I couldn't help the stirring in my heart.

I suppose my attraction to older guys was partly born out of my strong relationship with my mother growing up. She worked as a teacher, raising three children while still keeping a sense of humor. Bold and amiable, giddy and uninhibited, she was a spitfire who drew everybody's gaze when she entered a room. She had thick sandy-blonde hair, a contagious smile, beautiful shiny blue eyes, and she was never short of a kiss, a cuddle, or a dance.

My father was skinny, witty, light on his feet—he had a big heart, and his sarcasm and subtle comic timing made my mother laugh. I loved him for his humor and his quirks, always following us around the kitchen with a damp cloth; and rearranging the tableware we had set so that everything was perfectly aligned.

He was a meticulous cook, chopping his vegetables super-fine for salads, and he dressed tidily, taking great pleasure in clothes that were stylish but always comfortable. He also chose all the furniture and even bought my mother her finest outfits from high-end catalogues, everything matching. I did know that he took hints from my Aunt Sarah, who was particularly stylish and always noticed my shoes with a knowing roll of the eye.

But for all my father's charms, there were certain emotional lines he didn't seem to know how to cross. He was always there for us with a paycheck, music, and a whole lot of laughs, but not necessarily a shoulder to cry on. When you hugged him it was one squeeze, one pat on the back and you were through. I knew he loved me, and that he was an amazing dad by most standards, but perhaps I had always wanted more.

My mother was my emotional oasis, and I suppose what I was looking for in older men was that sense of physical nourishment, that "I will hold you and you will be safe" kind of thing. A blend of my father's stability and my mother's warmth.

My father always supported every venture I set out on, and I loved him for that. But initially he would never ask about my boyfriends, and one day when I came home with painted fingernails, he just about lost it. It actually gave him physical pain.

I said, "Dad, it's just nail polish!"

He squirmed and said something I couldn't hear.

"What?"

"Just...just...take it off will you?"

We were going to a dinner at his golf club, and the thought of one of his golf buddies seeing me with nail polish was too much for him to take.

"Okay," I said, "but one of these days you're going to have to wake up and smell the millennium."

He waved me away. I couldn't find nail polish remover, so I found myself frantically scraping it away with a butter knife as they were honking for me in the driveway. For my dad, it was a generational thing. My mom could not care less, but I granted his wish and never exposed him to that again. When he came to visit Barkley and me at the beach house, he remarked that since Thomas, my previous long-term boyfriend, I had "moved up the food chain."

I showed him my nails. "And look, no polish!"

Ironically, toward the end of the trip he started wearing his sweaters over his shoulder, Jilet-style, like Barkley. It was so adorable.

With Thomas, the first man I actually took home for Christmas, it was a different story. You couldn't get them away from each other, they hit it off so well, but Dad clearly didn't want me touching Thomas in front of our relatives. He acted proud of Thomas in front of everyone, but treated him as a friend of the family rather than someone I had been intimate with for years. I didn't complain and neither did Thomas, as he had always been semi-closeted himself.

Even though Thomas was my longest relationship, when he would introduce me to people as his friend, I would sassily whisper something in his ear to the effect of, "The friend who minutes ago had your cock in his mouth?" Nevertheless, Thomas was my first true love. He was connected to all these dynamic, incredible people and seemed to eat up life every day with such passion and extraordinary optimism—I felt lucky to even be in his wake, and eventually I ended up in his bed. He was an entrepreneur, publicist, and consultant, who would have many projects going on at one time—his life was rich and busy, a life I had imagined forming for myself.

The turning point for me was a particular evening toward the end, eating cheap Mexican food. By that time we had been in Colorado together eight years. He, of course, loved the joint. This was a man who ate peanut butter and jelly every day and had no idea what foie gras was.

I looked at his eyes, dark and beautiful, his faint beard. I wanted to crush him with love. I felt this amazing combination, as people who have spent a long time together often do, of love and abhorrence.

"You're so sexy," I said.

He didn't respond, just brought something else up, something I didn't want to talk about.

"Do you think I'm sexy?"

Again, no answer. Lately, our sex life had always been me initiating and him rejecting me a lot, and I truly wondered if he thought I was sexy anymore. *I need to live,* I thought to myself.

I noticed two guys at the next table, eating in a weighted silence, making loud clinks with their silverware, as if they were periods or exclamation points. I imagined they had sunken into a comfortable misery, knowing a new life was out there beckoning, but not owning the power to change. The point where silence becomes a scream, and life, all of a sudden, seems unbearably short.

I saw a little Mexican girl at another table pouring salt on an orange wedge and sucking it clean of juice. *Licking the wound.*

The following day I told Thomas that I was leaving.

He laughed.

"No, I'm serious. I'm done licking the wound."

"What?"

He laughed again and said, "Hold on, Pet."

He was on the phone.

"I love you more than anything. But I have to go now," I said.

He hung up the phone. It rang again and he took the call. He wasn't getting me. What had been stewing had come to a boil, and I could be capable of anything. I took off upstairs, to the kitchen. Thomas always had a giant container of different kinds of cereal, in his mind the perfect mixture of crunch, fruit, and fiber. He labored over the amounts, how it had to be 60-percent Raisin Bran, etc.

I picked up the container and turned it upside down, dumping it all over the slate countertop. Then I grabbed the milk—the carton clearly marked T for Tom with a blue sharpie—and poured it over the top of the cereal. The milk started dripping over the sides and it was a comforting sound.

Then I started emptying the cupboards, knocking everything to the counter and the floor, smashing the contents until it was a sea of broken glass, liquids, chaos. Thomas's assistant came down the driveway. For some reason, my heart went calm.

She came in as though entering a crime scene.

I ran into our room and weeded through our clothes, putting my favorites in a black trash bag. Then I started on the rest of my stuff, throwing the essentials into my gym bag: CDs, my photo album, an accordion file with my papers and records. I slung my guitar over my shoulder and picked up the bags. The whole time, Thomas was still on the phone downstairs, oblivious, and his assistant was cleaning up the kitchen.

Still in a fury, I grabbed the blender, a lamp we had gotten together, and the blanket we used to nest in. When my car got to the point where the only room left inside it was for my body, I came back into the kitchen. The assistant had finished cleaning—my whole episode vanished—and stood quietly leaning against the stove eating an apple. After all that he wouldn't even see a trace? I grabbed the apple out of her hand and crushed it under my left foot.

Four hours later I was in Arizona; everything was flat and arid and the colors had gone orange. I remembered thinking: I have three thousand dollars, I can do anything.

I knew that if I really wanted to sign a record deal I would have to move to New York or LA, and New York seemed too cold and too expensive.

I didn't want to hurt Thomas, but it was like a force was pulling me away. He had never even wanted a relationship, but I had taught him how to open his heart. I taught him how to hold my hand, how to sleep in on Sundays. I taught him how to cry.

A few more hours down the highway, I stopped at a family-style restaurant. All I could think about was how Thomas would have loved the place. He would have ordered breakfast even though it was nine at night. Waffles and peaches. I ordered a hamburger and fries. I never ate fries, ever, but everything had changed. My waitress had a look on her face that read *Take me away from here*. There was a soft beauty I could sense underneath her tedious misery. She brought me another lemonade without me asking. I ate the French fries slowly, feeling the grease dissolve on my tongue.

"You have any kids?" I asked her.

"What's it to you?"

"Just wondering."

"Yeah, I got a six-year-old and a baby girl."

"Husband?" I asked.

"What do you think?"

"No."

"You thought right." She filled my water and said, "What about you, pretty fellow like yourself, you married?"

"I was, I guess."

"What do you mean, you guess?"

"Yeah, I was. Until about seven hours ago."

"The poor girl, she's probably crying her heart out."

I tried to think of all the times I had witnessed Thomas cry. His mother's death. When he caught me smoking. The end of *Dancer in the Dark*. The morning after I came home drunk and cut my leg real bad. When I'd told him I wanted to give him the sun, to keep him warm.

"Oh, I think he'll be fine."

"Hmm?"

The waitress didn't hear the gender-specific pronoun and I decided not to elaborate.

"Nothing, can I have my check please?"

In the morning I wrote him a postcard.

> *Thomas-*
> *Please water the long ferns on the deck twice a week. Talk to them, too. I cannot possibly walk around without you in my heart. Please don't spend more than eight hours in front of that computer. There are moments when I can hear your voice.*
> *Love,*
> *Me*

When I arrived in Los Angeles, I went straight to the beach:

Venice. There were rows of closed tourist shops and a flat expanse of sand ending in the calm, greenish-gray sea. I got out of the car and sat on the hood. A dirty young man approached me, carrying a plastic bag in one hand and an old beaten-up guitar in the other.

"I'll play you a song for a buck or give you a poem for fifty cents."

I considered the proposition.

"Okay, sure, both."

He smiled again, more familiar.

"Money first," he said.

I reached into my pocket and collected six quarters and dropped them into his soiled hand. He started playing Bob Marley's "Turn Your Lights Down Low" and I leaned back on the windshield, the car hood still warm beneath me. Thomas's car, a hand-me-down. I remembered the day he gave it to me, how happy I was. He'd put the key on my pillow, like a chocolate.

After the poem, I asked, "How many do I get for the car?"

"What?"

"The car, and mostly everything in it. I need my pictures, my documents, my bag, but everything else." I wasn't sure quite what had gotten into me, but I had felt so caged by Thomas, so dependent on him, I just wanted to start fresh.

He smiled again, a smile that in no way indicated the difficult life he must have had. He walked around the car and looked inside.

"The blender?"

"Yep."

"Everything except the two bags on the front seat and the guitar. You already have one of those."

He sat back down, gazed out over the sea. There was the whir of cars on the highway in the distance.

"Five hundred songs and three hundred poems," he said, as if it was a highly serious calculation.

I started rolling a joint.

"I tell you what, just start playing and I'll tell you when to stop."

"Will do, man."

So there we were, sitting on my car on the edge of the Pacific Ocean. He played so many songs. Some I knew and started singing along with him. Every once in a while he stopped and recited a short poem. The songs were clearly better than the poems, but it was more than that. The sound of his voice, the clank of the old guitar, the swoosh of the cars speeding by on the distant highway blended with the roar of the shore. The pureness in his smile. I felt completely safe, which is the opposite of what I'd expected myself to feel. And then I thought about it: My life had been strung together in memory by these moments of safety, these "right place" moments. A rope of hope.

In the early morning I woke up and looked around, found the dirty young man curled in the shade by the car, fast asleep. I quietly went inside the car and retrieved the velvet pouch that contained my then life savings, three thousand dollars. I also took my favorite coat, my duffle of clothes and personal papers, the CDs, my guitar, and my photo album. As I picked it up, a picture of Thomas and me in the hot springs of New Mexico fell out. I couldn't leave it. I thought for a second about what I was about to do. The car had seen better days, didn't have much life left, but it was a fighter. I grabbed the title and signed my name, laid it and the keys gently next to his guitar and took off on foot.

I was not sure where I was going, but I knew this: whatever happened would be completely new, like the blooming of a cactus flower or the birth of a child. I remembered thinking, I am walking forward, and no one can stop me.

I moved to LA and the first thing I gave up was my car.

Although I had come a long way, I still had a lot to learn.

Several months later I met the millionaire, Barkley, then consequently Derek and Aden, and now here I was three years on, wondering if I would actually find emotionally available, long-term love. I had faith that this person was out there waiting for me, but unfortunately, this particular daddy on the plane to the BVI clearly wasn't going to be him. We drank two more mini wine bottles together, and he told me more about his kids, how one was in art school in New York and how he was going to the islands to visit his daughter. Perhaps we would like to meet?

"Not unless her name is Kevin," I said.

It took him a long, excruciating minute, but he started laughing uproariously.

The rest of our flight we sat in a peaceful silence. My mind kept drifting back to the new potential father figure—Timothy Meyer. If only my love life could fall in line as nicely as my career was. But I needed to focus, to follow through, and a small part of my stomach housed some butterflies that I hoped would make this recording that much better and not force me to freeze up.

# 11

Upon my arrival at the island where Damian Blue's studio was located, I was greeted by a man with dreadlocks in a three-piece suit who led me to a long white Cadillac convertible. He loaded my guitar in the trunk and said, "Meester Jackson, it is a pleasure to take you to Meester Damian."

The air was thick with moisture and the smell of roasting chicken. I rolled down the window and smiled into the night. Was this my life?

As the car curved along the shore, I started thinking about my new songs and where the weak spots were. After more than ten years of writing songs, the latest were the most developed bunch and also the closest to my heart. I was going to be working with Damian Blue! Nerves and excitement rushed through my veins.

The studio had plush couches and gold and platinum records on the wall, and Damian was immediately disarming. He took my hand and gave me a personal tour of the place, immediately making me feel at home. My nerves were calmed. He took great care as we worked on my songs, trying to get out of me the essence of what each song was about emotionally so he could convey that in the production. I was given a fair amount of creative control, which I relished. He even let me choose some of the instruments to be included and asked my opinion on mix issues, which I knew many producers never did.

"It's cool, man, I get it. This is your first record on a major. I want there to be as much of 'you' in it as possible. That's the point, right?"

"Yes," I said, smiling from ear to ear.

He had an unkempt, south Londoner named Roy doing beat programming; two pale, nerdy engineers from Scotland; and an amazing rhythm section (two cool cats from Miami).

Damian spent most of his time smoking in a big leather swivel chair, throwing out ideas with ease but also with an urgency that suggested he'd forget them if he didn't tell you right away.

"Use that hook as a pre-chorus, but don't give it away until the refrain. Make it a tease," he'd say.

His thoughts were inspired and effective, and shaped the songs, gave them more decisive hooks. This was why people were successful in the music business. Of course a lot of it depended on luck and timing, but it really was about having the right instincts.

I began to trust him and his erratic inspirations.

He showed me my own cottage on his property, and I slept long and peacefully to the sound of the lapping shore. I breathed in the salty air and listened to the seagulls in the distance. I thought their desperate wail would sound good on the breezy ballad I wanted to end the record with. I made a mental note to ask Damian if one of the technicians could record it.

Even though we were working hard, solid sleep and lots of fresh fruit and bread balanced it out. The meals were comforting and abundant, cooked by a big black man whose name was so hard to pronounce that everyone just called him Ed. The water was electric, postcard-blue, and the palms loomed over the dusty streets like oversized, upturned mops.

One night around two in the morning, as we were wrapping up, I asked Damian about his previous comment in our New York meeting.

"Do you really think Alanis will sing on something? I've been trying to find the perfect harmony for her."

"No, mate. I don't think so. She's in Korea."

Something deflated inside of me. That's it?

"But check this," Damian said as casually as if he were asking me to pass the salt, "she listened to your demos and wants you to open a five-city Canadian tour. I told Derek about it; he's contacting her camp."

"No. Way."

I was desperately trying to remain calm. I had played to five hundred, even one thousand people before, but opening for Alanis? Hello, she played stadiums!

It seemed like a clouded-over dream. I was going to play to fifty thousand people. What the hell was I going to wear?

"That's rad," I said. I had never said "rad" before in my life.

"It'll be a hoot," Damian said, scratching his beard. A hoot? I was pretty sure that this was also a virgin word for Damian.

"You know, I've worked with a lot of artists: big, super big, and huge. And I've never really been compelled to pull strings. But you've got something, Jackson. Something infectious. And I'm proud to help."

Was I hearing this correctly? I had to force my smile back, as I probably looked like a clown.

That night, I got a message from Neil ordering me to call him back ASAP.

"Hey, you. Listen, your dreamboat from *Interview* called me for your number down there. I gave it to him, dear, but you cannot, I repeat, you *cannot* tell Aden."

"Oh my god..."

"Girl, whatever you do, just keep it on the down low."

"He's so fucking sexy!" I could feel a tingle in my shorts.

"Sexy or not, Aden will get another ulcer if—"

"Don't worry. I can't believe..."

"And guess who called our offices today?"

"Alanis!" I said.

"Yeah, her agent actually, but how'd you know?"

"I'm on it."

Just then my cell phone beeped with a 212 number.

"Holy shit, that must be him. Gotta go."

"God help us..."

I clicked the phone over and attempted a nonconcerned hello, but it came out shaky and desperate.

"Hey there rock star, it's Timothy Meyer from *Interview*. I thought I might catch you before you headed back to LA."

"Oh, hi. Guess what? I saw you on the street, the Friday after the interview. You had on the same suit..."

"Never in the same week, my friend, you must be mistaken."

"No, it was you."

"Can I ask you a personal question?" His voice turned sly.

I was shaking at that point, opening the door to my cottage as if the air and the sight of the stretching sea might calm me.

"Why not?"

"Would you care to join me for two days in South Beach on your way back?"

"Um, well, let's see." My mind was racing. What would I tell Aden? How could I alter my itinerary? I would think of something. I would *have* to think of something.

"Well, Timothy, I'd have to say...certainly, I'd be honored."

"Right. Great. Settled, then. Eighteenth to the twentieth at the Delano. Do you need a ticket to Miami or do you already go through there?"

"I'm not sure."

"I'll have my secretary FedEx you a voucher just in case."

"Sounds great, Tim."

"Oh, one thing, Jackson. My mother told me to never let anyone call me Tim. So it's Timothy from now on, okay?"

"Will do, Timothy. See you soon!"

We hung up. Even though I rarely smoked, I lit a cigarette and called Neil back.

"Girl, you've got to change my flight. I need to be in Miami for a little detour. Booty calls." I was squirming like a kid in a candy store.

"You're gonna have to talk to Aden—"

"Just tell him I'm visiting a cousin."

"Oh yeah, he'll really go for that."

"Alright, tell him I'm seeing my old girlfriend Rita."

"You haven't seen her in ten years."

"Fuck it, he runs my career, not my life. Tell him it's personal business and he'll have to get over it. I won't miss anything..."

I heard the sound of shuffling papers.

"You're right actually; you don't have anything until the twenty-first. It says lunch with Kia Diamond. Who the fuck—"

"Oh my god, it's the soap-opera chick. Will you do me a favor? Get as much background on her as you can. What's his name—the movie guy—wants to set me up with her. Lonnie Simpson. It's all part of my hetero life."

"Am I hearing all this correctly?"

"Listen, baby, if he puts my song in Tom Cruise's little movie directed by Cameron fucking Crowe, I'll go *down* on her."

"Ew, don't say it."

"Okay, maybe not the carpet munch, but can you say major motion picture?"

"Oh, yeah. I'll fax you the new itinerary in the morning."

"You're the best, Neil. What would I do without you?"

"I don't know, but you sure wouldn't be humping Timothy Meyer in Miami."

I laughed, a little dizzy from the nicotine.

Later that night we finished preproduction—the skeleton of all the songs—and Damian burned me some CDs to listen to for a few weeks before we put on all the finishing touches.

# 12

For two whole days at the stark, gorgeous Delano Hotel in South Beach, I forgot about my career and everything else. Only the delicious anxiety of a new love affair lingered.

Timothy was a true gentleman. When I arrived at the hotel, reception gave me my own key, and I was led to a corner room with an oval window that spanned both the city and the beach. It was stunning. Timothy was hiding in the closet, and when he came out, I was not only startled by the surprise but by his undeniable beauty. We drank champagne and Timothy insisted on listening to my new tracks.

"I wish I could crawl inside your mind," he said. I didn't know what to say, so I just smiled, bashful.

"So many lyrics these days are so trite, so one-dimensional, but you have this gift of creating depth without getting sappy or sentimental."

"I used to work so hard to write simple pop songs, spending years trying to be something I wasn't. I feel so lucky that once I just started writing what I felt, people responded."

Timothy said, "I was a poet in college," and immediately blushed as if he wished he hadn't said it. It was adorable. He had innocence in his soft brown eyes and a genuine interest in me I found flattering, even though I wondered if it was partly because he thought I was slated to be a star.

It seemed polite to act as interested in his poetry as he was in my music. He was being so sweet.

"Oh, yeah? You know I'm always looking for lyrics—"

His laughter interrupted me.

"My stuff was preposterous," he said.

"I bet it wasn't—"

"Oh yes it was. The last summer of college I drove around

California with an ounce of pot and wrote about the stars and the universe. I had a whole notebook full of schlock."

Somehow I couldn't picture this older, distinguished, clever businessman driving around getting stoned and writing sky and earth metaphors.

"Wow," was all I could muster.

"Let's just be glad that notebook is somewhere lost in the attic of my parents' house."

That afternoon we lounged in a cabana next to the beautiful pool and ate tuna tartare and drank more champagne. The nice thing about being with him was that there were no uncomfortable gaps in the conversation. We were content in the silence. I lay with my head on his thigh and he stroked my scalp with the tips of his fingers. He was so gentle, so right, that something in the back of my mind was skeptical.

"I have a special place I'm taking you tonight," he said.

"Baby, we could go to McDonald's and I wouldn't care as long as I could look into your eyes."

I immediately regretted saying that. It was worse than cheese— it was Cheese Whiz, cheese product. Oh well, sometimes my words got the best of me, especially when I was love-struck. And besides, if you craved it, Cheese Whiz tasted good.

The place certainly wasn't McDonald's. It was down an alley and had no sign, and when we walked in, I felt strange about something but couldn't place why. Then I looked down. The floor was grass, real grass. The tables were low with giant gray bean bag-type chairs, and the whole place smelled yummy, like citrus and cinnamon.

After we were seated and received our drinks, Timothy said, "Look up."

The ceiling of the restaurant was a dome, a planetarium with a million stars, the solar system, the Milky Way.

"Holy—"

"Did I tell you how nice it is to have you here, Jackson?"

"No."

"Well, it is. In fact, it's more than nice."

We spent the entire dinner hardly speaking, just locking eyes, smiling, looking up at the Milky Way, and feeling the wavy grass under our feet.

In bed that night we made slow love. He kissed me carefully, as if I would break if he kissed the wrong parts. I surrendered to him completely. He ran his tongue along the bone of my waist and teased me to no end until finally taking my ready-to-explode cock into his warm mouth. In the morning, I woke up to him nibbling on my ear, and we kissed slowly until we both were erect and he stood up, parading around the room like he was on a runway.

"Get back here!" I said.

"How much do you want it?"

He waved his wand next to me until I finally jumped out and tackled him, brought him back to the bed. His smooth, salty skin tasted so good, I could have stayed there forever.

When it was time to leave, Timothy was arguing with one of the managers about being "wrongly charged" for something.

"It's not the money," he said to me, "it's the principle."

He gave me an envelope in the lobby and told me not to open it until I got to LA. As we hugged good-bye, he whispered, "Thank you for coming."

"Anytime," I whispered back, our lips brushing each other's cheeks.

A camera clicked, and my heart jumped. Did I really have to think about that yet?

"It's okay, Jackson, it was probably him."

He was referring to a chubby kid holding a disposable camera.

I put my sunglasses on just in case, and Timothy, the gentleman that he was, opened the door of the cab and put my bag in the trunk for me.

On the plane home, I was the only one in first class. The stewardess was bitter and looked like Judi Dench. I sipped San Pellegrino and ran the envelope back and forth through my fingers. I slipped it into my coat pocket and fell asleep dreaming about Timothy's hands, Timothy's smooth shoulders, his lips, and his slow, lulling voice...

"We're here, fella." It was Judi Dench in the sky, waking me up.

My friend Brian picked me up at the airport in his Jeep, and I threw my guitar in the back next to his massage table.

"So, how was it?"

"Surreal. Damian Blue is so fucking talented. I'm still pinching myself."

I hardly talked on the way home—distracted by thoughts of Timothy—while Brian went on in detail about massaging Kevin Spacey and dancing with him to jazz in the Avalon Hotel. I knew that he massaged Kevin, but I wondered if the rest was embellishment.

"Hmm," I said, "cool."

He finally turned to me and said, "Why you trippin'?"

I was running my fingers along Timothy's letter in my pocket, thinking of his perfect penis. I decided to read it in the bath with candles when I got home. I told Brian I was just tired. I wasn't ready to hear any New Age reasoning about why I should or should not fall in love with Timothy Meyer. Even Brian, Mr. Spiritual Healer, knew you couldn't control your own heart.

# 13

I ran a bath and paced my house, trying to wait until the water was ready to read the letter. I gave in before the tub was half full.

> *Dearest Jackson-*
> *You are, to me, already a star.*
> *Whatever this world has planned for you,*
> *like stars on cold nights, you will shine.*
> *This card entitles you to three nights in NYC with me.*
> *We'll stay at the Soho Grand*
> *and never go above Houston.*
> *Fuck it, we'll never even leave the room.*
> *My arms await,*
> *Timothy*

Wow. How quickly could I get to New York?

I called Neil and asked him about my schedule.

"Well, you're here in LA finishing the record mostly, interspersed with meetings and so forth. Then you're off to Maine for your family reunion. Then you're shooting your video—wait, yes, you have three days in between the reunion and the shoot."

"Yes!"

"What is it now, dear?"

"Timothy Meyer and yours truly, room service, and a view of Soho."

Neil laughed. "You are too much."

"What can I say? He adores me."

"He must be smoking some good crack. Listen, when the time comes, tell Aden the reunion was extended. By the way, what am I getting out of all this?"

"My eternal gratitude."

"I'll take a check instead."

"Neil, I know you too well, you could never blackmail anyone."

"Don't underestimate me—this is Hollywood, you know."

I called Timothy's office and confirmed the dates in New York.

"Consider it done," the secretary said.

The next day I was scheduled to have lunch with Kia Diamond at Chateau Marmont. The courtyard at the hotel was a little piece of Paris, with ivy crawling up the old walls and a peaceful, perfectly hedged garden. I was surprised to find her alone in the corner, quietly flipping through *People* magazine and sipping a Bloody Mary. She was dressed down in sweats and a T-shirt, with black curls framing her long, curvy face. Her feline-like beauty was alarming. She seemed at once delicate and strong.

"You didn't have to come you know; Lonnie is such a freak. He's been Dad's client for ages, and he always tries to set me up with guys."

I blushed.

"Oh, it can't hurt, right?" I said. "Lonnie seems to be a man of instincts—he's had a few good ones with his movies at least."

She rolled her almond-shaped hazel eyes. "Among other things." She took a large bite of her celery as if ravenous.

I decided not to push that issue and changed the subject. "So how do you like being on a soap?"

"It's strange, you know. People think it's a big deal to be on television. It's not like I'm changing the world. The writing on soaps is so atrocious that the worse an actor you are, the more successful you are. What I really want to do is make documentaries. The show is just a stepping stone, really. What about you? Music is your passion, or do you have some hidden, bigger agenda?"

"Oh, no. I couldn't think of anything else I'd want to do. Except maybe move to Italy and write a novel."

"Ha. You can do that after you're a star. Publish your memoirs."

Just then, Tobey Maguire came in with a small entourage. He looked like he hadn't slept in days, but even with rings under his eyes he was cute.

"Please," Kia said, "you can do better."

Ironic, that my first pseudo-hetero date recognizes my sexuality right away. I became mesmerized by the sunlight dappling her curls.

"Hey, do you want to get out of here and smoke a joint?" I said.

"That sounds groovy."

I couldn't tell if she was mocking me. She didn't seem like a person who used the word "groovy."

"We don't have to—"

"No seriously, let's go."

She downed her Bloody Mary and took the celery stick with her, which she ate noisily as we left the building. The juxtaposition of this delicate, lithe beauty chomping on celery like a horse was akin to a car accident. I couldn't look away.

An hour later we were perched on her balcony in Malibu overlooking the greenish, foamy sea, puffing an expensive joint. A tall, skinny, Brazilian-looking maid brought us iced tea with orange slices. She looked me up and down, and raised her eyebrows slightly at Kia.

"Ermolinda, this is Jackson."

She smiled, revealing perfect white teeth. She was the prettiest maid I had ever seen. She looked more like an exotic supermodel.

"Pleased to meet you," I said. She smiled a knowing, even slightly hostile, smile.

During the course of the afternoon, the iced teas turned into mojitos, and Kia and I each popped a Xanax. She described her father as a slimeball who screwed people for a living.

"An escort?" I asked, kidding.

"No, a lawyer."

"Oh, right, he and Lonnie Simpson work together." Now I remembered Aden mentioning that Kia's dad was the legendary showbiz lawyer Mark Diamond, but as with most of Aden's name-dropping, it had gone in one ear and out the other at the time.

She told me her dad had a place in town off Melrose that he worked out of and slept at most nights. Her mother was the famous Bree Diamond, publicist extraordinaire. She was throwing an opening soiree that night for the new hip restaurant in Santa Monica called Egg.

"Do you want to come?"

"Sure, why not."

Next thing you know we were getting our picture taken while getting out of Kia's SL5. We made our entrance into the restaurant, which had glass floors under which were thousands of pale brown eggs.

"I feel like I'm walking on eggshells," she turned and said to me.

"Ha!"

It was a festive, charged atmosphere—everyone pressed, primped, and glowing; voices and laughter sparkling; eyes darting. And though there were no celebrities in direct sight, one could feel their presence. It was an LA thing.

"Sweetie! Darling!" It was Bree, Kia's mother, calling out from across the room. She was carrying a phone, a Palm Pilot, and a purse, all in matching silver. She shuffled toward us through the crowd in her sleek, fitted black D&G dress looking perfectly restored, as if she slept inside Tupperware. The strange thing was, she looked even younger than Kia.

Noticing my befuddlement, Kia discreetly whispered, "The amount of money she's spent on her face could've fed an entire country in Africa."

"Right," I said.

Bree reached us and exclaimed, "Oh, look what we have here. Jackson, right? The-up-and-coming singer, deal with Virgin. I spoke to Clyde yesterday—he wants me to cover the launch of your album. I told him he couldn't afford me!" She was referring to Clyde Anson, the head of Virgin, who'd given me that foul cigar when I signed my contract. She laughed to herself, an erratic, monkey laugh that did anything but compliment her flawless fashion.

Before I could say anything, Kia pulled my arm and said, "Mom, we're famished, we're going to hit up the appetizer girls."

"Just eat the food, honey, not the girls."

Kia gave her a funny look.

We grabbed some lobster profiteroles and sashimi and went outside onto the veranda. A couple was fighting in the corner.

"Always with the drama," Kia said. "This town..."

I noticed that she was still beautiful despite the near-permanent look of disgust on her face.

"Par for the course for your kind of work, huh?" I asked.

"Well, at least in real life the script is better."

"Not always," I said.

"You obviously don't watch soap operas."

"Can't say that I do. Although I did watch *Little House on the Prairie* religiously when I was a kid."

"That's 'cause you had a crush on Michael Landon."

"Who didn't?" The Xanax and the mojitos were making my head swim. In a lovely way, of course.

"So, what's your take on Lonnie Simpson?" I asked.

"He's crazy. Literally. He's in a position to help you though, if that's what you want."

"Lately, I'm not sure what I want."

"Tell me about it."

After the opening, we went back to Kia's where we ate ice cream and watched *Harold and Maude*. It was a movie we both knew by heart. When it was over she rested her head on my shoulder and said, "You're sweet. You know that? Today didn't seem so bad with you around."

"Well, hey, I try."

"I get off the set at two tomorrow, do you want to go to Silverlake and get fish tacos?"

"Sounds like a plan."

She got up and stretched, her tanned and taut navel exposing a tiny silver ring. A perfect circle, partly obscured.

"Cool, meet me on the CBS lot on Beverly at 2:15. I'll tell them you're coming. Goodnight, Jackson."

She got up and languidly walked out of the room.

I made my own way out the door. As I was getting into my car, I heard two voices giggling. It was Bree, in the back of a limo with someone who looked like an older Johnny Depp. Maybe it was Johnny Depp. Whoever it was, it wasn't her famous lawyer husband, Mark Diamond.

There were four messages on my machine when I got home. The obligatory Aden and mother messages, one from Neil, and one from Kia saying, "Hey, I was thinking, you sure you want to be a rock star? I don't want to see you all cracked-out on VH1's *Behind the Music* in ten years, broke and bitter. See you tomorrow."

I giggled and lay down on the couch. After listening to my CD, playing some guitar, and reading the latest *Rolling Stone,* I fell asleep and didn't wake up until noon the next day.

# 14

I woke to the phone ringing. I don't know why, but I could always tell when it would be Neil.

"The artwork specs for the record just arrived, and Aden wants you to come over and look at them. Can you be here in fifteen?"

"Um, yeah, sure."

I had a poor man's shower (water splashed on my face and under the arms) and changed into a T-shirt I'd picked up at a thrift store purely to annoy Aden. Printed on the front were the words: "Silly Faggot, Dicks Are for Chicks". I thought he might appreciate it. Since I didn't know how to deal with Aden's obsession, all I could do was point my finger and laugh at it.

"Now that's taking it a little too far," Aden said when he saw the slogan.

Derek looked up from his bowl of Cocoa Puffs and laughed. "Keep it in the act," he said.

The artwork for the album was very cool—a Japanese anime-style drawing of a guy walking underneath a tree. There was no picture of me anywhere, which I liked. Let the music speak for itself. Egocentrism was out. I was amazed at how slick it looked compared to my demo and my first self-released CD. It was the real thing!

I approved the specs for the artwork and added a few people to the special-thanks list, including Timothy Meyer. Aden started to say something about it but Derek held out his hand. It was one of the few times I'd ever witnessed Derek exercise power over him. Remarkably, Aden backed down.

While pouring a second white-wine spritzer, Aden asked, "So how was your meeting with Kia Diamond, soapstress extraordinaire?"

"Let's just say she was nothing like I thought she'd be."

"How do you mean?" Aden was doing his squinty, *do tell* look.

"She's smart and kind of tough. And she really is exquisite. More than soap-star beauty."

"You'd have to be if you were the offspring of Mark and Bree."

"I met Bree, too, the other night. She's a trip," I said.

"Well, she's the trip that's going to get your career off the ground," Aden said. "This morning she signed the contract to publicize your first record."

"But she told me we couldn't afford her."

"Yes, but Virgin can."

"Right."

"You have meetings with some campus magazines tomorrow, and Neil is also going to conference you in with some European press—you know they're already spinning the single we produced."

"I know! It's unbelievable!"

"It will only get better, my friend. After you make your video, and all the press hits, everything will explode." I could see dollar signs in Aden's eyes.

I told them I had to run off to meet Kia for lunch.

"Oh, so this is becoming a thing?" Aden slapped me on the back. "Don't mind us, Romeo."

Derek put his finger in his mouth without Aden knowing.

I smiled.

On my way over to the lot I played my CD again, hoping to hear anything I could change to make it the best it could be. But I couldn't get in analytical mode because it kept reminding me of Timothy. Listening to it with him in the hotel in South Beach—his warm eyes, that supple skin. I couldn't wait to see him again.

The set for Kia's soap that day was a diner and a bedroom, sitting in each corner of the warehouse-like space, with hallways and dressing rooms along the sides. I found her in the hallway taking bobby pins out of her hair. As each strand fell, she became more and more real looking, the Kia I had first seen in the Chateau Marmont. The Kia of striking, natural beauty.

"Hey, kid," she said, like I was her little brother, "interesting shirt."

I looked down and remembered I was wearing the "Silly Faggot, Dicks Are for Chicks" shirt.

"Just give me ten," Kia said.

She dipped into her dressing room. While waiting outside I received several flirty looks from well-groomed actors, costume people, and set decorators. Apparently my shirt was being read as an ironic statement. Most of them looked like Ken dolls, and they were all dressed in black. I wondered how they dealt with the heat outside.

Kia burst through the door and said, "Your car or mine?"

"Yours is slightly more glamorous."

"Ugh, you sound like my mother. Listen, let's forget Silverlake and just go to Urth Café. It's right by my dad's place, so we can leave our cars there and not worry about parking. The clientele is kind of 818, but the food is delicious."

Kia was referring to the area code in "the Valley."

She gave me the cross streets for her dad's place and as we got closer to the house I had a strong sense of déjà vu. When we got to the driveway I froze in my seat. I had been there before. Oh my God. It was Mr. Cuddle's house. My Sunday-only lover, who never wanted me to stay through the night.

Kia knocked on the window and I snapped out of my trance.

*Pull it together,* I thought. *You've slept with her father. It's Hollywood. Pull it together.*

"Will your dad mind that we're using his parking space?"

"No, it's okay. I only come here when I know he's out of town. It's supposed to be his big work sanctuary, whatever that means, so my mom and I aren't allowed. I always suspected he just uses it to bang chicks."

*Yeah, chicks with dicks.*

She gestured toward a gate that led behind the house. "When I was in high school my friends and I would party by the pool when he was away." She gave a demonic little laugh. "It's handy having a daddy with his own private fuck pad."

What would I say? Should I keep quiet? I tripped over the curb and she laughed.

"Graceful, baby. Just don't do that on the red carpet."

We made our way down to Urth Café, which was crawling with coiffed, fake-tanned, Kenneth Cole–wearing industry types and their cell phones. After contemplating ordering a salad I settled on a ham sandwich. To my surprise, Kia ordered one too.

"The only reason to come here is the food," she said.

As we sat down, Kia started talking.

"I can't stand people who don't eat. It's so tired. 'Oh, I'll have a house salad, no dressing,' it's like, please, you're not a fucking rabbit. We're meant to be omnivores..."

Kia went on but I was zoning out, thinking of her father. I couldn't believe he was Mark Diamond, aka Mr. Cuddle! I had spent six Sundays in a row at that very same house, yet I had never gotten his last name. Lonnie Simpson's longtime client and Bree Diamond's husband—my movie-soundtrack contact, and my album publicist. The world was getting smaller by the minute. I suddenly felt a dose of Aden-style paranoia.

Mark Diamond was very cute, dark-skinned, with tiny hands and a tightly wrapped cocaine habit he'd bring out on the weekends only. He told me all about his routine: cocaine on Friday nights till three, pop an Ambien, then off to Malibu to play tennis on Saturdays (probably with Bree, I now realized). The fact that he regularly played tennis, that he had a little tennis bag, had turned me on, among other things: His place was always flawlessly neat, and there wasn't a single hair on his body—that beautifully taut, slick-skinned body he preserved so well for being forty. But in Los Angeles, forty was the new thirty anyway.

We would go to dinner every Sunday and chat aimlessly. He was funny enough, a bit dry for my taste, but the real pleasure was in the sex. I had wondered why he never wanted to linger afterward. Perhaps he had to get back to Malibu, to his wife and daughter, who I was now having lunch with. I scratched him off the true-love list.

"...binge and purge. I swear to God, on our set it's like Bulimics-Are-Us."

I noticed that Kia had the same high cheekbones as Mark. How was I going to tell her?

"...look at the fucking media! Every magazine model is airbrushed and their figure is virtually unattainable."

I noticed Kia's figure, which was healthy, supple, though of course still thin by anyone's standards outside of Hollywood. Real women have curves.

"They told me, the producers, that I needed to lose six pounds, can you imagine? I was like, take your six pounds and shove it up your ass."

I laughed. "They probably would have liked that."

Kia bit into her ham sandwich with animalistic verve. I sliced mine into fours for easier access. Role reversal.

"So what do you want to do documentaries on?" I asked.

"The irony and dichotomies within Hollywood."

"Political, satire, what?"

"Little of both. Michael Moore's a genius, but not as radical as him."

"Do you plan on exposing the lives of your parents?"

"Not exactly, although they are perfect examples."

Just then, a girl in unflattering spandex came up and asked Kia for her autograph.

"I love your show," the girl said, "and I really hope Brock dumps Lacey for you."

"The only thing Brock needs is a nine-inch cock," Kia said. I couldn't help but laugh. The woman pretended not to hear but was obviously mortified. She muttered a "thanks" and walked away. It was awkward to say the least.

"Bridge-and-tunnel crowd, they're the only people who watch our show," Kia said. I had heard this term in New York, but I supposed it was loosely applied to LA, too, meaning people from the Valley, from places outside Hollywood. I was confused as to why she wouldn't embrace her fans, even if they were slightly tragic.

After lunch we walked back to Mark Diamond's. She asked me to come in, but I quickly made an excuse that I had to go. We exchanged cell-phone numbers.

"Did you want Brock's number, too?" she said, smiling.

"I'm afraid I'm only eight and a half."

Kia smiled, and I felt a sense of protection that she was on my side. "Call me later."

Driving away, I immediately called Neil.

"Oh my God, do you remember Mr. Cuddle?"

"Of course," he said, "that lawyer guy with the hot body you were doing."

"Yeah. It's Mark-fucking-Diamond."

A Honda Element cut me off and I honked. Bitch.

"What?" There was a silence on the line, then, "How you get yourselves in these situations, Jackson, is beyond—"

"I've been hanging out with Kia on Lonnie Simpson's suggestion, how was I supposed to know—"

"Listen, believe it or not, Cher's people are on the other line so I've got to go."

"Is she doing Derek's song?"

"Yes, I'll tell you about it tomorrow."

One of the many ironies of all of this was that Derek had made a career writing songs for divas. And I was their "straight" artist.

What the hell was I going to do if Aden found out I'd been sleeping with Mark Diamond? Did Kia know he was gay? Did Bree?

This was all getting too strange.

# 15

When I woke up the next day, I realized I needed to work off some steam and think, so I beelined it to the Crunch on Sunset. I got there in record time and found a Stairmaster in the back corner, trying to avoid Jed, who loved to dish. Although I was usually game, that day I wasn't in the mood for socializing. All of this was happening so fast. I just wanted to be able to be myself, but I didn't want to sacrifice my success. Yes, I wanted teenage girls to buy my records, but no, I didn't want to hide my sexuality. Yes, I wanted to find true love, but after finding out that Mr. Cuddle was Kia's dad, I had serious doubts about my ability to pick the right guy. Something told me that Timothy Meyer was too perfect, that there had to be a catch.

I was vaguely aware of a girl two machines down, sweating like mad, her hair pulled back tight. After I stepped off, so did she.

"Hey, you want to go to the movies?"

It was Kia. I hadn't recognized her with her hair up.

"Sure," I said, "after I'm done. I could use an escape."

In the locker room I literally bumped into Jake Gyllenhaal. I said sorry and he just looked at me like I was a loser. I said it again, but his personal trainer just held out his hand as if to say *down boy.* Like I really cared that much about Jake-fucking-Gyllenhaal.

At the Sunset Five we saw the new Christopher Guest movie, which had us in complete stitches. Afterward, we went to Jones and got chopped salads and beers. In the dark corner of the restaurant, I broke down and revealed everything on my mind to Kia (except the fact that I had slept with her father): my apprehension about my career, my sexuality, Aden over my shoulder, Timothy Meyer. She seemed pretty unfazed by it all.

"Listen, Jackson," she said, "I knew you were gay from the start. But if you want to play straight, you can. Just don't be so nice.

Straight guys are assholes, in general. In a way, I understand where Aden is coming from. Hell, I've been playing straight for four years. It's hard enough getting work in this business without anything else for them to hold against you."

"What, you mean on the show?"

"On the show and in real life."

This I had to sit with for a minute. Of course I'd raised an eyebrow at her mom's comment at the opening—something about not eating the appetizer girls. But I guess I just hadn't processed it completely.

"Wait a sec—"

"I've been sleeping with Ermolinda since I was sixteen."

I remembered the iced teas on the porch in Malibu, the sexy maid raising her eyebrows.

"Well," I was clearly at a loss, "could you pass the butter?"

# 16

Damian flew to LA, and we did our last remaining overdubs on the record and started the final mixes. It was sounding so right, I felt really fortunate to have worked with such amazing people. When a fan buys a record, a lot of times they have no clue how much has to come together to get it to the point of being packaged and sold. One of the engineers had spent the better part of a day getting a sound for the bass drum! There were engineers, interns, studio musicians, graphic artists, managers, all making decisions—in a way my part was the easiest: show up and do what I do best. But I was so thankful at how far the project had come and realized I couldn't have done it alone. My record was ready to fly.

I headed back to Maine for my family reunion. On the plane ride I thought about Kia and her father, Mr. Cuddle, and how small the world actually was. I also thought of Aden and his quest to keep the world in a closet. All these people with secrets, and now I was one of them. I was going to have to tell Kia about her father sooner, rather than later.

The reunion spot was a secluded island on a large glassy lake, with six quaint cabins, all occupied by various members of my family. The morning after I arrived my mother came to my cabin and collected me for a skinny-dip.

"Morning, angel. Ready for a dip?"

"Sure, Mom. Hang on."

For some reason, skinny-dipping was something we always did together in my family, like say, gardening. Neighbors and such always thought it was a bit odd, but we never cared. I suppose we were exhibitionists, in our way.

My mom was the one I first came out to. Since she was worried about me contracting AIDS, it was hard for her to take, but she was completely incapable of hatred; she had an enormous heart and spread her good nature wherever she went. Plus, I had assured her that I practiced safe sex.

The lake was cold and crisp at that early hour but ran like silk over my skin, opening my senses and waking my brain. We swam out to a floating dock. The ladder was broken, so I hoisted myself up. When my mother tried, she fell clumsily back in.

"I'm not forty anymore," she said. "Get ready to bring out the oxygen tanks."

I reached out to grab her, but she refused my help and tried a second time, succeeding. She lay down next to me on the dock, both of us looking up at the early morning sky.

"The quiet is nice, isn't it?" she said. We lay there companionably, listening to the wind.

I wondered if the career path I was headed on would crumble because of the workings of my heart, which was basically what my music was based on. I wondered about Timothy, and why he hadn't ever given me his home number. I wondered about Kia and the maid, how beautiful they must be together yet how screwed up the situation was. I asked myself to simply let everything take its course and hope for the best.

"What's wrong, honey? You seem low."

"Well, this career thing is taking off and I have to play straight."

"How come?"

"Lots of reasons."

We sat in the stillness of the lake and listened to the distant loons.

I enjoyed quiet time with her. She was always the mother cheering the loudest at the soccer and hockey games. I'd secretly pray she'd tone it down. I used to make her duck down in the car if I saw someone who knew me, heaven forbid being seen with her. It wasn't that I despised her; it was that I felt her histrionics tarnished my burgeoning self-image as cooler than ice, with my feathered hair and Member's Only jacket. Don Juan in the making. Or maybe Cleopatra?

"Well, angel, I knew it was just a matter of time before your music was recognized, but no career is worth shutting down your heart for."

"Well, just in public."

"Ah."

I took her wrist and played with her bracelets.

"Do you have someone now?" she asked.

"Yeah. He's an editor at a big magazine."

"Holy smokes."

"I know."

I suppose it should have seemed strange to be hanging out with my mom, both of us naked, talking about the older man I was screwing, but it didn't.

"Just make sure he treats you well. You know, when you were a kid, you used to put on shows for us and the neighbors—"

"I know, in drag, right?"

She started laughing. "But you sang perfectly on key. Everyone loved it!"

"See? This is exactly what Aden's worried about. Can you imagine if something like that got out?"

"You always were very interested in my shoes," she said.

I placed her wrist back down.

"And the time I decorated the garage?"

"But it's all part of who you are. And it comes out in your songs."

"I know, that's what I try and tell Aden."

"He should talk—he's no Marlboro Man himself."

I laughed. "I know, right? Oh well, I'll figure it out."

Mother turned and squeezed my face together, giving me a big smooch.

"I know you will. As long as you keep being yourself and spreading your gift." Then she added, a tone lower, "Which of course, you got from me!"

She dove sideways into the water, her arms raised and a mischievous smile in her blue eyes. There was a glow around her head, her bracelets reflecting the low-angled morning sun, and I could feel the fresh, fresh air on my skin. That image of her would remain in my mind for years to come.

She was right—I did get my voice and my stage presence from her. My mom was known for her sense of high drama, conducting sing-alongs at dinner parties and being the first one on the dance floor. She always had a certain spunk, breathing life into any party. Even though Dad didn't lack in that department at all—he even played Big Jules in *Guys and Dolls*—my style took after her. Dad was the witty type, but Mom and I had too much emotional exuberance to pull off his dry delivery.

"What about my looks?" I said, jokingly. "Where'd I get those?"

She got back onto the dock, with ease that time, and looked at me with mock indignation.

"From me as well! What the hell would've happened if you got your father's nose?"

Just then she sneezed and the whole dock swayed. She may have spared me my father's nose, but the cost was my scaled-down version of her famous sneeze. Ever since I was a little boy I'd been terrified of her sneeze—a startled, screamlike explosion. And they always came in triplicate. Even our dog, Katzen, would briskly exit the room after she'd start in. Whenever Aden said my sneeze was loud, I told him it was nothing compared to my mother's.

"Okay, no more lollygagging you guys, breakfast's on!"

It was Dad calling from the porch of the main cabin. The sun was almost up over the trees.

"Race you," I said to Mom, and we smiled at each other and jumped off the dock, our privates jiggling free. We took off along the surface of the lake, our arms splashing white sparks off the crisp blue.

After breakfast, I noticed Dad wheezing a little on the porch. He had always had a strange breathing pattern, but it seemed different to me, shorter.

"I just heard the songs from start to finish. Nice!" he said. Then trying a little too hard to sound hip, he said, "It's got a cool vibe."

"Yeah."

I guess he could sense a hesitation in my response, because he asked, "You nervous about it?"

"Well, yeah, I guess."

"Not about the tunes, they're awesome!"

"No, it's the other thing."

He did this lip pursing thing that he always did when he was uncomfortable.

"Well, this Jaden character—"

"Aden." He always got Aden's name wrong.

"He's right, you know. Why let your personal life limit your success?"

He said the words "personal life" like he didn't approve.

"Yeah, I suppose so."

"Jack-in-the-Box, you know how many one-hit wonders there are out there? This is not a forgiving industry. I want to see you thrive. Just, you know, tone it down a bit."

My brother, Max, came out and overheard the last bit.

"Yeah," he said, "just do a lot of Sister Sledge covers."

Dad was at a loss. "What?"

To swerve away from Max's joke, I told Dad that they were auditioning top players for my backing band.

"Shouldn't you be there for that?" he asked.

"Derek is making the final decision and I totally trust him musically."

Dad looked satisfied.

"Okay."

Lots of stories went around at dinner that night between my family—Max and his son Tristan; my sister Rose's family, my mom and dad and me. Although Max was divorced, his and Rose's offspring, thankfully, took the pressure off me to procreate. Tristan was six years old, a beautiful, towheaded, precocious boy, who was my favorite nephew, partly because I had spent the most time with him. Max was a tender, salt-of-the-earth brother, and we had always enjoyed each other's company, even understood each other. Over the next few days we did all our traditional activities—swimming, canoeing, and singing songs around the campfire. Being with people who had known me my whole life could sometimes feel limiting, but it was wonderful, too.

On my last day I took a power nap in the afternoon and woke up groggy and giddy. I walked out to the lake and let my eyes drift over the water, escaping into the calm. The lakes in that part of the country were like pools of heaven left behind by glaciers over a million years ago, before humans came along with devices that eventually made more and more devices. Cell phones didn't work, and there was only one phone affixed to a tree by the long dirt road. It felt so primitive being surrounded by wood and trees, water and earth. It was grounding.

I thought about my upcoming visit with Timothy and reminded myself to keep a clear head, that I really wasn't quite sure whom I was dealing with.

# 17

The Soho Grand was elegant in a new-money kind of way. When I entered the suite, I saw a note that read "back in a flash" in that curvy handwriting that flooded my groin. I took a quick bath, and when I emerged from the bathroom this wonderful scent hit me like a punch. Timothy had plucked dozens of roses and covered the bed in hundreds of fresh, blood-red petals.

He was standing there naked save for his Rolex.

"Nice outfit," I said.

He told me to undress and get on the bed. I giggled with euphoria and obeyed, and he took my picture.

Like Whoopi Goldberg in the milk, I was immersed in velvety red. His semihard erection swung around as he moved over to the stereo and put on Prince's "Adore."

If heaven were actually a place, we were occupying it. Throughout it all, however, I saw flashes of Aden's face. I couldn't believe I was thinking about my career, in bed with a thousand rose petals and a hot older man. Was I becoming obsessed?

The rose scent was so thick it was intoxicating.

He looked at me with such grace and concentration.

"I could fall into your eyes," I said.

He kissed me everywhere—my armpits, my toes, the base of my back, and beyond. I felt beautiful. We barely left the bed for two days, except to pee, and I rationalized the sex as substitution for the gym. Once, while he took a bath, I got up and did five hundred sit-ups. The room service was splendid, and we even ordered a bottle of single malt. By the end of our stay, the room-service people seemed to regard us as exotic animals.

One afternoon, Timothy ordered ice and it took twenty minutes for us to finally receive it. He was curt and subtly cruel to the bellboy and said he would report him to the management.

"It's not his fault," I said, having much experience on the other side of the situation myself.

"You're right, I'll apologize the next time I see him. I just want everything to be perfect for you."

How could I argue with that?

I let him devour me, gave in to his seemingly endless greed. There were inches of his body I would stare at after orgasm, turns and shapes I'd taste—the back of his wrists, the inside of his elbow. He had a small ring through his firm navel that left a metallic sting on my tongue. A curving of gold into skin. A secret.

The last night we were staring at the lights of Soho from our large balcony (we had moved the mattress outside and put on old Beatles on the portable he tipped the concierge for) when he asked me what I wanted to be when I grew up. I thought for more than a moment. "To love." I answered. "And be loved."

He smiled and rested his head on my belly, the sparkling lights reflecting in his eyes.

"Me, too."

"No," I demanded, "you have to come up with your own answer."

Timothy didn't flinch.

"To love you. And be loved by you."

I laughed. He sat up.

Timothy seemed everything I was looking for. Stormy green eyes and a cool, clever smile.

"That song," he said, "'Fear of Falling,' is that about anyone in particular? Or just...life?"

"Right now it's about this," I said, and nibbled the hot stubble on his cheek.

The last night we simply fell asleep in each other's arms. He had a soft, adorable little snore—like a boy.

I felt safe from everything, free of all my worries.

When I awoke, Timothy was gone.

I looked around for a note, a signal, something. There was

nothing. I waited for a while and went to the hotel gym. When I came back, still no sign. I paced around the room, swearing out loud. *What the fuck?*

When I finally left the room, a well-dressed man swiftly approached me and said, "Mr. Poole?"

"Yes?" How did he know my name? I immediately thought it was a reporter and that that was it, my cover was blown.

He flashed some sort of laminated credentials. "If you don't mind, I'd like to have a few words with you."

My heart raced. What was this?

We stepped into an empty stairwell.

"We understand you've just been occupying a room that was purchased by a Timothy Meyer?"

This was like fucking *NYPD Blue.* He seemed to sense my nervousness and said, "This is nothing to do with you. I'm just looking for some information on Mr. Meyer. Have you known him long?"

The guy looked like James Woods. I was sweating. Could someone just yell *Cut!?*

"Um, a little while I guess."

"Do you know a Deborah Meyer?"

Oh, perfect. He's *married.*

"No, who's—"

"Do you happen to know where Mr. Meyer was headed?"

Even though I was still confused, I was relieved that he obviously wasn't a reporter. Or was he? How could I be sure?

"No. What is this about?"

"I'm afraid that is information I cannot disclose at present. Thank you for your time."

I was waiting for him to give me his business card, like in the movies. He didn't, just nodded his head and walked away.

I hailed a taxi to take me to the airport and immediately called Neil. The voicemail picked up.

"Neil, listen I need you to do something ASAP. Call Timothy Meyer's office and tell him to call my cell immediately." I wanted Neil to call so it would sound more official and not too desperate in case Timothy had a legitimate excuse.

Either I had watched too many movies or smoked too much grass, but while I was sitting on the plane, it suddenly occurred to me that I could have been bugged. I checked my clothes for a tracking device as discreetly as possible in the confines of an airplane seat. That's when I found the note in my jacket pocket. I recognized Timothy's wavy letters spelling JP on the outside in red. Even though I hated when people called me JP in high school, I liked seeing it written by him. My anger was temporarily assuaged, though I was still slightly disturbed by the whole detective thing. My heart lurched as I read:

> Jackson-
> Didn't want to wake the angel.
> Have to leave town for a while.
> Will you sing that song for me on my work voicemail?
> When I want to hear your voice, I'll know it's there.
> Talk to you soon.
> love t. meyer

I was relieved but still confused. Wouldn't he have known in advance that he was leaving town? Why had he just snuck off like that? I called his work number and asked for him, on the off chance he was there, wrapping things up before leaving town. His secretary asked for my name, and when I said who I was, her tone warmed up.

"Well, hello there," she said with her strong London accent, "I just saw a preliminary proof of your spread this morning. It looks simply *divine*, darling."

I had almost forgotten about the snowy car, the photo shoot.

"The boss has taken quite an interest in you. He left me a message for you that I'm to read word for word. Hold on." There was a pause, then she read, "I know you're going to be the next big thing."

My heart fluttered. I hoped he meant more than just my

music.

"Oh, and I heard they're spinning a pre-release of your single on WXPQ, what is it, 'Your Illusion?'"

"'Just an Illusion,'" I said, as masculine as possible.

"Right."

"Cool," I said, in a husky tone Aden would have approved. "When does the issue come out?"

"Tomorrow, dear. Do you want to leave a message for Timothy?"

"Actually, can you put me through to his voicemail?"

"No worries. Good luck with everything."

Timothy's voice came on, stately and professional. The phone beeped, and even though I was in 28B, in the middle of two people, and Timothy was probably married *and* a criminal, I sang "Fear of Falling" on his voicemail:

> *Love of flying, fear of falling*
> *Love of flying, fear of falling*
> *If I let go*
> *will you catch me*
> *If you catch me*
> *will you let go?*

The woman seated on the window clapped when I hung up. She was slightly overweight and smelled like mothballs.

"That was great. Are you a singer?"

"No," I said, trying to choose a profession, "I'm a broker."

That shut her up.

The image of the detective kept swimming in my mind, alternating with flashes of Timothy's gorgeous body, his soulful eyes. Was the guy really there for Timothy, or was it just a ruse to get dirt on me?

Either way, something was sketchy.

# 18

The morning after my return was the day of my first-ever video shoot. On the drive there, Neil filled me in.

"The director is very up-and-coming, he just finished doing J-Lo's video."

"Oh that's a good match for my image. Should I pad my ass?"

"Won't help, dear."

The shoot took place on a hillside north of LA that had been burned in the wildfires. The idea was "moonscape" shot in black and white. The label had given me a big advance on the record, but the video budget wasn't particularly extravagant. However, there were three assistants, yummy catering, and two trucks full of gear.

Neil had someone put a DIVA sign on my trailer. I had a trailer!

We worked well into the night and I was exhausted. Three cameras on me and my guitar, and a girl, of course, dressed in a billowy white dress, dancing down the ridge. She was a model, and after lunch I asked her why she hadn't eaten anything.

"I had lunch," she said.

"Really? What?"

"A Snapple and a cigarette."

Aden and Derek had to fly to New York to meet with radio promoters and weren't at the shoot, so Aden sent the straight patrol—these two guys he'd hired as "consultants." Neil was livid.

"Oh, what, because he doesn't trust me?"

"Whatever," I said. "We already decided on the outfit. What are they gonna do, make me play touch football with them during breaks? Hmm, now that's an option."

I was wearing the latest jean out of Norway, which still had the price tag—$1,200. For jeans! I felt like I should hang them on the wall or something. My top was an old black T-shirt with designs and words on the sleeves. It was surprisingly fitted without look-ing too gay, and underneath I had on a long-underwear shirt from Barneys. The label borrows the clothes, and the store or designer gets free advertising in exchange. The more buzz an artist had on a certain label, the more attention and perks you got.

The straight patrol ended up doing nothing except hit on the model.

I tried to put as much energy as I could into each shot, but I felt bizarre lip-synching and playing random parts of my song in various poses. In truth, the whole experience was more exhausting than glamorous.

When we were driving home, Neil was quiet.

"You looked great; I snuck a peek at some of the angles."

"Thanks, sweetie. I hope so."

The following night I met Kia for drinks at the SkyBar. The bouncer almost didn't let us in, but someone whispered in his ear and he said, "Right this way, Mr. Poole," handing me a drink card. From the way everyone was pining to get in, you'd think the SkyBar was the White House. It was just a little hut with a nice pool outside it. I noticed that seventy percent of the girls in the bar had boob jobs. They all looked like they were trying to resemble Laura Croft. We ordered mojitos and I told myself I had to come clean about her father.

"There's something I need to tell you," I said.

"You're pregnant."

"Girl, you spend too much time on that soap."

"Yes, but only for one more year, then I'm going to make moc-kumentaries that'll expose it all—and let me tell you, it's not going to be pretty."

I just blurted it out, "Your dad, Mark, I knew him before."

Her beautiful dark eyes caught my gaze and held it.

I went on.

"Is he, well, is he..."

"Spit it out."

I took a quick intake of breath and let it fly.

"We dated."

"What?"

"We dated. A few months ago. Well, it was really just dinner and sex. At the house, where I met you, where his office is."

This got her. It was too real to be a script. Kia turned to the girl next to her and bummed a cigarette. She didn't speak until after three or four drags.

"My mother once asked me if I knew anything; she said their sex life had been slowly dwindling. I knew he fucked around, but I had no idea with guys. Was he good?"

We were already on shaky ground, but somehow with Kia, I didn't monitor my conversations. Stuff just came out.

"He was fucking hot. The sex was totally incredible. Went on and on. He was, like, a dream guy for me. But there was one thing. He'd always ask me to leave right after we finished. I, well, me and some of my friends, referred to him as Mr. Cuddle."

She laughed. "Fear of intimacy."

"It's over now; it only lasted six weeks. Six Sundays actually, like a prayer of sorts." I took a long gulp of the mojito.

The Valley Girl next to me at the bar stopped doing her lip gloss long enough to smile at me for that one. Then she recognized Kia.

"Hey, are you like, Sasha on *The Young and the Restless*?"

"No," Kia said while taking her last drag, "that's my bi-polar lesbian twin sister." I couldn't help but let out a small yelp. The Valley Girl spitefully went back to her lips.

"Well, Jackson, you've certainly woven a web," Kia said.

"Are you mad?"

"He's an adult, Jackson, and so am I. Fuck it."

"I did."

"Clearly. It is weird to think about."

She put out her cigarette and sighed, switching gears. "So, do tell—who is residing in your web at the moment?"

"Timothy Meyer, but he seems to be in some kind of trouble,

and I think he's married." I told her about my wonderful time with him in New York, and then the weirdness of being approached by the detective.

"You know what, Jackson? You need to find a big hole and jump in it, stay there for a while. You seem to be a magnet for drama. I have a feeling this Timothy Meyer thing is leading somewhere...not the place to embrace, you know what I'm saying?"

"I know, and Lonnie Simpson, the hetero matchmaker, is crucial to my career at this point, at least on the film and television side. And he's a close friend of your father, whom I slept with!"

"That was the drama from two commercials ago."

"Aden's down my throat about anyone knowing I'm gay. What the fuck am I going to do?"

Kia waved at the waif bartendress in a purple sarong. "Two more, and make them doubles."

I laughed, which was good considering the fact that my stomach hurt and my brain couldn't process all the things that were going on.

"You know, I think it's really sinking in: You slept with my fucking father. He is so, SO busted."

"You can't say anything."

"Well, only if I must. I guess it is kind of creeping me out, though. He's like, double your age."

"I've always been into daddy types, what can I say? Not daddies in a leather-bar, furry sense, but distinguished gentlemen. Suits and handkerchiefs, men that hold the door and keep their knives in the right hand." My millionaire ex-boyfriend Barkley but preferably without the high drama and chemical imbalances.

"Well, he is a daddy, that's for sure," Kia said. "Oh my god, Bree would shit. They share the same therapist too, I wonder if...oh well," she said while preparing to slurp the second mojito, "such are the machinations of this warped town."

I wanted to know about her and Ermolinda, so I figured I'd divert her away from the your-father-was-my-fuck-buddy topic.

"So what's the deal with you and Miss Brazil?"

Her eyes went from their usual striking stare to watery and soft around the edges. The look said, *Do you really want to know?*

Yes.

"Well, she's worked for our family since I was a kid," she said. "It's slightly strange because in a way she was like my mother, then later became my lover. It's very Oedipal. But I was the one who initiated it, and now I can't imagine my life without her."

"And you're telling me it's weird that Mark was double my age?"

"Projection, I suppose." She said.

"Does your mother know?"

"She knows, but I think she's repressing it. At first she wanted to fire her but I wouldn't let her. Ermolinda is the best thing that ever happened to me. She knows what it means to listen, to really be there for someone. She's extremely altruistic, which is refreshing in this town."

"She certainly is beautiful."

"She liked you, too. She said you were like a lost animal, frightened on the outside but strong on the inside. She compared you, in Portuguese, to a truffle—bitter and sweet."

"You speak her language?"

"Of course, we've been together since I was sixteen."

We sipped our drinks.

After a moment I said, "What am I going to do?"

"Listen, I'll arrange for you to come by Dad's house, and you can tell him he must keep whatever happened between you two under wraps. In the meantime, you and I will go to the *Charlie's Angels* premiere together and get shot by everyone from *Us Weekly* to the *Times*. That will satisfy Aden, your label, and my agent. Voila."

"Wait a second, you're agent is—"

"Ironically, my agent is a lesbian, too. But I guess it's like your situation with Aden. Everyone in this town is so busy trying to be what they think will sell that nobody knows what's real anymore."

"This town is so twisted."

"Like a pretzel, baby."

"So wait, I'm confused," I said. "Do your parents actually ever sleep together?"

"Not anymore. Dad stays at the Melrose house, and Mom and I and Ermie stay in Malibu."

"Ermie? Cute. So why do they stay together?"

"It's called show business, Jackson, Hollywood politics. Most of their clients are interrelated. It's yet another façade."

We got drunk and then had cheeseburgers at Mel's. When I got home, I was too tired to even listen to my messages. I fell asleep with half of my clothes still on.

# 19

In the music industry, even the best solo acts typically go on tour with a band, which may be hired just for that tour. They are usually stellar musicians who can adapt to any sound and have been touring for years. Derek had chosen a bass player and drummer and I listened to their demos and approved.

I spent the next few days rehearsing with them in the Valley. When Neil first gave me the info for the rehearsal space, I cringed.

"Dear, you know I don't do the 818."

"Sweetheart, there are certain things," he said, "everyone must do in the Valley. Rehearsal spaces are one of them."

I was kidding him, of course, it was a Hollywood joke. The Valley was smoggy and filled with strip malls and women with teased hair who shoved their exploding bodies into neon Lycra jumpsuits. Well, not the whole Valley, but it was simply wrong.

There were four other bands you could hear through the walls housing the space. The bass player, a shy yet charmingly goofy hipster named Leroy, started jamming along with one of the bands, which was playing AC/DC covers.

"Sorry, I have a soft spot in my heart for Angus Young," he said.

Leroy, like many young musicians at the time, was a bit stuck in the Eighties. Even though it was well past the millennium, somehow shaggy Eighties-rock haircuts were in. During one of our first rehearsals Leroy showed up looking all retro and I couldn't help but to chide him.

"Ric Ocasek called," I said, "he wants his hair back."

The drummer Rico laughed. He had more of a mod look, like he could have been in the Cure. I wasn't sure if it was nervousness or if he was simply easily amused, but he was constantly laughing.

Except when he played drums—then he was completely serious, his lips retaining a flat line of concentration. He came from the brainy side, studied at Berklee College of Music. Leroy was more from the heart, self-taught. They were both exemplary. Aden approved highly of their masculine qualities and felt they supported my hetero façade nicely. Both of them knew I was gay, and Leroy felt Aden was misconstrued in his theories.

"I think it's more interesting if you're gay," Leroy said. "It's more of a story—the whole lead-singer minority thing."

"I know," I replied, "I thought so, too, but Aden is completely fixated on the young female demographic buying my records."

"You should tell him to wake up and smell his cappuccino," Leroy mused, "it's the 21st century."

Rico looked confused. "He maybe has a point, though."

We rehearsed for hours and got together a tight set. We gelled as a band and I felt confident we would shine.


The evening after our last rehearsal, I didn't sleep very well, my mind wandering again for some reason to Timothy and his mysterious trouble.

I called Neil as soon as I got up, and finally told him about Timothy's disappearance from the hotel room in New York.

"I thought he would have called me by now."

"I'm sorry, sweetheart, but maybe it's for the best. Aden's heard through the grapevine that Timothy is sketchy."

"Sketchy? Oh, and Aden's inside the lines?"

"Whatever. He heard from one of his lawyer friends that Timothy is not to be trusted."

"Great."

"Well, on the bright side, you got your advance wired into your account today."

In addition to the recording budget I received my own personal artists advance. I had been waiting for this day.

"Oh my god."

"Eighty large dear, and don't spend it all in one place."

"Holy shit. I'm rich!"

"Dear, that's nothing to what you'll get in royalties."

"I have to shop, immediately."

"Actually, you may not have to. The label is trying to get you sponsored by several clothing companies."

The next day was the *Charlie's Angels* premiere that I was to attend with Kia. In trying to figure out what to wear, I realized that I needed to rethink my whole wardrobe.

I had invited Jed and his straight friend Rich over to help me go through my clothes and see what to keep and what was too gay.

"Hello," Jed said, barging through the door, "whatever is Alexander McQueen is so mine."

"So, your manager wants you to dress straight?" Rich asked.

"Yeah, at least for now," I said, pulling out my entire wardrobe and plopping it on the bed. "But what is really straight nowadays anyway, with metrosexuality and people like Ryan fucking Seacrest?"

"Rich is metro," Jed said. "But not gay, unfortunately." He tried to ruffle Rich's perfectly coiffed hair but got his hand slapped down. "But you did have an affair with Robert Downey Jr., right?" Jed was holding my clothes up to his body and looking in the full-length mirror.

"I was just his trainer, you nut ball. So wait a second." Rich turned to me with a sincere expression, "You are compromising who you are for a record deal?"

"Well, not my whole self, just in the public eye."

"Well, you need to layer," he said. Rich was the type of guy who, though living in a tiny studio in the valley, wore a Rolex and drove a Mercedes. God knows how his PA job paid for it all; he probably had doctor parents in Connecticut. In LA, straight guys can be super groomed and even get manicures, but not rock stars. What the fuck? Jed slipped off his jeans and slid on my Silver vinyl pants.

"These are just too gay, I think you're going to give them to me."

"Nonsense. Oh my god, the last time I wore those was Halloween, 1999. I went to a rave in San Francisco in the Castro with Brian—"

"The wigga massage guy?"

"Yeah. The whole night we just roamed the streets like cattle, trying to stay away from fights and bodies keeling over. The silver pants were so fucking hot."

"Sexy-hot or sweaty-hot?"

"Both. I kept telling myself I should have opted for a more organic fiber."

"I'm sorry," Rich added, "but hemp just isn't sexy."

"Anyway, I wore a tight T-shirt with the word 'issues' on it and Brian wore one that said 'drama'. Even with all the craziness that Halloween in the Castro had to offer, our T-shirts were total hits. People pointed at us, saying 'Issues!' or 'Drama!' like we couldn't read. I remembered a guy with silver poles curving up from his shoulders and around his head. I asked him what he was and he said, 'A whisk!' as if that was a completely normal costume choice."

"Of course," Rich said.

"Now, if Aden had his way, my sexy pants would go to some Hollywood newbie, an extra on *Queer as Folk*. But I'm keeping them."

Jed gave me a pout.

"Take them off, bitch," I said.

Rich had found my men's black platform shoes.

"Wow. These are authentic," he said. "1950s."

"Yes, and they're not going anywhere." I gave Jed a mock-stern look.

"They remind me of how I met Barkley."

Jed perked up at the reference to an A-list Hollywood queen, of course.

"Do tell," he said, trying on a T-shirt.

"I had played a show in Newport Beach for tips, and this thirty-something man in a vintage suit left a hundred-dollar bill in the tip jar. He said he really 'connected' with my music."

"I bet he did," Jed said.

"I told him I would love to 'connect' with his bank account." Rich laughed.

"Needless to say, two months later there I was," I flung a scarf around me for effect, "in a helicopter flying over Victoria Falls in Zimbabwe, hiking the Himalayas, swimming with dolphins in New Zealand."

"No way!" Jed was impressed.

"Thirty-five countries in three months! And one night in Katmandu we got drunk in our hotel room and he put on the platforms and danced around. When he asked me why I lugged them on such a major trip, I said, in a tone not unlike Auntie Mame, 'Those shoes have been all around the world, darling.'"

"There's no way you can wear these," Jed said.

"Yes, but they're probably worth—"

"Keep them," Rich said. "You never know."

Jed gave Rich a friendly punch and picked up my tight Diesel jeans with the charcoal sheen.

"These are way too gay."

"I got those in London. I was staying with this hottie clothing designer I'd met in Greece in an abandoned church that guys used for cruising."

"Ooh, more gay history," Jed said. "I think I've heard of that place, in Mykonos, right?"

"Yeah. Anyway, he was being snotty that night and kicked me out of his flat, saying his sister was coming in to town and didn't know he was gay. 'You're a fucking clothing designer!' I told him. After making my dramatic exit I went to the Shadow Lounge and danced around a pole with this sexy older guy, but he turned out to be married. I ended up sleeping in this dingy hostel and got hit on by a fat girl from Ohio. I told her I was gay and she started crying hysterically. The next morning I bought her breakfast." I touched the pants for what may be the last time. "I still had these on."

"Poor thing," Rich said.

"What, the girl? What about the fact that I was downgraded from a penthouse flat on Kings Road in Soho to a ten-pound-a-night hostel?"

Jed put my see-through Gucci shirt up to his body to check if it fit him.

"So what's the story behind this one?"

"Oh, you know that cheesy club in New York? Go-go boys in showers over the bar?"

Rich rolled his eyes.

"Splash," Jed said.

"Yeah, a cute black guy shoved that shirt into my pocket there while he stripped on the dance floor. I don't know where he went after that, but I remember kissing someone while people gathered around to watch and thinking it should be porn."

It wasn't porn, it was my life, and it was about to go on the sale rack.

I relented. "Okay, you can have that one."

Jed pranced around and sung a house bass line.

Rich ended up taking a bunch of stuff for his lesbian sister, and I simply put the stuff I wanted to save in a big box and labeled it "My Secret Life."

When I came back from stashing it in my hall closet, Jed was pointing at a picture of Neil in my photo album. "He's cute."

"Jed, you've met him like five times."

"Oh."

We went through the rest of my clothes, then I whisked them out the door and said, "Who's driving?"

We were off to The Grove to do some straight-boy shopping. Or at least some androgyny shopping.

We strolled past the blonde mothers (or were they babysitters?) and the teenagers (or were they preteens?), and the first thing I picked out was a nice pair of DKNY khakis.

"No," Rich said. "Too Fire Island."

How did he even know what Fire Island was? Did he take an

Aden pill or something? Were they conspiring?

"Here you go," he said, pointing at a mannequin dressed like a homeboy.

"I wouldn't be caught dead in Tommy Hilfiger."

"You're such a label queen," Jed said.

"As if you weren't too excited about that Gucci top you just inherited."

We settled on some easy-fit Levi lowriders and a long-sleeve black T-shirt, several hoodies, a couple pairs of Pumas, and some butch belts.

"Listen," Rich said, "if you really want to do this, you should get a few pairs of boxers. I know you wear briefs..."

I looked at Jed.

"He asked me."

"Jesus, why don't you put out a press release."

On our way out of Banana Republic, I noticed two flirty teenage girls giggling and pointing at me, their young faces flushed with embarrassment. I gave them a smile and they looked at each other, giggling harder. I chuckled, too, at the irony that I'd most likely be more interested in their racquetball-playing fathers.

We ended up finding a suit that was not too prissy (I was clinging to Armani as Rich was leading me to Hugo Boss) and not too flashy. Understated, or, as Aden would say, "cool, but not icy."

We basically went with a lot of black, and I got a couple of Armani jackets that passed code, so I was happy. Even though we dropped a few grand, I still didn't know what I was going to wear to the premiere that evening. I thanked them by buying us iced mochas. Jed wanted additional thanks in the form of celebrity dish from the premiere, but Rich had something else in mind.

"What about getting me a date with Kia Diamond? I heard she's single, and she's fine," he said. Now, Rich was certainly a looker and actually seemed genuinely interested, but how could I tell him she was doing Ermolinda, the Brazilian maid?

"You can't compete with Ermie," I said with a smile.

He gave me an inquisitive, puppy-dog look, and he actually

looked irresistible for a minute.

"I'll see what I can do."

When we parted, Jed gave me the address of some producer's pad in the hills he was going to be house-sitting.

"There's a key underneath the flower pot by the gate; come by whenever—the pool is, like, huge."

"I don't even want to know what will be floating in it."

# 20

I met Kia at her dad's house before the premiere. She'd told me to come in without knocking, so I walked in unannounced to Mr. Cuddle, shirtless and gravely chomping on an apple. Kia was still in the shower. Mark gave me a smile that said, *I know this is pretty dysfunctional.*

"How've you been?" he said, putting his small, dark hand on my shoulder. He smelled the same—Vetiver cologne.

"Good, I guess. Lots of stuff going on."

"I'd say."

I cut to the chase.

"Mark, why didn't you tell me you were married or that you were *the* Mark Diamond?"

"What we had was—"

"Dinner and sex," I flatly interrupted.

"Yes," he chuckled. "That, too." He squirmed a little. "I felt it unnecessary to fill you in on the details of my—"

"Your other life?"

"Jackson, can you let me talk here?"

"Is that why you cut it off? Because we were getting too close?"

I remembered the sixth Sunday, when we cuddled for a record twenty minutes. He'd looked at me longingly and started to say something, but when I prompted him to say it, he got up and opened the blinds instead. A sweep of warm air came in. He turned around and smiled, and the light silhouetted his ripped torso. That had been my last image of him, until now.

"Me and Bree—"

"Bree and I," I shot in.

"Jesus," he said, and sat down. Even when sitting, his body showed no visible fat. "We're very good together in a lot of ways, but she doesn't—"

"Have a penis?"

He laughed and scratched his muscled shoulder, continued. "She isn't involved in certain aspects of my life nor I in hers."

"What, is she a dyke?"

"No, no. Well, probably experimented when she was younger, like anyone but—"

"Do you sleep together?"

Mark Diamond took the last bite of the apple and swiped at his bottom lip with his thumb. "Not in quite some time."

"I see. Well, I guess that's none of my business. If you don't mind, I'd like to pretend our thing never happened. With my record coming out and—"

"Lonnie Simpson on your tail..."

"Right, and Aden."

"It's a fine line, Jackson, and I've chosen to walk it a lot. What you do behind closed doors—"

"Is my own business? But I did confide in Kia about it, I hope—"

"Yes, well, Kia has her secrets as well."

I didn't touch that one. The clock chimed and Kia appeared in the doorway, her snake-like curls shaping her delicate face.

"Shall we?" she said.

"Right," I said. "Good-bye, Mark."

"Bye, Dad," Kia said.

"Good-bye, you two," Mark Diamond said with a knowing smile. "See you at the premiere."

# 21

Aden along with Kia's agent had arranged for a car just for us. We were to meet them at the premiere. It was obvious that both Aden and Kia's team had conspired to have us arrive together as a couple. I started getting a little nervous, so I poured a few inches of scotch over some ice in the limo bar. The ice clinked as we went over the bumps on Hollywood boulevard.

"How do I look?" I said.

I was wearing the black Hugo Boss suit with a loose, funky tie that had a spaceship on it. I had three days of scruff on my face. Grungy chic.

"Like Jackson Poole trying to be cool," she said.

"I'm not cool already? I have to try?"

"No, silly. I'm just fucking with you."

Just to mess with her, I gave her a prim look. "You know, for such a pretty girl, you certainly do curse a lot."

"Fuck," she said, "I broke a nail." She searched her bag for something. "This is why I don't like having these. My producers make me. They're so Barbie."

"You can put that in the mockumentary."

"Right."

I downed another sip of the scotch and could feel my blood warming, my head loosening.

"So, does your dad know about you and Ermolinda?"

"Dad and I know a lot about each other because we're similar, and I've always been closer to him than Bree."

"Hmmm."

"But I haven't talked to him about Ermolinda or his sexuality issues. We mostly just have an unspoken understanding softened by the large quantities of alcohol we consume around each other. It's super healthy."

We clinked glasses. The limo rolled slowly past the barricades erected down Hollywood Boulevard. It was the part of town where no one went to if they lived in Los Angeles. It was mostly overweight, squinty-eyed tourists (it's not that they were so large, just noticeable among the zero-body-fat LA hipsters) and random schizophrenics acting out one act plays with themselves. The stars embedded in the sidewalks were the novelty, along with the cheap trinket stores and dodgy bars.

Even blocks away the tents were set up, and every media company in the world seemed to be there. There were huge cutouts of all three Angels tied between the buildings over the street. The driver yelled back to us, "Okay, people," and Kia took my hand and swiped at some lint on my shoulder.

"Let me see the teeth, baby," she said.

I showed her.

"Perfect. Not that you'll really be smiling. But try not to close your eyes. It will feel like you're inside a light bulb."

"Great," I said.

The door opened and we walked the red carpet, arm in arm. It was just like she said—we were inside a light bulb. The flashes never stopped—they were numbing and sharp—and everything turned to slow motion. My every breath, movement, nuance was being photographed, and my record hadn't even come out yet.

When we got to the middle of the walkway, Kia turned and kissed me on the lips, holding herself pressed against me, making sure everyone got the picture. Was this a dream?

The first face I saw in the crowd was Aden, looking proud and cheering me on as if to say *Yes, you're 28 and you're straight!* Then I saw Derek behind him, frantically pointing at my crotch. I looked down and a shudder of horror engulfed me as I realized part of my zipper was down.

I tried to act nonchalant as I leaned down and, without moving my lips, whispered in Kia's ear, "My fly is unzipped. Help!" Ironically, the whisper must have looked romantic because suddenly an even bigger barrage of flashes went off in our faces.

Kia, the celebrity pro, murmured back, "You zip while I distract." She subtly positioned herself so her back was covering my front and did a huge wave to the crowd. Her gorgeous arm and glittering bracelet were like a red flag to a bull—a couple fans yelled "Kia!" and I could see everyone's faces fixed on her. I zipped up as inconspicuously as I could while being on live television and simultaneously photographed by hundreds of journalists. I already needed another drink.

Neil was behind Derek, rolling his eyes. We got to the end of the line, finally, and I managed to steal away to the bathroom.

I splashed my face with water and looked at myself in the mirror.

My upper lip still had a smudge of Kia's lipstick.

# 22

Not surprisingly, I found Aden, Derek, and Neil in the drink line. I'd lost track of Kia for the moment. Aden said, "Don't worry, it's very hip to look disheveled. It's actually a style in some of the New York clubs, the zipper-down thing."

The crowd was bright and beautiful, stars and their entourages, some with slow grace and glamour, some neurotic and fluttery, like injured birds. Was this the world I was entering?

All I really wanted to see were Drew Barrymore and Bjork, who were both nowhere to be found.

"I just hope it doesn't get printed," I said about the zipper.

"Not to worry," Aden said. He smelled like a combination of Altoids, CK One, and chardonnay. "You and Kia looked perfect."

"Yeah, a regular poster couple," Neil said under his breath. I pulled him aside and grabbed two champagne flutes off a passing tray. Neil whispered, "And the zipper thing is very East Village."

I laughed. "Can you fucking believe him?"

"I'm just happy he's a good drunk tonight. The bad witch is resting."

A little while later I went to the bathroom again and heard sniffing sounds in the next stall. The scotch and the champagne had made me dizzy, and I thought a bump would be the perfect antidote. I faked that I didn't know that anyone was in the stall and said, "Oh, sorry!" as I barged in. It was Aden and what looked like the blond boy from *Survivor*. Aden fed me two bumps to each nostril while continuing his conversation with the rugged, sexy, worm eater. I wasn't really listening, but they were talking about some restaurant in Paris that was booked solid for three years. *Whoopie!*

"But I can get in, of course," Aden said.

I almost said, "Yeah, because of your *husband*'s connections," but settled on, "Nothing a little smoke and mirrors won't fix."

Aden laughed his signature high-pitched nervous laugh and we all exited the stall. There was a big bodyguard type in a blue suit grooming himself in the mirror and checking his teeth. I let Aden and his *Survivor* toy leave ahead of me. I didn't want to be associated with the way Aden not only cheated on Derek but also flaunted it in his face. It was beyond comprehension.

I got closer to the mirror and realized it was what's-his-name, the guy who played Tony Soprano. He was checking his teeth. I wondered if he was as brutal and emotional in real life, if he would see a butterfly and start crying right after he shot someone in the head. His dichotomy of heartless bruiser mixed with vulnerable boy was magnetic on screen.

"Hey," I said, washing my hands next to him. What the fuck do you say to Tony Soprano? I didn't know his real name. I had to say something. I was in awe, it was my favorite show not counting *Six Feet Under*. So I decided to simply be honest.

"Sorry we were so blatant in there," referring to the illicit stall moment.

"Seen worse," he said, slipping an Altoid strip on his tongue.

I was watching Tony Soprano while he undertook his personal hygienic duties. I know Aden told me I had to get used to hanging out with stars, that they were just normal like me, but this was weird. He ran his thumbs through his hair, then stretched his big hand out to me.

"James," he said.

"Jackson," I said, "it's a pleasure."

His firm grip almost fractured my hand. As he left, he turned back, put up his hand, and said, "About your little snow party, fah-get about it."

I stood there stunned.

Outside I went directly to Kia and told her my night was made, that I didn't care what happened because Tony Soprano had just told me to, "fah-get about it."

"Cool," she said, looking around, making sure people noticed her. I couldn't believe Kia's alter ego. She was a completely different person when we were alone.

"You play this game well," I said. She looked at me with pity and a rueful smile.

"It's all a means to an end," she said. "Remember that."

That was what Neil always told me, and I suppose he was right, because now the great stuff was happening. My first advance had come through that morning (*eighty large* as Tony Soprano would say), and on top of the Alanis shows, I was to open for the Rolling Stones in England and Paris (even though they were all like, seventy). My album was due to be released soon, radio play was already in motion and climbing, and I had a video for Christ sakes! It was all too much to absorb.

"Let's go over there," Kia said, taking my arm and leading me to a table that had an ornate arrangement of sashimi and California rolls. She popped a piece of a roll in her mouth. "Yum." This is what I loved about Kia, the beautiful model-slash-soap star who not only wasn't afraid of eating, but also talked at the same time. Somehow she pulled it off, even while in celebrity mode.

The movie was overdone but entertaining. Drew, of course, was my favorite angel. Cameron seemed too flighty and Lucy Liu looked constipated. As we were leaving, we all huddled on the street beneath the ravenous eyes of the bridge-and-tunnel crowd, lurking like predators behind the ropes. It was easier before when we were focused on getting out of the car and dealing with the red carpet, but now it was just standing and waiting for the limo without any other distraction, so the crowd felt more obtrusive. But I cannot deny, I loved the attention. Who wouldn't? I was glad to be the sidekick, even though soon I would be the main attraction and I wondered privately how I'd handle it.

"How are you, kid?" It was Lonnie Simpson, who was to get my song in the next Cameron Crowe flick. I immediately stiffened into straight mode.

"Great," I said, sliding my hand off my hip to let it dangle loose and macho. "Nothing like watching three hot chicks blow shit up."

Lonnie Simpson laughed, while on the other side of our group, I saw Mark Diamond give me a conspiratorial look.

# 23

I had a few days off after the premiere. It was nice having time for some much-needed relaxation, working out with Jed one day and taking him up on his offer of using the pool where he was staying on another. Aden had told me about a publicity performance Bree Diamond was arranging to get me exposure with industry insiders. The goal was to convince the people with power that I was the next big thing so they'd push my album even more on radio, and with MTV and in stores. No pressure really. But I felt good about how well things were clicking with the band and I thought we'd be ready. I'd already started handing out the flyers Neil printed to advertise the show to "select people only" (Aden's edict).

Everything had been such a whirl that I'd been distracted from thinking about Timothy. But now that I had some downtime, he was back in my thoughts full force. Why hadn't he called me yet? He seemed so sweet and loving when we were together that it was hard not to imagine it going further. I loved the idea of being with someone who appreciated creativity and music. Barkley and Thomas were both so business minded that I never felt they fully understood me. But Timothy seemed to really get it, and I was a sucker for his soulful eyes. Not to mention his lips and his arms and his gorgeous hands...*better not go there.* I headed out to the gym again to work off some pent-up energy (and not in the steam-room).

After working out I ran some errands and saw Monica Lewinsky in the parking lot of Whole Foods. I knew she was a friend of Derek's, so I introduced myself and told her I was a friend of his, too. I gave her a flyer for the upcoming show. She had three men with her, presumably all fags, and she had accessorized with a little red bag that had *I heart Surfer Boys* on it. There were diamonds on her platform flip-flops, but she still looked like a fat girl in heels.

I tried to imagine if he were there, the worst thing I could say to make Aden cringe. Then I said it.

"Love the bag, love the shoes, let's do lunch."

"Sure," she said, "join us."

So there I was, dining on the little tables outside of Whole Foods with Monica and her tight T-shirted, big-lipped queens. Aden would have *loved* the scene. I secretly worried the tabloids would come by and get a furtive shot—not a good follow up to the pictures of me and Kia at the premiere. Luckily we ate our ahi salads and polenta in peace.

At the end of the meal, when her hunks had presumably gone to get the car, Monica pulled me close enough to her that I could smell the espresso on her breath.

"Listen, Jackson, Derek told me you're headed for the public eye and if so, I gotta tell you, be careful. We all have dirt, and yours can ruin you. You're still soft. Don't be so trusting. Even though sometimes you can't control it, your private life is not to be rummaged through, got it?"

This, coming from the girl who sucked the president's dick, was not to be taken lightly.

"Got it," I said, and went into the store for some groceries.

I got home and put the groceries away. Then I mixed a drink, lit candles, and opened a can of Pringles, which were so thin they gave the illusion of being less fattening. I came across a *CosmoGirl* left behind by one of the cleaner's daughters. I opened to a page that read "Finding Your Soul Mate" and skimmed down to Step One: List what you desire and what you despise in a partner. I started to jot stuff down:

> *The lithe, contoured body of Mark Diamond and the knowing disposition of Timothy.*
>
> *My soul mate must not wear pumpkin orange or eat Chinese food on a regular basis, nor listen to Celine Dion or Michael Bolton. Even if they only own one of their recordings and claim to not like it any more. Prohibited.*

*Tall and athletic, slim, skin that is primarily void of blem-
ishes (see Mr. Cuddle). Body hair must only be in the accept-
able places.*

*Eyes that are striking, a distinguished yet not too enervated
age, and a job that is both financially successful and not
without aspects of glamour.*

I mixed another drink and continued writing. I wasn't asking
much:

*I want sustenance, authenticity. I want a man, children, and
a career. Is that possible?*

There was no more space in the magazine, so I grabbed a piece of
scrap paper and continued. I was getting slightly OCD about it, but
hey:

*My ideal partner must be able to name, off the top of their
head at any given moment: three Prince albums, two French
cheeses, three islands in Greece, two of Lily Taylor's movies,
and Bjork's last name. Preferably they will own a car that
was made before 1969 or after 2003. Cat owners take a hike,
dog owners rule.*

*Anyone who swims the butterfly or does push-ups with claps
in between them is absolutely forbidden.*

*Flossing, chewing with mouth closed, sleeping in the nude
(and late on Sundays), all extremely significant.*

*In the way of sex and sexuality, my ultimate other ought not to
be shy or frigid, but sensual and liberated. Not inclined, when
it comes to fornicating, to define the when/what/where/how,
but able to act purely on impulse. Like an animal, or the beating of the heart.*

I put the list down and sipped my drink, wondering if Timothy
would make the grade. It would definitely help things if he weren't

missing in action. One thing was certain: No matter how hot Aden's quick neurotic breaths were on my back, I would not let him interfere with my desire for love.

I called Timothy's voicemail and hung up. Then I called again and left a message.

"Timothy, it's me, Jackson. Just, um, thinking of you."

# 24

Neil called to give me a heads-up that Derek and Aden were going to be stopping by my house with a surprise. I confessed that I had called Timothy.

"Girl, don't you know that acting too interested can sabotage?"

"Since when did you write the book of love?"

Neil had recently been through a messy break-up with a lover of three years who he'd thought was the one. I realized, after the fact, that the comment could've sounded harsh so I added, "I don't know, I guess I am a little pathetic."

"What did you say in the message?"

"Just that I was thinking of him."

"Whatever you do, don't drink and dial."

There was a knock at my door and looking through the peephole I saw Aden, slightly perspiring, and Derek, smelling my bushes. I opened the door.

"Please, delightful managers, do enter."

"Place looks great," Aden said. Why was he so cheerful?

"So, what's the surprise?"

"Close your eyes," Derek said.

I obeyed, and he put something in my hand. I immediately knew what it was. My CD! It looked so cool!

"I feel like I just gave birth."

"And you didn't have to do any Lamaze classes!" Derek said. Then he showed me the *Interview* spread, which was huge and glowingly positive. The pictures were complimentary, and I certainly didn't look gay in them.

The three of us looked at each other, beaming, then Aden whipped out a split of champagne and said, "Shall we have a small toast?"

We sat and sipped on my little porch, and I read all the liner notes and made sure everything was in there—thanks to my family, friends, and everyone else who had gotten me there. After a few minutes of enjoying the moment, Aden started to grill me on what to say during the slew of interviews I was about to face.

"Just watch the sibilance when you say the letter 'S'."

Normally I would have laughed at him, but sitting there with the CD and the article in my hand and listening to one of the men who—with the extreme administrative help of Neil and the connections of Derek—had gotten me there, I simply said, "Okay, Aden, no problem."

"All these interviews will fuel the radio support we've been rounding up. By the way, several of the radio stations in Europe are already playing your demo single in heavy rotation. The phones are off the hook!"

After Derek and Aden left, I called my brother and Kia—telling them how excited I was to actually see the finished product of my CD as well as the big article.

Lying in bed, I thought how bittersweet it was to have the magazine but not the man. He knew the article was coming out, and I'd left two messages. Where the fuck was he? I looked once again at Timothy's name in the liner notes and remembered I didn't even have his home address to send him a copy of the CD. What if something was really wrong?

# 25

I drove all the way to Silverlake for a fish taco and to think. I had to find out about the Timothy Meyer mystery. I remembered my friend Kane, the private investigator. I still couldn't believe how well she'd done for herself since our restaurant days. She now had a house in Bel Air and a body that even Demi would die/pay for.

At the seedy Silverlake taco place, I was on my cell phone while eating, just like most of the other patrons. Kane answered in one ring. I remembered that she always had, like clockwork.

"Kane here."

"Hey, it's Jackson."

"Baby doll, how are you?"

"Great, sort of."

"What can I possibly do for you that some steroid-pumped lumberjack in a flannel shirt can't?"

I jumped into it right away, explaining the situation of having a wonderful time with Timothy, then his deceptive disappearance, and the official-looking man accosting me in the hotel.

"I'm a private detective," she said, "not a stalker."

"I just need the skinny on him. He's been unreachable for days, and the detective or whoever he was freaked me out."

After giving me a bit more of a hard time about not aiding stalkers, Kane agreed to meet me that afternoon. She picked the place, in an eerie part of Burbank that was utterly nondescript. Los Angeles was so vast that there were places where you felt like you could have been anywhere, the landscape void of any symbols that grounded your sense of place. I think that was the reason why some Los Angelinos tended to look lost, whereas in New York they looked like they knew exactly where they were and where they were going. I wanted to be one of those people. Direct and determined. I parked right outside and smelled chorizo cooking next door.

Kane strutted into the place just as I was sitting down at the bar. Before even saying hello, she ordered a Macallen 12 on the rocks. You have to love a woman who drinks scotch. The walls of the bar were black and lined with pictures of old, mostly dead movie stars. The bartender was an old Columbian woman with sharp eyes. Kane and I each took a gulp and turned toward the other.

I looked at her deadpan face, eyebrows just plucked, a sensible Chanel suit, and a sleek silver cigarette case rolling through her long, manicured fingers. Detective to the stars.

"I'm telling you, your gay phase is over, Jackson. It's now or never, dear; my peach is ripening."

I winced. "Don't say 'peach'."

"Would you rather I say 'cherry'?"

"Something nonperishable would be preferred." I gestured at the bar. "So tell me, did you pick this place just to bolster your image as a hard-boiled detective?"

She laughed. "You caught me. That, and I like the scotch selection." She raised her drink and we clicked glasses. "So, do you have a home phone or address for your disappearing friend?"

"No, he was always elusive about it."

"First red flag."

"I know, but darling he's 'Richard Gere sexy'." Aden's constant pop-culture references had clearly rubbed off on me.

"I don't care if he's fucking 'Benicio Del Toro sexy', it's a red flag. Fire engine red."

She paused, then said, "Richard Gere sexy" after a two-drink minimum?"

"No, at all times, trust me. Here, I have his cell."

"Out with it," she ordered. "You know I'm only doing this so one day you'll turn straight and marry me."

*Why does everyone want me to be a breeder?*

I wanted kids, just not with a woman.

"Okay, sure, baby," I said, "I've even preordered the sports channels."

"No doubt to see the football players in tights," she said.

"I prefer soccer—more skin. But come to think of it, it's all quite homoerotic."

"Okay, what's the last name again?"

"Meyer. Timothy Meyer." I spelled it for her. "He's the senior editor of *Interview* magazine."

"Anything else you can tell me?"

I couldn't think of anything else that I hadn't already told her. *He's gorgeous. He's a great kisser.* I was pretty sure that wasn't what she was looking for. I shook my head.

"Right, I'll see what I can dig up."

Kane downed a second scotch while we caught up, and she filled me in on her last breakup.

"So, I was like, 'I'm ovulating', and he was like, 'I'm out of here'. Fear of intimacy I suppose."

"Perhaps you could have brought it up more subtly?"

"Look at me. Do I look subtle? Do I look like a fucking people person?"

I laughed.

"Don't you want to have babies someday?"

She was right. I had confessed that to her at one point.

"Yeah, but using a turkey baster. 1-800-SURROGATE."

"How romantic!"

"Well, Aden's happy, now that according to *Us Weekly* I'm dating Kia Diamond."

"That tramp? I heard she was a dyke."

"Maybe you should be one, too."

"Sorry, honey, I'm not about the womb broom."

"What?"

"Forget it. Listen, I'll give some of my East Coast contacts a call and see what I can come up with. Until then, think paternal. My ovaries are about to shut down. Ciao, baby."

Kane marched out of the bar with confidence, gathering looks along the way.

On the drive home, I thought of some new song lyrics and called my machine to record them. That was what I usually did, and then worked on the melody later, going back and forth between piano and guitar.

> *I signal you to answer but you disappear*
> *Now you're just a whisper ringing in my ear*

When I got home, I set up my place for writing. Lit the candles, opened the blinds, spread out the paper on the floor. I always wrote on the floor. Perhaps it was the most grounding, a place where I could figuratively get to the bottom of what I wanted to say. I worked for hours, getting most of the way through a song before crawling into bed.

The next day the interviews started, and continued for what seemed like a week but was actually only a couple of days; *Spin, Blender, Details, Rolling Stone.*

Of course they all wanted pictures, which was its own special torture, given the hetero mandate. The first photo shoot was so stressful I felt like I was going to have a breakdown, but Neil told me to just forbid Aden to come anymore, and after that they were better. The most memorable was the one with an up-and-coming independent photographer in his huge loft studio in downtown LA. The guy was unbelievably serious. We had to wait until the exact moment when the natural light came through the skylight. Apparently he only shot between 5:45 and 5:55 P.M. While we were waiting, his assistant told us he'd shot Moby the day before.

Most of the interviews I did over the phone, walking around my house in sweats with no shirt on, quietly eating a piece of fruit or sneaking drags of a cigarette.

A couple of them were in person, at various offices and restaurants around the city. I thought of interviews with my favorite stars I had read and remembered the journalists always including a line or two about the restaurant they were sitting in. Now they would do this with me!

Most of them were the usual surface questions, but some

tried to pry deeper into personal territory and I had to adjust my answers accordingly. Even though he was annoying, Aden's advice had helped tremendously, and I think I came off pretty professionally even though I was somewhat new at it. They were divided into the real answers and the given answers, which were not all lies, just not the whole truths. They would have to do for now because I wouldn't dare say the real answers.

*Who were your favorite singers growing up?*
Given answers: James Taylor, Sting
Real answers: Madonna, Sister Sledge

*What was your worst job before you landed a record deal?*
Given answer: Waiting tables
Real answer: Go-go boy

*Describe your perfect morning.*
Given answer: Eating ice cream off a Playboy bunny
Real answer: Eating Richard Gere

*No, seriously.*
Given answer: Okay, getting up with a beautiful girl and staying in bed till noon, then going to the beach and drinking margaritas
Real answer: Getting it up for Richard Gere and staying in bed till noon, then going to the beach and drinking a '91 Bordeaux with Camembert, green olives, and a baguette

*What was your favorite subject in high school?*
Given answer: Math, English
Real answer: Talent show, home-ec

*What did you have for breakfast this morning?*
Given answer: Corn flakes
I-wish answer: Richard Gere
And so on—you get the picture.

The journalists were respectful for the most part, and I didn't come across as an inarticulate heroin addict. Aside from not saying anything homosexual, I tried to simply be myself. That's what Derek had said to me in his warm, compassionate way.

As much as I liked to make fun of Aden's paranoia, I felt lucky that there weren't any direct questions about my sexuality. I didn't know if it was Kia's red-carpet kiss, or if Aden's madness really was just that and nobody cared if I was gay or not. It was as if I were walking a thin line, and if I fell to my right, I would float into a soft cloud of fame and fortune, and if I fell to my left, I would swan dive into a bottomless hole.

# 26

On the morning of my publicity show for all the industry insiders, I stayed in the bathtub until I was pruned from excessive soaking and thinking. I was just about to light up half a joint when Kane called me with news about Timothy. I got out and toweled off. Somehow I didn't want to hear what she had to say while sitting in the tub.

Apparently the man I had spoken to in New York was a private detective.

"What?"

"And, are you sitting down?"

"Yes."

"Timothy is married. Anyway, they're getting a divorce, and his wife, Deborah, is trying to get dirt on him for the settlement. This guy's all over the place, Jackson. He's not just a one-time philanderer; he's been cheating on her for years."

My heart dove. He was married, and a player? What was the deal with me and married men?

"Fuck," I said.

"Maybe you should take up barn animals."

"It's not funny, Kane; he was so fun and so hot." I couldn't admit to her that I thought of him as true boyfriend material.

I walked into the kitchen, poured myself a glass of OJ, and chugged. Then I put the juice back and slammed the refrigerator door shut.

"Every gay guy in Hollywood is hot," she said. "And so are you."

"Thanks."

"Now fuck me already."

"Kane!"

"What? I have to act quickly. And god knows I can't raise some kid with a football-watching, ball-scratching straight man. No, my kid needs to be classy, you know, have taste. So how about it, can you hook me up with the white stuff?"

"What, a bump?"

"No, Einstein, sperm."

"That would be way too *Queer as Folk.*"

"Think about it, sweetie. Your blue eyes, my black curls."

"Kane, it's all sweet, but now's not the—"

"Your voice, my legs."

"I'm getting scared now."

"Okay, listen. If you want to know anything else on this Meyer character let me know."

"Okay," I said, sitting down in my breakfast nook, a damp towel still wrapped around my waist. "Thanks."

Talking to Kane was always a bit like walking into a whirlwind. I tried to weigh the good and bad of the news I had heard. He was married but getting divorced—how could she really know he was a player?

I thought back to our weekends in Miami and New York. Timothy had seemed so sincere, so present. I remembered the gentle way he touched me, the broken sunlight streaming in through the window and across his face. I wanted so badly to believe his feelings for me were real, but how could I know for sure?

I decided to call Kia. I filled her in on the latest developments, and she told me, "You need to take a break from all this, dear. Drink some tea and do some tai chi."

"Tea is boring. I just can't believe all of this. I haven't even thought about my show tonight!"

"Well, you better, because the whole lot is coming. I overheard Lonnie say Clyde is flying in from New York."

Shit. If the head of my record label was coming, I'd really better be on point. I was suddenly glad I hadn't smoked that half a joint. I needed to keep a clear head.

"Come over before your sound check and do some yoga with me and Ermolinda."

"Okay. I just feel like such a dork. A fucking detective asked me questions outside our hotel room, and I was still trying to tell myself he was a perfect catch. In fact, I still want him to be!"

"We've all been there, honey."

"I suppose I haven't really, not this way. I've been lucky."

Yoga with Kia and Ermolinda consisted of light stretching on the deck while listening to Dead Can Dance. I don't think the stretching did much for me, but it was nice watching them together. They drove me to my sound check in the house Mercedes, giggling at each other like I wasn't even there. Was I asking so much to have that kind of relaxed, day-to-day sweetness with someone?

The walls of the House of Blues Foundation Room on Sunset Boulevard were covered with giant posters of my face. The stage was set with candles and draped with dark red velvet. I was to perform solo as well as with my band, who would be sitting in for some of the songs so the crowd could see what my touring show would be like.

"The guest list is unbelievable," Aden said, "but I'm not letting you see it. I just want you to be yourself." Derek's mantra seemed to have rubbed off a little onto him. For once he wasn't obsessing over how hetero my hair was or whether or not I was going to accessorize—perhaps he was keeping it all inside. It felt good, like I actually had a supportive manager.

Backstage before the show I tried to breathe and empty my racing brain. Kia was massaging my hands and Neil was copying the set list for Leroy and Rico.

"Your sound check sounded great, sweetie."

One of the tech guys raised an eye at Neil's term.

"Um, I mean dude."

We laughed.

"Fuck, Neil, I'm so nervous."

"Jackson, I'm not even nervous. This is the easiest part. You're going to be great."

After they announced me, I walked out alone to a packed, standing audience that looked ready to pounce on me. I picked up my guitar and started the first number. I tried not to think of Timothy.

> *I wanted to give you the world*
> *A smile on the face of a girl*
> *A tear of joy in the eye of a boy*
> *You were worthy of this and so much more*

There were suits, beautiful girls, and gay boys in the audience (Aden couldn't control the fact that, yes, it was Hollywood, we were everywhere) and I tried to connect with them all. I even saw Jed (he'd actually left the gym) in the back with someone's arms around him. Another rung on his ladder to fag heaven I assumed.

I sang from my heart and prayed that my knees would stop shaking. Then I fell into the rhythm. It was my most natural of states—my sexuality proved irrelevant at times like these. During one song, "This Life," I almost started crying. Instead of letting the tears come out I used them, channeled them into my voice, my emotion. You could hear a pin drop in the Foundation Room that night.

Rico and Leroy joined me onstage, and I noticed Leroy checking out some girls in the front row. He had this way of moving his head—like a bird—that was magnetic. They loved him. Rico was as serious as ever, keeping a perfect beat. I was so happy to have them behind me, and my nerves slowly dissipated as the set went by and the crowd cheered harder for each song.

After the show I went outside for some air, and Neil brought me some chilled Evian. I turned to him and said, "That's it."

"What?"

"That's it. That's what it's all about. All this craziness, trying to be somebody, putting on airs, dating married men on the sly, all of that gets thrown out the window when I'm up there. I just love making music."

"And it shows. You were mesmerizing tonight. Stunning, even. I overheard Clyde turn to someone and say, 'see what I'm talking about?' But now comes the hard part."

"What?"

"You've got to go in there and schmooze."

"Ugh, no. What about Burundi?," I pleaded.

"Burundi will have to wait, dear."

He led me inside to a blur of adoring smiles and kisses and handshakes. I was so pleased at everyone's reactions. I felt this huge perma-smile cementing my face. Thankfully, somewhere in all the madness, someone handed me a drink. It was Bree Diamond. She had on an ice-blue clingy dress with fuck-me boots.

"Well, Clyde told me you were a star in the making, but he didn't tell me you could croon like that. Honey, I had to check my panties."

She started in on that high-pitched monkey laugh. Again it contradicted her immaculate fashion sense. As a matter of fact, it sounded a bit like Aden's laugh. Go figure.

"Thanks for the drink," I said.

"Listen, baby, we've only just begun, but everybody and their mother is here." It was true. In the corner I saw David Geffen and Barry Diller. At the bar, sipping martinis, I noticed Calista Flockhart and Harrison Ford. He looked sexy, but even with my Daddy complex, he was too old. I didn't have a *Grand*daddy complex.

The label head Clyde Anson pulled me aside. I secretly prayed he wouldn't break out one of his cigars.

"Listen, kid," he said, "whatever may happen in this crazy business, whatever transpires, I want you to know you're one of the few artists I've signed on talent alone. And you proved that tonight."

I didn't know what to say. What did he mean? What was there besides talent, and was I missing it, whatever it was? But he seemed sincere, so I took it as a compliment.

"I'm glad you think so," I squeezed out.

I continued to move through the glamorous crowd, and my mouth started to cramp from my smile.

Lonnie Simpson stopped me by the buffet table.

"Hey, Jackson! You were really on tonight. Congratulations. By the way, how are things going with Kia?" He gave me a teacher-to-student smirk.

"Oh she's..." I almost said fabulous, but went for something more hetero. "She's a knockout."

"Hear, hear."

He smiled and clinked our glasses.

I saw my friend Brian—masseuse to the stars—in the corner, in a tank top that showed off his tattoos. I was grateful for an old, familiar face I could roll my eyes with.

"Can you believe this?"

"I know, girl, did you see Mr. Geffen and Mr. Diller?"

"Yeah, they're too cool to say hi."

"Whatever," Brian said, switching into his black girl mode, "they all in the kool-aid but don't know the flavah."

I laughed.

"Getting any new clients among all these movers and shakers?" I asked.

"Girl, I'm always workin' the work."

Aden had come up from behind us while walking someone to the door and heard Brian call me girl.

"Easy," he said.

Brian just rolled his eyes and went on talking.

"Liza's here, from Paramount. I told her she needs to fly me to New York next week if she wants to work those boulders out of her shoulders."

"So, what did she say?"

"The usual, call my assistant."

Brian started rubbing my shoulders and I squirmed away.

"Oh, right," he said, snapping his fingers, "you a breeder now."

We laughed and I finished my drink.

"Listen, I gotta fly, film at eleven."

"I'll be watching," Brian said.

On the way home, in Kia's car, we heard my song, "Got Even" on the radio.

"Oh my god, I'm not a radio virgin anymore. This is the first time I've heard myself!"

Kia hollered and started driving really fast.

When I got home I listened to my messages. The first one was from the detective guy in New York wanting more information, which freaked me out at first. How did he get my number? Then I remembered I was listed in the phone book. Duh. With all the increasing publicity, I'd need to get an unlisted number. The next message was from the mystery man himself, Timothy Meyer.

"Sunshine, you were flawless tonight. Meet me at the Santa Monica pier tomorrow night at seven. By the Ferris wheel."

He had been at the show?

This was all too cryptic. Why would he call me as if nothing was different? And did the detective somehow know he was in LA? I was really not interested in being involved in someone's ugly divorce.

I fixed myself a nightcap and sat on the porch watching the scattered lights of Laurel Canyon. I wished Neil was there; his simplicity, the goodness of him, were grounding. I was sick of duplicity and bigwigs and private investigators and such. But underneath it all, I was happy the gig went well, and I thanked the stars that my song was being played on the radio.

# 27

The next day I did what I had to do when the world was over-whelming. I got it all out on the Stairmaster. Even at the high-pro-file Crunch on Sunset, I was able to tune it all out and simply sweat. I had weeks' worth of toxins to release, and it was liberating—as was the quickie with the hot Latino daddy in the steam room.

I didn't see Jed around, so I decided to swing by the house he was sitting and use the pool again. It was a sprawling infinity pool, and being a Pisces and an avid swimmer, very inviting. If no one was there, I planned to take a skinny-dip.

On my way up to Jed's place, I listened to a message on my cell from Neil.

"You are not going to believe the feedback from last night. The phones are crazy! I've sent out press packs to like, everyone and their dog. Get this—Madonna's manager asked for one too! I'd say total victory. Call me."

I wasn't as excited as I should have been. Even though I had worked out some anxiety at the gym, something was eating at me. It was so gratifying having the career thing starting to work out after all the dues I'd paid, but I also wanted love. Real love. And I had been chasing it and deluding myself and sleeping around too much. On some level, I knew that hooking up with the guy in the steam room was one way of evening the score with Timothy. Like screwing around with some stranger—no matter how hot—took the sting out of him being married.

He'd had the nerve to ask me to meet him tonight after disap-pearing and then calling out of the blue, and the sick thing was, I couldn't wait to see him again. But Kane had confirmed he was divorcing his wife, so part of me wondered what could still happen between us. I wanted to become an adult. Have a family. Gays were doing it everywhere. Why couldn't I?

I almost turned around and headed over to Clean Slate to celebrate what was working in my life, but since I was nearly at Jed's house-sit, I decided to keep going. I remembered that the owner's cars had been left in the driveway, so I parked on the street and walked up the side entrance that came out by the pool. I heard a male voice, then another, then splashing. So much for my skinny-dipping plan. Although, if it was Jed and someone mellow, maybe it would be okay. I looked through the slats of the wrought-iron gate and saw Jed standing in the shallow end of the pool, his tanned back to me. He was holding and kissing another guy, but I couldn't make out the face. Then Jed dove away and revealed who it was—my heart plunged.

It was Timothy Meyer.

Jed swam back to him, and Timothy reached out and tenderly pushed the hair away from Jed's eyes. "I wish I could crawl inside your head," he said.

That was the exact line he'd used on me! The same inflection, the same look in his eye. I felt so stupid. How could I have been drawn to his bullshit? How many other guys had he said that to?

I turned around and sat against the gate for what seemed like an hour, unable to move. Even though I'd obviously had some doubts about him, I was stunned. Not only was I pissed at Timothy, I felt completely betrayed by Jed, who knew I had been seeing Timothy. I'd told him all about our trysts in South Beach and New York. Some friend.

I turned and watched. Their laughter seemed unreal, like it was coming from a TV someone had left on. In all actuality, it shouldn't have surprised me that much, but I was bewildered, frozen. After a while they went inside and I heard glasses clink. Screw them. I have my own toasting to do, I thought.

I got back into the car and drove to the offices of Clean Slate.

Neil handed me a schedule of more interviews, photo shoots, and appearances.

"What's wrong?"

"Nothing, just a little tired," I said.

"Well, honey," Neil said, while putting on my as-yet-unreleased record, "with the amount of buzz and prerelease press this record is getting it's bound to debut at the top of the charts—and stay there."

"Really?" Would Timothy have been true to me then?

Not likely. He was obviously a player through and through. Kane had even told me that directly, but I'd stupidly chosen to focus on the fact that he really was getting a divorce. I felt like an idiot.

Some fans had shown up to have me sign some of the advance copies of the record. I found myself distracted by the music (it was always weird to socialize while your own music was playing) and also by the scene I had witnessed in the infinity pool, playing back in my internal VCR. Jed, that little whore.

Derek grabbed me and pulled me out into the hallway.

"You okay, baby?"

I'm not sure what it was—Derek's warm, concerned eyes; all the new developments with my music; Timothy and Jed—but I just lost it. I wept all over his cashmere sweater. He just waited and held me. After a bit he said, "I know, Jackson, it's all happening very fast."

"Oh, you have no idea," I said, trying to break out of my tear spell, "you know who Timothy Meyer is?"

This was probably not in good judgment, but considering my volatility it was unavoidable. I had to tell someone like Derek, someone wise and seasoned—even if he did sometimes act like a kid. I told him the whole story from start to finish, and when I was done, he said, "Excuse me, I'm going to go get a Valium. Maybe two."

I laughed.

"Listen, Jackson, I think the best thing you can do is concentrate on yourself. Get some rest, eat well, and stay focused. I've got the keys to Cher's house in Malibu. I'm going to send you down there for three days to unwind. Don't worry about Aden; I'll cover for you. In fact, it's really not a good idea for him to hear any of this, so why don't we keep the whole saga to ourselves. Come here."

Derek took the sleeve of his shirt and wiped at my eyes.

"But you must do one last thing. You must go to the pier, or wherever it is, and tell this Timothy character you're not interested. End it. Simple as that."

"The problem is, I still am."

"Even after you saw the tramp with him in the pool?"

"I don't know. Yes, I guess. Isn't that pathetic?"

"Well, you're going to have to get over it, like you say in your song."

"It's not that easy." People always assumed I lived all of my songs.

"Listen, you'll wake up tomorrow and realize it is. You've got your whole life ahead of you and we need you to be brave. There are plenty of guys out there who will make you happy, whom you deserve," he giggled a little. "Just don't be seen with them in public. If you really feel strongly about him, then maybe you can forgive him, but you have to do what you feel is right."

"Can I ask you a personal question?"

"Of course, baby."

"Well, you're with Aden, but you guys never even touch each other. Why are you with him?"

Derek straightened his sweater and smiled.

"I have my reasons," he said.

I looked down at my watch; I had twenty minutes to get to Santa Monica if I was to meet Timothy on time.

"Derek, I've got to go."

"Okay, come by tomorrow and pick up the keys."

"Where is Cher?"

"I don't know, probably in New York; that's where her plastic surgeon is."

"Are you sure it's okay?"

"You're our golden boy, Jackson, remember that."

He kissed me on the cheek and wiped the last tear away.

# 28

The Santa Monica Pier was hopping with tourists and blonde joggers. I approached the Ferris wheel and saw Timothy, two ice-cream cones in his hand. He handed me one of them, and I threw it into the ocean.

"Whoa," he said. "What's up, sunshine?"

"Not much, you tell me."

"I've been crazy, sorry I haven't called. I wanted to surprise you at the concert, but I couldn't find you."

"That's funny, 'cause I was the last one there."

"What's wrong?" he said, like nothing possibly could be.

"You and Jed, that's what. Not to mention you're married."

He squirmed in his sweatshirt, looked at the ground. I noticed a slight twitch in his cheek, the same cheek I had tasted with such passion during our time together.

"Shit," he said, "I know you probably think I'm—"

"An incredible asshole."

I felt electric. I had the upper hand.

"Jackson, listen to me. Jed's a boy, that's all. He's got nothing to offer, really. I saw you in all the papers with Kira—"

"Kia."

"Kia. I figured there might have been something you weren't telling me."

He was suavely trying to deflect the accusation.

"Kia's my friend," I said. "You didn't tell me you had a wife!"

"We've been separated for months. I'm—"

"Is that why she hired a detective to spy on you?"

He squirmed some more. The cheek twitch was now spasmodic. I was basking in his discomfort. Some screaming kids ran by us with cotton candy in their hands. He pushed me a little.

"What the fuck," he said, turning sour, "Who are you—"

"Never mind," I said. "I had a really great time with you but I have to say good-bye now. I can't operate like this."

"Is it Kia?"

He started to cry. I was absolutely flabbergasted.

"I only want you, Jackson," he said feebly.

I flashed on him touching Jed so gently, with the same sweet look in his eyes that had made me feel he truly cherished me.

"Why don't you try auditioning for Kia's show," I said, and held up my hand as he started to speak. I walked away, simple as that. But of course it wasn't simple at all, and I felt my heart break a little.

Cher's house looked like a giant pillow of white from the outside. Modern lines with huge plate-glass walls and the sea crashing around it. I spent most of the time sitting at the Steinway grand piano that was perched in a dome-shaped room. The sand underneath the glass floor looked alive from the runoff of the waves.

Lying on the porch alone, something came to me: I wasn't going to get the kind of real, long-term relationship I wanted if I kept going for sexy, overly-private hotties. The warning signs were there from the beginning with Timothy and even Mark Diamond, and I'd just ignored them. Timothy did have positives, however. I was drawn to his confidence, his romance, and his interest in music— or was even that just a line? Regardless, it was time to let it go.

I spent hours playing, singing, and just sitting. I was trying to find melodies and words to express what I was feeling, but the melodies were too dark and minor-ish, and the words came out confused and fleeting. Was I ever going to be able to follow up my debut with an album like it, the one I had written as a dreamer, not as one who had landed the dream? I supposed it was an obvious dilemma to the artist who receives fame, but I guess I never expected to actually arrive at that crossroads.

It felt nice to be in such an opulent place. I could have this myself, I thought. But before my head got too big, I went back to the piano and started writing.

*I am more*
*than you think I am*
*How can I forgive?*

Shit. Nothing was clicking.

I undressed and thought: *I am walking through Cher's house naked.*

I started up the Jacuzzi and got in. I imagined Cher in the exact place I was, with her glam squad of assistants and stylists, getting ready for a party. *Do you believe in life after love?*

Well, yes. But I wanted love first. You could be the most famous person in the world but where were you without love?

John Lennon said it the most simply: *All you need is love.*

# 29

Derek was correct: A respite at Cher's villa did me wonders. I'd even managed to keep the Timothy and Jed thing out of my thoughts the last day I was there. I drove back toward Hollywood feeling refreshed and ready to go. I told myself it was simply time to concentrate on my music, my career. After all, I was about to go to Canada to support Alanis and then to the UK to support the Stones. I secretly fantasized about brushing Alanis's hair and kissing Mick Jagger. I remembered in high school when his lips were on every torn T-shirt and patched pair of jeans in sight. A rock-n-roll iconic image up there with the Nike swish or Macintosh's bitten apple.

I called Neil to check in.

"Listen, Aden was looking for something in my office and found the itinerary for your New York visit. He's been badgering me for info all day. Girl, you need to call him immediately. I can't keep blowing him off. You know how he gets."

"Shit."

"Just call him."

"Okay."

"Ciao, rock star. Good luck."

I hung up the phone and decided this was a conversation better handled from home. When I got back to my place, I did a shot of Patron to prepare for the call. What the hell was I going to tell him?

I dialed his number and he picked up on the fifth ring.

"Aden here. J? Hang on."

He put me on hold long enough for me to pee and water my plants. Pure passive aggression, because I knew he was dying to grill me about the trip. Some manager.

"Hey. Now listen, I saw you added a stopover in New York after your family reunion. Why didn't you tell me you were going to be there so we could set up some publicity? This relationship is never going to work if we don't retain a strong channel of communication, if you're not straight with me."

"No pun intended?"

That got a slight laugh out of him.

I couldn't think of a good lie, and I knew he'd torture it out of me eventually anyway. "Okay, listen. I've been seeing Timothy Meyer. A little bit."

"Jesus fucking Christ." I could hear him pacing, along with the sound of ice being thrown hastily into a glass. His voice rose. "I have this whole conversation with you, and then you go sleeping with a fucking major media mogul!"

"Well, it was behind closed doors, like you said."

"You know that's not what I meant."

"Aden, he's not going to spill anything. Anyway, it's over now. I ended it with him the day after the publicity concert."

"Right, Jackson. How can a person who writes such evolved lyrics be so naïve? I quit yesterday, but fuck it, I need to go get some cigarettes right now. Derek? Derek! Can you tell Mauricio to get me some American Spirit Lights? NOW!!"

"Aden, I've got to go to the gym. We'll talk about this later, after you smoke a cigarette."

All I heard was an exasperated sigh, then the phone clicked. He'd hung up on me, the diva. As infuriated as Aden was, conflict was essential to his well-being, he thrived on drama. But I knew from his tone of voice that he'd be okay after half a pack and a couple of cocktails. Realistically, he had to know that I wasn't going to stop having sex entirely. Wasn't it enough I was giving up all signs of public gayness?

I actually would have liked to go to the gym, but I realized now I would need a new one if I didn't want to run into Jed. Instead, I played my phone messages while I unpacked my bags.

Timothy had left a slew of messages while I was at Cher's.

Apologetic: "Let me explain. I just want to talk to you."

Desperate: "I just want you to sing me another song."

Drunk dial: "Are you listening? Where are you!"

Angry: "Who are you? You're nothing."

Guilty: "I'm sorry, I just want to hear your beautiful voice again."

I called Neil and filled him in.

"Psycho," he said. "Listen—just delete all future messages without listening. And whatever you do, don't call him back. It will just encourage him."

I didn't check my cell for two days, and when I did, there were more messages from Timothy, in various states of distress.

"I'm getting a divorce," he said in one of them. "Please, just call me."

Another drunk dial.

"Jackson, I'm down, I'm down on my...Jed is a stupid boy I hired, he's just...and Deborah, she's a bitch I've never...I've never loved her. Please just, call me...let's go to the Hamptons or something, work it out..."

I erased that one before he finished. Jed was a rent boy? Apparently, as much of a fuck-up as Timothy Meyer was, he cared about me. Either that or he was a highly delusional schizophrenic mess. Most likely the latter. The last message was from the detective again. I hit delete before he finished talking.

The next few days I was thankfully distracted by heavy rehearsals and tons of press. Between the radio shows, photo shoots, and rehearsing, I was exhausted. After one shoot, Aden would barely look at me. Was he still mad about the Timothy thing?

I whispered in his ear. "It's over, I swear."

"Whatever," he said. "Your car's waiting for the next meeting."

That evening I took a bath and was sprawled on my bed when my phone rang. If it was another phone interview from some magazine, there was no way I was going to take the call. It was Kane, so I picked up.

"Listen, I just found out that the IRS is pursuing your lover boy for unpaid taxes, and he's run up huge debt. I thought you might like to know."

I was suddenly grateful I extricated myself when I did.

"Yeah, he's basically psychotic. He's left me like 500 messages."

I remembered at the Delano one of his credit cards got refused and I hadn't thought twice about it. His impatience and rudeness to the waiter made more sense now.

Before I fell asleep, the phone rang again. A 212 number—New York City. I let it go to voicemail.

# 30

I didn't sleep very well, my mind distracted by thoughts of Timothy. When I got up I called Neil right away, and told him the latest news about Timothy's debt and IRS fraud.

"I'm sorry, sweetheart. But at least you got out early."

Neil was still trying to wrap his mind around the end of his long-term relationship.

"Can you imagine what insanity you'd be experiencing if you were still seeing the guy?"

"Right? His crazy phone calls are over the top enough already."

"You're not listening to them are you? That's like the gateway drug to more of his bad medicine. And you had better not be calling him back!"

"No, no! What would I even say to him? Anyway, he's not calling as much as before. I think he's finally winding down."

I knew it was a sickness, but part of me was sad that all the dreams I'd pinned on Timothy were over. It wasn't that I missed him so much anymore—he was acting like too much of a freak for that. But I still wanted a good, solid relationship so much. I knew it was dumb to fall for strange guys and expect it to be all joy and rapture. But how could my instincts have been so wrong?

"I really thought we had something. But I'm already getting jaded. Part of me wonders if that's why Timothy has been so wigged—because I'm going to be famous, or whatever I'm going to be. Am I always going to have to worry now that people just want a piece of me for something?"

"Well, you're very attractive, Jackson; let's not forget that."

Those words sounded strange coming from Neil.

"Thank you, sweetie," I said.

My crush on him had never completely faded away; I'd just never acted on it, knowing he worked for my management company. But I liked the thought of romancing someone my own age for a change. Unbeknownst to Neil, I had even written a song about him.

> *Loving you*
> *It's as easy as walking*
> *Simple as rain*

There had been a few occasions where I could have simply leaned over and kissed him, but I'd held back. Looking at his previous boyfriends, I didn't fit the bill. They were dark, burly types with big square faces, and arms as big as my legs.

I just liked being around Neil. He not only had a certain maternal charm but was also filled with good humor and gossip. Also, I felt the crush was healthy, in that he was actually younger than me.

That Friday we were over at Aden and Derek's place while they were getting ready to go to Monica Lewinsky's birthday party. Monica had sent them special instructions—stickers and feathers they had to place on a cardboard cutout with a picture of them. It was an art project, all part of Monica's cute little birthday plan. Derek had all the stuff spread on their dining room table.

"Jesus," he said. "What the hell?" He tried to arrange the feathers and then just threw them up in the air. Aden was already halfway into a bottle of chardonnay and being subtly hostile toward Derek as usual.

"Why you must wait until five minutes before we're supposed to leave is beyond me. Derek, just—"

Derek was frantically flipping through photographs.

"I can't find a picture of us!"

Neil and I shared a raised eyebrow look that said *Burundi* loud and clear. Out of an entire stack of photographs, there were none with the two of them together. Aden and Derek redefined dysfunctional. It was all too uncanny, and it was not a pretty night at

Camp Neurosis.

I was smiling at the absurdity of it all and Aden looked at me as if to say, *and you're not helping matters.* I could tell he was still pissy over the Timothy thing. If he only knew that Timothy was borderline psycho!

"Fuck it, I'm not doing this," Derek said, and stood up to pace around the table. Neil and I took over the project for him. We cut out two separate pictures of each of them and pasted them together, along with the feathers and the scratch-and-sniff stickers. I put a banana right near Aden's head.

"How do you even know Monica?" I asked Derek.

"Herb took her photograph, she's actually a sweetheart."

"I would have so gone down on him too. Can you imagine? The power in that cock!" I said.

"I know how big it is, the shape, everything," Derek said with his boyish smile.

Neil winced. "Ew," he said, "power or not, that girl is not right."

"So, do tell. How big is it?" I asked.

"Well, I'm sworn to secrecy, but let's just say he proves that size really doesn't matter."

"She's just a kid, really," Aden said, downing the rest of his glass. "But there will be other celebs there; I'm sure it will be very A-list."

"Yeah, Monica's just so A-list," I said.

"Yes, well, we already know you prefer magazine editors, Jackson."

*And don't forget entertainment lawyers like Mark Diamond.*

Thank god Aden wasn't telepathic.

After we finished the pathetic little party invite thingamajig, I handed it to Derek. Aden downed another half glass of wine, and Neil looked at me and whispered, "God help us."

Since Neil had the key and knew their alarm code, they scooted out before we did and left us in an awkward, eerie silence. The house was so stark, so modern, that it gave off the feeling of being unlived in. That day had been record hot for Los Angeles, and without thinking twice I took off my shirt, turned on the patio speakers, and jumped in the pool. I'm not sure what got into Neil, Mr. By-the-Book Neil, but he came out with a martini shaker and a bottle of Grey Goose.

"What about Aden?" I said, playing into a little role reversal. Besides, I knew Aden probably kept a keen eye on their liquor inventory.

"Fuck Aden," Neil said, "consider it a bonus for dealing with their crazy asses for three fucking years."

He poured two martinis and we each took a big gulp. The vodka was smooth and cold, much like the newly treated water from Derek's pool over my skin.

"Jesus, what's gotten into you?" I said.

"I don't know, Jackson, a lot of things. You know that guy I was seeing, Pedro?" He took another sip. After his long-term relationship breakup, his rebound had been a super-hottie model.

"Yeah, the one that did the underwear ad."

"Yeah, well, it turns out he's a fucking rent boy; can you believe it?"

"Jesus, this seems to be going around—Jed is, too. How do you know?"

"Well, I sensed something was up when I saw his penthouse apartment in Beverly Hills. Trust me, it wasn't bought by residuals from Fruit-of-the-Womb print ads."

The vodka was taking effect.

"Fruit of the womb?"

"Don't start."

"Loom, honey. Well, at least he's not married and wanted by the IRS."

"True. Ugh, dating in this town is such a nightmare."

Neil took off his shirt and dove into the pool. His hair was curly and tight, and when it was wet it lost its perfection. The effect was quite charming. The sun was going down over the Hollywood hills and I could hear the occasional quiet purr of expensive cars.

We sipped our martinis and started making up lyrics to the music that oozed out of the outdoor speakers. Neil's version was something like an Italian Eminem.

> *Aden's on crack and he don't know jack*
> *The house is wack and that's a fact*
> *Jackson is cool, sittin' in the pool*
> *My boy's a ho and I told you so...*

Neil was coming undone, and no matter what he sang it was funny to me. Just being there was enough contentment to forget about everything. Nothing mattered. I looked up at the sky, which was now saturated with red and pink clouds. Yes, this is it... you can't describe it, but it's something like this—getting lost in the moment.

We poured another round of martinis and I found Aden's stash of pot. I rolled a joint and Neil surprised me by sharing it with me.

"What if this was our house?" I said to him. "What if we were married and this was our house, and we were like, big A-list queens."

"A-list, shmay-list," he said while slowly dragging on the joint. He blew it out and continued. "We'd be farther up the hill, darling, not down here with the minions."

"Oh, yeah?" I said, swimming closer. "And if this were a movie, now is when I'd kiss you."

Neil said nothing, just looked at me. Finally, he closed his eyes and I kissed him. His lips were round and full, and we barely used our tongues, as if that was a mystery yet to be solved. The kiss continued as we sank under the water. We came up laughing. After our voices died down, it seemed strangely silent. Everything looked different.

I started to sing.

> *Coming up for air*
> *Rising to a very new, somewhere*
> *Coming up for air*
> *On the last breath around*

After our little romantic swim at Derek and Aden's house, Neil and I carefully put away the physical and emotional evidence and made it appear as if no one was there—not even a ripple in the pool. On the ride home I started to say something but couldn't find words. It was a moment where we were happy with only our breathing.

"Tomorrow is the big day."

Neil was referring to my record coming out. There had been so much hype, so much press, that it was bound to do really well.

"We're having a get-together at Clean Slate. Don't be late. Hey, I'm a poet."

"A cute poet."

I pecked him on the cheek.

Later I met Kia at her super-fancy gym (I couldn't bear to see Jed after the Timothy thing) that overlooked the sea in Santa Monica.

"I heard you again on the radio. And Ermie said she heard you twice."

"I know, it's weird, huh?"

"It's great, Jackson. You should be so proud."

"Hmm, funny word choice. Maybe I should just walk into the offices tomorrow and shout, 'I'm here! I'm queer!'"

"That would be effective."

After the gym I did two more college-radio spots and then rehearsed with my band again. Both Leroy and Rico were unsuccessfully hiding their excitement about going on tour with Alanis and then the Stones.

"We're going to be fighting off the chicks," Leroy said.

"Easy, killer," Rico said.

"I'm going to put a cucumber in my pants."

When I got home, I checked my messages. The first was from my mother, calling from Boston.

"Sweetheart! We heard you on the radio!! We are all going to the store tomorrow right when they open. Call me tomorrow."

Then there was one from Timothy that sounded completely sane, as if he had never left all those creepy ones.

"Heard you on the radio. Good luck tomorrow."

I went to bed thinking, my record is going to be in stores tomorrow. People all over the country are going to listen to it at the little stations, come in and ask about the song they heard on the radio, and pick it up. It was real. I was a recording artist.

The next morning I slept late and then went for a long run in the canyon, and returned to a message on my cell from Aden, which was slightly garbled. The next one was from Neil and it was loud and clear.

"Girl, you debuted at number four on the *Billboard* charts. Aden is frantic to talk to you. The whole office is partying; someone broke out a case of Veuve Cliquot. I knew you would place, but number four? Get over here fast."

I got into my car and drove to Clean Slate, and when I entered, everyone cheered.

"Jackson! Jackson!," everyone yelled. "Number four!" Derek was holding up the *Billboard* chart. An intern passed me a glass of champagne and I downed it in one long gulp. "Okay, well, here's to rising from four to one!"

"Hey, I'm just happy my name is on there!" I said.

Aden pulled me aside and said, "Now that you're a bona-fide success, I'm not holding the Timothy Meyer thing against you." Then he added, "At least not today."

"Thanks," I said.

He looked at my small blue Gap bag and said, "Is that a purse?!"

I threw it on Neil's desk and said, "Of course not. It's a butch bag."

Neil rolled his eyes. I remembered my dad asking the same thing about that bag. It wasn't that bad, really.

I got away from Aden, and Neil handed me the *Billboard* chart. "Jesus," I said, "is this what all the publicity does?"

"It's not only that," Neil said, "it's the fact that everyone loves your single—the DJs, the radio-listening public. It spread like wildfire. It's your talent, baby."

"Hell yeah!"

We all touched glasses. I didn't really know many of the people there—interns and secretaries thankful that their usual Tuesday afternoon had become a champagne party.

We played the record and everyone danced.

It was my party and I did what I wanted to.

# 31

My first-ever stadium show was in Toronto. Of course it was technically Alanis's stadium show, but I still had to get up there and perform in front of thousands of people. We drove up to the loading dock before the show and I ran onto the stage area, charged with joy. During sound check I was mesmerized, looking out into the vast, empty stadium. Millions of bright orange seats. Would they all be filled? I was amazed that I was standing there.

I ran to my dressing room to see if all my needs had been met. I had worked with Aden on the "rider," which is a list of what an artist requests to be in the dressing room. The bigger an artist you were, the more ridiculous your rider became. AC/DC's drummer only drank blue Gatorade, and promoters would have to FedEx bottles of it all around the world. Normally, opening acts just got what was given them, but since Aden was all for acting like I was already a star, we had submitted a rider—and sure enough, everything was there! A case of Fiji water, a bottle of Grey Goose, strawberries, a honey bear, and Fig Newtons. Even in Canada they found me Fig Newtons!

I'd insisted Neil come on tour with me, and with the help of Derek, Aden finally agreed. We had adjoining rooms in a Hilton with views of the city. When we first arrived, there were hordes of fans waiting to see Alanis, who wasn't even staying at that hotel. A bogus tip, we supposed.

"I'm here!" I said, as we walked by unnoticed. Neil laughed. My video wasn't going into rotation until the following week, so no one really knew my face yet. Most of the initial press would be hitting in the coming days and weeks.

"Get used to it," Neil said with his boyish smile, "they'll be here for you soon enough."

I took a long bath and did a little yoga to relax. The bellman slipped a fax under my door and I saw the letterhead: *Interview* magazine. It was from Timothy. Was he on crack?

> *Knock 'em dead kid.*
> *I know you will.*
> *I will be rooting for you.*
> *T Meyer*

Did he honestly think he was going to get somewhere with all this excessive attention? He reminded me of a pushy salesperson—not taking no for an answer.

Neil barged in as I was reading it and snooped over my shoulder, enough to see the letterhead.

"Girl, you need to lose that fanatic."

"I know, whatever."

"Doesn't he have a clue?"

"Apparently not."

I will remember the few moments before my first major stadium appearance forever. It was like there was something swimming in my veins: a drug, the anticipation, the pride, the stage jitters, all of it.

When I walked onstage, the crowd was in a total uproar—I had experienced applause many times, but none of this magnitude—but when they realized it wasn't Alanis, a lot of them went back to talking. I changed the set list and bumped up the single, cueing Rico and Leroy of the switch. Leroy went with the flow, but I could tell at first that Rico didn't want to deviate from our rehearsed set. But sure enough, as we played a song they were already familiar with, people gradually started checking us out. My senses were overloaded. I could smell the antiseptic on the microphone, see a lighter held by someone in the very last row.

I had gotten "briefed" by Aden again before the tour about butching it up. I found myself monitoring my hand movements and worrying that my hair had too much gel in it. Aden had gotten under my skin. Halfway into the third song I tried to follow Derek's advice and just be myself. I thought of what my professor/lover Patrick always said in my college acting class: *Get out of your head, get out of your head.*

I finally loosened up a bit, and the crowd became more energetic. Aden wasn't there anyway; he was in the Hamptons and was to meet us in London for the first Stones show.

That first night playing to all those people was a culmination of the years of struggle, waiting tables and making demos, trying to be pop, trying to be folk, trying to be rock, trying to be the next thing, and finally reaching it by just doing what I did best; and being myself. But was I? There was something in the back of my mind, even with Aden not around, that stifled my gayness. But I knew deep down I had gotten here not because I liked to suck cock but because I was a talented musician. Imagine that.

After the show, I felt like a truck had hit me. I was extremely happy but exhausted at the same time. I sat with Leroy and Rico and talked about some of the kinks in the set.

"You should go on longer and vamp at the end of 'Go,'" Leroy said. He loved to improvise.

"Okay, good idea."

Rico voiced his concern about the impromptu set change because he didn't like to have two songs back to back with the same type of drumbeat.

"I think the change was smart; I just want to be prepared. That way I'll switch up the bass drum rhythms. Too much four on the floor otherwise."

We agreed to keep the single at the beginning of the set and move a couple other songs around.

Leroy said, "Okay, time to meet chicks."

"You guys go; I'm going to chill. Great job tonight!"

Neil and I went to our suite and shared a bottle of Veuve. We clinked our glasses together, the bubbles rising in tiny thin lines.

"This time, I don't care about the incidentals!" Neil said.

We sat by the window looking at the skyline of Toronto.

"You are truly amazing, Jackson. Even after all this time, you never cease to blow me away."

I tried not to blush.

After the bottle was done, I pulled out a joint that I'd gotten from a huge, longhaired roadie for Alanis they called "Mom." He told me it was "creeper," meaning, don't smoke too much 'cause the effect takes a while, then creeps up on you.

I ignored Mom's warning, and sure enough I was soon dancing in the terry-cloth hotel bathrobe. Neil, to my surprise, joined me once again in the pot smoking (he rarely did), and I put on a little show for him.

I was camping it up, singing my single like I was Madonna or Kylie Minogue.

"This will be my debut video," I told him, "Aden will love it."

By the end I was naked, lying on the bed. Neil approached me and brought his face inches from mine, and I thought: *This is it. We're finally going to have sex.*

But instead of feeling those full, moist lips against mine for the second time, he whispered, "Jackson, we should go to bed. You've got interviews tomorrow, and we've only just started the tour."

I looked into his glazed-over, almond-brown eyes and smiled.

"Okay," I said, "to be continued."

# 32

The fan response greatened at every show. The single had already caught on, and though it was hard to win them over, when we'd break into it, I turned from a random opening act to an artist who was striking their memory chords.

Aden had told Neil toward the middle of the tour that the video was in heavy rotation in Canada, and I could tell because people started to recognize me. It was in rotation in the UK now, too, so hopefully we'd be well received during the Stones tour. More press had come out, and more radio stations were adding the single to their playlists.

Toward the end of the stint, a man who introduced himself as the VP of Universal Canada was sitting with his daughter in my dressing room after the show.

"Hey, there's the rock star," he said. "Great show."

"Thank you."

I shook his hand firmly and then kissed his daughter's hand. I noticed an *Advocate* I'd been reading peeking out from under a shirt on the dressing table and tried to subtly cover it up.

I was smiling uncomfortably. What would a straight guy do? Subtly flirt with his daughter? It was sinking in how much was riding on my success, how everything had to be played out a certain way.

I looked in the ice bucket and said, "They forgot the beers." I turned to the daughter, who was wearing two different colored tank tops—a strap look. She had on low-rider Seven jeans and very cute black heels. I wanted to compliment her on the fabulous ensemble but settled on, "Would you like a Coke?"

She blushed, "Diet, please."

Neil walked in just in time. I looked at him and said sternly, "Neil, we need some Diet Coke in here."

"Is that a Martin you play?"

Mr. Exec was apparently instrument savvy.

"Yes, it's a Martin."

"Open-C tuning right?"

Wow. He was spot on. I downplayed my excitement to appear butch.

"You got it."

The daughter looked proud of her father—how cool would it be to have a dad who takes you backstage?

"Well, we just wanted to say hello, but I want you to know, Jackson, me and everyone at the label are very impressed by your growing success."

"I'm just stoked to have the chance." Stoked? Where did that come from?

"Well, keep up the good work, and thanks for the great show."

I completely shunned the thought of flirting with this guy, who was getting more attractive by the second.

"Cool," I said.

Neil came back with the Diet Coke as they were leaving, and the daughter took it to go.

After they left, Neil said, "Girl, tell me you were not flirting with that guy."

"No. But he was kind of cute. He's a VP at Universal Canada, and he liked the show!"

"Of course he did, darling. You rock."

On the last of the Alanis shows, my secret wish came true. We had to share a dressing room (the other ones were being renovated) and Alanis's stylist was called away to take a personal phone call. Before he left he handed me the brush, motioning for me to finish brushing her hair. It was surreal, sitting there running the brush through her silky brown hair that cascaded down her back. Neil came in and rolled his eyes. Alanis told me that I brushed as well as I sang.

"Thanks," I said. "I didn't know you had a chance to catch my set."

I'd only met her informally up until that point and hadn't realized she'd even been watching my shows. She was sweet and comforting.

"Of course I have, Jackson, I watch the first half until I have to go into vocal warm-up."

I was in heaven until the panty-wadded stylist came back in and gave me a snarl.

"I'll take over from here," he said. I handed him back the brush. It was the last of the shows, and I told her I'd love to open for her again sometime. She agreed, and actually invited me to a private party she was throwing for Bono's birthday the following night. One of her assistants (with purple hair and three nose rings) gave me an invitation made of metal, only an address was etched on it.

"That will get you and a guest in," Alanis said. "The only catch is, you have to wear white."

"Thank you." I felt awkward yet glowing.

I heard the crowd yelling and Neil grabbed me to lead me to the stage. Halfway through the first song I realized I still had the metal invitation in my hand. I waved it in the air, and it caught the light and reflected beams onto the sea of heads. I took the mic off the stand and paraded around the stage, knowing it was the last show of my first stadium stint. In the beginning the stage felt so vast and I just stood in the center, but now I was owning it. Leroy and Rico approved and became more animated as well. Leroy was doing variations on his bird-head movements and Rico twirled his sticks with masterful precision.

At the end of the show I did something I'd only dreamed of doing—I shook all the grasping hands in the front row as I exited the stage.

*This is it*, I thought. *I'm a fucking rock star.*

Bono's birthday was great, except I never saw Bono. I'm not sure he was even there. The metal invitations got Neil and me into the main party area, but the VIP invitations were copper. Who knew?

They were serving Cristal like it was tap water and there were tons of groupie chicks, a lot of whom congratulated me for my performance the previous night. I smiled and genuinely thanked them. I was still basking in the newness of it all.

I ended up meeting one of my earliest inspirations, Sarah McLachlan. She had heard my record!

"I was so into your first album," I said. Neil squeezed my arm a little.

"Thanks. I'd wish you luck, but I don't think you'll need it."

If you only knew.

The next day we were off to London for the Rolling Stones shows. As we landed in JFK for a brief layover, I couldn't help thinking of Timothy. Something inside me still lusted after him, even though I knew he was wrong. The forbidden fruit—gorgeous on the outside but rotten in the center.

London was exciting—so much style and diversity.

We went to a private club with Stud, the Rolling Stones's tour manager. George Michael was there and I was tempted to pick his brain on the whole sexuality issue within pop music, but he seemed angry and belligerent. On the way out he punched the doorman. The eighties were over and it wasn't pretty.

The shows were incredible, but I never got to meet the Stones. All in all, the UK crowd was a bit more adult—less screaming but lots of intent, listening faces. Every show was like a small stepping stone in my confidence as a performer. Leroy and Rico were gelling more as a rhythm section, and each night they watched the Stones from the wings.

Of course, Aden claimed to have talked to Mick for twenty minutes, but Neil and I knew the real truth. They were untouchable. They were whisked in and out of the venues with virtually no contact with anyone. I also got to watch from the stage, however, and noticed Mick had on a lavender silk scarf one night. I pointed at it in front of Aden and said, "Look!" even though I knew I couldn't compare it with my situation. The Stones were at the stage where they could do anything. People would pay to see Mick Jagger fart.

Neil had been a little standoffish since we'd arrived in the UK, and I wondered if it was because Aden was around so much.

The last night, Neil and I had adjoining suites again. He knocked on my door, wearing a short tank top and sweats, asking if I'd like to join him at the hotel gym. I found myself mesmerized by the thin trail of black hair leading from just below his navel to the Adidas striped sweats that sat low on his waist. He nonchalantly played with the bottom of his shirt, lifting it up slightly, revealing a little more.

"Give me a minute," I said.

Hotel gyms were always the same. A tiny room made larger with mirrors, a couple of machines and one of those medicine balls. We worked out in silence, and I wondered if he knew what I was thinking. Being five-star, this particular hotel had a little steam room and two showers in the dressing room.

"Oh, look, his and his."

Neil peeled off his top. I was never bashful with my body, but at that moment I blushed taking my shorts off to reveal my growing erection. Neil, who was usually shy about his body, jumped out of his sweats and barely tried to cover himself with the towel.

We sat opposite each other in the dark, cloudy steam room. I sensed someone else in there, and as Neil's toe tickled the side of my knee, I giggled. The person got up and left, and we were alone. The steam rose thick around us, smelling of eucalyptus. Neil's toe searched further up my inner thigh. By then I was completely hard, and his foot expertly played around my groin. I had to concentrate in order not to come. The sound of the steam was loud but soothing—white noise.

When the steam stopped, he kissed me, and all we could hear were our quick breaths and the occasional drops of moisture from the ceiling. He stood up and turned around, revealing his perfectly rounded, milky butt cheeks. I kissed each one. Then the door opened, and we frantically grabbed for our towels, sitting down next to each other this time. When the steam grew thick enough again, I rested my head on his shoulder, and he brushed one of his fingers gently across my lips.

# 33

When I arrived back in LA, my album sales had grown and huge promos of me were plastered on billboards around town. I turned away when I passed them at first, since it struck me as slightly creepy seeing yourself with a six-foot nose and a forehead as big as a car. Nevertheless, it added to the adrenaline building in my blood.

Letters had come into the office via Virgin, and I felt like my whole world was resurfacing in front of my eyes. Suddenly people I hadn't heard from in years cherished me. Neil had put them all in a giant duffle bag, which I emptied out onto my floor. Letters of all shapes, colors, and sizes, even care packages!

One letter, in the shape of a heart, was from a fourteen-year-old girl from Ohio. It said, "Jackson, would you come to my prom with me?" and had a picture of her, braces and everything, her hair done up on top of her head. Maybe Aden's hetero plan was actually working.

Another letter creeped me out—a loose bullet and a magazine cutout of a man's torso with smeared ketchup on it. What the fuck? I tossed it immediately.

Thankfully, the weirdness of that letter was immediately erased by a letter from Autumn!

> Jackson-
> You are everywhere now! And to think, I kissed you in a police car! I am back in art school, dating a tired-ass guy who writes bad poetry and fixes motorcycles. I am so happy for you and you must look me up if you come to the cultural epicenter of Olympia Washington!
> Your first big fan,
> Autumn.

I smiled and wondered if she was still doing the pickle trick at the local bar.

My former professor Patrick, the subject of my single, was next:

*Jackson-*
*So glad to hear you're doing so well. I am still teaching and still single. Enclosed is a T-shirt that my niece would love you to sign. I'm enclosing an SASE to return. I've also enclosed a picture of Spickett, a Cambodian boy whom I've adopted.*
*Love always,*
*Patrick*
*P.S. Fool still asks about you.*

His cat was still alive? The poor mangy, red-haired thing was blind and half deaf, thus the name, "Fool." His child, Spickett, looked like a small, skinny, Cambodian Elvis. I looked at the T-shirt—merchandizing I didn't even know existed. It showed half my face and my name written horizontally in cursive. I signed the shirt on the sleeve to be arty, and prepared its return.

I also got a letter from Electra, Patrick's secretary, the one who always provided me a knowing smirk after my frequent office visits. She gave me dirt on both Rita and Patrick.

I was reminded of that crazy afternoon of my breakup with Rita, the culmination of my bisexual phase. Apparently she was now married, no kids, touring the country with a children's theater company for inner-city youths. Electra reported that Patrick had gone on to head a theatre program at a prestigious college in Chicago. I was sure he was probably still sleeping with his students.

Even though I barely knew Electra, other then her conspiratorial smile when I would walk out of Patrick's office, her letter suggested "getting together soon." It was bizarre being contacted by all these people from my past.

I remembered I was supposed to go meet Kia for crepes. When I told her about the letter from Electra and voiced my apprehension about all these people in my past who could leak the fact that I was gay, Kia was concerned—a seasoned closeted star.

"You need to write her back and explain your situation regarding, you know..."

"You can say it. Gay. Gay. Gay."

The teenagers next to us in the creperie giggled.

She gave me a quelling look. "Seriously, that stuff can get out so easily."

"I can see the headline: Rock Star Does Nasty with Professor!"

"Yeah," she said, "and His Name Is Patrick!"

"Well, what am I going to do, call everyone I've ever met? There must be dozens, if not hundreds, of people who know. And who's to say that my contacting them would actually prevent them from doing something bad? The whole thing is impossible."

"I guess you just have to hope for the best."

I told her about my impending crush on all things Neil and our soft-porn moment in the steam room. She said he wasn't right for me because he was, besides being a little fem, too short. "Never date a guy who couldn't kill a spider."

I tried to picture Neil killing a spider. Maybe she was right, but she didn't seem herself. I was so excited about Neil, and I would have expected her to root me on. I wasn't going to let her dissuade me, however, spider killing aside. Neil was dreamy.

Kia excused herself and went to the bathroom twice during our meal and hardly touched her crepes. I noticed circles under her eyes and that her hands were shaking. Her usual fragile beauty had gone a step in the wrong direction. She looked like she was about to break down, like you could snap her in half.

"Are you okay, girl?"

"Sort of. I've been doing some crystal. The show is threatening to write me off, which would probably be good. My mom's not talking to me because now the Ermolinda thing is way out in the open, and I can't reach my father."

"Wow, that's a lot."

"I've been thinking about the name you had for my dad, Joe Cuddle?"

"Mr. Cuddle."

"Yeah. For as long as I can remember, he was never affectionate with me physically. It's weird to think that you probably hugged my father more times in six weeks than I have my whole life."

"I'm sorry to hear that."

"Whatever, fuck it." She waved her hand as if she was shooing the thought away. "Your Neil's nice but too simple. I see you with someone more, more..."

"Fabulous?"

"Well, yes. And rich maybe."

"Oh, so now Neil's white trash?"

"Listen, just forget it."

The easy banter I'd gotten used to with Kia now felt awkward and tense. Neil was real, was like family to me. I couldn't have felt more detached from Kia at that moment. We sat in silence.

She went to the bathroom a third time, long enough for me to pay the bill and check my messages on my cell. Finally, I ventured to the ladies room and knocked. Nobody answered, so I opened the door to find her keeled over in a pool of her own vomit. It was a scene that paparazzi dream of stumbling upon. Thankfully, she came to as soon as I called her name. She was still slightly out of it and very embarrassed. I felt sorry for her, the fallen soap star. It wasn't easy being a product of Bree and Mark's LA society. I cleaned her off and got her into a cab without causing a scene.

I sat on the curb in silence watching the cab turn the corner.

I felt a loss, a deep sadness, but also an epiphany. From the first time I'd met her, Kia had dictated the tone of our time together: casual, mutual needs, taking nothing too seriously. But this was an evolution. I sensed that Kia and I had run our course, at least for now. She had been like sand slipping through my hand—beginning with a nice sensation and then silently dropping away.

# 34

Unbeknownst to me, Kia and I were photographed in the creperie by a paparazzo, who sold the image to *People*, which I found
out from none other than Timothy Meyer, who was now borderline psycho. He left yet another message on my machine telling me
that I "looked forlorn" in *People* and was everything all right? Of
course, Timothy, just peachy. Did he think I was that stupid?

This time, I left him a message.

"Listen, Timothy, I'm really over you contacting me. Can you
give it a rest? I need to get on with my life." *With people like Neil
who really care about me.*

A few days later when I was at the store I flipped through *People*
to see the photo with my own eyes. I was relieved for Kia's sake
that it was just a picture of us eating, the caption saying something
about our "blossoming romance." I put the magazine back without
buying it. There was a small picture of Monica Lewinsky in the
corner of the *National Enquirer*'s cover and I picked it up, thinking
about what a strange thing it is to be in the public eye. It felt surreal
to be standing in a store looking at pictures of myself and people I
knew, just going about our daily lives.

I opened the *Enquirer* and gasped at a picture of me—naked
save for a superimposed black rectangle—on a bed covered with
rose petals. It was the photo Timothy took of me in the Soho
Grand Hotel. I was in shock. The blurb said:

### Jackson Poole—Rockstarlet?

*Virgin jumpstart Jackson Poole posing in a New York hotel room
where sources say he was hiding out with entertainment mogul David
Geffen. The singer's people could not be reached for comment.*

Clearly Aden would not be fielding those types of calls. It went on, but I dropped the magazine and walked out to my car in a daze.

My impression of Timothy Meyer had now reached an all time low. I rushed over to Clean Slate and opened the door for what I thought would be the last time, a pup with his tail between his legs.

Aden was sweating. He looked at me with cold, glaring eyes while lighting a cigarette. Even the secretaries from the other company that shared the offices gave me dirty looks. David Geffen? What the hell? I had only met him once; he didn't even know who I was before the record deal.

Derek was on the couch in the hallway eating Jujubees and breathing quick breaths. He wasn't looking at me, just methodically popping the candies one by one into his mouth. Even angry, Derek was cute. I started to explain.

"I had no idea how deranged this Timothy Meyer was. He seemed so sweet; we had such a great time at first. He's trying to get back at me because I cut him off."

Aden hung up the phone and stepped to the doorway. "I'm too old for this," he said.

I started to talk but he slammed the door to his office in my face.

I could see Neil through the glass in his office. He was calm—the grounder of Clean Slate.

Derek was twitching his head in a way that scared me. He looked like someone out of *One Flew Over the Cuckoo's Nest*. Without looking at me, he handed me a *Variety* with a page over-turned. I read:

### Virgin Records Bought by Universal

*Yesterday, Universal Music Group acquired Virgin Records, a move anticipated to cause a major restructuring of Virgin's list. A slew of artists have already been dropped from the label...*

There was a picture of me with question marks and money signs bubbling out of my head, along with Riff, the Puerto Rican rapper that Virgin had just signed.

"Universal wants to talk with us," Neil called out from his office door, "I got a call a couple of minutes ago. They're reviewing all the artists on Virgin's roster. Apparently they're being very selective about who they keep."

Derek, who up until that moment I'd never heard raise his voice, stopped the twitching, threw down the Jujubees, and screamed at Neil, "What? And when were you deciding to tell us they'd called?!"

"I was waiting till Aden—"

"Fuck Aden!!"

*Obviously you don't*, I thought.

Neil just put up his hands.

Aden slammed down the phone and opened his door. "That's it, Neil, let everything go to voicemail. This is a fucking circus; Jackson, do you realize what you've created? I got a message from Universal as well."

"What we've all created," Neil said sternly. It was the first time I had heard him speak that way to Aden. I wanted to move into his arms, to run my fingers through his tight black curls. Instead, I moved closer and reveled in the smell of lemon soap from his skin.

Derek said, "If they do sign you, they're going to slap you with a morals clause that would make a nun nervous."

"Great," I said.

"Listen, we'll all go to New York, meet with the Universal execs, and win them over. We did it with Virgin and we can do it again," Aden said.

I appreciated him not mentioning that last time I didn't have an erratic ex-lover spreading gay rumors about me.

Aden said, "For now, please, gentlemen, let us get a drink."

"Or twelve," Derek said.

# 35

The next morning I tried to distance myself from my problems by having a long brunch with Brian, who filled me in on his latest massage conquests. A producer had flown him to the set of a movie in Vancouver, and he was starting to rake in the dough.

"I think it's in the air," I said. I decided not to elaborate on my second chance with Virgin. I was happy for him, and after I paid the check, he said, "No more sugar daddies for you, huh?"

"That's the plan," I said.

I went home and took a nap on my couch. I was woken up by a phone call from my mother. She sounded different—parched and drugged. I was worried she'd heard about the *Enquirer* story, but what she said was far worse.

"Jackson, you know how Dad's been having some breathing trouble?"

I could feel what was coming, hear it in the way her voice shook with instability.

"No."

"Sweetheart, I don't know how else to tell you. Dad just had a heart attack. We're at the hospital now."

I sank down on the floor. The word itself brought me to my knees. It was something I could never, ever have prepared for. He was so healthy!

"The doctors are with him now, we don't really have any info yet. Don't worry, angel, he'll be back to new in no time."

I tried to keep it together so my mom wouldn't have to deal with me being upset on top of her own worries. I got the name of the hospital and told her I would catch the next flight out. I hung up and just stared at the wall for a minute. Then I called the airline in a daze and explained that I needed the earliest possible flight.

What if my dad died before I could get to him?

I spent the next few minutes comatose on the couch, memories of my dear father swimming around my head. I had never seen him cry. At that thought, my own tears started to come. I was finally in a place where I could show him that all of my work was starting to pay off, to prove that I was successful. And this was what happened?

After packing my bags, I called Neil's cell phone instead of the Clean Slate number. I couldn't face talking to Aden right now. I told Neil what was up—that I couldn't fly out with everyone to New York for the Universal meeting but would try to meet them there. His concerned voice almost started me crying again, so I hung up quickly.

When I got out of the shower, my brother, Max, called.

"Mom's freaked out because apparently he'd had some arm pain and some flutters and was keeping it secret. I told her to calm down, that he's going to be fine. By the way, we saw the article but he doesn't know about it."

I sighed. "Good. I will be there tomorrow."

"Cool. We need you here."

I sensed insecurity in his voice, that like me, he truly didn't believe Mom's "going to be fine" comment.

"Okay, Bro. See you then."

"Alright, buddy. And don't worry."

While traveling to Boston, I noticed eyes on me, and one girl asked for my autograph. Because of the state I was in, I refused. I just wanted to be anonymous, alone with my thoughts. My celebrity status all of a sudden seemed very unimportant.

I took a cab straight to the hospital. When I got to the right floor, I saw my mom at the end of a long corridor and ran down it to embrace her. Max and Rose came over and made it a four-way hug.

"The doctor says he's stable," Mom said, "at least for now."

Rose went to get coffee, and Mom and Max and I stole some leftover wine from an empty room down the hall that looked like it had hosted a party. Seeing the aftermath of someone else's celebration in such a strange place highlighted the stakes we were facing: joy and gratitude, or sorrow.

"The doctors are so vague," Mom said. "They think he'll recover quickly, but there's more test results we have to wait for." She reached for my head and pulled it into her. Max sat on her other side, gently rubbing her shoulders.

"He'll have to completely change his diet, and they want him to take medication," Mom said, while her tears dropped into my hair. "You know how bad he can be about things like that."

I held her for a long time and let out some more tears of my own. I had always been closest to her, but my father's love and support were always there. Music was our glue—making up for my lack of interest in golf and the fact that unlike my brother and sister, I didn't have kids. My earliest memory of him was playing John Prine songs next to the fireplace in the living room among our sleeping Labradors.

When we finally got to go in and see him, he saw we'd been crying and spoke to my mother.

"Don't alarm the children. I'm just fine."

I felt a weight lift, an ethereal sense of relief, at seeing his animated eyes. He looked exhausted and weak, but he was still himself. Mom was gripping his hand like it was a life preserver. Not surprisingly, he was the calm one. Now it was my mother I was worried about.

"This was just a wake-up call that I need to change my ways. It's nothing for you spring chickens to worry about."

We got to spend a few minutes with him before a nurse came in and shooed us out again. For all his efforts to put as at ease, it scared me to see how weak he looked. He must have sensed my anxiety because he said, "Everything is going to be fine, right, Jack-in-the-Box?"

His pet name for me had always been Jack-in-the-Box because of the tireless energy I had as a child.

"Or should I call you 'rock star' now?"

Rockstarlet, I thought. And who knew how long even that would last.

# 36

The doctors said the tests wouldn't be back for forty-eight hours, so there was nothing we could do but wait it out in the drab, lifeless waiting room—why do they paint hospitals beige? I suddenly felt overwhelmingly angry with Timothy for planting the *Enquirer* story. The last thing my father needed right now was a scandal about his gay son. There was a time when I first came out that I might have relished my father being forced to confront who I was. But now I just felt protective of him.

When I initially came out to my mother, the first thing she said was, "We can never tell your father."

He probably already knew. Don't all parents? How many evaded girlfriend questions and solo homecomings until they get a clue? He told me that whatever I wanted to do or be in my life he would support. Now, he still never really asked me about my boyfriends, but how could I complain? Some parents disowned their own children—for choosing to sleep with someone of your own sex? To me, unfathomable. There were certainly worse things children could do to disgrace their parents. I never felt one should cling to it as his or her only identity; it was simply another aspect of themselves, like long arms or red hair. That's how I saw it.

I remembered him sending me a postcard shortly after my mother gave in and told him. I still cherish it. It's a picture of four obviously male feet on a bed near an open window. The caption read:

**Who is to mind what these affectionate people do, so long as they don't do it in the street and scare the horses?**

While the sentiment is sweet, I always wondered whether it was his subtle way of saying he approved but also a warning for me to be careful not to flaunt it. Like the time I came home with black nail polish on my fingernails. That, to him, was crossing the line.

An old soda machine hummed in the corner, and a few orderlies walked past, smiling to bring us cheer.

Now that my dad was sick, the scandal of my own life seemed so unbelievably trivial.

Max took my mom home and I slept on the hard chairs next to the soda machine.

In the morning, Max reassured me it was okay to go to my Universal meeting.

"You saw him, Bro, and you did your time tonight so don't sweat it. The tests will be back tomorrow."

I went in to say good-bye to my father, who was eating his canned peaches.

"Mmm, fresh from the vine," he said. I admired his resilience, or rather his capacity for denial.

"I'll come back right after I'm done with my meeting," I said. "I tried to postpone it but—"

"Listen, Jack-in-the-Box, don't worry about me. You go about your business and just check in once in a while. Okay, kid?"

When I was in college, he would always end our conversations with, "Okay, kid," and it inevitably brought a smile to my face.

"Dad, I'm coming right back, whether you like it or not."

I thought I noticed his eyes well up, but he could have just been sleepy.

Max and Mom dropped me at the airport early. I was completely out of sorts—too many dark things on my mind. I tried to distract myself by calling home and checking messages.

There was another one from Timothy.

"I got your message and I'm sorry; it was just a stupid prank. I was mad at you for not returning my calls, but it was so good to hear your voice. Call me at my new number..."

How dare he say it was just a prank! My whole fucking career was in jeopardy, not to mention giving my sick father something else to worry about if he found out.

I was furious. I called his new number and left him a seething message.

"DO NOT EVER CONTACT ME AGAIN!" was the jist of it.

One of the other messages was from the detective saying he still hadn't been able to locate Mr. Meyer and would greatly appreciate my help. "You will be well compensated for any information you can provide." So now they were upping the ante to bribery?

I called the detective's number and got him in person. "This is Jackson Poole. As I told you before, I don't have any information for you about Timothy Meyer. But here's a freebie: If you're so eager to talk to him, stop bothering me and call him yourself." I gave him Timothy's new number, then banged the phone down.

# 37

New York looked different. It was as if I saw people more closely, could read their pain, their loneliness, and their despair. And also in turn, I saw people's happiness, their ease, worlds not cluttered with tragedy. I supposed it was part of growing up that you live through things and suddenly the world doesn't revolve around you. It was hard to concentrate because on this particular trip, it was about me but my mind was with my dad.

We were to meet with Peter Montgomery, VP of Universal, at a conference room in their offices. We met outside, all of us having a hushed cigarette. This time we were in black and passed easily as Manhattanites. I had removed all of my jewelry, which Aden checked for right away. He was pacing on the street, very anxious, and snapped at me.

"If you hadn't slept with Timothy, who knows if we'd even be suffering through this."

Thankfully, Derek intervened, clearly considering the situation with my dad, "Aden, that's enough." I'd called from the airport in Boston and updated Neil about his status.

"Okay, I'm sorry, but listen. This is it. It's all riding on this meeting. Just let us do most of the talking, and if you do talk, easy on the hand movements."

I couldn't even respond, but Neil did by simply giving me a hug. In the elevator, we all rode in silence until Derek said as the door opened, "Into the fire we go."

We sat in the cold, intimidating conference room, and someone handed me a bottle of water. I spilled it onto my shirt in the first sip. My hands were shaking. Peter, a handsome man with white hair wearing a green sweater, spoke about whether they would keep me on the new label.

"I wish it wasn't an issue, the gay thing, but it is."

"We are aware of that," Aden shot in, "and you should know about Jackson's blossoming romance with Kia Diamond. It's no problem to have them photographed again together."

"Gentlemen, and Jackson especially, I'll be straight with you. I don't care if your deepest desire is to fuck sheep. If you want to join the Universal family, none of this is possible." He slapped down the file with the *National Enquirer* blurb, along with an Internet blurb none of us had seen, one that said something like "Virgin Star Light In the Loafers."

"Yes, well, as I explained repeatedly on the phone, the Geffen rumor is entirely untrue. Jackson doesn't even know the man. And the photo was leaked from a shoot for one of those avant-garde music magazines—Derek, do you remember which one?" Derek looked like he was genuinely trying to remember as Aden continued with a hand motion like it was an unimportant detail. "You know how publishing is these days—everyone wants the most over-the-top image they can get."

"Like I said," Peter went on after sipping his single malt, "I don't care about the details; I care about the perception of our buying audience...listen, I've got a niece who's a raging lesbian at fifteen for Christ sakes. But this is a job, and look at it like this: Jackson's career is a spaceship, eh? And it has lifted off and the smoke has started to billow out from under him. I've seen it before gentlemen, believe you me, and these sort of trivialities, so to speak, can kill the power on the rocket."

Neil snuck me a look that said *Ooh, big metaphor.*

I smiled.

"I got a great response from our Canadian VP, who met you after the Alanis show. But I have to ask—do I have anything to worry about if I authorize signing Jackson?"

"Nothing, Peter. Nothing at all."

Aden kissed up to him a little more, buttering his dry toast of a speech.

"Undoubtedly," he said, "what we have here is a rocket whose launch will not be deterred. We shall see to it. As I mentioned,

Jackson has been dating a lovely girl—a soap star. We'll arrange some photo ops with the two of them to put the public's mind at rest."

*Yeah, maybe a shot of me watching her go down on Ermolinda.*

"Well, that is promising news. We have big plans for you, Jackson. You're selling like crazy, and we think you can go far. I've been considering having you headline a big-venue tour in Europe, as well as having Universal do a campaign in support of you as Best New Artist for the Grammy's."

Was I hearing this correctly? I straightened my back and nodded even though I could've screamed. To think, this major opportunity was being held in front of me, and it would all crumble if all I did was soften my wrist or say the obligatory "You go girl."

He handed over some papers.

"Now, you obviously will want to have your lawyers look over this."

We all said our good-byes and I allowed myself a smile while shaking hands.

Derek turned to me with his bright eyes. I loved the way he swam through life. He looked at us, the people around him, as if he had just come across us, another fish in an ocean that goes on and on. He had been here before. He knew it would be all right. Hell, maybe Aden even put out.

# 38

I sat on a neighboring stoop outside the hotel and called home. Max picked up on the first ring.

"How'd it go?" he asked.

"More importantly, how's Dad?"

"The same. He's a little weak, but he's fine. The doctor said he's completely stable, so we're all pretty relieved. Kind of unclear as to why they're keeping him. We'll know more in the morning. So is Universal taking you?"

"I think so."

"Rock!"

I smiled into the phone as some kids skateboarded past me.

"I just...I don't know, I can't really enjoy it right now. I'm just thinking about Dad."

"I know, but you should just enjoy it, dude. He certainly is. The nurses are fighting over him."

"No way."

"He's totally busting their chains."

"Nice."

Later, we met up in my room at the hotel and our lawyer explained the contract. Among other things, it said that any homosexual "or otherwise deviant" behavior on my part would void their contractual obligation to me entirely. Basically I couldn't be an "out" homosexual as long as I was signed with the company.

Since touring and production expenses are part of an advance against future earnings, without Universal in the long term I wouldn't see a dime from the thousands and thousands of records I'd already sold. But how long would it be? Apparently other artists and even movie stars in old Hollywood had been legally bound to basically stay in the closet. Although some gay performers still hid that part of themselves, it had been going on forever. I somehow didn't want to perpetuate the cycle, but it was a job. A good job that I fucking loved.

I took a long walk in Central Park with Neil. The clean spring air did not go with the confusion I was feeling.

"This is so jacked. What the hell?"

"Nothing will really change, Jackson. You'll simply have to be more careful."

"Not working my new sarong on Fire Island?"

"We have another name for sarong. It's called so-wrong."

He grabbed my hand and kept it in his. Here we were, basically deciding I could not be "out" in public, and Neil was holding my hand, an act we had never committed in public before, regardless of my new addendum.

I looked down at my hand resting in his.

"Neil, this is not a good start."

"You're right," he said, and guided me into the shade of a tree, kissing me hard and fast.

"Oh, that's better."

He looked at me adoringly and I thought of what Aden had said. We must take the deal and all of this had to stop.

"Am I supposed to stop living my life?"

"For now, yes."

"We'll just go to other countries..."

We turned to each other and said the word together.

"Burundi."

We laughed, but after the laughter died, I felt a pang of anxiety hit my lower stomach. I could not go on playing a role that wasn't me, but I would never give up a career I had worked so hard to make.

"Neil," I said, "book me through Boston on the way back; I need to see my dad again while I'm on the East Coast."

"No problem, sweetheart, we figured."

As we left the park, he took my hand again, but then yanked his arm back.

"Shit. Sorry."

"Let's just get to the room," I said.

"Right?" he said, and scooted up ahead.

He went to his room first, then showed up at my door in a robe and a cowboy hat a fan had thrown on the stage at the London show. There was a red scarf around his neck.

He opened the robe and flashed me really quick before I grabbed him and pulled him inside, slamming the door shut.

"Zero points for discretion but ten for hotness," I said, reaching under the robe and running my hands over his warm skin.

Sex with Neil was comfortable. Our bodies were the same size; our features complemented each other's gracefully. Afterward, we sat side by side against the headboard, Neil wearing nothing but the cowboy hat. He gently touched my nose and said, "You can do this. I'll be there for you all the way."

There was a rapid knock on the door, and Aden called out. My heart started to pound. Neil jumped up and ran into the closet. I smiled at the sight of his cute little butt, with the sheet halfway wrapped around him.

"Just a sec!" I stalled Aden and put on my Diesels. "I was just taking a shower."

With the closet completely shut and Aden's assistant after-sexed and naked inside, I opened the door of my room.

"Hey there. Sorry to...um, am I interrupting something?"

"No, what is it?"

"I need to make copies of your new deal and..." Aden picked up Neil's little red scarf, "and actually, I'm looking for the owner of this particular scarf."

My heart picked up a few beats per minute. For some reason, I had the urge to laugh. I looked at the closed closet door and so did Aden.

"Neil left that in here; I think he went for a walk."

"I thought you both went for a walk."

I ran my hand through my dry hair.

"We did, I—"

Aden gave me a look.

A look that said, *I suspect Neil is in your closet but I'm going to leave to avoid further embarrassment.*

"Listen, just tell Neil to ring our suite ASAP."

"Sure," I said, noticing a condom wrapper on the floor and covering it with my foot.

"And by the way, you are with us in going forward on this thing?"

"I think you mean going straight?"

"Precisely," Aden said, laughing that high-pitched neuro-laugh.

Nice of him to ask.

"Yes."

When he left, Neil got out and giggling ensued.

"Shit, I need an alibi," he said.

"Neil," I said, "I think he knows. How obvious is it?" I looked down at my still half-erect penis making a lump in my jeans. "Aden is a smart man."

"Maybe he didn't want to say anything until you've signed the new contract," Neil said. "Let's just move forward and from now on keep it on the way down low. And that means no PDA and no registering at Bed Bath & Beyond."

"Right, we'll just make it Pottery Barn."

Still giggling, Neil snuck out of my room with the hat on. My secret cowboy.

# 39

Boston was rainy. Max picked me up from the airport with his son, Tristan, my prized nephew, who had just turned seven. The ride home was relatively quiet aside from Tristan's bright-eyed questions.

"Uncle Jackson, are you, like, a rock star now?"

"Sort of," I said. "But I'll always be your Uncle Jackson." That sounded so Hallmark and rehearsed. But that's what family brought out sometimes.

I remembered attending a doctor's visit with Tristan when he was four. The receptionist had been cooing at him in unnerving baby talk, asking him if he was excited for Christmas.

"Duh!" he replied.

I just about peed my pants.

Halfway home from the airport we stopped at a small bar. Max pulled me aside while Tristan was distracted with the orange lollipop I had brought him.

"Um, Jackson, I want you to know, well, um, Dad's gonna have to get a bypass. But they say there's an extremely high success rate."

"They always say that."

"He looks a little weaker, too," he said gravely.

"Papa's sick," Tristan said, orange lipped. "But he still makes me smoothies."

I held back a tear with a blink.

"That's great T, I hope he makes me one too," I said.

Max smiled. He was like an older Tristan, still wide-eyed and slightly naive, but determined and on point. He was the sibling I most connected with and most admired. He wasn't gay, but he didn't care.

"How is Neil?"

I had forgotten that the night after Neil and I first kissed in Derek's pool, I drunk-dialed Max and went on and on about how fabulous Neil was.

"He's great. Except it's sort of, well, thin ice because of business issues."

"Sorry about the *Enquirer* thing—what a nightmare to have to deal with. You weren't with David Geffen were you?"

"Hell no."

When I came into the house, my father was asleep in front of the TV. My mom was asleep as well in their bedroom. Max told me that he loved me and took the angelic Tristan, who was asleep in his arms, to bed.

The house held an eerie quiet, and Dad looked so ultimately changed that for a moment, since everything was so completely still, it seemed like he wasn't alive. When I heard his familiar chuckle of a snore, my heart went soft, and I just sat next to him and listened to him breathe. Life seemed unbelievably precious.

A few hours later I woke to my father's sleepy figure trying to get up from the chair.

"It's me," I whispered. "Jack-in-the-Box."

He stopped dead and stared at me, and for a moment I saw his face before the attack, his young face looking intent and sincere through the pale sheen of exhaustion and medication.

"New York," he said, concerned.

I shushed him.

"Done, I came back for a bit before I head back West."

I helped him up, walking him into the bedroom. I got him into the bed and pulled the covers up to his ears. Role reversal.

"Good night."

"Good night, Jackson."

On my way out my mom grabbed me from her side of the bed, her voice thick with sleep. She whispered so Dad couldn't hear.

"Thank you, sweetie, your father... he needs you."

"I know," I said.

"Good night, angel," she murmured.

"Night."

I got into the bed in my old room, the same bed I slept in when I was Tristan's age and the same bed in which Chris and I explored each other's teen-age bodies. I couldn't sleep. It seemed as if my life was filling fast with the good and the bad, the reward and the price.

# 40

On the way back to LA, I picked up an *Us Weekly* for something to tune out with. Unfortunately, the cover page had a small picture of Kia from the day she threw up at the crepe place. Apparently the paparazzi had shot us the whole time we were there after all. I turned to the article inside:

## SOAPSTRESS CHECKS IN TO POSH MALIBU REHAB

Soap star Kia Diamond checks into Life, the upscale Malibu rehab...There was another larger photo from the day at the restaurant. Kia looked deathly. I wondered if the paparazzo who took it cared that he was profiting off of someone else's pain. Probably not or he'd have picked a different line of work. There was a smaller picture of her, disheveled but still beautiful, coming out of a car, presumably at the rehab, and another one of the two of us kissing at the movie premiere. The caption read, *With pop star Jackson Poole.*

After what I'd seen in the restaurant, I supposed it was a matter of time until she ended up in rehab. I wondered where Ermolinda fit into the drama. I remembered the promise Aden made to Universal—having us appear in public together as the hetero cover story. Would I have to find someone else to stand in for Kia? My stomach turned—it was one thing to hide; it was another to actively create lies.

I stopped off at Tower Video and bought a *Harold and Maude* DVD for Kia, then got her some flowers and had everything sent to her at the rehab. When I got home, my foyer was brimming with another slew of fan mail dropped off for me by Neil. I couldn't believe the things people sent. Adoring letters, personal stories—it was strange to receive such intense yet ultimately impersonal affection. The fans didn't really know me, yet they thought they did. It was flattering but also slightly unnerving, especially when I came across a letter with nothing but a dead bug inside. What the hell did that mean? I looked again and there was a picture included in the package. A woman who had no teeth. Was it a joke?

People sent pictures of themselves with their grandmothers or pets, stale chocolate, fake flowers, invitations to art openings and parties, lipstick-kissed cards with phone numbers—it was all a bit overwhelming.

I started making a small pile of letters and packages that looked most interesting. There was no way I could read all of them, much less respond.

I noticed a letter with a return address in my hometown. The name sounded slightly familiar.

> *Jackson-*
> *Dude, you're kicking ass. It's been a long time since we hung out. You were always so funny, and so talented. I can't believe all those great times we had together. I enclosed a picture of you and me at my 3rd birthday party. Dude, call me when you can, I got a favor to ask.*
> *Later,*
> *Russell Coleman,*
> *Good Gardens Co.*
> *AKA "Rusty"*

In the picture, Rusty's tiny arm was around me and I was slightly out of focus. There were two fingers held above Rusty's head, presumably the sticky fingers of some other naughty partygoer whose body was outside the frame. The cake candles gave our faces a demonic hue. The picture was slightly unsettling, not to mention I really had no idea who Rusty was. Then it hit me. He was the guy that drove Chris and me home on that fateful night in high school—the start of my first gay experience. Rusty, the drunken townie who ran the lawn-mowing business. No wonder he didn't even leave a number. It probably hadn't changed.

How could I suddenly be so sought after? I supposed it simply came with fame, but it was weird not knowing if people were genuinely interested in me. Even my ex, Barkley the millionaire who dressed very Great Gatsby, was back on the Jackson wagon. His letter was a monogrammed invitation on Tiffany's paper, and I knew before I even opened it that it was from him.

> *Darling Rabbit,*
> *You've way surpassed my dreams of your virtuosity striking gold. May I, one last time, sneak you away to Monte Carlo for a small gathering in your honor? Enclosed are the details.*
> *J'adore.*
> *Barkley*

He had nicknamed me Rabbit because, well, figure it out.

Ironically, he had never considered my music career a practical venture. "It all leads to drugs and death," he had said. I remembered feeling sad for him that he could have such a cold, hard view of the world. In response, I said something like, "Yeah, I might as well just kill myself now. Do you have any arsenic?"

Then I told him seriously that I could not live without hope and romance.

He was charmed but not exactly convinced.

The invitation was all silver with an asterisk at the bottom announcing that Jackson Poole might be performing. Barkley always was a cheeky one. But unlike Aden, it was less about name-dropping and more about creating a fantasy world where everything was always fun and glamorous. I had been enticed by it myself, until I realized that it never seemed to go any deeper. The guests were to meet at a private jet at Long Beach Airport for a direct flight to Monte Carlo. I couldn't think about whether or not I would attend, especially with Dad's bypass coming up.

I sat frozen on my couch, swimming in opened and unopened letters that were like a pile of wayward leaves around me. It seemed that with all of this sudden interest and flashes from the past, I was only sinking deeper.

The next morning I took a long hike to clear my head and returned home and made a smoothie. After my first gulp, there was a knock at my door. It was Rita, the third corner of the Jackson-Patrick triangle, the college girlfriend I'd met in dance class. How the hell had she found me after all these years?

"Rita?"

She barged right in the door and strolled around like she owned the place. She still looked pretty in a tough-girl way.

"What...what are you doing here?"

She picked up a roach from the ashtray in the kitchen and lit it, blew out a hit while talking. "Nice crib."

Was this really happening? Did Aden contact her or something?

"Um, thanks," I said apprehensively.

She started casually rifling through my fan mail.

"I can't believe you're a fucking rock star! Who knew?"

"Rita, what—"

She saw the letter from Patrick.

"Holy shit! Did he tell you he's a father now—I think the kid's name is, like, Spigot. Weird. I read this article about you hanging with some soap-star chick. Yeah, right."

She took a sip of my smoothie. I wasn't really scared. It was part of her act; she had always been like that.

"I was the last, right?"

"What do you mean?"

"The last girl you slept with?"

I remembered Autumn and the kiss in the cop car, our romance during that crazy summer when I did the Northwest coffee-shop circuit.

"Pretty much."

"You know what that feels like? You know what it *felt* like? Took me years to get over. As a matter of fact, I'm still not fuckin' over it."

I wasn't sure what she wanted to hear. Did she have some delusion that she'd turned me gay? Or that she wasn't "woman enough" to make me straight? It wasn't her at all, she was beautiful and smart—it was just the timing.

"Listen Rita, can we go somewhere?"

I thought it would be better if we got on neutral ground. She agreed to go out.

The Standard hotel was busy with young industry hipsters with good hair. There was a real, live person displayed in a human-size fish tank behind the reception area. Rita was beside herself.

"What the hell..." she said, tapping on the glass. Inside was a stoned model in his underwear with his head on a white shag pillow. He was reading a Danielle Steele paperback as if it were his bible. Rita was still tapping.

"Rita," I said, "stop it or they're going to kick us out."

We sat by the pool on the neon-blue Astroturf and ordered vodka gimlets. I definitely needed something strong. She gave me a long look and her anger seemed to dissipate.

"Okay," she said after taking her first gulp, "so when I asked if I was the last girl, you said pretty much. What the fuck does that mean?"

I laughed. Rita was the type of girl who could cuss all the time and somehow it seemed okay, like Kia. She had a tough look about her but also an unexplainable tenderness. Even after all these years, she still had the power to draw me in. I felt as if I could have been back in her apartment in college, drinking ginger ale and doing bong hits.

"There was one girl on the road—Autumn. But why would you even care?"

"Why? Well, you were my first love. Remember?"

"I thought Patrick was."

"No, he was *your* first love."

"The whole thing was jacked."

"I know. Listen, Jackson, I don't want to beat around the bush. The past is the past. The real reason I'm here is to raise funds for the children's theatre I'm involved in—one of my investors lives in the area. It's a great cause—we work with inner-city kids who'd probably be dealing drugs if they weren't involved. And they're genuinely talented."

She took another sip. She always had an amazing affinity for children and an unbelievable power to disarm them.

"The bottom line is, I need three thousand dollars and I want you to come on board. I've raised seven, but we need ten large to take the company to Europe."

Sounded like a great project.

"Fuck, look at it as a form of alimony. You were my college sweetheart and you left me for our gay professor." She took another sip of her gimlet, sighed, and said, "Thank god *that* soap opera is over."

Perhaps it was the gimlet, the beautiful breeze, or simply the fact that Rita had never changed—still the hard-ass I loved—whatever it was, I took out my new silver D&G checkbook holder and wrote her a check for three thousand dollars.

Later when we hugged good-bye, she said, "Give me a call if you ever want to talk. I still have the same number."

I laughed. "Are you serious?

"Yep."

"No way," I said. "444-TITS?"

"Yep," she said again. We laughed.

"Will do, baby-doll."

Her big brown eyes moistened at the sound of her old nickname coming from my lips. But she quickly snapped out of it, punched me in the arm and walked away. *Ouch*, I said to myself, holding my arm, *that kind of hurt.*

As I was getting into my car, I saw Aden drive by in his Boxster convertible with some twink in the front seat. I wondered, as I had many times, how Derek put up with him.

"It's called selective denial," Neil used to tell me.

I ducked so Aden wouldn't see me. Just then a teenage girl came up and asked me to sign her notebook. I knew something had changed because I didn't even flirt with her hot father. Was it the fame? Neil? I wasn't sure, but I was thankful for it, considering the last thing I needed was more homo scandal.

# 41

The following morning I woke to the smell of bacon and panicked. Was someone in my house? Obviously. The housecleaner? Then I realized with a smile that it had to be Neil. He loved to cook breakfast and he knew where the hiding place was for my extra key. I laid back and became lost in the sounds and smells of a home-cooked meal. Sure enough, a few minutes later, Neil came to my bedroom door with a tray.

"Now don't get used to this, dear. I'm just feeling especially altruistic this morning." He kissed me and placed the tray on my lap. It was eggs Benedict with real bacon and tomato, a dish he knew I loved.

"I even made the hollandaise from scratch," he said, "what can I say? I love being domestic. By the way, your kitchen could use some more effective organization."

"You know me, I don't use it much," I said, tasting the wonderful balance of the salty bacon, the creamy sauce, and the sweetness of the tomato.

"I can tell. I saw your fan mail spread out all over the counters. Anything interesting?"

"Flattering, but a bit strange. People are strange."

"Jim Morrison was right, huh?"

"I would have to say so. Yesterday my girlfriend from college knocked on my door."

"Rita? No way!"

"Way."

"What did she want?"

"Three large."

He laughed, assuming it was a joke, and I decided not to elaborate. Besides, I still loved Rita, and I believed in her cause—I didn't want to make her out to be a money mongrel.

After I finished he took my plate away and came back with a mimosa. I was in heaven.

"What are you wearing?" he said, as we clinked glasses.

Of course he knew I slept in the nude. But it was his excuse to pull the covers back. Once my privates were exposed to the air, I built into a rock-hard morning erection. Neil blew on it and kissed my inner thighs, teased me for what seemed like eternity. When his mouth finally took in my cock, I came within seconds. I was red with embarrassment.

"It's okay," he said, "this morning was for you, on your time."

We laughed.

I took a bath while he cleaned the kitchen, and I wondered at my luck being with someone so nice.

"So, are we boyfriends?" I asked flirtatiously when I came out in my robe.

"You know, you should really invest in some Tupperware."

"I guess that's a no."

"Boyfriends? In a perfect world, yes. But not only are you not allowed to have a boyfriend but I'm not supposed to be—"

There was a knock at my door. I answered it while Neil hid in the pantry. It was Aden. Again? He barged right in, fury on his bloated face.

"Where is he!? I know he's here!"

He started frantically searching around, opening the closets and even the cupboards, as if Neil was the size of a cereal box. He was clearly in one of his odd, hungover states.

"Excuse me—"

"I saw his car, Jackson! I've been trying to track him down all morning. He used the company credit card yesterday and I need it back right now."

He was acting crazy, even for Aden. Were dealers taking plastic now? Or was the card thing just a ruse so he could check up on Neil and me? My mind had to work fast.

"His car is here because he went to see Antonio."

Neil had a friend who lived near me. But I needed a reason why he wouldn't have parked at Antonio's house...

"Antonio's driveway is being redone." That would have to work.

Luckily, he skipped the pantry and went into my bedroom. I was starting to get quite annoyed.

"Aden! What the fuck—"

"Listen, Jackson, I've told you before, if we are going to continue a working relationship then the communication lines must remain open. I know you're screwing Neil and I don't know who I'm more angry with, you or him."

"Aden, I am not doing anything with Neil. Now will you kindly get the fuck out of my house?"

"You tell him, wherever he is, that he is to call my cell immediately. As for you, Jesus, Jackson, look how far we've taken you! Is this our payback?"

"You mean how far Neil and Derek have taken me?" That was mean, but I was really irritated, Aden having disrupted such a perfect, blissful morning.

"I know you're going through a lot and fame can bring on irrationality, but one of our fucking employees?" He gave me a disgusted look and stormed out.

Neil came out of the pantry and snuck a look through the blinds as Aden's Audi pulled out of sight.

He turned around and stared at me with an extremely serious, volatile look. He was red in the face. I had never seen him like this and it frightened me.

"The answer to your question from before," he said, before slamming the door, "is no, we aren't boyfriends."

I followed him out.

"Why is this my fault?" I screamed after him. "What the hell did I do?"

"Nothing," he said.

"What are you...just wait, Neil, let's talk—"

"There's nothing to talk about, Jackson. We can't do this."

I could feel tears forming and managed to say, "Wait," once

more. But it was too late, he was gone. After all these years of winding through the maze of discovering my sexuality, and all kinds of dating experiences, I had finally found someone who seemed right. Neil was exactly what I was searching for. Only I couldn't have him.

Now his job was on the line, Aden was psycho, and Neil was taking it out on me. I didn't even get to thank him for the breakfast and the blowjob. Is this what one wishes for when they dream of being famous?

I turned off the ringers to both my home phone and my cell. I had a fleeting impulse to talk to Kia but knew she couldn't take calls at rehab. She didn't owe me a shoulder to cry on, especially while dealing with her own drama.

Later at the gym, I saw Jed and he tried to be coquettish. It was so intentional and affected that I was getting nauseous, so I decided to unleash.

"I didn't know you were a rent boy," I said.

"I'm not, who told you that?" Jed tried to disentangle his earphones.

"A little bird."

"What?

"Timothy Meyer."

"Who's that?"

Poor Jed looked honestly confused. I realized Timothy must have given him a false name. So Jed hadn't betrayed me after all, at least not intentionally.

"No one, really, just some guy I dated. I had decided to tell him I loved him when I found him in a pool kissing you."

Jed waved to someone across the gym, turning on a dime from being totally busted to smiling his plastic smile. He may not have known who Timothy was, but he was still a little bitch.

I pushed by him, nudging him with my shoulder.

"Later, trollop," I said. That was one of Derek's words.

In the sauna after my workout, someone kept staring at me. He looked familiar, but I couldn't place it. Then it hit me. He looked like John Leguizamo, but it obviously wasn't him because this guy was a super fag.

"Are you Jackson Poole?" he asked in a tawdry tone.

"Yes," I mumbled, and left immediately. I wasn't in the mood for celebrity-to-fan small talk, especially when naked. It was only starting to sink in: I was a real celebrity.

As I was leaving, the Leguizamo look-alike sauntered up to me with a permanent marker in his hand and his towel pulled back.

"Sign my butt?"

# 42

Needless to say, I didn't sign his butt, but I couldn't help laughing all the way home, which was needed therapy. Thoughts of Neil and his stone-faced look in my kitchen kept hovering in my mind like a gray-cloud lining, along with the image of my father's frailty after his attack. Dad didn't deserve to be sick, and Neil and I didn't deserve to be pulled apart. I couldn't do anything at that moment to help my dad, but at least I could talk to Neil.

That night I went to his house, but no one was home. I went to my old stomping ground Akbar, the anti-Hollywood, mixed bar Neil still frequented, but he wasn't there either. I checked my cell, no messages, not even from Aden. I wrote a letter on a napkin while sipping a pint.

> N-
> *I never got to say thank you for breakfast. That was the sweetest thing anyone has done for me in a long time.*
> *I keep thinking about my dad being sick, and I'm scared.*
> *If I don't have the people I care about, what's the value of success?*
> *I need you now more than ever.*
> *Big love,*
> *J*

A tear fell, staining the word "love" and making it look distorted.

A troll-ish looking man bought me another pint and tried to talk me up. I accepted the drink but quickly downed it and left. On my way back home, Derek called me on my cell. I knew something was seriously wrong because Derek rarely called anyone; everyone called him if they wanted to speak to him.

"Aden's had a nervous breakdown. I need you to come over here, Jackson."

"Is Aden there?"

"Yes."

"Derek—"

"Listen, just get over here."

When I arrived at Camp Neurosis, Derek looked calmer than he sounded on the phone. I suppose since Aden was always the one in control, Derek had to make up for him at a time like that. Sedatives undoubtedly helped.

"I guess he went on a serious bender. Ever since the articles came out he's barely slept," Derek said, the slight waver in his voice negating his cool exterior.

I tried to calculate how long it had been. Several days at least, though it felt like much longer. Aden's erratic behavior at my house made a little more sense.

"The thing with you and Neil put him over the edge."

"What am I supposed to do, Derek?" I said, my eyes brimming with tears. "I mean, I don't even fucking care anymore. I'd rather work in a bank."

Derek laughed, which was one of the reasons I loved him. Even under the direst of circumstances he could see the humor in any situation.

"Seriously, though," I said, my voice quivering, "is this what it's about? Living a lie? Finally you get somewhere, but you can't be yourself and you end up hurting the people around you? I signed the thing with Universal, but what are they going to do now? Follow me around?"

"No, it will all die down, believe me. Celebrities have gone through far worse scandals than this. It's bound to blow over. But the Neil thing, we do have to talk about that."

He looked completely serious. The Derek I knew, the fifty-year-old silly boy, was washed clean off his stern, pale face.

"What would you do?" I said. "Can we really control the workings of our hearts? I've had a crush on Neil since day one."

"It's the timing, dear, with all of this. Aden feels very betrayed, after all the work he's put in. Not only by you, but by Neil."

"Well, he and Neil have their own issues."

That stopped him in his tracks. Even the dog, Blake, perked up in his fleece bed, and looked at Derek with concern.

"What do you mean?"

It was asked in the sort of tone one uses when you damn well know the answer.

Shit! Backpedal.

"They're just so competitive about all the business stuff it can be kind of hard to be around sometimes."

Thankfully, Derek seemed appeased by my answer.

Derek said, "Well, listen, go in and talk to Aden; he's in bed."

I walked into the eerie silence of their bedroom. Aden was sleeping and his face looked troubled. A bottle of pills sat next to the bed. Days of a cocktails-and-cocaine diet and now what? I looked at the label on the pill container. Demerol. Oh, that should help.

Even though Aden was obviously down for the count, I started talking to him, hoping subconsciously my voice would seep in and he would hear me. I took my time.

"I never meant any of this to happen, Aden. I always sailed through my life, not lost, but certainly not overly concerned about being found. I love to play music, you know that. You love my music, I think. I know. That is if you really love anything besides chardonnay.

"Anyway, I'm sorry I slept with Neil. That was the wrong timing, the wrong choice. It doesn't matter now because he's not even talking to me. We all make mistakes, Aden, and though you try and act all together I know you're not. Look at the way you treat Derek. I know I'm not in your shoes...they're too expensive...but I see how you treat people and frankly it's cruel.

"With Neil it's one thing, because you work with him and lots of stressful stuff comes up for you, but with Derek? There is a man who has nothing but compassion, nothing but a big, loving heart, and you treat him like a doormat. If I was lucky enough to have someone like Derek in my life, a funny, brilliant artist like him, I would give him the world, do you know that?"

Blake joined Aden on the bed and stared at me strangely, as if protecting him, deflecting my words.

"But you know what I think I'm realizing? None of it matters. Neil, Timothy, the contracts and the fame, and all this pretending to be somebody else. What matters to me right now is going back to be with my father. He's getting a heart bypass, Aden. So why should I care about myself, or my career, I mean please..."

My tears started to collect and fall as I continued.

"The reason I play music is because of him. He bought me my first musical instrument—a pair of drumsticks and a snare—when I was five. He didn't care that it would make noise, and I would just bang on it out of time. Eventually I learned, and after drums it was piano, then guitar, and now here I am. He is going through so much, Aden. That is *real* tragedy. Everything else fades in comparison."

Aden started to quietly snore, and my crying turned into heaves. I had never prepared for any of this, but especially not the thought of losing my father. Max had told me the operation had an eighty percent success rate, and that other twenty percent was a little piece of fear lodged in my throat.

Derek, who had been listening from the doorway, came up from behind me and held me. When I regained control, I looked up at him and noticed he too had damp eyes. His father had passed away the year before. But maybe that wasn't why, maybe it was because I was talking about him, sticking up for him. Had he ever heard those kind of affectionate words about himself?

"Go home, Jackson. Get some rest. Everything will be on hold. Go to Boston until after the operation. Your family needs you."

I returned to my house exhausted, but before I went to sleep, I phoned my mother to check in. Her voice seemed resolved, like something in her had accepted what was happening.

"Some days are better than others," she added, sensing my

despair.

"I'm flying back tomorrow."

"Good. I need you here. I just need everyone here. Is it alright with your managers and everything?"

The last thing she needed was for me to elaborate on those issues. If I had a bus I wouldn't take her there.

"Of course. See you soon, Mom. I love you."

"I love you too, angel."

I fell asleep to the sound of the wind through the oleander outside my bedroom window and dreamed that Dad was in a giant field. I kept running toward him, but when I got there it wasn't him; it was just his shape in the grass created by shadow and light.

# 43

When I arrived at my parent's house, my sister, Rose, came out to the taxi and grabbed my bag. She was a sporty, conventional type who was pretty when she wasn't worried. Before the reunion and Dad's last hospital stay, I hadn't seen or spoken to her in a long time. I suppose it was simply that we had dissimilar lifestyles and that created a slight chasm. But we were family and always would be, and seeing her again was like looking at a warm, foggy picture of my past.

Although I could tell she was sad, she was good at masking it with maternal efficiency. She offered to make me something to eat but I wanted to find Max and get the lowdown on how Dad and Mom had been doing.

"Where's Max?"

"I'm not sure. Dad's sleeping I think, but you can go in and see him. Mom is in the laundry room. She's been cleaning all day to distract herself."

I thanked Rose for helping with my bag, and went up to my room. When I came down, I ran into Max in the hallway. He gave me a hug.

"We saw the new *Enquirer* article. And Tristan brought it in to Dad. Sorry."

"Shit! There was another one? Was he upset?"

"Well, yeah, at first." He saw my face. "But not with you! He went on a little bit about the sleazy state of journalism today, but then he let it go. What else can we do? Honestly, I wouldn't worry about him."

As if timed, Tristan ran up to me and blurted out, "What's a faggot?" He pronounced it "fag-goat." He held up a second picture of me in the *National Enquirer,* which was just one of my generic publicity stills with a huge, hot-pink feather boa photoshopped in. Pathetic. Somehow I didn't think Timothy was the source, if only because it was so totally lacking in style. I was sure Aden was having a fit somewhere, but right now, I just couldn't make myself care. My dad's well-being was all that mattered to me right now. Tristan pointed at the photo again to get my attention. Downside: my label might drop me. Upside: I actually thought I looked kind of glamorous.

I told Tristan, "A faggot is someone who likes chocolate and sleeps in the nude."

He smiled but knew I wasn't being straight with him.

"Is that really you?" he asked, giving me one of his handsome looks.

"Yes, but they painted the scarf on. Last time I checked I didn't own any boas."

"What's a boa?"

And so on and so on. It was probably the only time in my life when I could have cared less about everything—my career, myself. I was thinking only about being there for my family. The threat of tragedy opens your eyes. Only mine had been closed so long the light was blinding.

"My uncle, the fag-goat," Tristan said, jumping around the room.

"Sorry," Max said, raising his hands.

"Just think of me as having an alternative lifestyle," I told Tristan.

I went in to see my dad. His eyes lit up when he saw me and I was immediately warmed. I had thought the photo might have put him off.

"So, tomorrow's the big day, huh?"

"You got it." It was awkward. Even though Max told me it was okay, I remembered how he'd reacted to my painted fingernails. Now a boa for all the world to see?

I saw the article by his bed and turned it over.

"Oh, forget about it," he said, waving his hand.

"Can you believe it? I've never even worn one of those."

"The miracles of modern technology."

He looked weak but was still sharp as a tack.

"Listen, Jack-in-the-Box, I realize now that you have no control over what other people say about you. You just have to take the ride. And as long as you have some big secret, other people will always have power over you. I have faith that you will be a success no matter what you do."

"Really?"

"I was wrong to think you can keep it a secret."

I felt the urge to hug him, but settled for grabbing his shoulder.

"Now get out of here so I can take my tenth nap of the day."

"Thanks, Dad."


On the way into the hospital, Dad was grabbing Mom's butt.

"Stop it, dear," she said, even though it made her laugh, which was nice to see.

On the way into the operating room, Dad was singing Italian songs and some of the nurses were whispering about him. He was a hit.

During the surgery we all waited in the hallway—reading, pacing, on our cell phones, napping in the uncomfortable chairs. I kept looking for the doctor to come out of the doors. It was nerve-wracking.

Mom, Max, and I sang some songs with my old guitar which we'd brought, and a few family members of other patients gathered around to listen. Rose joined in singing harmony. A woman holding a baby in her lap said, "You sound good; you should start a band."

We smiled.

The doctor finally came out and I held my breath.

"Everything went fine. We'll keep him in intensive care until the anesthetic wears off, then you can see him."

We jumped around the hallway like children.

"Yay!"

A few hours later when he was coherent, we each went in to visit one by one, as the doctor requested. I brought the guitar in. The room smelled like rubbing alcohol, and my father looked a little caved in, as if he had begun a slow retreat inside his body. He was sleeping. I started softly strumming and singing.

> *We don't survive*
> *Like oceans and stars*
> *And heroes they come from unlikely places*
> *But lucky things happen while we're here*
> *Holding mirrors in our hands*
> *In hopes that one day*
> *They'll catch the light*

When I finished the song and put down the guitar, his eyes slowly opened and locked into mine. He reached out his hand. Once he had hold of my hand he closed his eyes again, as if knowing that he was out of harm's way.

After he came home, I could see right away he was on the road to recovery. He grumbled about being weak and having to take medication, but I saw him reading a book about the Ornish heart program and he kept saying things like, "When I get back to the golf course..." Mom was completely rattled at first, always worried he'd miss a dose of his medication or do too much. But he told her to stop worrying, and we could all see little increments of improvement every day.

Once I started really believing he was going to be okay, images from LA reappeared in my mind—Aden furious at my door, Neil frozen in the closet, Derek despondent in his hallway.

"So, Jackson," Dad said as I was getting ready to leave for the airport, "you ready to go back and be a rock star now?"

"I'm not sure I ever was."

# 44

I returned to my LA pad and took a long bath. I checked my messages and was relieved there were no new ones from Timothy. It seemed telling him off had worked. Finally.

When I put my jeans back on, I noticed the wadded-up note I had written to Neil. I called all of his voicemails. I wondered if everyone had seen the *Enquirer* sham photo—especially Mr. Universal exec. But surely that happened to other stars. What was true in the tabloids? Basically nothing. Still, it was sinking in what was really on the line.

The next day at Clean Slate, Neil hardly looked at me when I walked in. It was beyond awkward.

"I looked for you the other night," I said.

"Oh?"

"Neil? We have to—"

Aden bust through the door and Neil went back to work as if I was just another intern. It hurt. On top of that, Aden was especially cruel.

"It's your fault if all our hard work is ruined, Jackson. And what is with that belt? This isn't an episode of *Queer Eye*."

I hadn't even realized what belt I was wearing and became unglued. I was fed up. I ripped the belt off dramatically and threw it into the trash, making a little scene.

"There. You happy?"

"I wish it was that easy."

I wished like hell Derek was there.

"Well, in case you care, my dad made it out of surgery okay."

Both Aden and Neil softened.

"Shit. Is he alright?"

"Yes."

I stepped outside for some air.

Derek arrived and we had a phone conference with Universal VP Peter Montgomery on speakerphone. He said we had to "face the music" and that he "had some concerns."

Thankfully the meeting wasn't in person because we were all freaking out. He went on.

"I know you can't control what the *Enquirer* does—they've given us plenty of trouble over the years. As long as there's no smoking gun—Jackson kissing another man for instance..."

He laughed as if that was absurd, and we followed suit.

"...we can still do damage control."

We let out a collective breath.

"Our legal team is deciding whether or not to try to muzzle them with the threat of a libel suit. Sometimes it works, sometimes it doesn't. In the meantime, we need those girlfriend photos in the press. I'm not happy that it's been days since we talked about this and you haven't gotten anything in print yet."

Aden started to say something, but Derek laid a hand on his arm.

Peter continued, "Now, I've got a story in front of me here saying that your girlfriend Kia Diamond is in rehab. Drug addiction is no problem; you're a rock star after all. But what concerns me is that you can't be seen together if she's locked up somewhere."

Neil and I exchanged a glance: *Is this guy for real!?*

"The key question is will she be out soon? We need some pictures in the press ASAP to offset these rumors."

Predictably, Aden jumped in like the sycophant he was, "I've already looked into that, and unfortunately she'll be there for a while."

Was he lying about looking into it? The whole conversation was making me sick.

"Well if you know she's not a possibility, what are you doing about it?" He sounded like a principal or a mean boss.

Aden said, "Well, we're going to have to resort to a fake relationship." Neil rolled his eyes at me behind Aden's back. As opposed to my true-love bond with Kia?

Aden blurted, "We would have done it sooner, but Jackson's dad has been sick. He's been with his family since our last meeting."

*And the dog ate my homework.* I felt sleazy hearing my dad used as an excuse like that. I gave Aden a quelling look.

Peter actually sounded sincere when he said, "I'm sorry to hear that, Jackson. Is he doing better now?"

Perhaps cutthroat businessmen did have hearts somewhere.

Aden looked at me and gestured impatiently toward the phone. I cleared my throat and leaned toward the desk, "Um, yes, he made it through the surgery and is recuperating now."

"Good, good." Peter was instantly all business again. "Well in that case, I'd like to see some photos in the press by the end of the week."

We all looked at each other like, fuck! Two days!

"Now, let's get down to the important stuff. As I always say, it's about the music. Judging by your performances opening for Alanis and the Stones, and the boost in your sales in the last few weeks, I've decided to start you big for your own tour. It will be a combination of theaters and some smaller venues, and I want to start you in England to capitalize on the good numbers in your market there. You'll swing through the rest of Europe, plus Asia as well, then take a break before doing your U.S. tour leading up to the Grammy's."

We all stared at the phone in awe. A little speaker that could've slit my throat was now adorning it with jewels.

"We've worked up some dates starting in a couple of weeks."

Aden started jotting something down. Neil wiped his forehead.

"I know it's soon, but I believe in striking while the iron's hot. We've got to launch your rocket fast and hard, Jackson." I looked at Neil and saw him starting to giggle. I could feel myself starting to laugh, too, so I looked away quickly to Derek, who was calm but had a twinkle in his eye. We were being given another chance. Would it be the last?

"Jackson," said the little speaker, "I want to hear something from your mouth only...are you committed to this? Can you do this with your family issues? We're pouring a lot of assets into you, and I need to know you're solid."

Aden pushed me toward the phone and I pushed him back. Chill!

"I can assure you, Mr. Montgomery, I am 100 percent there."

"By the way, who are you dating now?"

"This trainer at my gym."

Aden almost had a conniption until I followed it up with "She's a hottie."

"Good, well, if you can't get Kia out of the rehab than the trainer will do. Trainer to the stars?"

"She is now," I said.

Group laughter.

After the call with Peter, Aden was busy on the phone calling Bree Diamond to set up the fake girlfriend appearances.

On the way out, I took the opportunity to talk to Neil in the parking lot.

He touched my face gently and said, "Sweetheart, obviously I can't be with you. Not now at least."

"I know we can't be together openly," I said. "But we could—"

"Listen. Think about what we've worked for; it's not worth it."

I looked up at the smoggy sky. I thought he was right, but something in me still didn't want it to end.

"Neil, I don't understand. You were the one who kissed me in New York, not even hours after the meeting with Universal. What's changed?"

"Jackson, I'm so sorry I did that—no, actually I'm not. What we've had has been wonderful. But I'm sorry I didn't think it through first and realize what this was really going to be like. Worrying about Aden barging in, wanting to hold your hand in public and realizing I shouldn't, fearing the paparazzi is going to pop out and ruin your career at any moment because of me."

"But if I'm willing to take that chance—"

"It's not just you, Jackson. I wasted too much time in my teens and twenties hiding who I was and who I was with. And I realized at your house this is just another closet. I can't go back. Maybe someday we can still be together but not now."

What could I say to that? He was right. He deserved more than some furtive relationship. "Well, I can't argue with that. I just hope I won't lose you completely. I love you, Neil. You're my best friend."

"I know, sweetie, and I love you too."

We threw caution to the winds one last time and had a long hug good-bye outside his car.

"Burundi?" I said.

"You better believe it."

# 45

The next morning I dreamed that my father was sitting in the corner of my bedroom. He looked young, maybe thirty. He told me to be careful, and he smiled. I woke up with a shudder, staring at my empty chair. I wondered if the vision was a premonition of some kind, so I called home immediately.

"He's doing great," Max said. "He's outside doing his laps right now. They've got him on a slow-building exercise program, but of course he's already jumping ahead."

"Great, I'm relieved to hear it. He's always been a trooper," I said. The phone beeped. "That's the other line, I'll talk to you soon."

Neil was calling with the details of the fake-hetero publicity stunt Bree Diamond was arranging with Aden's guidance.

"She's got someone lined up, but I suggested Rita. Didn't you say she was in town?"

"No. I'm not going to use her that way."

"Okay, well, you have to be at the Ivy at one."

I found myself primping in the mirror. What the hell was I doing, checking if I looked good enough for some stranger, when my heart was still hurt from the Neil episode?

"What's her name?"

"You're going to laugh. Isis."

"Isis? Is that her real name?"

"Fake as her tits I would imagine."

I met Isis at the Ivy, where she was waiting for me in a sundress. She was the eye candy in a new thriller with Matt Dillon, and apparently it was a mutually rewarding outing. The idea was for us to be shot eating together, and then arrive at the opening of the new Prada store in Beverly Hills. Isis had a salad with no dressing, and I found it hard not to stare at her cleavage. Her breasts were like foreign objects I couldn't understand. Mono-boobs.

"So, what was it like opening for the Stones?"

"Well, it was great, other than the fact that I never met them."

"Wow, how come?"

"Happens all the time. I knew the drummer of a band that opened for Bob Dylan for an entire world tour and never shook his hand."

"Wow."

I had a feeling "wow" was one of Isis' signature words. What was I even doing? I had to remind myself it was for my career and how important this was. I looked at Isis. She looked like she could've been twelve and spoke that way as well.

"What's it like working with Matt Dillon?"

"Wow. It's like, amazing. He's so talented!"

*So is your plastic surgeon,* I thought, once again staring at her tits.

When we got to the store, there was press galore. Once again, I was inside a light bulb. I had my hand on her waif waist, and she rested her fake blonde hair on my shoulder.

It was true how the press fattens you up and then digs their teeth in. This time the questions were more intrusive.

"Jackson, is it true you've had sex with men in public bathrooms?"

I laughed. "Not that I can recall..."

"Mr. Poole, how long have you been bisexual?"

"Actually, right now I'm really into barn animals," I said, grabbing Isis and pulling her even closer.

"Jackson, is your father dying?"

What? Did I hear that correctly? I had the urge to punch the woman, but instead I took a deep breath and said, "He's in perfect health, thanks for asking."

The artillery continued.

"Jackson! Jackson! Is this your new girlfriend?"

"I couldn't say at present, but she looks beautiful, doesn't she?"

"Jackson, will Kia Diamond be sad to see you with another girl tonight?"

"Kia has a lot on her mind right now, and she knows that I care for her tremendously."

"Jackson, is it true you saw Kia Diamond doing drugs?"

"I don't believe so. But I do see some moisturizer on your cheek. Rough morning?"

When we finally got inside, I realized I probably would have to buy something. Prada was never really a part of my wardrobe and I had a silent rush inside knowing that now I could actually afford it.

Afterward, I dropped Isis off at her hotel and she kissed me good-bye. I was afraid of touching her rock-hard breasts.

"Wow. It was great meeting you," she said.

"Wow. Bye," I said.

I immediately called Neil.

"I feel so weird, like I'm living a lie. Even if I was straight, I would not be hanging out with someone like her!"

"I know, but I'm proud of you. As much as I don't approve, I think you did the right thing."

"Thanks."

"And Aden saw you on *Access Hollywood Live*—he's appeased for now."

"It already aired?" I guess it really was live. "Well if it satisfied Aden, I'm sure it'll be good enough for Peter Montgomery, too."

I took a long nap when I got home. When I woke up, I ran a bath.

Max had told me Dad was alright, but I wanted to get him on the phone and hear for myself.

"Jack-in-the-Box! What's up with the busty blonde?"

I couldn't believe it traveled that fast. TV was weird.

"Just a stunt."

"Well, you okay with that?"

"Not sure."

"Well, if not, give her my number."

Dad was clearly doing fine.

# 46

Now that I knew my dad was really okay and my hetero career obligation was fulfilled—at least temporarily—I decided to take Barkley up on his invitation to Monte Carlo. I felt unsettled about giving the world the impression that the tacky Isis was my girl-friend, and I was still conflicted about my feelings for Neil. I knew I should consider myself lucky that our friendship seemed to be surviving, but my disappointment over losing him as a lover was still roiling under the surface. It would be great to get away for the weekend and clear my head.

As it turned out, Barkley's party was just another Hollywood A-list party transported to southern France. But it was exactly what I needed—a plane ride to a foreign land, sunshine, French food, and lots of really expensive champagne.

Everyone seemed so genuinely pleased with my attendance. Young men with names like JP and TJ who had previously "thrown shade" at me were now licking at my bootstraps. Strange how that works.

"Oh my god, you're, like, such a star." JT said, clutching his clear-plastic cigarette case.

"Did you get to meet Alanis?" MJ inquired.

"I did," I said.

"What's she like?"

"She's...she's..." I couldn't think of what to say that would fill his expectations, so I told him the truth.

"...just like everyone else."

Barkley looked smarter than ever in a cream three-piece with a monogrammed handkerchief perfectly placed. Full regalia, as I referred to it. Or armor. There seemed to be a weariness or sad-ness beneath his usual charm. I pulled him aside at one point and thanked him for everything. We walked out onto the veranda overlooking the rocky beach and green-gray water, the burnt orange sun almost down for the night.

With everything that had been going on in my life, I felt like I was floating, misplaced in the world. But I was also relieved. Like moisture into the soil of my mind, something had sunken in. I felt a wonderful sense of fearlessness. I cared less and less what people thought.

The veranda was far enough up the hillside that the German tourists and French families below looked like colorful dots spotted randomly against the white rocks. The excited screams of kids playing carried up to us on a slight wind.

I'm not sure what had gotten into me, but I wanted to elicit honest responses from Barkley about his life.

"Is this it?" I said, looking at the lapping waves.

"How do you mean?" he said, fixing his bowtie and dusting off his square shoulders.

"Your life, is this it?" I gestured back toward the party. "Surrounding yourself with opulence and pretty boys to look at? What happens when they leave? Are you just empty again?"

"Well, yes, I suppose."

Maybe Barkley was in a different space than I'd seen him in before because I could see moisture forming on his forehead. He seemed unnerved by what I was saying. He touched my cheek and said, "What's gotten into you?"

He didn't know about my father's heart attack, and I decided not to share. So much was changing in my life, and I just wanted to make sure that in the process, I didn't lose the things that were important to me.

"I care about you, sweetheart," I said, "and to be honest, you're better than this. You have more to offer. You're clever, you're a forward thinker." I pointed in to the party again, where a young bleached-blonde boy of no more than twenty was lifting a key of powder to his nose.

"You have more to offer than your money and rounding up pretty boys. Have you ever tried to have a conversation with any of them? They might as well be real-live magazine cutouts. So vacuous."

"That's not fair—"

I supposed I was being a tad judgmental; some of them were, in fact, pretty smart. But still.

"How far can one go on beauty alone? Don't get me wrong, I've used my looks in my life quite a bit, but I'm finally realizing that beauty comes from inside. People told me that, but I didn't really know it. Being in LA has skewed my vision of that for too long. But now I'm getting it back. I don't care what Aden says about me being too old or too gay, fuck it. I'm just being myself."

"Was that your self on *Access Live*?"

He had a point.

"Well, from now on."

He stared out at the bay as some drunken kid from inside the party called his name. Barkley looked uncomfortable, confused, which I had rarely seen from him.

"I should—"

I grabbed his hand and looked into the face I once thought was "the one." How many times had I thought that about people I now realized I hadn't had true intimacy with? I'd seen the emptiness in Barkley's eyes before, but somehow I hadn't connected it to what was wrong with our relationship. I remembered thinking how ironic it was that someone could be so secure financially and so insecure emotionally.

"There is more than this, Barkley. This is all fun and good, but it's not going to get you what you want."

I noticed him fighting back the emotion building in his face and was reminded of a morning at the end of our relationship. We had been in this posh homo-tel in Greece, and after refusing to let me drink some juice before we went to the beach, he ended up grabbing it from me and spilling it before I stormed out. He came out on the balcony and screamed, "Where are you going!" as I scooted past the other guests around the pool.

"If you really loved me, you would have given me the juice!"

I'd yelled.

A man who was lounging looked up from his magazine and said, "It's not about the juice."

The man had been right.

"I'm sorry about your father," Barkley said. I guess he did know.

"Me, too. But he's getting better already." We walked back over to the edge of the balcony and stared off into the distance.

"Maybe it's corny to be so affected by the fear of losing him, but I feel like it's taught me a lot. I'm no longer so worried about what I'm supposed to do, what I'm expected to be. Life is too short."

We turned and held each other for several moments, the burnt orange turning to soft violet in the sky. The quaint villas of Monte Carlo looked stunning in that light. When we let go of each other, I saw his face again, shadowed only halfway, regal and stern.

He raised his champagne flute and we clinked our glasses together.

"You're our rock star princess!"

"Right."

Again, someone drunkenly shouted Barkley's name. He patted my arm and then walked back into his party.

I couldn't believe how quickly I'd gotten tired of hearing that expression directed at me. Rock star, that is. But I supposed it was better than boy toy or pothead, roles I had clearly grown out of.

I took out my cell phone and called Neil. There was no answer, and I hung up without leaving a message.

The sun was gone, the magnificent color drained from the sky, and I was alone on the villa's deck. There were only a few people left scattered on the rocks below, packing up their things. I could hear the chant of the water moving over the stones.

I thought about what Barkley had said. I was still living a lie. Somehow I knew that would all have to change.

# 47

When I got back to LA, I listened to my messages. Neil was the only one I'd told about going to Barkley's because I didn't want to hear another anti-homo lecture from Aden. Even though I was only gone through the weekend, Aden had left me several messages, each one progressively longer and more irritated than the last.

"Jackson, are you there? Pick up. It's extremely rude of you not to return my calls. Bree Diamond was waiting for confirmation of your appointment, but I assured her you'd be there. Make sure to tell her how grateful you are that she set up that photo opportunity with Isis. Are you there? You know, if you don't have the courtesy to show appreciation for all that people are doing for—" I hit delete.

I needed to rush if I was going to make it on time to the appointment he'd made for me with Bree.

The Diamond Mine offices were flowing with overdressed, underpaid interns trying to squirm their way up in the hierarchy of Bree's PR palace. A pretty girl in what seemed to be every shade of beige—and pulling it off—asked for my autograph.

"It's for my roommate," she said, blushing. "She's, like, a big fan."

I noticed her pretending to be nonchalant, stealing looks at me while I signed.

"Tell your roommate she looks great in beige," I said, handing the signed paper back to her.

The receptionist, clearly an after-picture for plastic surgery, smiled but her face didn't move.

"Bree's been expecting you. Please have a seat."

It was strange being in the public eye. More people pretended not to notice me than people who actually looked at me.

A well-dressed cutie summoned me through the giant silver doors into Bree's world. Exotic plants hung in her glass-roofed penthouse office, and a small fountain gurgled in the corner. It smelled of orange essence and housed an enormous black desk and two modern chairs. I couldn't decide whether to choose the right or the left. Bree was on the phone. For the first time, I saw Kia in her face, that breakable confidence in the eyes.

She pointed at a chair and whispered to me while still on the phone, "Oh, just sit down will you?"

I zoned her conversation out, staring up at the crooked light coming through the glass ceiling. She hung up about five minutes later. I had sunken slightly into the chair, and when she slammed the phone down I bolted upright.

"Well, my dear boy, you certainly caused a stir. I knew Isis was our girl. What did you think of her?"

"Wow," I said.

She threw her head back and laughed her screeching monkey laugh.

I was at a loss. Her phone beeped.

"Hold all my calls," she yelled at the secretary through the speakerphone.

"Oh my god, between taking on a gay rock star, my daughter becoming a bohemian lesbian addict and leaving her show, my husband sleeping with the gardener—"

Had someone actually told her I was gay? Aden? Kia? I guessed it didn't matter, since her job was to keep things like that out of the press.

My brain caught up with her reference to her husband.

"A male gardener?" I tried to act like I assumed Mr. Cuddle was straight.

"Yes, but let's not bore each other with my asshole husband's recreational fuck-ups. Let's get on to you, dear. You're looking a little peaked, you okay?"

She lit an extra-long, thin cigarette and went on, without letting me respond.

"Listen, dear, I've got you on the BBC when you get to London and you're to be live again on KNRS, oh, and a press conference tomorrow, uck, in the Valley of all places. Anyway it's going to be correspondents from papers all over the world. There are some things, pumpkin, that are worth the trip to the 818."

I laughed and she went on, "You need to speak with Aden, by the way, he said he's been trying to reach—"

"I know." I'd had enough of Aden's messages.

"Well, call him, you little lamb. I'm sending a car to your house at noon tomorrow. Dress down."

"Okay," I said.

"By the way," Bree said, as she walked me out of her office, "I know you slept with Mark. So did most of the 310 apparently."

I made a "whoops" face.

"You know what, Jackson? It's a two-way street, and this vixen's had her share." With that, she turned around and worked that walk back to her office in the sky, interns nervously swerving out of her way.

# 48

After stopping by Brian's birthday party for a couple hours, I finally called Aden back on my way home. When I first met him, I was honored by his interest, and even though he clearly was moved by my music, now it was all starting to be about me being a money machine and raising his status.

"You have to stay in contact with me if we're going to do this." We?

"Listen, I have just the right actress in mind to play your personal-trainer girlfriend in the press."

"No thanks. Isis was plenty. And to be honest Aden, I don't see the need for additional lies that will be shown for what they are when I am out of the closet later in my career."

"That's never going to happen, Jackson. You'll always have to be in the closet."

I had a vision of my worst gig ever, the cage above the sports bar. No, I will not always be behind bars. Closets are for clothes.

The next morning Neil and I were brunching at the Avalon Hotel in Beverly Hills. It was our first solo meeting since our "breakup." The decor was sixties minimalist, with comfy cabanas sporting white fluffy couches around a pool shaped in a figure eight. Neil told me that my "outing" in the *Enquirer* didn't seem to have had any effect on my record sales. They were still climbing steadily. Now I even had a fan club led by three famous Asian drag queens in Hong Kong.

"Let's not share that little detail with Universal, shall we?" I said.

Neil laughed. "I've got a present for you," he said. He put the belt I'd thrown in the trash at Clean Slate on the table.

"My belt!"

"Right? How could I let such a *Queer Eye* item be thrown away?"

"You are the best, sweetie." I grabbed his hand, which I instantly knew was the wrong thing to do. All the friendly affection we used to show each other now had a U-Haul's worth of baggage attached to it.

There was the inevitable awkward silence of us not talking about all that had gone between us.

I decided to break it. "Has Aden ripped you a new one over us?" I asked, semi-jokingly.

"No, as a matter of fact, we haven't even talked about it. After all this good fortune with your career, we're all just strollin' down the denial aisle."

I took the cuff of his shirt in between my thumb and forefinger.

"Neil, you know I love you."

The waiter, a slick Italian queen who looked like he got around, interrupted us with a loud voice.

"Do you fancy a drink to begin?"

We both went red in the face, then simultaneously burst out laughing.

The Eur-ho was not amused.

"Two mimosas," Neil said.

The conversation was easy, like old times again. I told him about my weekend with Barkley, and we both bitched about Aden for a bit.

It wasn't until we were about to leave that Neil said, "Remember at the end of *Lost in Translation* when Bill Murray whispers something to the girl, and you can tell it's the most perfect thing, but you don't hear it?"

"Yeah."

"Well, I feel like saying that to you, whatever he said."

We exited the building, and I had to lean up against a tree outside the hotel to gather the importance of his wish.

"What is it?" Neil asked.

"That's one of the nicest things anyone has ever said to me."

We sat on the grass and watched the cars go by.

I was to go on a world tour in a matter of days. They had hired a new tour manager so Neil could stay home and man the office, but I knew he wanted to come. It was something he had dreamed of.

"What's the name of that tour-manager guy, the one they hired for me?"

"Rex."

"Well, you better train him on the phones 'cause you're coming abroad with me," I said.

"Jackson, that's sweet of you, but Aden—"

"Fuck Aden," I thought of Derek and impulsively added, "Did you?"

"What?"

"You know what I mean."

Neil lay back on the grass and lit a cigarette.

"No. Heavy petting."

I waited while he had a few drags, but he didn't elaborate.

"So he's basically always wanted you?"

"No. I hope not."

"Come on, Neil."

"Let's put it this way; Aden's all over the place. He's always got something going on, and the worst part about it is that Derek has to know but just turns the other way."

Neil got up and stretched.

"But Aden and I, that was three years ago and we were on ecstasy for Christ's sake. We only kissed."

"I thought you said heavy petting? Anyway, he is going to approve you going on tour with me or I'm firing him."

Neil put out his Ultra Light and spun around with a boy's excitement.

"I've got to start packing then. For every climate!"

"That's right, baby."

# 49

I still had a little while after seeing Neil until the press conference Bree had set up, so when I got home, I called my parent's
house. I told my mother I wanted to fly her and Dad, Max, and
Rose to the final shows of the tour in Hong Kong. After telling
Mom the news, I heard her voice perk up in a way I hadn't heard
since Dad got sick.

"Will Dad be well enough to travel by then?" I asked.

"I hope so, honey, but we'll have to check with the doctors.
They say he's doing great, but it's no picnic recovering from this
surgery."

I really hoped Dad could come. I wanted to fly him somewhere
for once in my life. He had always shared with me so generously.
One of my strongest childhood memories was him handing me
a crisp five-dollar bill in the rain outside my middle school. One
Christmas, he gave me a hundred dollars to wrap a present for him.
He always told me that the best presents came in envelopes, and
he'd always have one for all of the kids on the tree. Those envelopes were portals to opportunities I have cherished my whole life:
recording my first demo tape, buying my first beat-up Buick.

"Well, I'll email you the itinerary and you guys can let me know.
You'll stay with us in a nice hotel. Everything will be taken care
of."

I heard Max in the background.

"He wants to take us to Hong Kong," Mom told him, "adults
only."

I said, "Well, I hope so, because I have a fan club there run by a
group of drag queens."

Max and his ex shared custody of Tristan, and I knew she'd be
happy to get extra days with him.

"Get out! Drag queens?" Mom said.

I heard Max laughing in the background.

"What shall I wear?"

"Think winter in Hong Kong," I said, and then added, "whatever that means."

"Oh, Jackson, I'm so excited!"

"You deserve it, Mom."

"We all do, angel," she said as her voice grew softer, "We all do."

The car Bree had arranged pulled up outside my house. She'd told me to dress down, so I just checked my hair and made sure I had some mints in my pocket. I was half expecting a taxi driver's impatient honk, but the limo driver got out and knocked on my door. He walked ahead of me down the driveway and opened the limo door for me. It seemed excessive to be alone in a car that could seat ten. I turned on the TV and it was *Access Hollywood* replaying yours truly and Isis walking into the Prada store. I smiled, but started to get nervy thinking about more press. As I watched the TV, I realized that I'd handled it pretty well, but this was to be a major press junket with media and journalists from all over the world.

As we drove up to the location in the Valley, I could see hundreds of people out front. At first I thought it must have been for something else. Then I realized they were waiting for a look at me, can you imagine? I hadn't planned on this sort of fan stakeout. I ducked as we drove by, and immediately called Bree on her cell.

"I'm so sorry, Jackson, I should have sent the car earlier," she said, "the word got out. Listen, here's the backup plan. Have the driver take you around to the alley behind the Domino's Pizza across the street. Ask for Romeo, he'll explain everything. Good luck, sweet cheeks."

So, there I was, in the back of Domino's Pizza with Romeo, who was totally hot. He peeled his uniform off and threw each item at me one by one, an unintentional strip tease. I felt like I'd been transported to a porn video, only without the bad music.

"You need the hat," he said. "What are you, a movie star?"

"No, singer." The hat was sweat stained and smelled of garlic. "This is hilarious."

Romeo, sporting a shimmering six-pack stomach, handed me two large, empty pizza boxes.

"Easy, just go through the kitchen and out front," he said. I was counting the muscles on his stomach. Was it a ten-pack? Jesus. He put on just his apron, which emphasized his gorgeous shoulders.

Unfortunately, I had somewhere to be.

I pulled the hat down low and made my way across the street. It was a struggle getting through the crowd. Someone knocked over my pizza boxes and noticed they were empty. A girl yelled, "JACKSON!" Suddenly I was mauled from every direction. At first it felt strangely erotic and blissful, but then fear and panic started to sink in. I tried to move forward but couldn't.

Then I heard a familiar voice yelling and realized it was Derek. The crowd started to part and I saw him squirting a large machine gun water pistol at my perpetrators. He whisked me into the building and we collapsed just inside the doors, half soaked.

"Oh my god," I said. I was in shock.

He laughed and said, "It could have been much worse. Think about Michael Jackson. Or Paul McCartney in his day."

After I got cleaned up and back into civilian clothes, Bree touched up my hair, and then led me toward the press junket.

"So, who's Romeo?" I whispered to her.

"Oh, he's door number...fuck it, I've lost count."

"Hot," I said.

"Hot as my husband?"

"Close," I said, and we laughed.

She pushed me out into an array of flashes and clicks, all freezing me in time.

I looked and smiled. I was nervous, but there's nothing like being mauled by an out-of-control mob to put a press conference in perspective.

The publications weren't as "dishy" as the Prada store experience. There were a lot of serious questions regarding my inspiration and my upbringing. A couple of them did ask about Isis, and I was deflective without appearing anxious. Halfway through a sip of my Evian, I noticed my pinkie up and immediately put it back on the bottle. For the most part I was butch.

# 50

When I got home I showered and slipped on a pair of shorts so I could enjoy the warm weather. I started working on a new song called "Blind" that was partly about my father. I did my usual writing ritual of lighting candles and laying out the paper. I opened the windows and the smell of fresh-cut grass mingled with the sweet scent of the flowers under the windows. The soft breeze felt good on my bare arms and chest.

I sang the lyrics as I picked out the guitar part.

> *Staring at the sun*
> *I may go blind*
> *Searching for these things*
> *I may never find*
> *Sitting in the corner*
> *You came into my mind,*
> *you told me to be careful*
> *This time*

The gardener from next door came up to the screen door and said, "Sounds good, Chico."

Something in his smile told me that he was a good soul and that to him I wasn't Jackson Poole, I was simply a "chico."

He was tall and lithe, with big beautiful lips and eyes the color of sun-drenched wheat.

"Yeah?" I said.

"Yeah," he replied, smiling again and revealing perfect teeth.

I had always seen him working next door but figured he was straight. He had never looked twice when I was shirtless, washing my car. But now, something had changed. There was something inviting and sensual in his stare.

"You play well." His skin was such a soft, beautiful brown, like cinnamon ice cream.

"You want to make some lemonade?" I asked impulsively. As he entered I checked for paparazzi. Thank god my home address still seemed to be a secret.

I squeezed some lemons, and then he took over while I played him a few songs. After performing to so many large audiences, I realized that playing to one was just as rewarding, if not more so. I paused and asked him what his name was.

"Emilio," he said with a third-times-a-charm smile.

He picked up the guitar and started playing a syncopated Spanish song expertly. I dropped a lemon on the floor while watching his beautiful hands on the strings.

The lemonade was never made.

His skin tasted salty and sweet, a perfect combination. The phone rang twice during our encounter, and although both people left messages, I was too far gone to recognize their voices. He dabbed at my ear with the tip of his tongue, and I stroked his huge cock through his briefs. He stopped occasionally and stared into my eyes, and I briefly worried he was recognizing me but I knew he wasn't, it was simply part of the whole Latin love thing. He was intense—he tasted every part of me, and I him, and he held our cocks together as we simultaneously came.

How pleasurable sex with strangers can be.

Lying on the wood floor, staring at the fan, I thought about all the times I had experienced this sort of rushed, passionate sex with someone I hardly knew. On some level I knew this might be the last time I would be able to do something like this, and it made the intensity that much stronger. I knew Emilio had no idea I was famous. For all I knew, he might have a wife and three kids. But it was mutually rewarding for us: I was about to go on tour and he was about to go finish the neighbor's lawn.

When he left, he turned around and smiled, and I threw him a lemon.

"For prosperity," I said.

The messages that had come in during our interlude were from Aden and Derek, respectively.

Aden wanted to remind me to use Kyle Brown as my alias in hotels. Derek asked me to meet him at Formosa for drinks at nine to say an early good-bye before I left on tour. He sounded hushed and sad.

I finished writing the song and took a power nap. I woke up, dressed, and almost tripped on a lemon as I headed for the door. I laughed out loud, a strange thing to do when you're by yourself.

Formosa was dark and smelled of gin. Derek loved all the old, seedy Hollywood hangouts. I suspected Aden wouldn't be there, as he was the opposite, only hanging out in sleek, new places where he could see and be seen by "important" people.

Derek was nursing a gin and tonic and flipping through *Billboard* magazine. He looked handsome in the diffused light of the booth, but also slightly forlorn. I suppressed the urge to touch his face. He showed me my name on the *Billboard* charts. I'd moved up another spot.

"Look, baby, I always told you so," he said.

"I know. It's all been a lot to grasp. But I'm happy."

"You've done mighty well, I'd say."

I ordered a beer and he looked at me strangely.

"It doesn't matter, you know," he said authoritatively, "you can order a froufrou Cosmo for all I care."

"Not the place for it," I said.

Derek updated me about the upcoming tour. "Now, this one is really important for you, and I know you guys will kick ass. I've made sure you have your own sound person, not just the random house guys. And I've faxed him the effect levels I want on your voice. We need to be consistent with your sound on the record."

"Cool."

He gave me some tips for not being recognized while traveling.

"By the way, Domino's is hiring," he said.

I laughed. "You know every time I see you, I'm guaranteed a laugh."

"Not bad, huh?" he said, referring to himself.

"Not bad at all."

Derek sipped his drink from the little straw, slurping a little. He was such a kid!

"I'm worried about Aden," he said after a minute.

"What's up with him?" I asked.

"He's been getting into the whole Scientology thing, spending all his time with this guy Justin."

"He does seem different," I said.

"That's exactly what scares me. And I think he's fucking him."

"The Scientology guy?"

"Yes."

Even though I had always wondered, and even asked, I'd never received an explanation as to why Derek had put up with Aden for so long, so I flat out asked him again.

"It's like a comfort thing," he replied softly, "knowing the person's going to be there." He wiped at his forehead with a cocktail napkin. "What am I saying? It's a fucked-up codependency. But what relationship isn't?"

He had a point.

I told him about my gardening lesson.

At first he looked worried. "Are you sure it was anonymous?"

"Well, maybe not anonymous, but Emilio is a good guy." Unlike Aden, Derek actually believed that some people had good hearts. He grinned.

"Tell me everything, you tramp," he said. "Was he hung?"

"Like a horse," I said.

"I always knew you liked equestrians."

"Especially Mexican ones."

"Don't stop there," he said.

Derek and I both had a penchant for "dishing," so I explained my encounter in detail while we huddled in the booth like teenage girls.

# 51

Neil had told Leroy and Rico about the European tour when we first heard about it, and Leroy had actually canceled some dates he'd previously booked with a country star. We met at our usual rehearsal space in the Valley. I thanked Leroy for his loyalty.

"Country gets old," Leroy said. "And I just can't hang out with people who say 'y'all.'"

"Okay," I said, "I'm gonna teach y'all a new song."

It was important as a live act to update the set list, so we learned a new cover song that I wanted us to play, a funky version of Seal's "Crazy." It was important when doing covers to make them original—add an element that makes the song your own. We worked out a building drum solo in the middle, followed by Leroy and me trading licks on the guitar and bass. There was an unspoken respect among us, and I felt grateful once again that we were such a good team. For the first time I felt I was a truly professional musician, especially when my stellar band mates told me they dug my new song.

When we packed up, my drummer Rico asked, "Hey, did you get that Isis girl's number?"

"You don't strike me as a fake-tit kind of guy," I said.

"He's a drummer," Leroy said, "He'll sleep with anything that walks."

We laughed and Rico punched Leroy as we left. We got tacos and talked about how we could rearrange the set list. Although they both had an impressive track record, I could tell they were really excited about the tour. Especially since most bands—even big ones—flew coach, and we were going first class.

I gave them the itineraries Neil had supplied me, complete with hotels, sound-check times, and the updated rider that included the preferences I'd asked Neil to get from them.

Rico said, "Cool, Reese's Pieces!"

It was nice to be able to impress people whom I respected and admired. They had both been professional musicians at least as long or longer than I had.

After rehearsal I saw Brian and he gave me a massage. I'd insisted on paying him now that I was a big-time rock star. He worked wonders. After he was done, we sat and lounged by the pool in the house he was staying at. He didn't approve of my hetero ruse.

"Yeah, but what would you do, Bri?"

He was silent.

"I guess you're right. But it's going to come out, I mean please. I had a client ask me the other day about you. I held up my hand and said 'no comment.'"

"Good answer."

When I arrived home, I got some juice and sat down with my mail. There was a Priority Mail envelope with a return address from Kane. Inside was a note and a folded-over piece of newspaper which I opened up. Timothy Meyer's face was looking out at me from the corner of page twenty-three of the *New York Post*. He still looked hot, but he no longer did it for me.

### Magazine Honcho Nabbed for Tax Fraud

*Timothy Meyer, Senior Editor of the celebrity magazine* Interview, *was arraigned in the New York Judicial Court yesterday on charges of tax evasion and consumer fraud. Bail was set at $250,000, an unusually high amount, according to legal experts. "Flight risk is one factor in determining bail," said prosecutor Susan Holland.*

*Mr. Meyer is the husband of Deborah Meyer, daughter of oil magnate Drake Mellon. A source close to Ms. Meyer reported that divorce proceedings for the couple were initiated several months ago. "I would be extremely surprised if she paid his bail. He's already taken out second mortgages on all their properties," the source said.*

*Mr. Meyer is currently being held in the sixteenth precinct and was unable to be reached for comment.*

Holy shit! I couldn't believe Timothy was in jail! And to think I had been falling in love with him. I read Kane's note.

> *Jackson:*
> *Here's your man. All I know is, the wife's family is NOT happy. I'm told they want to pay off Timothy's debts to avoid a scandal but she won't allow it.*
> *Call me,*
> *Kane*

It was a little weird realizing that part of the reason he was in prison was the very debt I had participated in accumulating. The Delano and the Soho Grand were not cheap. I thought again of his credit card being declined. The part of me that had been seduced by status and luxury was gone, and thankfully so. Now I had earned my own.

I called Neil while slowly shaking my head.

"You'll never believe where Timothy Meyer is."

"Far away from you, girl."

"He's not even close."

"Well that's good. Oh no, you didn't talk to him did you?"

I didn't tell him I'd left a message for Timothy when I was in Boston. Neil would not approve, even though it had worked.

"No, no, he stopped calling me, thank god. But listen to this article my friend Kane sent me." I read it to him.

"I am telling you, girl, you better watch your—"

"I was so done with him before all this."

"Me, too. Okay, what are you wearing on the plane?"

"Neil, he's in jail!"

"Well at least he wasn't lying about being separated from his wife."

"So now you're sticking up for him?"

"Whatever, just bring sweats for the plane, it gets frigid. And I'll bring extra vitamin C. Those things are germ tubes."

I read the article again to make it sink in deeper. I'd been dating a criminal!

Thankfully, I was about to leave the country.

# 52

The next morning I took a long shower and did a mask, then played guitar for while. After picking up some last-minute items at the drugstore, I went by Derek and Aden's place so I could play Derek a hook I'd come up with for one of the new songs.

I knocked and then peeked in when no one answered. "Hello?" I called out. It was eerily quiet. They were probably out by the pool, and their "Do Not Disturb" sign wasn't flipped over, so I strolled in.

I was walking by their bedroom when I saw Aden and some guy—presumably Justin?—in the throes of passion. Drugged up passion, it seemed like. They were barely making any noise, which somehow added to the creepiness of it. I couldn't believe it. In Derek's bed!

I left quickly and called Neil from my car.

"Figures, Derek's in Nashville tonight; he gets back in the morning."

"So I have to meet Aden for brunch tomorrow, while poor Derek drives himself home from the airport? Great."

"Jackson, I don't mean to be harsh, but it's not like Derek hasn't signed up for this kind of thing. He could leave Aden any time, but he chooses not to."

"He still doesn't deserve it. What time are we leaving tomorrow?"

"Not till late—10:02 P.M. We get to go to sleep on the plane and wake up in London!" Neil was clearly excited about the tour.

"I've got to talk to Derek..."

"Listen, Jackson, it's not for you to get in the middle of, okay? Just make sure you're packed and your bills are paid, and let's get the fuck out of here."

I was driving fast down Sunset and had to swerve away from a prostitute crossing the street in red stilettos.

"Shit," I said.

"What?"

"Nothing. Will you just try to get me some time with Derek in the afternoon? I'm not going to tell him what I saw; I just want to talk to him before I leave."

"Will do, sweetheart."

The next morning I woke up early and finished packing, mostly just the basics. I was to go shopping with Neil in London for stage wear.

I dressed in my favorite Diesel jeans and a white long-sleeve T-shirt. I was to meet Aden at The Standard hotel for brunch. Normally I would have had to lessen the impending stress of being in his presence by luxuriating in a joint, but ironically I didn't feel the need to this time.

We greeted each other politely. A strung-out waitress in a yellow apron dully took our orders. Aden, of course, wanted everything on the side.

I broke us in by telling him again that there was no way Neil was staying, that I needed him on tour, and that we weren't sleeping together anymore.

"It's fine," he said, 'it's already arranged." Something was up, this was not like Aden. I don't think I'd ever suggested anything to him that he didn't initially reject.

He stirred Splenda into his coffee. He looked calm and wasn't fiddling with his glasses or darting his eyes.

"Can Rex, or whoever he is, answer the phones and run the office?"

"No, I will," he said firmly.

The thought of the party-till-four and get-up-at-noon Aden running Clean Slate Management somehow didn't fly.

"Okay, great. It's settled then," I said.

"There is the matter of the deposit we gave Rex's agent to book his time. Fifteen hundred, which I feel should come out of your end, frankly."

"Fine," I said. "To me, Neil is worth way more than that."

"A couple of reminders for the tour—don't camp it up, don't accentuate it. The coolest thing you have going for you is that you're not typically flamboyant, at least when you perform. If you're too obvious, people will lose interest. Always exude a certain mystery. Mystery sells."

"You know what, Aden? I'm just going to be myself."

He started to say something, then stopped, waited a minute, and finally said, "Yes, exactly. But remember the basics on the press outings. No umms in your speech, stay away from anything too personal, maintain a smile, and if there are cameras, blot your forehead with a napkin."

"Wow, you don't quit do you?"

"Jackson, it's in our best interest."

I could hear his greed oozing out of the word "our." I knew at that moment that Aden would not be my manager forever. The parting would have to be done in a tasteful fashion, and there would be miles of bureaucracy involved, but eventually it would be worth it. Bottom line, where my career was headed, this was not the person I wanted representing me.

He laughed when I paid the check.

# 53

I got home and called my mother.

"Did you look over the itinerary?"

"Yes, angel," she said, "but Dad can't come. And Rose has to be here for a conference, so she's going to look after him. So, it'll just be me and Max...beware!'"

"Are you sure it's okay?"

"Yes, he insisted, Jackson. I wouldn't leave if he weren't already so much better. Plus, you know how he gets. He wore me down until I agreed to go."

"Well I'm glad you guys can come. Can I talk to Dad for a minute?"

"He's asleep."

"Will you tell him how sad I am that he can't come and that I'll fly back through Boston so I can see him?"

"Oh, he'll like that, honey. By the way, you wouldn't believe it, but I got stopped in town today. They asked me if you were my son and I said, 'Of course!'"

"You know I got it all from you."

"That's what I told them!"

After we hung up, I emailed Neil the dates to fly Mom and Max to Hong Kong. As tour manager, he'd be dealing with all the travel arrangements on the road, along with any other issues that came up. I was so thrilled he was going to be there with me. This was it. I was leaving that night! My bags were piled by the door. I was sure I'd forgotten a million things, but I didn't care.

I hadn't heard back from Neil or Derek about seeing him that afternoon, so I looked out my window and started eating a plum. I saw Emilio, his long, wiry arms working some soil in the neighbor's garden. I felt flushed, so I took another shower during which my mind was filled with images of Emilio in his garden mixed with flashes of us having sex. I came as the warm water coursed over my back.

I was putting on my robe afterward when I heard a knock at my door. Had Emilio been summoned by my erotic thoughts of him?

I opened the door and laughed with pleasure at the unexpected sight of the startled, bright-eyed Derek.

"Oh shit-fuck-damn, I didn't mean to—" I had never seen him so flustered. I realized he was upset.

"Come in, come in."

He immediately started pacing and talking. What was it with people pacing in my house?

"Okay. Fuck, you're leaving tonight and I can't...I can't even come to any of the shows because of this stupid musical..."

Derek was doing a made-for-TV musical—the theme song and background music. He wasn't very happy about it, though he usually enjoyed the work. It was more that Aden always kept him in his own little hell.

"I haven't seen Aden in three days, and there's all this paperwork for you that has to be finalized."

I knew our demo-management deal was for a year only, so was the paperwork about me renewing my contract? I drifted out of the conversation for a minute thinking about loopholes to dust off Aden. I had nothing but loyalty to Derek and Neil, but Aden embodied everything I had to get free of.

Derek said, "Would you testify? Seriously?"

"What?"

"If it came down to it, and I'm not saying it will, would you testify?"

"Derek, honey, I don't know what you're talking about."

Derek sat down on the couch at that point, and it was like he'd folded into a wounded animal. I sat down next to him and heard a strange noise—a cry?—come out of him. With his ruddy face and moist eyes he looked even more boyish and innocent than ever. If only.

"He's been stealing, Jackson, from Clean Slate."

Something sank inside me. I felt sour. This was a whole new level beyond adultery.

"Aden's always done the books, but he's been so off and on lately that I called in an accountant to handle all the increased paperwork. We've never managed an artist who got signed to a huge label, and I wanted to make sure you were taken care of."

Classic Derek. He didn't make a big show of what he was doing like Aden did. He just quietly got it done. But what the fuck had Aden done with my money?

Derek saw my expression and rushed to clarify, "Sorry, don't worry. All your numbers look fine. The money is missing from the company's general account."

Whew. But not for Derek.

"Are you sure he didn't just mix up some digits? You told me he wasn't sleeping before, plus he was doing drugs—"

Derek cut me off. "No, there's no mistake, and he's actually cut way back on the drugs. It was a check in his handwriting dated three days ago—$25,000 to the Church of Scientology."

My jaw dropped. Derek uses his god-given talent to write music for the fucking Olsen twins to pay the bills, and Aden gives the proceeds to the Scientologists? Un-fucking-believable! I had an unwelcome image of Aden and Justin screwing in Derek's bed. Ugh. Erase.

"I don't know what to say. That's truly awful."

"After all I've done for him. I know I'm pathetic. I know I am."

"Derek you could never be pathetic. You are the most creative and kind person I know."

In the long hug I gave him there was no Jackson Poole, rockstarlet, and no Derek Jacobs, legendary songwriter, just two friends connecting in the world.

Derek seemed a little more collected afterward. "I hate to even ask you, Jackson, and I hope it won't come to this, but like I said, would you testify if I need you to?"

"Of course I would testify, Derek. Of course I would."

"You know Jackson, he really isn't all that bad. He actually has a sweetness about him that no one sees. He means well, or rather, he meant well. But this is the last straw."

I didn't want to touch that sweetness comment. Sweet like poisoned candy? But then again, who was I to judge after falling for the likes of Timothy Meyer?

"I think you have so much to give, Derek. You are so refreshing—in a city of posers you are just yourself, and I love you for that, I always have. And I'm not going anywhere."

"Yeah, just around the world."

"Well that's not that far nowadays."

"Be careful, it can be cruel out there."

"I will."

We hugged again and I could see him morphing back to his usual, go-with-the-flow self. On his way out he turned back to me.

"Don't go too crazy out there. Remember, everything in moderation."

"Including moderation," I replied.

He laughed. "Call me from the road if you need anything."

# 54

Neil had one of Clean Slate's interns drive us to the airport. We met up with the crew, my band, and several groupies at the gate. The groupies were several nice girls and a guy in his early twenties, all of whom had bought tickets for my opening shows and were on the same plane. It was strange to think that people planned vacations around my performances.

This one girl, in a flowery dress and looking quite wholesome for LA, said that she had followed me from my first record.

"It got me through my mother's death; I listened to it nonstop for months."

I was moved by her sincerity. And to think that she was referring to a self-produced recording without truckloads of cash behind it. It seemed like reaching her was just as powerful as reaching millions.

On the way to the gate, my drummer Rico said kind of jokingly, "So, am I gonna have to protect you from the hordes the whole tour?"

"Who knows," I said.

"Sky's the limit!" Leroy said.

Neil slipped me an Ambien and I was out for most of the flight. I woke up feeling groggy but peaceful.

Our hotel was in Leicester Square, near Piccadilly. London was the greatest place to people-watch. Londoners had a mix of styles, running the gamut from businessmen to punkers, that I had always admired. There were cinnamon-skinned Indians with big black eyes, high-cheeked Asian tourists with flawless fashion, the hard rock crowd with piercings and giant safety pins holding their clothes together, prissy schoolgirls in uniforms, dirty pub boys, and the suits and the suave-sters, all filling up the Tube and the foggy old damp streets.

Bree had scheduled me for another press junket, starting with the BBC. I was relieved at how polite they were. They brought me tea and I drank it too fast, burning my lip. I started talking funny, and they seemed amused, playing it off as nothing. After that, there were some photo shoots—one with the acclaimed photographer Brice Walker. I was nervous as hell, seeing as this guy had not only shot everyone from the President to Madonna but also had a reputation of being "intense."

The shoot was outside the city in Brighton, on the famous stone beach.

I didn't realize until that day, doing press back to back after traveling, how exhausting it is. Even though I was just sitting there, it took them three hours to do my hair and makeup.

Brice was really tall and Nordic looking, and had two assistants named—I'm not kidding—Hanz and Franz. When we were finally ready to shoot, Brice came out of his little tent and took a couple of shots. I was extremely self-conscious, partly because of Brice but partly because of Neil, who was watching. He still had a market on a corner of my heart. After a few minutes, Brice looked annoyed. He told everyone to take five, and he pulled me aside and we walked along the shore. Neil tried to come, but Brice put up his hand.

"So, what is it; what's going on?" he asked.

I didn't know what to say. He was so serious, staring at me with rock-hard eyes.

"Listen," he went on, "I've been doing this for a long time, and you're hiding something."

Oh my god. Was he psychic?

"Hang on, I'm going to try something. Stop right there."

We were under a bridge, and Brice took the camera he had been carrying and placed the lens inches from my face.

"I want to see something that's only Jackson. I don't care if it's joy, pain, sex, anger. I just want you to own it."

I looked into the lens as if I were looking at myself, and I felt my fear lift. I felt confidence burn through my eyes. He snapped and snapped. When we got back he yelled, "That's a wrap!" Hanz and Franz were very confused.

We had a few days before our opening at the Royal Albert Hall, and Neil and I shopped in between more publicity obligations. I dressed in disguise, in a hip-hop hoodie and baggy pants. No one seemed to notice me, or if they did, they weren't bothered. Though feeling pangs for Derek and his predicament, I was glad to be out of LA.

On the last day before the performance, I noticed a man looking at me and wondered if it was a mere coincidence that I'd seen him out of the corner of my eye three times that day. Were we being followed? The man was probably about forty and had fierce, deep-set eyes that were partly shadowed by the bright orange visor on his head. He resembled a young Christopher Walken. The third time I saw him, I could have sworn he gave me an intentionally threatening look. After seeing his crooked smile a cold chill ran through my belly.

"You need to show off your ass," Neil said, clueless to what I had just witnessed.

"What ass?" I said distractedly.

"Exactly, we need to find things that *accentuate*."

"Did you see that?"

"See what?" he asked.

"Him."

But when I looked again the man was gone. I ran out onto the street and looked for him. A few blocks down I saw the orange visor intermittently poking out from a sea of heads. I had an urge to run after him, but Neil told me not to worry.

"He probably just thought you were cute," he said. "C'mon."

I was still freaked out, but I tried to put it out of my head.

We settled on a bunch of designer retro T's and a slew of jeans. For shoes, I chose a pair of black square-cut Kenneth Coles, and some sporty Prada numbers that were comfortable enough to move around stage yet still stylish enough to make a statement.

We went for fish and chips, and Neil was beside himself.

"This shit is so good!" he said, his full lips slightly shiny from the grease.

That night, after a disco nap we went to the Shadow Lounge and drank champagne. They had recognized me and gave us a private booth. I wanted to dance with Neil, but I wasn't sure which would be riskier: the danger of being photographed holding another man or feeling Neil's warm body in my arms again.

We left early and went back to our separate rooms at the hotel.

Although I was excited about what lay ahead, as I drifted off to sleep, I couldn't shake the image of the man with the orange visor out of my head.

# 55

The Royal Albert Hall was stunning. I felt like a king just being there. We got a tour of the place and they showed us the Queen's box. I remembered the John Lennon line he'd said from that stage years before. He told the crowd to clap their hands, then added, "And you aristocracy up in the boxes, you can just rattle your jewelry."

I loved that.

It was my first major headlining show, and although I had played stadiums, now everyone was there for me and it felt different. I was happy but also felt a larger sense of responsibility, like I really had to kick ass. Leroy looked at me from his post at the side of the stage at one point like, *What's gotten into you?* I was stamping my feet, using the mic stand as more of a prop, and taking more risks with my singing. This was it. I had to step up to the plate.

The crowd was rapt. I could feel the energy surging from the audience and it fueled me. I sang my heart out into the mass of yellow and orange lights. I had come so far and this was only the beginning. I felt so lucky.

My opening act for the tour was a seventeen-year-old British girl called Jess who could sing her tits off. Well, what she had of them. I was so amazed that I asked her onstage during my set to sing backup on "Fear of Falling." She picked it up quickly and sounded incredible. We hung out backstage after the show.

"I didn't realize I'd heard you before until tonight," she said, "but I've heard your single a few times."

She giggled beneath her stringy curls. She looked like she could have been the daughter of Meg Ryan. It was all about her hair, strawberry ringlets that framed her baby blue eyes, which seemed curious yet seasoned. Although she appeared so young, she had an air of sophistication about her.

We ate warm cookies and drank red wine while Leroy and Rico were on the other side of the room chatting up some cute British girls.

I asked her if she was allowed to drink.

"It's Europe, mate. I've had wine since I was thirteen. Dad's on tour with me, and he approves, as long as I don't get pissed."

Neil entered the room, leading a man of about forty, who was unbelievably handsome in a very English, scholarly kind of way. I blushed.

"You were great, pumpkin!" He said, ruffling Jess's hair.

"Yeah? Thanks! Dad, this is Jackson," Jess said.

He was her father?

He was a little shy, shaking my hand with a limp wrist. But he looked me right in the eye. Don't even *think* about it, I told myself.

"I'm Liam," he said, loosening his already loose tie, "You sounded spot-on out there."

"Thank you, thanks a lot. It sure was a rush."

"Tell me about it," Jess said, "I haven't performed for more than fifty people until tonight. I was going mad. The crowd was keen though!"

She was so cute, and so nascent. I took an immediate liking to her in addition, of course, to her father.

Neil told us they were going to let the after-show pass-holders into the backstage bar. He also told me there was someone by the name of Lord Geoffrey who was claiming he knew me through Barkley, and wanted access backstage.

Oh my god, I thought, crazy Geoffrey.

"Sure, let him back," I said, and took another sip of wine to fortify myself.

"Who's Lord Geoffrey?" Jess asked.

"Oh, the sidekick of this millionaire I dated whose dog drinks Pellegrino."

Liam started to speak but apparently thought better of it.

Lord Geoffrey had claimed he taught Barkley how to dress,

among other things. He said he was the former head of the VIP
room at Studio 54, that he'd made leather gowns for Nancy
Reagan, and that he started the Ford Modeling Agency. No one
really knew how true his claims were, but he talked such a precise
game it all seemed believable while you were with him. Truth or no
truth, Lord Geoffrey always brought laughter and intrigue to any
situation. And there was no doubting he was filthy rich.

I saw him approaching from across the room, wearing a white-
on-white suit and a giant red scarf. His bald head (*scalptual,* he
called it) beamed under the lights. I caught his small, bright eyes,
and he winked at me. Sixty going on twenty-five.

We kissed on the right, left, and then right again, the Euro-chic
ritual.

"Jackson, darling! Oh, I must say, dear, you've simply outdone
yourself! I remember seeing you in that horrific little dive in Long
Beach! Now, here you are, dear, in all the glamour! The Royal
Albert!"

I tried to interject a few words, but it was always a lost cause
with Geoffrey. He was like a human radio.

"I missed you in Monte Carlo, dear; Barkley said it was fabulous.
I was at a country party in Tuscany and just couldn't pop over. You
know how it is, darling, everyone pulling me in all directions—I
feel like an octopus! Listen, dear, I've brought two fabulous Nordic
supermodels and lots of special treats. You must join us, we have a
car waiting. Door sixteen."

Geoffrey was literally pulling me out of the party, but not before
Neil handed me three hundred pounds sterling and our spare hotel
key with the address on the back.

"Remember, dear," he said, "you're a public figure. Be careful.
Don't do anything I wouldn't do."

I stopped to give Jess a hug and told her I'd see her the next
day.

"I'm so excited you're on the road with us."

"Me, too!" she said.

Liam was looking at Geoffrey like he was an exotic animal that might attack any minute.

Ten minutes later I was sipping cognac in Geoffrey's stretch, staring at Elga and Niko, the two skinny, gorgeous, legs-up-to-their-chins female models from northern Sweden. They spoke no English yet responded with alacrity when handed a mirror full of cocaine.

"Yes," they said in unison. "Yes, yes." Apparently that was the only word they knew. Not a bad one, I supposed. Better than "maybe."

We went to a club that had four rooms with different DJs, and bowls of fruit everywhere. When we entered, Geoffrey did runway up and down the dance floor, flicking his scarf and being faux-dramatic. The crowd ate it up. Then he grabbed a stock of irises out of their container and threw them in my arms.

"For you, my darling! The superstar!"

In the bathroom, when no one else was around, a gorgeous guy with dark hair and light eyes kissed me. It was literally painful to walk away from him, but I knew I had to. I gave him the last iris in my hand.

I escaped into the alley, smoking a cigarette and wondering just how many toxins I had consumed. I started talking to a guy who at first seemed like just another hipster stuck in the eighties. But then I realized it was Boy-fucking-George! Seeing him older and un-airbrushed, I hadn't recognized him, probably because he didn't have the signature braids in his hair. He was drinking from a gold flask, his eyes painted blood red.

He told me he'd been at my show earlier. His manager had sent him to see Jess, but he stayed. He said he liked the show. I felt tiny next to such a legend.

I told him this was my first big headlining tour, and that given the state I was currently in, I wasn't exactly having a good go at moderation.

"You'll find a way quickly, otherwise you'll sink fast," he said. "But no matter what, you'll have to go clean and then have a comeback, it's the way it works, it's a cycle. Be thankful you're at the start, it's the best bit."

"I saw a fucking *bus* with my picture on it."

"That's not the least of it. Wait till they make a doll!"

We laughed. He told me to follow him and we got in his car. The last I'd seen of Geoffrey he was grinding with two boy toys in a corner of the club, so I didn't think he'd miss me. Boy George yelled something in French to his driver, and we were off. He took me to a private club where everyone knew him, and we drank champagne and talked shop.

"I'm happy to be out of LA; it's so crazy there—like everyone's out for themselves."

"It's not only in LA. Just make sure you've got a good accountant and watch the money. It goes quickly, believe me."

He started getting a tad flirty, so I excused myself. He gave me his cell number and told me to call him when I returned to London. Boy George's cell number? Amazing. I'll file it next to Simon LeBon's, I thought.

# 56

The next series of shows were packed so tight that the cities seemed to blur together.

I seemed to spend most of my time in hotels, doing phone interviews and getting ready for the next performance. It was a ritual for me, preparing for a show. I would start with a long bath, of course, then sing songs of some of my favorite singers before heading over to the venue. Shawn Colvin, Van Morrison, Chris Martin from Coldplay.

The odd thing was moving from the small, tight dressing rooms with their lighted mirrors and walking out onto the enormous stage with the roar of the crowd. It was like suddenly going from my most intimate place to my most exposed state. When I was onstage I tried to spread myself to everyone in the audience. All those people cheering for me and wanting me to shine took me to another place, and during the performances I sometimes left my body. I was living in and out of a dream, and the stage was dreamtime.

In Paris, when I squeezed in some time to shop, somebody broke into my hotel room and stole—get this—my underwear. Nothing else. What kind of eBay freak was that? So, for the rest of the tour I wore French underwear.

In Rome, we finally had two days off, and Neil, Liam, Jess, and I explored the city together. Leroy and Rico had taken a train to the beach for an overnight. I had so much Italian food and red wine that I gained five pounds.

We mostly took planes, but from Rome to Vienna we drove in a huge luxury tour bus. It was every band's dream to have a tour bus. In my first band in college, we drove around in a van with five people and two dogs. You can only imagine the smell. This was slightly different, seeing as Neil and I were lounging on a double bed watching *Six Feet Under.*

"I never really got this show," he said.

"Oh my god, it's brilliant. I love Claire."

"Well, they're using your song for the final episode."

"No way!! I can die now."

"You are such a freak."

A pillow fight ensued, until Leroy came in and made us watch some bad European soap opera because he wanted to gawk at the female lead.

Backstage in Vienna, I showed Jess my little potbelly.

"Oh please, that's baby fat," she said.

"And you should talk. You are a baby."

"Exactly! So I should know!"

We did some vocal warm-ups together and Liam walked in, stood there awkwardly for a moment, then left.

"I know you have a crush on him," she said.

"Wait a second. What makes you think I bat on that team?"

"Um, duh!"

"What?"

She went into the backstage bathroom and pulled out my extensive line of hair-care products. I laughed.

"Okay, but mums the word. And your dad? Are you crazy?"

"Don't even try to play me. It's obvious. Besides, I think he might be gay, too."

I have to admit at that point my curiosity was piqued.

"Really?"

She grabbed my arm. "He's been divorced for years, hasn't re-married, and he's got an amazing shoe collection."

I chuckled.

"Oh, I've slept with my share of daddies. And some of them were fathers, too," I said.

"Really? That's kind of odd."

"Not really, just turned out that way."

"Oh! And he cuts off the crusts of his sandwiches, makes them into little triangles."

"Total fag," I said.

That night after the show the four of us went to dinner, as Leroy and Rico had dates—why was my band getting laid and not me? It was great to go out and dine at ten o'clock and still have the city totally alive. It was all so Euro.

On the walk back to the hotel, Neil and I lagged behind a bit. There was a layer of fog clinging to the ground that hid our feet, and we held hands and kicked our legs up out of the mist like kids.

I joked with him that he was all over "Daddy Liam." The two of them had been talking to each other and laughing throughout dinner.

"Hardly," he said, "that man was too busy checking you out."

"I wish. But Jess told me she thinks he's gay."

He tried to act uninterested but cracked a smile. We knew each other too well.

"Really?" his tone matched mine when I had received that very information.

"That's what I said."

The peaceful feeling of being with Neil was erased when I noticed someone keeping pace with us across the street. It was dark enough that his features were hidden, but cutting through the fog was something I had seen before. An orange visor. I could have sworn it was the same man from London, giving off the same threatening vibe.

"Oh, shit. That was the same guy I saw in London, I swear."

By the time Neil looked he was out of sight.

"Girl, you're trippin."

"He had that orange visor on."

Neil brushed it off, but the image lingered in my head.

# 57

Germany was kind of a lull in the tour—Jess was sick, and I was overtired and anxious about seeing the strange man with the visor again. Was he following me? The show was not our best, and the crowd was a little indifferent. Oh well, can't win them all.

Cape Town, South Africa, was unbelievably stunning. I couldn't have imagined a city with such majestic beauty. Billowy clouds formed what looked like tablecloths over giant mountain ridges, and cocooned within were little scenic bays filled with light-turquoise water and warm sun. It was a heavenly place.

I felt the tension from Germany melt off me, and even took time to send postcards to everyone I knew, including Kia in rehab. I sent a long letter to my dad, since I still felt bad he couldn't come to Hong Kong.

Neil was taking Liam to a gay club that I had heard about and always wanted to go to, and it took a lot of strength not to join them. It was simply too risky. When they left, I sat alone in my room, sad and stifled. I couldn't even go to a gay bar! What the fuck? Even though it was South Africa, it was a high-profile place with some popular NYC DJs—I had seen the flyer. Even though I was bummed, I put it out of my mind, remembering what my old boyfriend Thomas had told me: Sacrifice. Nothing good comes without sacrifice.

Our second day there, just before sound check, Neil told me the news.

"Derek is breaking up with Aden. He's finally doing it."

"Thank the Lord," I said, "what happened?"

"He walked in on him and the Justin guy."

"You are not serious..."

"And our accountant discovered outrageous amounts of personal expenses charged to the company, including LA hotel bills.

They had a somewhat open relationship, but Derek's finally had it. And apparently, Aden wants to claim half of the house, which is all Derek really has. The whole thing is a nightmare."

I thought of Timothy Meyer and his similar fall from grace—thankfully he was history.

"What about my contract?"

Neil did his famous eye roll.

"Jackson, I know it's hard to believe, but this is not about you right now."

"Meow."

He laughed a little and went on. "We'll sort all that out. Probably what's going to happen is Derek will stay president of Clean Slate, and Aden's job will be taken over by—"

"You."

He did his best game show–host smile.

"Naturally," he said, "but it's not going to be easy. He's not going to leave without a fight. Your contract isn't up for renewal until a month after we get back, so let's not worry about that yet. I've arranged for Derek to join us in Singapore and Malaysia if he can finish the children's film in time. He needs to get out of there. Apparently Aden is off the deep end. He started into the Scientology thing, got clean, and then relapsed big time."

"Ooh, scary."

"Anyway, kick some ass for Derek tonight, will you?"

And that we did. It was an outdoor venue with the ocean nearby, the waves adding impromptu percussion. People were dancing and swaying their arms and the atmosphere was charged. Leroy broke a bass string, and while the roadies changed it, I sang an a cappella song I had learned as a kid from my father. The crowd silenced in a good way, people listening intently.

I dedicated the last song, "Affliction," to Derek.

"This one's for my chief manager back in LA. He's about to rid himself of an affliction."

Neil smiled from the side of the stage.

After the show I called Derek but got no answer. I took a walk on the moonlit beach and ran into Jess by our hotel.

"So, you're firing your manager?" she asked.

Word travels fast.

"Well, sort of."

"I can't do that, 'cause Dad's my manager. Well, I suppose I still could, but it would be highly unlikely."

There were many successful artists in the past who had dealt with horrific managers and ugly disputes. Underneath the music and the good vibes, there were sharks making money, and it wasn't always pretty.

"You're lucky to have him. There are people whom you think of as family, but they're not. Even people who've been with you from the start can drop away like sand. You're left counting your true friends on one hand."

"Hey, can I use that as a lyric?" She asked.

I pushed her and we fell into the sand. We looked up at the sprawling, velvet sky spotted with thousands of tiny stars, and she held my hand. It was peaceful, there with no one else around, and we lay silently for a while. The headlights of passing cars intermittently lit up the side of Jess's youthful face.

"You know, this has been quite fun so far," she said.

"A whirlwind, huh?"

"In a good way," she said.

"You know what? You're right."

"I'm always right," she said sassily, and rolled to her feet. "See you tomorrow, handsome."

I could see her mischievous grin in the moonlight. I laughed and threw some sand at her legs. "Goodnight, you naughty girl."

With that, Jess walked back toward the hotel and left me alone with the water quietly lapping the shore and the sound of distant voices. It struck me that laughter sounded different in foreign countries.

I started to get sleepy and drift off but was suddenly startled awake, my heart racing and muscles tensed. I realized someone was walking right next to my head, despite the huge empty stretches of beach all around. Shoes crunched inches from me, grains of sand hitting the side of my face.

The person didn't excuse himself, just kept walking down the beach as if he hadn't done anything. I was about to shout something at him when he reached into the bulky bag slung over his shoulder. As he turned back to glare at me, a passing car's headlights illuminated the unmistakable orange of the visor he was putting on his head. His hateful expression burned in my brain even after the lights had passed. There was no doubt that it was the same man from London and Vienna. Up close, and by myself, his threatening energy was even more terrifying.

I felt dizzy with shock and fear, but he just casually turned back the way he was headed and kept on walking. I was paralyzed for a few long seconds, then scrambled to my feet and rushed back toward the lights of the hotel. The back of my neck felt naked and exposed, but I forced myself not to look back.

I couldn't find Neil anywhere in the hotel, and people were looking at me funny. I had started to sweat and I was out of breath. I threw my hands up in the lobby when I heard Neil's voice.

"Jackson, what are you doing?"

"Where were you?" I practically screamed.

"I was in the conference room contacting our next venue, what happened?"

He led me to the small lobby bar and I explained that it was him, the same guy from London and Vienna, I was sure of it.

"Jackson, I'm sure a lot of people have orange visors."

I was angry that Neil was brushing it off again. What the fuck? I wasn't crazy.

"Neil, not with that face—those eyes."

I started looking around the bar. People were noticing me—because of my music or because I was so distraught?

"Listen, let's go up to the room and chill for a while," Neil said. "I'm sure it was a misunderstanding."

"Neil!"

Leroy and Rico were approaching, laughing with drinks in their hands.

"Let's not bring this up to them," Neil said to me. I supposed he was right.

Rico was concerned and said I looked like I had seen a ghost.

"I'm just tired," I said, and went to my room.

Neil arranged for a massage therapist to come to my room and work on me. She wasn't as good as Brian, but it definitely helped.

Before I went to sleep, I checked the closets and under the bed. Was I just paranoid? The sighting had to be a coincidence. *Please,* I thought. *Please don't let this be something bad.*

# 58

The next morning the first thing I thought of when I woke up was the terrifying face of the man with the visor. Cape Town had gone from paradise to a place of fear, and I was relieved that we were leaving that day. We'd been to so many cities on the tour, and I'd only seen him three times, so I hoped I wouldn't see him again. We were starting the Asian leg of the tour, and it would take a truly dedicated psycho to follow me there. Or so I told myself.

I called home to check in on my family during our stopover in the Seychelles, a cluster of tropical islands that resembled an underdeveloped Hawaii. My mom answered and told me how excited she was about the trip. I told her about parasailing and snorkeling, and then asked to talk to my dad.

"How are you feeling," I asked.

"Fine, Jack-in-the-Box, just fine. Getting a little better every-day."

"Easy on the sweets now, right?"

"Yeah, yeah."

"Hey, I went gambling last night. Won big."

He was a "craps" man, who always seemed to come out ahead. I remember as a kid watching him shake the dice in his long skinny fingers, a look of dead concentration in his eye. After he'd rake it in, he'd hand out bills to Max and Rose and me. One time, when I was about ten, he gave us a twenty each and I bought a bag full of candy bars. A kid's dream.

"How are the shows going? You break any strings?"

"No, but my bass player did, and I sang the lonesome-road song!"

I could feel him smiling.

"That's great. You keep in touch now, okay?"

"I will." Dad handed the phone over to Max, who asked me how

I was doing.

"Sometimes I feel like this is happening so fast that I need witnesses to share it with me."

"We'll be there, dude."

Max was the only person who could get away with calling me "dude." I was excited to show him what my show was like now, to have him see me in front of such huge crowds and with my new band. It meant more to me that he liked it than if ten thousand screaming fans did. That's the way it always was. You could bask in oceans of adoration from strangers, but what your friends and family thought carried the most weight.

I remembered as a kid being so obsessed with Sting and the Police. There was an article I'd read in which Sting mentioned that when he heard Bob Marley he wondered why he even was a musician. Everyone had their admirers, all the way up the chain.

At the show in Singapore, the stadium was only half full, and they all seemed to be there for the opening act, a trio of twelve-year-old girls who were basically singing karaoke.

We arrived back to the hotel later and I opened a FedEx package from Bree. Neil, Jess, and Liam were with me in the elevator.

It was copies of various entertainment rags showing photos of me.

"Look, that's us!" Jess squealed.

Sure enough, there was Jess and me on the beach in front of our hotel in Cape Town, splashed on the pages of *People*. I was throwing sand at her, and both of us were laughing. The picture quality wasn't phenomenal because it was at night, but you could clearly see our simpatico expressions. The photos were in European mags as well. An Italian one that was apparently an *Enquirer* equivalent had a picture of me and Neil captioned, "Jackson Poole, with millionairo Neil Dechaump."

"Where the hell did they get that last name?" Neil said.

"Who knows, but at least you're a millionaire."

"I wish."

"I cannot believe this," Liam said. "You're everywhere."

He was right. It was extraordinary how quickly it was spreading. There must have been thirty magazines.

Jess was still looking at the one of us.

*Jackson Poole Dating Underage Singer.*

She put her arm around me. "Hi, honey, I'm home."

I read Bree's note:

> *Jackson,*
> *Good work, kiddo! I've also sent copies to Clean Slate and Universal.*
> *By the way—next time how about picking someone above the age of consent?*
> *That might help,*
> *Bree*

We parted in the hallway and Neil came into my room. I pointed at the picture from Cape Town.

"That's the orange-visor guy."

"What?"

"He must be the one who took the picture! There was no one else on that beach, Neil. Who else could have taken it?"

"Well that's a relief," he said. "If the guy is just a stupid paparazzo, he's not going to actually hurt you."

"But why was he so hostile and creepy?"

"I'd be bitter, too, if I had such a shitty job."

"It feels deeper than that, Neil. I keep telling you, the guy is seriously scary." Still, I had another piece of the puzzle, and that somehow felt reassuring.

Neil went to his room to make some phone calls, so I went by Liam's room. Jess had gone to the hotel pool.

"I hope you're not upset about the pictures of me and Jess," I said.

Liam didn't care at all.

"Are you kidding? Jess loved it, and it's free publicity!"

I felt as if a huge weight had been lifted.

Neil and I stayed up late watching a B-movie (a shared weakness) and drinking wine.

# 59

The more I thought about it, the more relieved I was to know that the guy in the orange visor was just a paparazzo. He was probably the angriest, in-need-of-therapy photographer on the planet, but at least now if I saw him again, I'd know why he was there.

Besides South Africa, Hong Kong was the place that truly blew me away. It was like being in a different world. Driving into the city, there were trees on the side of the highway with leaves bigger than the car—fantastical, like out of a children's story.

I slept-in the first day and realized that everyone but Jess and me had already gone out sightseeing. So she and I went out and just wandered the streets, reveling in the strangeness of it all. I realized it was the first time on the tour that I'd walked through crowded streets during the day, and it was a relief realizing that people didn't seem to know who I was. When people did look at me, I got the impression it was just because I was a light-haired westerner in a sea of dark-haired people.

"You know Dad's with Neil today," Jess said.

I had suspected as much but made out like I didn't.

"Oh?"

"Yeah," she was twirling one of her curls and smiling through her words, "I sort of think they should get together, don't you?"

"Well, I guess so..."

"You don't sound keen."

"Well, Neil and I actually had a fling recently, and although we're not together, I care about him a lot. I guess I'm a little protective."

"Don't worry, Dad won't be a bad influence..."

"No, I know; it's just, maybe I'm a little jealous."

"Ha!" Jess was beside herself. "Jackson Poole? Jealous? That's a good one. Listen, Romeo, you can have anyone you want!"

I thought about what she said, and it really wasn't true—especially with the label breathing down my neck. I'd always had my share of romances, but since the Timothy Meyer fiasco and my too-short experience with Neil, I hadn't had anyone. Well, besides Emilio, but random sex with gardeners didn't count.

Besides, I didn't want just anyone. I supposed it was simply a time to be alone. The last thing I needed was relationship drama. Anyway, on the tour up to that point, most of the obviously interested parties had been girls. Cute ones, too. Maybe I would have to experiment and Aden would finally get his wish. Not.

Jess and I went down a beautiful street of open-air markets, all the colors of the rainbow shown in food, fabric, and spice. It was an attack of the senses, and I felt like I could have kept walking through that maze of culture forever.

"Isn't this amazing?" I said to Jess.

"Beyond," she said. "The stimulation is unreal."

We bought nuts and beers, and sat on a bench and people-watched. Being around Jess felt comfortable. She was so disarming and extremely mature for her age.

"So, do you have a boyfriend?" I asked.

"Kind of," she said. "But he's in school up north so it's kind of hard."

"Is he going to be pissed about our picture?"

"No, he probably won't even notice. He's not that in tune with pop culture. He writes bad rock songs and fixes vending machines. He's kind of dirty. Not dirty-dirty, but unkempt-dirty, I kind of like that sort of thing. Don't ask me why."

"Nothing like a manly man," I said in my deepest voice.

"You," she said, "you're just fine the way you are."

When we got back to the hotel, Neil and Liam were talking at the bar.

Liam was happy to see Jess, but Neil seemed a little sheepish when he saw me.

"What did you two get into?" I asked.

Liam blushed and looked down, avoiding my eyes.

"Oh Dad!" Jess said. "You're terribly cute when you're embarrassed."

Neil started to blush, too, so I grabbed Jess and scooted away.

"Bye, we're going to go shop like maniacs now," I said.

As we left the hotel, a gaggle of Asian girls swarmed around us with notebooks. I was wondering why I was so anonymous before. They were all in school!

Jess pretended she was my girlfriend and they all looked at her, memorizing her outfit, tentatively reaching out to touch her shiny curls. It was nice for my ego, considering I was definitely still feeling a tinge of—something—about Neil and Liam.

When I got back to my room later that night there was a package for me inside my door. For some reason my heart fluttered and I had a sinking feeling. Was it a bomb? I had obviously watched too many B-movie thrillers. It looked completely harmless, and I told myself that since it was inside the door, someone from the hotel had to have put it there.

But I was still completely freaked out. Feeling like a fool, I called Neil and asked him to come up to my room.

He didn't seem fazed by the package at all and was nice enough not to tease me about it. Maybe he still felt bad for not believing that I was being followed by the paparazzi guy.

As I watched Neil casually pick up the package and put it on a table, I thought of Kia's comment that he couldn't kill a spider for me. How wrong she was! He opened it up, pulling out a bundle folded in tissue paper.

"It looks like a present," he said.

He turned back the tissue to reveal a cloth doll with its eyes gouged out and its mouth sewn up with thick black thread.

He dropped it as if he'd been burned. "Whoa!"

"Oh my god!"

We stood there speechless for a few moments, the only noise the groan of the minibar fridge. Then Neil, like the hero in a suspense film, took things under control. He called the reception desk and asked them who had delivered a package to my room. Apparently no one knew anything about it, so he told them there were to be no packages left for me without previous inspection. Then he called Jess and Liam and asked them to come sit with me while he tracked down hotel security.

"Don't touch it again, in case the police can get evidence from it."

"Are you kidding? I haven't touched it at all!" The thought of it made me shudder.

"I'm going to go talk to the concierge about how to deal with the local police. Will you be okay alone for a few minutes until Liam and Jess get here?"

I nodded.

After Neil left, I avoided looking at the freaky doll. Just being in the same room with it raised the hairs on the back of my neck. Suddenly the realization sunk in. I might truly be in danger. What kind of person makes something like that and goes to the length of breaking into someone's room? I felt paralyzed by a saturating fear. Was this the price of success? Would I have to live the rest of my life looking over my shoulder?

Jess and Liam arrived a few minutes later. Liam insisted I needed a cup of hot tea and set to work making it.

"My Lord, what the hell is this?" he asked when he saw the doll.

I didn't answer, and they seemed to realize how shaken I really was. Jess came and sat next to me until Neil returned with the police, and Liam got me more tea as I answered questions through the police interpreter. When I tried to explain about the paparazzi guy, they didn't seem to understand why I connected the doll with him. How could I explain the animosity I'd seen on the man's face?

"Mean," I said, "bad." It was useless.

While the police were talking to me, a porter came and moved all my things to a new room down the hall. When the bustle was over, Neil walked me to my new room and tucked me in.

"You realize you are the best tour manager ever, don't you?"

"And friend, too, I hope." He gave me a chaste kiss on the forehead. "Get some rest. Everything will look better in the morning."

# 60

Neil was right about things improving in daylight. When I woke up, I was embarrassed about all the fuss I'd caused over a stupid doll. I'd gotten fan mail just as weird back home and had barely raised an eyebrow over it. There was probably some logical explanation for how it ended up in my room—probably a porter trying to make a bigger tip for going the extra mile.

I decided to pretend the whole thing had never happened and focused on my mom and Max's arrival that evening.

Jess helped me prepare their suite. Just to be silly, we made a goofy sign out of licorice that said "Welcome to Hong Kong, Mom and Bro." Jess was such a charming mix of worldliness and innocent enthusiasm that she was the perfect person to be around right then.

I'd told Neil I wanted them to have the best suite in the hotel, and he had clearly come through. The view from their windows was breathtaking. I ordered a bottle of champagne to be put on ice just before their arrival, and Jess oohed and aahed over the fresh flowers I'd had placed throughout the rooms.

"It's so lovely you can do this for your family," she said.

I couldn't wait for Mom and Max to see it all.

Later that afternoon I was scheduled to do some press and meet the three drag queens who were the head of my Hong Kong fan club. I wasn't sure how the drag queens had snuck by Aden's hetero-conformity campaign, but I was looking forward to the change of pace.

Neil had arranged a private lounge in the hotel for the press interviews, which were more absurd than usual because of the language barrier. English truly was the universal language, but in Hong Kong even some of the people who seemed to have the vocabulary down were hard for me to understand. I must have said, "I'm sorry, could you repeat that?" about a hundred times, and I had no idea if anything I said would actually be quoted correctly. Of course, their English was better than my Chinese, so I couldn't really complain.

After the last interviewer left, I was surprised to see Leroy and Rico appear, along with Neil, Liam, and Jess. Apparently drag queens were a bigger draw than reporters.

The drag queens came in a few minutes later wearing matching black leather dresses and clear-plastic high-heeled shoes with live fish swimming in them. They were stunning. Judging by Rico and Leroy's stares, I had a feeling they might soon be doing some deep questioning of their sexual identities.

Jess kept staring at the fish; she couldn't get over them.

"I need a pair of these!" she said in a girlish tone I hadn't heard before.

The girls' names were unpronounceable, and like the Singapore triplets, only one of them spoke English. Her name was something like "Zoochi," but she said we could simply call her "Sushi."

"No, that's what's in her shoes!" Jess said.

Sushi said she had received overwhelming responses from teenage girls who loved my single.

I smiled and said, "That's so great."

I felt slightly embarrassed as they stared at me, these three pale geisha faces with big, startled eyes framed by black bobs. They were men? You certainly couldn't tell. They were beautiful.

Sushi lit a cigarette and dramatically blew the cloud of smoke to her left. She asked me, "Are you top or bottom?"

I couldn't help but laugh. Jess answered for me.

"So sorry, but that is personal information. But if you asked me, I'd say top."

"Jess!"

Leroy and Rico were visibly shocked by Jess's audacity.

Sushi turned to the other girls and spoke rapidly in Cantonese. They all laughed.

A photographer and an assistant walked in and Neil got up to greet them.

I stopped Neil and looked inquisitively at him.

"I told them they could take a shot with you for their monthly newsletter," he said. "They take fan clubs very seriously here."

"What about Aden and the label?"

"Dear, we are so far from home, and to be honest, they aren't really as concerned about this particular market."

So there I was, posing with the three Asian Robert Palmer video girls, well, guys, in our chic Hong Kong hotel. I was finally having a rockstarlet moment on my relentlessly hetero first world tour! I figured if the people at Universal ever complained about it, I could just claim that I thought they were women.

We were all chatting and eating some fruit when the hotel concierge peeked his head in. "Mr. Poole," you have a phone call. "Would you like to take it now?"

Thinking it might be my mom and Max, I told him I would take it on the phone in the room. When it rang, I picked up and said hello but there was nothing. I said hello again and heard a distorted male voice whispering four words, spread apart: *I...can't... hear...you.*

The line clicked and went dead, and I stood there in shock, the phone still held to my ear.

"What is it, Jackson?" Neil asked.

I tried to snap out of it. "Someone playing childish games."

I told Sushi and the other girls I'd enjoyed meeting them and excused myself. Neil followed me out into the lobby.

"What's going on?"

I was upset but trying to hide it. I told him what I'd heard on the phone.

"What do you want to do?" he asked.

"I'm not sure there's anything I can do. Isn't that what the police said?"

"Unfortunately, yes."

"Anyway, I realized this morning that none of this is so different from the freaky stuff I was getting in the mail in LA. Celebrities have bizarre stuff happen to them all the time, so if this is the price of being famous, I better just get used to not letting it affect me."

Neil knew me well enough to know that half of what I'd just said was bravado. He still looked concerned, but he knew I was right. What else could we do?

We went back into the lounge and I said another good-bye to Sushi and company. I didn't want them to think I was rude for rushing off so abruptly.

I met Mom and Max at the airport at seven that night. Mom was tipsy on cheap wine from the plane.

We had a group hug.

"Welcome to Asia!"

"Oh my," Mom said, putting on lipstick, "what a flight!"

"Long," I said.

"I slept," Max said, dreamy eyed.

"Dad still okay?"

"Yes," Mom said, "I told him I may run off with a Chinese billionaire!"

"Yeah, one that comes up to your waist," I said.

"Rose is with your father and he's doing absolutely great, thank God."

We gathered their bags off the carousel.

A young girl ran up and asked me for my autograph.

"Do you want mine?" Mom asked. "I'm the fabulous mother!"

The girl didn't understand her. Max just laughed.

"I'm so happy you guys are here!" And I truly was. What was the point of being on a glamorous tour if you couldn't share it with the ones you loved the most?

We made our way through the airport to the limo I'd arranged, and toasted with champagne on the way to the hotel. I knew their flight was endless, so I'd planned a quiet dinner at the hotel's four-star restaurant for their first night. The show wasn't until that Friday, so we had three days just to play.

The next day, I met up with Mom and Max for brunch. They were both jetlagged so we decided to take it easy. That afternoon we indulged in a little retail therapy. Mom went crazy buying colorful tops, while Max and I concentrated on shoes. For a straight guy, Max had an extraordinary appreciation for shoes. I found a kitschy green belt I thought Kia would like and a cheetah-print handbag that was perfect for Bree.

There were seemingly endless miniature gadgets, and Max and I debated which bizarre golf accessory would be best for Dad. Max was arguing for a laser sighter that helped you line up your shot, but my favorite was a motorized golf tee with little blades that were supposed to pop up and trim the grass around your ball. It looked like it would break after about two uses, but it was so absurd, I couldn't resist it.

I enjoyed the shopping, of course, but the things themselves didn't hold as much importance to me as they once would have. What I cared more about was being with my family. I was happy, aside from occasional thoughts of the creepy doll and phone call, and images of the paparazzo's hate-filled face. Whenever I thought of him, I made myself take deep breaths until I could shake it.

Coming out of a store, my mom's watch beeped.

"What's that for?" I asked.

"Oh, it started out as the alarm for me to give Dad his meds, but now he does it himself, he's very good about it. I just keep it on to remind me to check in with him. Can I use your cell phone, angel?"

I'm sure it cost a fortune to use in other countries, but it certainly was nice not to have to stress over those things anymore.

"Sure, here you go."

After she was done, I said hello to my dad, who was in good spirits.

"I'm coming on the next tour," he said.

"You bet. I'll just make sure there are golf courses near every venue."

"Perfect," he said.

We got ice cream and met up with Jess in the square. She said that Neil and Liam had gone on an adventure together.

"Hmm, I wonder if that adventure involved KY," I said.

Max laughed, but Mom didn't get it.

"What?" she asked, rearranging her shopping bags.

"A lubricant," I said.

She still didn't get it.

Jess, Max, and I started laughing as we all walked back to the hotel. Mom kept asking, "Oh come on, kids, what?" which just made us laugh harder.

That night we all had dinner at a crazy restaurant with a giant circular exotic fish tank in the middle.

My mom had sushi for the first time and liked it, although at that point she was most likely too buzzed to taste anything. She started telling stories about my drag performances when I was five. Sushi and her harem perked up.

"You wouldn't believe him!" She was carrying on loudly. I didn't mind; I was just happy to see her joyful after everything she'd been through with Dad. "He would wrap this old turtleneck around his head just so, so it looked like hair. Then Rose—that's his big sister—would do makeup on him and he'd wear one of my funky dresses, you know, from the Sixties?"

"Funky," Sushi said. "We know funky!" They giggled.

"Even Daddy was keeled over. I'll never forget, you sang happy birthday to him one year like Marilyn Monroe!"

Max was laughing, though I remembered when we were younger he used to be embarrassed by it all. Like my father, he was a supportive person by nature, but they were both suburban dads, so their threshold just wasn't at the same level as mine.

I noticed he was quite keen on Sushi and Co., and I had a feeling he wasn't quite putting all the puzzle pieces together.

"They're guys," I whispered to him.

"I know that," he said, though clearly he hadn't. His looks for them turned from flirtatious admiration to a more detached curiosity.

Later he leaned over with attempted nonchalance and asked about Sushi's sister. "Is she...you know?"

"I'm pretty sure she's the genuine article."

The sister's English was as good as Sushi's, and pretty soon Max was lost in conversation with her.

Neil was talking with Liam most of the dinner, and when it came time for the check, they started battling over who was going to pay it. I stopped them by paying it myself.

After dinner we danced in the lounge attached to the restaurant. Well, I should say Mom danced, with the help of Leroy, Rico, and Sushi & Co. It was quite a sight. Neil, Liam, Jess, and I watched with our mouths half open. When Mom started grabbing Sushi's ass, Max and I decided to draw the line and take her home to bed.

We got her back to the hotel and into her room, but she stopped in her tracks at the sight of the view from her window. The sparkling lights of Hong Kong were spread out far into the distance.

"It's like champagne!" she said.

Max and I laughed and steered her into the bed.

# 61

The next morning Mom, Max, and I had a delicious room-service breakfast in their suite and decided to just wander around and see more of the city. We took a ferry to a giant market and had dim sum for lunch, then walked along the crowded streets.

"Boys, I'm going back to the hotel for a little nap; I'm still a little jet-lagged." Mom said.

After Max and I walked her back I said, "Jet-lagged or hung-over?"

Max laughed. "Probably both." He glanced at his watch. "And it's around the time she likes to check in with Dad. At first I thought the whole alarm thing was about making sure he was okay, but now I think it's more for her, just to reassure her that he's still there."

"He really is okay, right?"

"Yeah, he is, but you know how she gets."

"Drama," I said.

"Capitol 'D.'"

"So, you plan on making the moves on Sushi's sister?"

"I could go for a little Asian persuasion."

After Mom's nap we went out for coffee and I was startled by loud screeches from a growing group of girls outside the coffee shop. Mom and Max just looked on as I furiously signed all of their Hello Kitty notebooks. I was cornered and had nowhere to go. It was similar to the feeling outside of the junket back in LA—strangely blissful but also scary.

That night when I got back to my room, I played guitar for a little while to unwind.

I stared at the lights of the city for a while, then peeled off my clothes to take a bath. When I pulled back the shower curtain my breath stopped, then I screamed. Someone had written something on the tile in red—it looked like blood. It was the same phrase I had heard whispered on the phone earlier.

*I can't hear you.*

I threw my robe on and ran out of the bathroom, slamming the door. I called Neil and they moved me to yet another room. The police were called again, and Neil started to arrange for a bodyguard. I sat in my new room, stunned, while Neil put the hotel manager on the spot in the hallway.

"This is completely unacceptable," he was saying.

The manager seemed genuinely upset and baffled about how it kept happening.

Before I went to bed, I slipped a note under Max and Mom's door saying I'd changed rooms—I used bad plumbing as an excuse.

That night I barely slept, and when I finally did, I woke up sweating bullets. I still hadn't gotten out of bed when the phone on the nightstand started ringing. I was scared to answer it but told myself at worst it could only be another spooky voice on the line.

When I heard Derek's voice, I was flooded with relief.

Derek told me that Aden was asking for more severance than he'd offered, and he was going through Derek's stuff and claiming things as his. Though part of me wanted to unburden all my stalker fears to Derek, it obviously wasn't the time, and in a way I appreciated that his drama took my mind off the subject.

There was a silence on the line and I could tell he was crying a little.

"Sweetheart, I am so sorry," I said into the phone. "About everything."

"It's just, you think you know someone, for years. I feel so stupid."

There was a knock on my door and I heard my mother call my name. I wrapped a sheet around me and opened the door.

My mother burst into the room and grabbed some of my Dermalogica moisturizer. "I just love this stuff, Jackson, you must get me a truckload."

Max was right behind her, saying, "Mom, he's on the phone!"

He dragged her back out and whispered to me, "See you in the lobby."

Derek continued, "But I also feel good this is happening now; I'm sick of it."

"Well, that's understandable. I hope you won't take this the wrong way, but frankly we all were. No one deserves that kind of treatment, Derek."

"I know, I was in major denial."

"Listen, I'm really sorry to do this, but my family's here and they're waiting for me..."

"Oh, I'm so sorry—"

"No, I'm so glad to talk to you! And I'll be home in a week's time."

"I know."

"Will you be okay?"

"Yeah, I'm at Cher's. I'm so sorry I couldn't make it to Singapore. With the Aden thing it was—"

"Don't worry."

I remembered when I was in crisis and he sent me to Cher's house. It seemed like another lifetime ago that I was worried about Timothy Meyer.

"Get in the top Jacuzzi for like, an hour," I told him, "then eat popsicles and stare at the sea. Worked for me."

"Okay. Hey, listen, Lonnie Simpson wants to commission the two of us to write the title track for the new Sandra Bullock romantic comedy. So think love song, okay? I'll work on melodies; you work on lyrics, deal?"

"Deal. Sounds great, baby."

"You have a show tonight, right?"

"Yep."

"Okay, knock 'em dead."

Mom and Max were waiting for me in the lobby and we all had breakfast at the hotel restaurant. I kept looking around for an orange visor, because though I tried to suppress it, I'd had a sinking feeling inside since the note in my bathroom. I couldn't dismiss it as odd fan behavior anymore—I was being violated. Was all my good fortune too great to be without mishap; without impending tragedy?

Neil found our table and introduced me to a burly guy named Ace who was to be my main bodyguard.

When they left, I explained to Mom and Max that it was just a precaution because of my growing number of fans in the region. They'd seen the teenagers crowding me for autographs, and my mom accepted it at face value. But when she went to the bathroom, Max said, "Tell me what's really going on, Jackson."

I tried to play it off. "Some weird stuff has been happening, that's all." He didn't look convinced.

After breakfast, Mom went to write postcards and I briefed Ace and the other bodyguard, a wiry Asian guy who went by Tommy, on everything I'd experienced. Max insisted on sitting in on the discussion, and Neil was there, too. I gave Ace and Tommy a description of the paparazzo whom I suspected might be doing it, and it was gratifying that they seemed to be taking everything I was saying so seriously.

Ace explained that I'd be spending the most time with him, since he was going to be working the day shift. He gave me a rundown of what to expect and some extra safety precautions. Tommy, whose English had a British-inflected accent, explained that he would be stationed outside my door at night to make sure no one came in.

"We'll both try to be as unobtrusive as possible," Ace said, "but if something happens, we'll need you to follow our lead."

Afterward Max said, "You think it's just a prank?"

"I really don't know. But listen, you can't tell Mom. I don't want her knowing, and I also don't want the info getting to Dad."

"Will do, Bro."

The production company that was putting on the shows had hired us a car and a driver for the day, so we explored the city some more. Ace was as good as his word, hanging back a bit to give us privacy but constantly monitoring our environment. I felt much safer with him around, though still jittery.

In the afternoon, we drove to the utmost point above the city and then took a steep tram for the final climb. The view was magnificent. Hong Kong was like ten New York Cities lined up next to each other. It was unfathomable. In spite of my growing success and fame, it made me feel curiously small and humble.

Max took a video of Mom and me goofing around on the platform, the city like Lego colonies in the distance. The air was thick with humidity, and there were surprisingly few tourists around.

Max thanked me for bringing them there, and Mom gave me a hug.

"This has all been so amazing, sweetie."

We were standing in a triangle, open to the city, when Mom's alarm went off. I realized I had forgotten my cell phone at the hotel, so I couldn't give it to her to call Dad. My mind suddenly raced with anxious thoughts. What if something happened and I couldn't call for help? I had no way of knowing whether the stalker was violent, and even with Ace there, it would only take seconds for a psycho with a gun to shoot me if he really wanted to. Fear for Mom and Max's safety filled me. What if the stalker was watching us right then?

As my thoughts spiraled rapidly into ever-darker visions, a wave of fog suddenly moved over the top of the mountain. Within seconds we were gently covered in thick blankets of white. We couldn't see two feet in front of us. I felt my anxiety fade into a sense of peace and calm.

Mom, Max, and I slowly came into a three-way embrace, holding each other above the giant city, the beautiful lush white fog all around us. The wisps of cloud gave an ethereal look to their faces, the moisture caressing our skin. I had never been one who believes in higher powers or ghosts, but I could have sworn I felt Dad's presence at that moment. And I'm pretty sure Mom and Max did too.

# 62

The next day, Jess and I were hanging out backstage at the stadium, getting ready for the show. Mom and Max were lounging on the plush couches.

"This is so cool," Max said.

Mom was dancing around and singing.

"Your mom is so brilliant," Jess whispered to me.

Leroy and Rico were sound checking. I was happy to be with my family and Jess, but even with Ace outside keeping guard, I still kept seeing the bloody words in my head. Someone was in my shower writing that. They had to be seriously twisted.

Mom held Jess's hair back as she put on eyeliner; then she and Max went to their seats in the VIP section on the side of the stage.

Jess and I did our vocal warm-ups.

"I wish..." Jess's face got serious and forlorn, an expression I had yet to see.

"What?" I said, feeling like I wanted to protect her, like she had become the little sister I never had.

"I wish my mom was here. Your mom is so cool!"

I had never asked the mother question, though obviously I'd noticed that she wasn't around and that Jess and Liam never talked about her.

"Where is she now?"

"I don't know. She left. But I don't really want to talk about it right now. Maybe some other time."

As Max, Mom, and I watched Jess perform from the wings, I speculated about her mother and where she might have ended up. How could anyone leave their own child, especially one as warm, funny, and wise as Jess? She was so strong onstage; she had an undeniable star quality. I couldn't imagine being at her point when

I was that young. She had experienced so much and yet was only just beginning her adult life.

"Wow, look at all the lights!" Mom said.

"There must be twenty thousand people out there!" Max was in awe.

Before her last number, "Forgive," Jess told the audience, "This one is for my mother, wherever she is."

I'm not ashamed to admit I cried like a baby. So did my mom, of course, and I think even Max got a little choked up.

After Jess's heart-wrenching, soulful ballad I went to my dressing room to have what Neil referred to as "my moment." It was when I looked in the mirror at my real self, before I gave my public self to the world. Or in this case, a stadium full of twenty thousand screaming Chinese teenagers.

Neil called in.

"It's time, princess."

Ace led me out of the dressing room to the wings. Even though it was strange having this burly guy follow me wherever I went, I felt more protected.

I walked by Mom and Max, and they both gave me a good-luck squeeze on the arm as I entered the lights.

Leroy and Rico came on from the other side, and we did our ritual head nod and wink. Rico started the beat of our first song, and the crowd went crazy. I was still in awe that all of these people in such a foreign land knew who I was and had paid money to come see me. A couple of times I played to the side of the stage and could see smiles from Mom and Max.

Toward the end of the show, I dedicated "Just an Illusion" to my dad. Looking at the side of the stage again, seeing my mom, Max, and Neil, I felt unbelievably blessed. They were the architecture of my life, the pillars on which I stood. This fan craze, though lovely and intoxicating, was fleeting and unstable. My ground, my anchor, were the people close to me. I vowed to never take that for granted.

As the last chords of "Just an Illusion" faded out, someone on the balcony directly in front of me unfurled a huge vertical banner. I read the words "I can't hear you" and suddenly the whole stadium went dark. People screamed with excitement, thinking it was part of the show. I felt terror in my blood, sliding through my veins. My face felt hot and I couldn't take a deep breath. Someone grabbed at my arm and I panicked. Ace called out, "It's okay, Mr. Poole, it's Ace. We're going to get somewhere safer now."

He led me to the wings by the light of a few emergency bulbs. I tripped over wires and banged my hip on something in the darkness. I started to really fear for my life. What if the stalker was in the crowd somewhere or even on the stage? The words *I can't hear you* swam through my brain, over and over. Neil rushed by with a flashlight and told me Liam and Jess were fine. "I'm going to make sure Rico and Leroy made it off stage okay."

"Where are Mom and Neil?" I asked, but he was already gone. I pulled away from Ace, panicking. "Where is my family!?"

Ace and I found them in one of the side stage rooms, which had an emergency light on. Mom, Max, Jess, and Liam were all there, along with some of the crew. I hugged my mom first.

A few minutes later Neil arrived, and I took him aside and told him about the banner in private. Max had given me a look when I walked in, and was distracting Mom by prompting her with stories to tell Jess and Liam. She seemed to believe the whole thing was a lark, and I didn't want to scare her. The stage manager came in and informed us that it was simply a circuit gone awry and the lighting system had been tripped—apparently it was a glitch that had happened before, and he was very embarrassed and apologetic. It was not intentional. I told him sincerely that I didn't mind at all, and he looked relieved.

I took a deep breath, and boom—the lights went back on. But what about the sign? Neil understood it was serious, but it was hard to make the people working at the stadium understand. Finally they agreed to send a security guard into the crowd to see if the person holding the banner was still there. Ace had been shadowing me closely the whole time, and said, "In a crowd that big, the guy could just drop the banner and disappear. I wouldn't expect to find anything."

I really didn't want to go back onstage. Mom was telling Jess about some of her own performance horror stories. I wasn't really listening, but heard the words, "the show must go on," and realized if I didn't go back onstage, I'd have to tell her what was up. I stalled by saying I had to go to the bathroom, and Ace and Neil followed me into the hall.

In a remarkably short period of time, a security guard arrived with a shaken looking Chinese teenager in tow. In thickly accented English the guard told us, "He says someone gave the sign to him outside the arena and said you would love it. He doesn't read enough English to know what it says. I think he's telling the truth." Did that mean the stalker hadn't come into the building at all? I noticed the kid still standing there, trembling. I smiled at him. "Please tell him thank-you for the kind gesture." I gestured for the autograph book in his hands and signed it, "Don't kill the messenger, Jackson Poole."

Max came out into the hall. "Mom just said she can't wait to hear the final number."

I'd told her before the concert that I was going to end the show with her favorite of my new songs. She said she'd been listening to it all the time back home, but she'd never heard it live. I realized I had to do it. I had to go back out there.

Ace and Neil both told me I was crazy.

"You've already done forty-five minutes, Jackson. For a lot of people, that's already a full show," Neil said.

I thought of the kid getting suckered into holding the banner, and all the other kids out there, waiting to hear the rest of the show. Maybe the stalker hadn't even come into the stadium. It was one thing to switch my hotel room, or hire a bodyguard, but if I let this guy prevent me from doing my job—from doing what I loved—where would it ever end?

Ace led me out to finish the show.

In the wings, looking out into the mass of people, I felt like I was staring over a cliff. I scanned the crowd for an orange visor, or anyone with hair that wasn't dark. It was the same bobbing sea of glossy black, everyone watching and listening as Sushi & Co. lip-synched to a Sly and the Family Stone song. In an effort to lighten the mood, Max said, "Look, it's Sushi in the middle, and rice and wasabi on either side."

I waited for the end of the song and then walked on stage.

*Keep it together,* I told myself.

I tried to slow down my breath, but it was speeding up rapidly. I felt strangely exposed, as if anyone in the audience might hurt me at any moment. What if the stalker had a gun trained on me right now? My heart was on double time. I looked to where the sign had been. It wasn't there.

I went up to the microphone to sing.

But nothing came out.

I flashed on the doll with its grotesque sewn-together lips. My dad in the hospital. The stalker and his mean face. I was shaking and started to sweat uncontrollably. I held on to the microphone stand for balance, but suddenly my knees gave out like pins being knocked down. My vision clouded over, and the last thing I saw was the halo of Neil's head hovering over me in the spotlight as he tried to pick me up.

I awoke to Neil still above me, holding my hand and looking more scared than I'd ever seen him. A kind-looking Chinese man in a white doctor's coat was gently holding my other wrist. "Your pulse is normal now."

My first thought was, *I'm not dead.*

I was disoriented, cloudy. Painkillers?

The doctor spoke slowly and clearly and made me feel calm. He explained, in expert English, that I had experienced a panic attack, and I should not be alarmed.

"A panic attack?" At the sound of my own voice, tears of relief filled my eyes. I touched my throat. *I can't hear you.*

"I thought—I was afraid..."

The doctor gently patted my hand. "There shouldn't be anything wrong with your voice."

I looked at everyone's concerned faces. Jess, Liam, Leroy, and Rico were crowded around, and Ace was standing watch.

"Where's—"

"Your mom went back to the side room because she forgot her camera. She didn't see you fall," Neil said. "Max just went to get her."

I was confused. "How long was I out?"

The doctor looked at me with compassion. "Not long. Your friends told me all you've been going through. Stress has a powerful effect on the body."

He recommended a special herb formula and was demonstrating some relaxation exercises when my mom came in, totally frantic.

"What's wrong? What happened!?"

"Mom, I just fainted, it's nothing at all."

"We were up all night after you went to bed," Neil lied, "he was just dehydrated."

That seemed to work.

"Well, no more of that, Jackson; you have to take better care of yourself."

"I will, Mom, I promise."

Worried mothers must be universal, because the doctor didn't say anything.

The stadium manager came up and announced that the rest of the show had been cancelled.

Max and Neil basically carried me back to my hotel room, with Ace keeping guard nearby. I was too exhausted to even think. I fell asleep the minute my head hit the pillow.

# 63

The next day was my second and last Hong Kong performance and my mom and Max's last full day in Hong Kong.

I woke up and called Derek at Cher's house, explaining everything that happened.

He seemed to understand how scared I was and started telling me about all the people he knew who'd dealt with stalkers and crazed fans.

"You know what? You get in a position of success, fame, whatever it is, and people want a piece of it, or they're bored, jealous, whatever. It happens with *every* big celebrity. But you have to remind yourself that it's almost always more of a nuisance than a threat. My friend Courtney Cox was getting over-the-top, weird stuff, like rotten fruit and videotapes with static, and she was completely terrified, but then it ended up just stopping when the stalker moved on to another celebrity. Courtney was like, "What, I'm not good enough for you anymore?""

I laughed.

"Just try not to worry, and focus on why you're there. The one thing they can never take away is your talent, remember that. Just do what you can to stand proud and rise above it."

"But I lost my voice!"

"Honey, you will never lose your voice. You just let it get to you. Just remember, your gift is more powerful than any prank or creepy message."

I was amazed that with all Derek was going through he was so level headed and sincere with me.

"Derek, thanks, I'm glad I know you."

"Break a leg, or at least the stalker's arm."

Neil wanted to cancel the show but I refused. Derek was right.

I wasn't going to let some asshole in an orange visor keep me from living out my dream. Even though I hadn't seen him again since the beach in Cape Town, I was convinced he was the one behind everything.

Ace knocked on my door and told me Jess was there to see me.

"Send her in," I said.

She walked in like she was a zombie in a horror flick.

"I can't hear you..." she whispered creepily.

I laughed.

"That's my boy," she said. "As long as you can laugh about it."

"Well, I'm not going to let it get to me."

Just then the phone rang.

I picked it up but didn't say hello.

"*I still can't hear you,*" a voice said.

I started to panic for a brief second until I heard my mom singing in the background.

"Max, you asshole!"

I turned to Jess, who looked amused. I said, "What, did you guys plan a conspiracy to desensitize me to this bullshit?"

Jess gave me her mischievous smile. "I guess great minds think alike."

Max was laughing and apologizing at the same time, "I'm sorry dude, I couldn't resist."

Leave it to my nearest and dearest to try to torture me out of my fear.

Mom got on the line.

"Angel, you okay?"

"Yes, Mom, I'm fine."

"You sure?"

"Yes."

"No more fainting?"

"Yes."

"Promise?"

"Promise!"

I went back to the stadium early with Leroy and Rico, and we played a few songs just to get me over any remaining fear of the place. It sunk in that this really was the last show of the tour and that we'd succeeded in rocking our way through Europe and Asia.

"Thanks, you guys," I said, "for all you've done. You both kick ass every time we perform, and I'm proud to share the stage with you."

They acted like it was no big deal, but I could tell they were pleased.

The incident had made the local news, and Neil told me several American reporters in Hong Kong had come out for the last show in case more histrionics ensued.

But the show was a success and drama free. Security was tightened and the fuse system in the venue was backed up. Before I cued the band to start the first song, I grabbed the microphone and yelled, "Can you hear me now!?"

The audience roared and raised their hands in the air.

Leroy and Rico put their hands up, too.

The crowd sounded like an angry lion.

After the show we were escorted to a special bar that was reserved for us by Sushi & Co. And guess what they served? Sushi! The street out front was mobbed (apparently word had gotten out that the after-party was there), but we were whisked in through a tunnel that led from the building next door. It was all very James Bond.

Once again Mom was in rare form, and I saw Max with Sushi's hot sister. I sidled up next to him at the bar and noticed him blush when the bartender placed two froufrou drinks in front of him.

"Are you double fisting, or are you hoping for some action with Sushi's sister?"

"Um, actually I got her number the first night," he said.

"No way! Did you—"

"Twice!"

"Where is the justice that my entire band and my brother are getting laid and not me?"

"Dude, you got enough going on."

It was the first time he had been laid since separating from his wife, and I could tell he was practically beside himself. I watched him strut back over to her with a bounce in his step.

Jess and I settled ourselves in the VIP booth, drinking sake and watching the mayhem. Ace stood just far enough away that we were protected but he couldn't hear our conversation. The room was filled with roadies and production staff, and a few groupies. There were also a few people I was told were Cantonese celebrities, although I didn't recognize them.

A guy who looked like a gay Jackie Chan on Valium asked me to dance. I told him, "No, thank you," and Sushi came up to me a minute later and scolded me.

"Shame on you J-boy, he big star in Hong Kong, he do big commercial."

"I'm sorry, not my type, sweetheart."

Sushi smiled and pulled her clingy black skirt a little further up her thigh. She batted her eyes, and asked, "Oh, J-boy like me though?"

"Sushi, you're a gorgeous girl, but I'm not into chicks with dicks."

Jess laughed.

Before strutting her stuff back to the dance floor, Sushi gave me a saucy look and said, "Once you try, you never go back."

Jess and I giggled and drank more sake.

Neil and Liam were dancing suggestively, and I noticed Jess smile as Neil dipped Liam.

I admired the openness and affection in Liam and Jess's relationship, and being around them had gotten me thinking a lot again about having a kid. I wondered if I was unselfish enough to be a good parent, and if I'd have the courage to sacrifice everything for my child if I had to.

"Go, Dad!" Jess yelled as Liam twirled Neil across the dance floor.

I imagined if your kid was as incredible as Jess, any sacrifices would feel easier to bear.

She was still cheering Liam and Neil on.

"How much of that sake have you had, young lady?"

"Young? You kidding, I came out of the womb at thirty."

"That makes you almost fifty," I mused.

"Mentally, that's how I feel sometimes."

It seemed clear that everyone was getting laid except for Jess and me, so we decided to go back to my room and order room-service french fries and watch bad Chinese TV. When I asked my mom if she wanted to go to the hotel with us, she just laughed and kept on dancing.

When we got to my room, Tommy the night bodyguard was waiting. Ace said goodnight and Tommy checked the room before taking his post outside the door.

"All clear, Mr. Poole."

"I keep telling you to call me Jackson."

"Yes, Mr. Poole."

We ordered extra fries for him and a Coke, since he was going to be up all night.

"Can you believe Neil and Dad?" Jess asked.

I was flipping through the channels on the TV. "What?"

"Are you still jealous?"

"Why would I be?"

"Duh, you and Neil."

"What about me and Neil?"

Jess was mixing mustard and ketchup together for her fries.

"Quit trying to be coy."

"Well, we had our time, and it was great, but it wasn't meant to be. I'd be an idiot to let jealousy get in the way of our friendship. I feel it, but I fight it off."

"Understandable."

"Besides, I think Liam and Neil are perfect together."

"I'm glad they'll still be able to see each other while we're in LA."

"Ugh, don't remind me I have to go back to that hellhole."

"It can't be that bad!"

"My dear, you have no idea. It takes fresh young things like you who have talent and natural beauty and grinds them into insecure Barbie clones."

"You think I have talent and natural beauty?" She was grinning at me, a smear of her mustard-ketchup blend on her chin.

"Of course, you goof. But you're missing my point. I'm dreading going back."

I thought of the Aden and Derek drama and all the posers like Jed, who were an inevitable part of life in LA.

"Well I'm excited to go," Jess said. "I'm recording a couple of songs, and I've already decided I'm going to go the beach every day."

I had an idea, and before thinking it through I asked, "Will you stay with me?"

"You mean at your house?"

"Yes, I've got a little extra room that could be yours."

"Of course, Jackson!"

I suddenly had an image of my house—all those windows for my psycho stalker to peer through, or worse, break and then climb through. What if the stalker knew my home address? He'd found me in all these different cities with seemingly no problem. I immediately regretted inviting Jess. I didn't want her involved.

"The only thing is, well, what if the stupid stalker comes back? I would hate to have you—"

"Oh please, Jackson. I'll fight him off with my super powers!"

"Okay, but if anything fishy happens, I'm sending you back to the hotel with your father, deal?"

"Deal."

While I was saying good-bye to Mom and Max in front of the hotel the next morning, some people gathered around. I guess the news reports about the stadium blackout had made me more famous among the non-teenage set. My mom kissed me and told me how proud she was of me. She got a little emotional saying good-bye, and I reminded her that I'd be seeing her in less than a day in Boston. My flight wasn't until later that night, so I'd hired a limo to take them to the airport. I held her arm as she got in, and she immediately started playing with the gadgets inside, turning on the stereo and searching for a radio station.

"This is so wonderful, honey."

I hugged Max for a long time and gave him a peck on the cheek. Just as I kissed him, I heard the rapid clicking of a professional camera, a sound I'd come to recognize after all the publicity I'd done. When I looked for the source, I saw the paparazzo/stalker, a gloating sneer on his face.

"Thanks," he said, "that's the big money shot." He took the orange visor out of his back pocket and threw it at me.

"Here, fags like orange," he said.

I grabbed it automatically, then stood frozen in shock.

Neil, who had been taking pictures of us with his phone, yelled, "That's him! That's the guy!"

Ace was already in the process of jumping on him, pinning him to the ground. People standing nearby seemed confused, but one person cheered.

"You cannot legally detain me. And I will sue you if you don't let go of me right now."

Everything was happening so fast that I just stood there.

"He's right," Ace said. "We don't have a legal right to hold him."

He let the guy up with obvious regret.

As he walked away, the paparazzo turned around and said, "You chose to live a life in the public eye. I'm just doing my job. And if my equipment's damaged, I will expect payment."

"Fuck off," Max said.

Mom was in the limo, clueless, saying, "Boys what's going on out there?"

I was still in shock but knew I wanted her out of there.

"Nothing, Mom. You guys are going to be late. I'll see you in Boston."

Max had bounced back more quickly than me and was trying to reassure me. "What a loser," he said. "He's the guy who never got laid in high school."

I laughed in spite of the adrenaline still rushing through my veins. I said to Max so Mom couldn't hear, "Just get her to the airport, okay?"

Max got in the limo and my mom called out, "Bye, honey!"

I leaned in and said, "Safe travels."

As the limo pulled away and I walked back into the hotel, the crowd began to disperse.

Neil and Ace walked on either side of me, and as we crossed the lobby to the elevator, Ace said, "Are you all right, Mr. Poole?"

Strangely, I was. I was still stunned, but something felt different.

"Why do I feel better about that freak all of a sudden?"

Neil scoffed. "I don't feel better. He was a fucking asshole."

"Yeah, but he seemed—I can't put my finger on it." As aggressive and psycho as the guy had just been, it was as if the venomous hostility I'd felt from him during our previous encounters had vanished. "He just seemed like a generic jerk—like an average, everyday closed-minded bigot. Do you know what I mean?"

"All I know is, I need a stiff drink," Neil said.

I realized I still had the orange visor in my hands. Somehow I wasn't so scared anymore.

As we walked by the trashcan near the elevators, I threw it in. "Buh bye."

# 64

My flight back to the U.S. was uneventful. I had told my dad that after the tour I was scheduled to perform at a benefit concert for cancer research in Boston, so he would get to see me play after all. It was just an extended layover, but I was glad to see him in person. I gave him his golf-gadget present and he loved it.

"I'm gonna try this right away!"

"Wait, you're already going out on the golf course?"

"Doc said I could."

He did seem to have quite a renewed vigor, and I was thrilled to see him normal again.

At the fund-raiser, I recognized one of the speakers immediately. It was Chris, my "first time," high-school love. I wondered if he was still "feeling heterosexual." His voice was the same, especially the way he moved quickly through his r's and over-pronounced his t's.

Dad and Mom were watching the show from a lighting booth above the balcony—their own little VIP suite. I played a short set and dedicated my last song to my father. It wasn't a stadium, but I was happy to have him there. I could tell from the way he kept grinning at my mom that he was having a blast.

Chris greeted me after the show with a warm hug. He had the same bright, inquisitive look in his eyes, but his face had fleshed out, grown broader. What do you say? We hadn't seen each other in fifteen years.

His daughter, Julie-Ann, jumped into my lap and looked at me with such adoration and pride that I felt suddenly emotional. Looking at her innocent face reminded me I wanted to have a child of my own.

My mother barged into the backstage room and said, "Chris! Oh you dear thing!" He turned red when she kissed him.

She turned to me and said, "Can you believe it?"

*That I fucked him in high school or that his daughter is on my lap?*

"I know," I said, feebly.

"You too were such buds! I couldn't tear you apart!"

Chris looked at me, smiled, and we all looked at the floor.

"Where's Dad?" I asked Mom.

"You're not going to believe this...he's signing autographs!"

My mother couldn't get over seeing Chris again. She told the story of when he and I were suspended from junior high school.

To counteract, I told the one about how Mom saw this lady on the golf course in Prout's Neck, Maine, and said to her, "I know you from somewhere!"

It was Barbara Bush.

Hello?

Chris hugged me again when we said good-bye. It's peculiar how an embrace can lose its power. I remembered hugging him in high school and feeling a surge of electricity, like there was a current of strength and beauty coming out of him. But that spark had died. He had become someone else. So had I. I pictured myself in Chris's shoes. Had I chosen that life, I would be living a lie even more than I was now.

That night, lying in my childhood bed feeling restless from jetlag and too much sugar, I couldn't sleep. I was reluctant to go back to LA. It had been so refreshing being abroad and away from the beauty-obsessed, money-driven, narcissism mecca that was Los Angeles. There were many times that I had bought into all of that myself, even thrived on it. But everything that had been happening—my dad's health crisis, the stalker scare, even meeting such good, grounded people as Jess and Liam—had made me realize that life was too short to worry about things that really weren't important.

It was time to simply live.

# 65

On my last day in Boston I got up early for a good-bye breakfast with my family before my flight. Dad was excited about his first day back on the golf course. Neil had emailed me pictures of the tour and we all gathered around the computer to look.

"There's our limo!" Mom said.

I noticed the creepy paparazzo in the background of some of the pictures. I printed them out on my dad's prized printer and packed them in my guitar case. I didn't quite know what I would do with the images, but it felt reassuring to have them just in case any more weird things happened.

At the airport in Boston more people were looking at me than before I left for my tour, and I realized how much I was going to miss the relative anonymity of Hong Kong.

Several people nodded and smiled at me, and I got a couple of long stares. Bree's publicity machine had undoubtedly been working overtime in the U.S. while I was away.

A cute, bashful guy came up to me and said, "You're a hero now."

He was adorable, and for a fleeting moment I imagined asking him to join me for a drink. But if even if I hadn't still been bound by Universal's hetero-only mandate, I didn't have time.

I rushed to my gate, and as we were boarding the plane, I was struck by how overstyled the passengers were. I could always pick out the waiting area for a plane to LA by all the blondes, boob jobs, Botox, and tiny cell phones. I entertained the thought of moving to New York as I had many times before, only now it could be a reality. I could afford the huge downtown loft I had dreamed about or the brownstone in the West Village. Also, I'd be closer to my family. New York had its superficiality, of course, but it by no means dominated as much as it did in Los Angeles.

When the plane landed in LAX, I put on my sunglasses and a Kangol hat. Cliché celebrity disguise, but it was surprising how well it could work. The walkway from the plane to the gate was filled with the sound of cell phones being turned on. Ugh, LA.

"Yeah, forty large now, plus more on the back end," said a metrosexual in a suit. "Time to go cheat on the wife."

"Oh my GOD! I got the part," said a no-body-fat Cameron Diaz wannabe with a bad dye job and too much makeup, "I have to be nude but it's totally, like, artistic, you know? It's, like, art."

I suppose I was just as bad though. I turned mine on, too, and gasped at the number of messages. The phone instantly started ringing. It was Neil. He said, "Oh my god, I've been trying to reach you all morning! Where are you right now?"

"Sorry, I didn't have my phone on. Are all those messages from you?"

"Shit! I'll give you all the details later, but right now, Jackson, where are you?" He sounded a bit frantic.

"I'm about to come through the gate at the airport. Aren't you meeting me?"

"Yes, but don't move!"

I stopped where I was, inspiring angry looks from the passengers trying to pass me. "Neil, tell me what's going on! You're scaring me."

Even though the paparazzo was more of a known quantity now, I still worried for a second this might be about him.

"Just stay where you are. Are you wearing your hat and stuff?"

"Yes, Neil, but I'm not...what is going on?!"

"Okay, after you go through security, take a sharp right."

I hung up the phone and walked out with the rest of the crowd from the plane.

I could see a group of photographers in the distance and heard a familiar voice. It was Brian in some sort of robe, telling everyone to let Jesus heal them and passing out flyers. What?

I skirted the scene and Neil grabbed my arm as everyone watched Brian, who was getting louder and louder, drawing all eyes to him.

Neil led me to Brian's little car in the parking garage, and we waited for a minute until Brian came running up. He was throwing off his robe and tossing his flyers, which were actually pictures of Florence Henderson.

As we peeled away laughing, I said to Brian, "Mrs. Brady?"

"I'm telling you, girl, she will heal you!"

As we got on the freeway, the car went silent, and I got a distinct feeling they weren't telling me something. Then Neil put a *National Enquirer* on my lap. There I was on the front page, kissing a man.

"Oh my god, it's Max," I said.

"Outside the hotel in Hong Kong, remember?"

The headline read: *The real Jackson Poole on tour with his gay lover!*

"That fucker."

Neil told me Clean Slate and Diamond Mine's plan.

"Aden contacted your parents to get a photo of you and Max that shows you're obviously family, and Bree is using her contacts to get the story aired right away."

My phone rang. Was this the sound of my career being flushed down the toilet? I looked at the caller ID. Speak of the devil.

"Hi, Bree."

"Listen, don't panic. I had you scheduled for *Oprah* in a couple of weeks, but I think I can get you bumped up to counteract this *Enquirer* bullshit."

"Do you think it will work?"

"Everything I do works, don't you know that by now, darling? I expect special presents for this one. Do you know who I had to fuck for that slot?"

The call-waiting beeped. I gave Bree my undying thanks and clicked over to talk to Derek.

"Don't worry, this will all blow over," he said.

"I hope so, Derek, or my career is toast."

"Always assume the best, kid. Other people have weathered far worse storms than this."

I hoped he was right. "Well, at least our escape from the airport was fun. And I look good in the picture."

"That's the spirit," Derek said.

"I still can't believe this, though. I'm kissing my brother!"

Neil was giving Brian directions to his house, not mine, and I looked at him quizzically.

"Your house is crawling with media."

"Are you kidding? Shit! I've been dreaming of taking a bath in my own bathtub for the last week."

I forgot that I was still on the phone with Derek.

"Sorry, Derek."

Dead air. The cell had died because we were on the south part of La Brea.

Brian dropped us off, and Neil and I lounged in his fabulous garden, which was overflowing with life. He made us drinks.

I told Neil about my escape to New York idea.

"Girl, I'm coming with you. This town is beyond tired," he said.

"So what's the deal with Aden?" I asked.

He offered me a cigarette but I refused. He lit one up anyway.

"He's off the deep end, apparently. Derek's been staying at Cher's. They're not talking. I don't know why Derek doesn't just kick him out. It's his fucking house!"

"We've been trying to figure out that logic for a while now."

"It's been a nightmare being back in the office with Aden constantly looming and trying to get me to tell him Derek's plans. I just want it to be over." Neil started watering the flowers. "Speaking of which, you have a meeting with—are you ready?" Neil paused for effect, "Mr. Snuggle, or whatever you call him."

"Mr. Cuddle?"

"Yep. Mark Diamond is handling the litigation for Derek, and they've drafted something that will essentially lay Aden off and pay him out. Aden's requested ridiculously high numbers, but Mark says he'll bring it way down. He says Aden doesn't have a leg to stand on, especially regarding anything of Derek's."

"Thank God."

"We're all praying that none of this will go to trial."

"It's too bad about Aden. I mean, as much as we can't stand him, he did a lot for our careers."

"I know, but he's still a dickhead."

We laughed.

"So how's the Liam thing? He's here with Jess, right?"

"It's good, yes. Actually, the four of us are meant to do dinner tonight at The Crescent, where they're staying."

"But wait, Jess was going to stay with me!"

"Yeah, but honey, where would that be? I don't know if Bree's publicity is going to be enough to fight off the media's thirst for your gay blood. When I went by your place earlier, I practically got assaulted pulling into your driveway."

"Jesus."

"Well you can stay here with me for at least a little while, and if we have to, we can find you someplace with a gate and security."

"God, no wonder celebrities end up being such reclusive freaks! Somehow I just never thought it would happen to me." I got up and stared at the flickering lights of the East side. "Anyway, Jess could still come stay with me if I end up having to hole up somewhere like Marlene Dietrich. I'd be even more in need of company."

"Well, you should tell her that tonight. Maybe instead of meeting at The Crescent I can cook dinner for everyone here."

I could see the Martha Stewart wheels in Neil's head turning at the idea of entertaining. It was probably his wet dream right now to make Liam a home-cooked meal.

"That sounds great. Especially if you make your curried chicken thingy."

"I'll call and invite them. By the way, Jess starts recording tomorrow, and she wants you to sing on her record."

"Cool! I'd love to."

"Well, it's not that simple anymore, sweetie. Now you're like a commodity, and there's a bureaucracy and loopholes to manage such a thing. Since you're not on the same label it may be tricky.

Plus, Aden could potentially make a claim for part of any revenue you generate before he's officially severed from Clean Slate. Derek doesn't want Aden to have any grounds for suing you later, so he said he thinks you should wait to sing on Jess's record. He's hoping the settlement will be finalized this week."

"No problem, she probably won't be at background vocals for a while anyway."

"Background? Girl, it's duet or nothing, I say."

Neil seemed so much more assertive, more confident. I wondered if it might be due to his newfound romance with Liam. I told him they seemed very sweet together, and admitted that I'd thought Liam was cute the minute I met him at that first show in London.

"I know, girl, I was like, simmer down! I hate it when people always use this word, but he's just so adorable!"

He waited for me to follow him inside, where he put his little apron on.

"There is one thing," he said, while he pulled stuff out of the freezer.

"What?" I asked.

"He's uncut."

"Ew!"

We laughed. Neil and I shared a slight aversion to uncircumcised penises. We just didn't want to deal with all that extra skin, preferred them pulled tight and neat.

"I know, it's so weird. But you know, I think I could get to like it."

I watched Neil start preparing the food and was mesmerized. Some chefs were true artists, like painters or musicians. Neil was one of them.

"You should do a cooking show."

"Cooking with rock stars?"

"Yeah. I'll tell my people to get on it."

"I am your people."

# 66

Jess and Liam arrived at Neil's with wine and dessert in hand.

"Not only did I have to drive on the right," Liam said, "I had to dodge the prostitutes."

"Oh, you went through that part of Hollywood."

"That was Hollywood?" Jess asked.

"Yeah" I said. "People don't realize that most of Hollywood's a dump."

"Everyone wait a minute," Neil said. "Bree said to watch *Access Live*."

"More drama," I said.

Liam and Jess said together, "We heard."

"At least refill my drink first," I said as I turned the TV on and lowered the volume. Neil obeyed and opened a new bottle of wine, and we all toasted to Jess's new record. Then I heard my name coming from the TV. Neil turned the volume up.

They were billing it as an "expose of tabloid journalism."

"And what is *Access Live? 60 Minutes?*" Neil said.

They went to commercial but not before showing a teaser with an icon of my face.

Jess said, "It's so strange. On one hand you've got these nasty paparazzi who have no respect, and on the other, fans who are so impressed they're shaking when they talk to you."

She sipped her drink and continued, "I was so proud on the flight to LA when this lady asked me for my autograph. But then I noticed that she wouldn't meet my eyes. It was like she thought I was this important person, and she had to be extra respectful or something. It made me sad." She got up to help Neil with the appetizers. "Do you know what I mean?"

"Exactly," I said.

"That's the one thing they don't tell all the kids who dream of being a star. Everything changes."

"It sure does."

The show came back on and they showed a picture of Max's wedding, his ex and him kissing with cake in their mouths, and yours truly as the best man, standing next to our mom and dad. The family resemblance was unmistakable. The expert held up the *Enquirer* story, using the photo as an example of how easily an image can be used to imply something that isn't true. He said, "The frustration for celebrities is that they could literally bankrupt themselves of time and money trying to counter all the false representations. It's a no-win situation."

We cheered. Bree had come through once again.

We were already pretty buzzed when we sat down to dinner. The food was way better than the trendy Crescent Hotel. Neil had outdone himself once again, and Liam was eating the food as if he was relishing the formation of new taste buds. Wine, laughter, and yummy food—sometimes that was all life was about.

When Neil and Liam were outside smoking, Jess and I settled in on the couch.

"Jess, does your mother know, I mean, about your career?"

She looked at me hard, as if seriously contemplating her next words.

"I had this piano recital in fifth grade, and I practiced so hard. She helped me prepare for it—she was the first musical person in three generations of our family. I got my talent from her. Anyway, the morning before the recital she watched me practice it once more, then drove me to school. She always watched me until I got right to the door of the school, then I'd turn and wave.

This time she called my name when I was just a couple steps away from the car. When I turned around, I could see she had tears in her eyes. She told me, 'Don't worry, you're going to shine.'"

I could hear Liam's laughter through the screen door. The crickets seemed to get louder in response. A thrumming heartbeat.

"And..."

"And that was the last time I saw her."

I hugged her and she rested her head on my chest. She said quietly, "I often wonder if she meant I would shine in the recital or I would shine in the rest of my life."

Liam and Neil barged in, still laughing, until they saw the expression on Jess's face.

"What's wrong, my dear?" Liam asked, suddenly terribly concerned.

"Listen, I'm going to leave you two—" I said.

"No, stay, I don't care, Jackson," Jess said.

Neil pretended to look busy rearranging the magazines on the table.

Jess looked at her father with the intensity of a wingless bird trying to take flight.

"What was it, Dad? Why did she leave?"

Liam set down his drink.

"Oh, Jess, we've been through this before—"

"Yes, but you always held something back, I could tell. Well, I'm old enough now. I want to know. I need to know."

Liam turned red and started to perspire. Neil tried to leave the room but Jess shouted, "No! Tell me, Daddy, tell us." Jess was clearly emboldened by a little too much alcohol.

Liam said, "This is not a matter for—"

"Just tell me."

Liam turned away, and then faced Jess again. "She knew I was homosexual, okay!" he blurted out, his arms shaking and his eyes wild. "Are you happy?"

Neil sat down quietly and we all looked at the floor for what seemed like an hour, then Liam quietly went on.

"A 'friend' of hers told her she'd heard I'd had a male lover in college. Then somehow another friend heard, and another, and pretty soon our whole circle knew. She was ashamed and embarrassed, and I suppose she never really loved me anyway, in that way mind you. We were friends, partners more than anything. We never had," he paused, glancing sharply at Neil before looking back at his daughter, "romance."

"Well you bloody well conceived me didn't you?"

We all laughed, and suddenly the tension in the room lifted a bit.

Liam began to softly cry. Jess went over to her father and hugged him.

"It's okay, Daddy. You're the best family I could've asked for. I just needed to know."

The two of them walked out into the kitchen, leaving Neil and me alone in the room.

"Well," Neil said, after a big combination sigh and eye roll, "who needs daytime TV?"

# 67

The next day I woke up at Neil's and wondered when I'd actually be able to go back to my own house. He'd gone to work already, but there was a note on the kitchen counter.

> J-
> *Fresh fruit and lemon yogurt in the fridge.*
> *I had an intern drive your car over.*
> *See you at the races.*
> *Neil*

I called Derek to check in.

"See? I told you so," he said. "Bree and Aden's scheme worked." Leave it to Derek to give props to Aden even after everything he'd done to him. He was such a good person. "And the intern who picked up your car said there was no sign of anyone at your house, so it should be safe to go home."

"Whew." Big relief.

"One more thing—I want you to sit in on the phone conference I've scheduled with Peter Montgomery from Universal tomorrow afternoon."

"There's a terrifying thought. Do we have to talk to him?"

"You don't, but I do. His secretary has already called me five times. It can't be avoided. Don't worry though, it will be fine. I set it up for tomorrow so Aden won't be there. Have you forgotten that the last time we had one of these calls, you ended up dining with the mighty Isis?"

I laughed.

"Isis the wonder boob. Okay, but I have to tell you, I'm feeling less and less comfortable lying about all this stuff, Derek."

"Don't worry about it; leave the talking to me. Come by the

office at two o'clock."

"How can you be sure Aden won't be there?"

"We'll make sure he's occupied somewhere else."

On the way home, I stopped by the post office to pick up all the mail that had been held during my trip. There was an envelope from Kane, postmarked just a day into my tour. I opened it on the way back to my car.

> *Jackson—*
>
> *A brief update: I heard that Timothy Meyer was released on bail yesterday, and that the wife's family is planning to pay off all his debts so the charges will be dropped. Some people have all the luck, huh? Apparently they don't want their name tarnished by the scandal of having a convicted felon in the family. I hear the wife is pissed, but she's got to take some consolation from the fact that he spent at least a few days in prison, right? I've got some exes I'd love to have put away. I'll let you know if I hear anything else.*
>
> *-Kane*
>
> *P.S. Still not knocked up. Have you thought any more about my proposal?*

So Timothy was out of prison. When I thought of the fact that it was his stupid David Geffen rumor that started all the paparazzi hell I'd been going through, I sided with his wife. A little time in prison couldn't hurt. I could feel myself getting angry when I remembered him calling the Geffen thing a "prank." Classic user—completely unconcerned with how his actions affected other people.

But at least he was relatively tame compared to the freak I'd been dealing with lately. Compared to that sick doll and sabotaging my concert, Timothy's calls and drunken phone messages seemed like nothing in retrospect. If I could trade him for the paparazzo guy, I would.

It suddenly occurred to me that I could ask Kane to research the paparazzo just like she had Timothy. I didn't have much for her to go on, but at least I had the photos of him from Hong Kong and the fact that he'd sold the picture of me and Max to the *Enquirer*.

When I got home, there was a flower box propped against my door. Neil must have had them delivered to welcome me home. So sweet! I got in and threw down my bags, setting the flower box on my kitchen counter. When I opened it, I found a dozen dead, decapitated roses and a note: *I still can't hear you.*

At first I felt the familiar surge of fear, but then I found myself getting angry. I finally get home and this is what I am welcomed by? What the fuck! Does this guy have a life? He already got his stupid shot of Max and me.

I threw the flowers in the garbage and slammed the lid shut. I wanted to put my hand through a wall. I checked the whole house for anything else, and locked all the windows and pulled the shades. Was I not even safe in my own home? I was just a singer! Not a child molester or a white supremacist!

I called Kane and told her in brief what had been going on.

"I need to hire you to help me with this, Kane."

"What, you think everything up to now was free? Ha!"

"Seriously."

She could sense I was freaked, and told me to meet her at the same old-school bar with the movie posters where we'd met before. "Bring the flower box and the photos."

I drove fast to the bar and ordered a drink. If people were noticing me, I wasn't noticing them. I had one priority. This had to stop.

When Kane arrived, she asked for the whole story from beginning to end, speedily taking notes on her Palm Pilot.

When I finished, she sipped her drink and sat back like a therapist.

"Well, we can't know for sure that your paparazzo is the one doing all the other freaky stuff, but that orange visor does suggest an intentional terror agenda. It sounds like he wanted you to know he was there, which doesn't necessarily jibe with him just trying to get a gay photo. If that's all he was after, he wouldn't want you to be on your guard."

I downed the rest of my drink and signaled for another.

"It's an important detail that only the *National Enquirer* published the photos. That means it was an exclusive, and I may have an easier time tracking him down.

I gave her the box of dead roses and the photos of him.

"Oh, lovely. Just the type of guy you want to take home to meet Mom!"

The bartender noticed Kane taking notes, and the pictures spread out on the bar.

"Are you a detective?" he asked.

"No," Kane said with a hair flip, "I just play one on TV."

She dug for more info about all the little incidents—the phone call, the doll...I told her everything I remembered.

"Well, I can't be certain, but it sounds like it's just scare tactics, with no real intent to harm. There's been no escalation of threats, and the way you described your confrontation with him outside the hotel doesn't suggest an obsessive fixation."

I gave her a look. "That's quite a fancy term for a hard-boiled detective."

"Honey, half my clients are celebrities. If I wasn't an expert on this shit by now, I wouldn't be able to do my job. Some people think if you haven't been stalked, you haven't hit the big time yet."

"Gee, that's comforting. I can be officially famous right before I'm officially dead."

"Well I don't want to give you a false sense of security, but my feeling is that if this guy really wanted to hurt you, he'd have done it already. I don't think you're in any physical danger."

Derek had said the same thing. I took a deep breath.

"Does that mean I can go home?"

"Like I said, I can't make any promises, but my gut feeling is it's okay." She threw down a twenty for our drinks. "But, if you'd feel more comfortable with a bodyguard, I know a great one I think you'd like. He's six-three and has biceps the size of my thighs."

"I'll take a rain check."

"Yeah, well, it's sunny out."

We walked out to our cars.

"I'll be in touch when I have some info. In the meantime, sexy, lay low." She slid into her car. "By the way, your brother's cute. If you can't come clean for my gene pool, then I may have to tap the metro brother."

Whatever. I appreciated her help, but her relentless quest for sperm was beyond tired. I waved good-bye and got in my car.

I rolled down all the windows and cranked Missy Elliot on the stereo. I was singing along at full volume when it suddenly hit me: The cloud I'd been under for weeks had finally lifted. I'd believed Kane when she said she didn't think I was in danger. It was as if I'd been holding my breath without realizing it, and suddenly my lungs were full again.

I drove to the gourmet grocery near my house and stocked up on all the foods I'd missed while on tour. Jalapeno stuffed olives, sliced papaya, blue corn chips, avocados. I also picked out three different kinds of bubble bath in addition to my staple, Rain. I was feeling adventurous, expanding to tropical fruit bubbles.

When I got home, the house didn't have any of the creepiness I'd felt right after finding the flowers. I opened the windows and created a little nest on my couch with pillows and blankets.

I called Jess to see if she still wanted to stay with me in light of the latest stalker news. I also told her what Kane had said.

"Are you kidding? When can I come over?!"

"Let me talk to your dad for a sec?"

Liam said it was okay with him as long as Jess was comfortable. When Jess got back on the line, she accused me of being old school. "What am I, eight years old now?"

"Like it or leave it, my dear."

We made plans for me to pick her up the next day after her recording session.

After getting off the phone with Jess, I fell into a brief nap, and got up and fixed myself some nibbles. Then I played guitar for a while and just enjoyed being in my own space again. I watched some TV, read some magazines, had a glass of wine. Stars are normal people, too.

When I lay down, the feeling of being in my own bed with my own sheets was delicious, delightful, de-lovely.

# 68

The next afternoon I went to Clean Slate for the phone conference with Peter Montgomery. Even though Bree had managed to counteract the latest *Enquirer* story, I was nervous. I saw Neil as soon as I walked in and asked him if Aden was there.

"Derek got his old friend at Aden's hair salon to bump up his appointment by an hour to clear him from the office before the conference call." Neil looked around to see if anyone was nearby, then added, "But he was gone even before that. He left at like 10:30 for a 'lunch date,' and I saw his Scientologist waiting for him in the parking lot."

"What a skeeze."

I walked into Derek's office and he noticed my nerves. He rubbed my shoulders a bit. "You're just here as a formality, believe me. Don't worry your pretty little head."

Neil came in and we gathered around the phone once again. Peter's secretary put him on.

Derek didn't mention I was there, just updated Peter about what Bree was doing to offset the latest rumor. He mentioned *Access Live* and *Oprah*.

"What can you do?" he said. "You know how these tabloids are."

"Be straight with me, Derek, do you think the kid is gay? Where there's smoke there's fire, and he's got an awful lot of smoke coming out of his tailpipe."

Neil was trying not to laugh.

"What was that story they had right after the spread about Jackson?" Derek said. "Something about sewer rats running the Pentagon from a secret lair in the subways of New York?"

Peter laughed. "Point taken. Well, tell him to keep his chin up. His album is still flying off the shelves, and there's no celebrity that hasn't been the butt of an ugly rumor at some point in their career."

After they got of the phone, Neil said, "I heard an ugly rumor that Peter Montgomery is a homophobic asshole."

"That's 'cause he's secretly in love with Rod Stewart," I said.

We all laughed, partly out of relief at another crisis averted.

After leaving Clean Slate, I picked Jess up from the recording studio and showed her around my place. I walked her around to the starting points of all the hiking trails nearby. "There's no beach outside the door, but the hills are quiet and beautiful."

"It's lovely, Jackson. And if I want to go to the beach, I'll just call a taxi."

I got her settled in the loft room over my garage.

"It's not exactly the Mondrian," I said.

"I don't care, I love it," Jess said. "There's something about hotels that saddens me. I'd much rather be a guest in someone's home, however humble. Besides, England never really discovered the futon, and I think they're quite comfortable." She looked angelic with the sun rays from the skylight swimming across the top of her curls.

"If I were straight, I wouldn't have to look any further," I said.

She blushed, which I rarely saw her do.

"That's sweet, Jackson. I actually feel the same way. I hope that doesn't make me your—what is that terrible word you use over here? Fag hag?"

I laughed.

"Can't a woman enjoy the company of gay men without becoming a hag?" she asked.

"When I get my place in New York, you can have your own wing. The Jess fag-hag suite."

"So you are moving to New York?"

"The more I talk about it, the more it sounds real."

"Well, keep talking, baby. You're way too cool for this town anyway."

She had only been in LA for three days. I reminded her of that fact.

"Yes, but I know, I can tell."

"It's crazy, isn't it?"

"It's LA LA land."

"Yeah, and it's about to be BUH BYE land."

Jess laughed.

After a brief chat with Neil to set up my time with Derek the next day, Jess and I watched movies and ate popcorn. I noticed her scrapbook sticking out of her bag. It seemed uncharacteristically girly, like how a ten-year-old would have it.

"What's that?" I asked. "It's cute."

"It's kind of naff, like a security blanket or something. But it makes me feel grounded when I'm on the road."

"Can I peek?"

"You can peek, but no mocking comments, please."

It had the usual scrapbook stuff, plus tons of mementos and pictures of what I presumed to be her mom. On the last inside flap was her birth certificate. The more I glanced at it, the more it seemed to basically be a shrine to her mom. Her emotion at Neil's was even more understandable now.

The next morning we got up and had breakfast, then took a short hike. When we got back, I asked Jess if she wanted a ride to the recording studio, but she said she wasn't due until that afternoon.

"I'll have to catch up with you later then. I must get to Cher's villa and write a little ditty for Sandra Bullock's new movie," I said, mocking the LA persona I was beginning to despise so much. "'Cause I'm too fabulous for words."

"You go, girl," Jess said.

I gave her the number of a cab company and drew her a little map so she was geographically situated.

The Pacific Coast Highway, the beautiful stretch from Santa Monica toward Malibu, was pretty empty, and I drove fast with the windows down. Cliffs were to my right, and on my left was the gray, glassy wonder of the ocean. I arrived at Cher's house and entered through the kitchen door, punching in the code I remembered from when I'd stayed there. It was t-i-g-e r, after the name of the first Chihuahua she and Sonny had owned.

I walked in on quite a sight. The kitchen was strewn with little white and yellow globs that looked like snot. The place reeked of smoke. What was going on?

Derek was on a stepladder, looking frazzled, wiping up the bits on the ceiling with paper towels.

"Should I even ask?" I said.

Derek looked genuinely distraught to be caught amid the chaos, like a kid who had done something terribly wrong. I couldn't help but laugh.

"I put some eggs on to boil and took two pills I thought were aspirin but they put me to sleep!" he yelled.

I could barely hear him because the fire alarm was going off and an extremely loud recording of a voice was instructing the "homeowner" on what to do. The only problem was the recording was in Spanish.

I looked at Cher's kitchen covered with exploded eggs and the pot burned black. Being on the Atkins diet on and off for years, Derek was constantly making egg salad.

"Precaucion! Deje por favor el premesis usando la salida mas cercana a usted!"

"What the fuck is it saying?" Derek was getting a bit frantic.

I messed with the knobs to see if I could change it to English.

"Hola! Usted huele humo no lo hace precaucion alarmada!"

I started laughing again. After a minute, he started laughing, too, as the recorded voice continued to yell at us in Spanish.

The firemen called and we couldn't find the phone. We paged the phone and found it inside the grand piano. They called back and finally turned the alarm off remotely. There was a great calm. I helped Derek clean the rest of it up.

"Thank god Sylvester wasn't here today. That girl would have lost it," Derek said.

Sylvester was Cher's highly dramatic, effeminate Puerto Rican houseboy. He was the one who lived there the most out of anyone, which is why the alarm had been programmed in Spanish. When I had stayed there previously, he'd given me such a long lecture on dos and don'ts, I thought he'd never leave. He ended by telling me to wash my hands before touching the piano, insinuating through gestures with his little finger that I had been touching myself. You never knew if he was joking or not, but you didn't want to be on his bad side. Apparently Cher worshipped him.

When we sat down at the piano, I said to Derek in a stern Sylvester voice, "Did you wash hands first?"

He laughed.

"Can you imagine if he had seen the egg mess? He would have had a conniption."

After a moment Derek started playing a melody and I hummed along.

"It's supposed to be a love song, but for teens," he said. "Girl meets boy. He sees her at the top of the stairs. And 'I can't believe my eyes it's really her' type of thing."

"Can it be a him?"

"Oh, the eternal question. Well, dear, for the general public it will be a girl-boy romance. But we can visualize sheep if we want to."

We brainstormed all afternoon, taking breaks to eat apples and yes, egg salad (Derek made another batch, this time with the timer on). The lyrics and music gelled as we threw out ideas, our instincts clicking with each other as we took turns playing bits of melody at the piano. We were on fire. It was like the feeling William Hurt described after getting fed information from Holly Hunter while on the air in *Broadcast News*. We were a machine.

> *If I'm dreaming,*
> *Don't wake me up*
> *Cause I'm breathing you in*

*And it feels all right*
*I'm taking this in*
*Tonight*

By the end of the day, we had the song. As we were singing it, Derek on harmony, I noticed him looking at my hands playing the chords. When he noticed me noticing him, he looked away.

# 69

The next night, Neil picked Derek and me up and we went to the Crescent Hotel to meet Jess and Liam for dinner. Liam had fetched Jess from her recording session earlier so they could have a little family time in the afternoon.

On our way through the lobby we passed the usual film industry posers, along with a group of people desperately trying to look indie rock. We made our way to the tables around the pool. When Jess saw me, she immediately grabbed me and gave me a big kiss. A camera flash went off. I looked over and saw Jed, already putting a camera back into his bag and heading for the exit.

"What's wrong?" Neil asked, "You've gone pale."

"Nothing, I just—that was Jed who took that picture!"

Neil gasped and said, "Rent boy Jed?"

"Yeah."

Once the initial shock wore off, I found myself not caring. Maybe Derek's advice not to take any of it seriously was fully sinking in. As long as it wasn't my homophobic, asshole stalker, people could take all the pictures of me they wanted to.

Neil said, "Great, a new Hollywood hyphenate: social climbing-rentboy-celebrity stalker-scumbag."

"I'm pretty sure that combination has been seen in Hollywood once or twice before," Derek said dryly.

*Yes, and one of them is your ex-boyfriend.* I was so glad Derek was finally freeing himself from Aden's clutches. He deserved to finally be happy.

Jess asked how I knew Jed, which took us on a detour to the Timothy saga. After introducing Derek to Jess and Liam, I explained the whole story. The waiter-actor-model couldn't get a word in edgewise.

Liam was more animated than I'd seen him before, looking earnestly interested and gasping in all the right places. The Timothy-Jed pool scene was a scandalous hit, except with Neil, who started rolling his eyes.

"Timothy Meyer is so two months ago."

"Shhhh!" Jess said. "You're just saying that because you've heard this before."

Derek pretended to be apathetic but was hanging on every word, despite having heard the story before.

When I explained that Timothy was the one who first outed me to the press, Liam looked horrified. "What a mess," he said.

"Completely," I said, "but I've moved on."

Jess said, "And I thought heterosexual romance was bad! If every time I met someone I had to not only worry that they'd break my heart but that they might ruin my career, too, I might never date again." She looked at her dad. "It makes falling in love seem very brave."

Liam blushed.

"Falling in love is brave no matter who you are," Derek said, and we all toasted to it.

It suddenly occurred to me that I was happier just sitting there with them than I had been at any of Barkley's glamorous parties or even meeting Sarah McLachlan at Bono's birthday.

Liam and I ended up in the men's bathroom at the same time.

I'd gotten an idea of something I wanted to do for Jess after seeing her scrapbook. Kane had been so successful getting the dirt on Timothy that I thought she might also be able to find Jess's mom. "I don't mean to be nosy, Liam, but do you know where Jess's mom went when she left?"

"Why do you ask?"

I didn't want to tell anyone about my plan in case it didn't work out, so I told him part of the truth. "I just can't understand how someone could leave you and Jess without notice. You're both such wonderful people. How could anyone not understand that there's nothing better out there than that?"

He blushed.

"I'm sorry, Liam, I didn't mean to put you on the spot."

"No, it's okay, Jackson. To be honest, I've wondered that many times myself—not about me, but about Jess. Isabelle adored her. And I know she never would have left if she had any doubt that I would do everything I could to give Jess a good life. But she had a troubled soul. It was like she couldn't just let herself be happy with a normal life."

It struck me that the bathroom at the Crescent was an odd place to be having such a deep conversation, but I felt touched that Liam was opening up to me. Like Neil, he seemed to be letting go of old restraints. And of course the two bottles of wine we'd already had at dinner probably didn't hurt either.

He continued, "At any rate, I don't think even she knew where she was going when she left. I've tried a few times to track her down—for Jess's sixteenth birthday, before her first paying gig—but none of her old friends knew where she went, and both her parents have passed away."

We both finished washing our hands, and he crumpled his towel up in his fist. "When I'm angry with her for causing Jess so much pain, I imagine her drowning her sorrows in some dank pub in Newcastle. But I prefer to think she's found her dream, and one day she'll come back into Jess's life again."

We both threw our towels in the trash.

"Listen, Jackson, I must tell you," Liam said, with alcohol-edged emotion, "It's been quite scary having, you know, Jess being so swooped up into this life of celebrity, and...oh bullocks!" He stared at me and laughed. "I'm just saying I'm glad you've taken a liking to her and that she's quite keen on you as well. You seem like a nice balance, the two of you, and she needs looking after. I may not be, well, she's growing up..." His eyes started to well up.

I couldn't think of what to say, so I did what my heart wanted to do. I gave him a hug.

A buffed-out, supermasculine Guido dude from the 818 entered the men's room at that moment. He looked at us with disgust and we started laughing.

Liam camped it up as we left, which I had never seen him do

before. I guess he was completely "out" now, and it was great to see.

"C'mon, darling," he said in a high-pitched voice, "let's go flirt with the foxy waiter."

Back at the table, Derek's body language had closed inward a bit, and I asked him if everything was okay.

"It will be," he said. "I'm glad you're back." I looked at him, wanting more. He dabbed at the corner of his full lips with his napkin.

"I just want to go back to my house. I love Cher's, but it's not home. After we sign the papers tomorrow, the break will be complete. Can you believe it's come to this?" The napkin was now dabbing at his forehead.

"Better now than later." I said.

"The irony is that I don't even want to live in LA anymore. I mean, look at this place."

I looked around at the people in the restaurant. It was like one big Prozac- and Botox-induced fashion ad. When you really looked at people, you could see right through them, as if their perfect exterior images were transparent.

"I know. Two words," I said. "New. York."

Jess overheard and said, "I love New York. There's like this breath there, this giant breath, and you can feel it; it's like waves."

"No more wine for you, sweetheart," Liam said, veering briefly back into fatherly mode. The rest of the dinner he was strictly in boyfriend mode, now comfortable with his hands on Neil, and Jess didn't seem to mind. If only every family could be so adult about it, so accepting. After all it's just two people who like each other.

As we were leaving, Jess pulled me aside and whispered, "He fancies you."

I mouthed the word *who* and she gestured toward Derek.

After Neil and Liam said their good-byes, Derek, Jess, and I piled into Neil's car. Jess took the front seat so she could pick out a radio station. In the dark back seat on the way home, I could have sworn I felt Derek's thigh slightly pressing against mine. I pressed back.

# 70

The next morning I let Jess borrow my car, since Derek was driving me over to Mark Diamond's to sign the papers. We were silent in the car. Derek laid his head on my shoulder at a red light, and it was as if I could feel the weight in his mind, a weight that after a few signatures I hoped would soon be lifted. As of that afternoon, Aden was no longer going to be in our lives. I was so happy, most of all for Derek. Sometimes, I had discovered, the strongest happiness is the kind you feel for someone else.

The gate to the guesthouse at Mr. Cuddle's house was open. We made our way back toward the pool, and Mark's office.

"You're sure Aden's not going to be here, right?" I whispered to Derek.

"God, no."

We went in and sat down, and Mark showed us all the different papers. There were some severing my ties with Aden, and a whole stack involving him and Derek. Aden's signature was already on the documents, and it was strange seeing his familiar writing. Like a ghost in the room. Mark was talking legal jargon, but I wasn't listening. I was looking at Derek from a different place.

We signed and came out to the courtyard where Mark had some champagne chilling for us. Derek and I toasted, but it was an oddly joyless moment. It was like toasting to surgery. It wasn't cause for celebration, but it had to be done.

Afterward, I drove Derek home and got him settled in.

"Are you going to be all right?" I said.

"Yeah, sure," he said, but I wasn't convinced.

"Listen, I'll just stay for a while, okay?"

A while turned into us watching the *Sopranos* and drinking schnapps and eating ice cream.

I woke up in the middle of the night leaning against him on the couch. I had been dreaming about Timothy Meyer, and my first instinct was to squirm away. But then I remembered where I was. This was Derek; I was home.

I woke him up and he started mumbling gibberish, which made me giggle. After he became more conscious, he sleepily told me to grab whatever I wanted and take the guest room.

The next morning I woke up before Derek and took a skinny-dip in the pool. The morning air was cool and still, a few birds waking up in the trees. I got out and went to the pool house. It was always stocked like a spa, with piles of fresh towels, bottles of sunscreen and lotions, and a bunch of robes hanging against one wall. I slipped one of the robes on and was walking out when I saw Derek coming onto the patio. His hair was a mess and he looked adorable. I felt this urge to take him in my arms, but I told myself not to think that way because the Aden breakup was so fresh.

Derek looked at my robe and all of a sudden turned pensive.

"What is it?" I asked.

"Oh, nothing, sorry."

"Something's wrong, sweetie, I can see it."

Derek balanced on his right foot, then his left. Finally he stood straight and looked at me. "It's just—I gave Aden that robe and he only wore it once. He said it was too old-fashioned, like me."

"First of all, this is a fantastic robe! And second of all, I'd rather be old-fashioned than a pretentious prick."

He laughed. "Thanks, Jackson."

We went inside to make breakfast. As I was washing fruit, we heard the nominations for the Grammy's on the radio.

I was nominated for best new artist.

Both of us acted like we didn't hear it at first, and then we started jumping up and down. I couldn't figure out which was more surreal: that I was making breakfast for Derek in Aden's robe or that I'd been nominated for a Grammy.

Then I realized Derek must have known already. I looked at him.

"They called us at Clean Slate yesterday, but I wanted you to hear it for yourself."

"Oh. My. God," I said.

"What?" Derek asked.

"What on *earth* am I going to wear?"

We laughed.

I turned my cell phone back on and listened to the messages:

Bree said, "I'm setting up a press conference for you, and you better get ready for a week in New York on talk shows—start your Crest whitening strips now," she warned.

Neil tried to sound nonchalant in his message, but the excitement in his voice was obvious. "Have you heard the news yet? Call me!"

I looked at Derek pouring coffee into two mugs and realized I wanted to just revel in this moment with him for a while before the inevitable circus began. I turned the ringer off on my phone and leaned against the counter next to him. He started scrambling egg whites.

"Are you sure you don't want to boil them?" I asked.

"Very funny," he said.

I finished washing and cutting the fruit, and we ate outside on the patio. The sky was so blue, more so than it had ever seemed before that moment. Derek knew I couldn't wait to call people.

"Fuck the rest of the breakfast. Get on the phone!"

I turned my ringer back on and called my parents. My mom said, "My angel, my little Jackson! I knew when you were five years old you were going to be a star! Holy smokes! Can I tell Max?"

"Sure, and tell Dad I'm finally going to get to fly him somewhere."

"So we can come to the ceremony?"

"Of course, Mom!" I heard my dad in the background saying, "I wouldn't miss it for the world!"

"And I'm sure there will be an after-party, too," I said.

"At Bungalow 8," Derek said, grinning at my look of surprise. Bungalow 8 was a premier NYC hotspot that had to be booked months in advance. I realized it meant Derek had had faith that I would be nominated. I melted.

I heard the call-waiting beep and got off the phone with my mom to talk to Neil.

"My god, Neil, I feel like I'm pregnant or something."

"Well, let's not go that far. But you know what? From the day I saw your demo in the stacks at Clean Slate, I knew this day would come. I did. All I have to say is, I need to go shopping."

I called Jess's cell phone next.

"Where were you last night, you little vixen! Did you get some?"

When I told her about the nomination, she screamed so loud I had to hold the phone away from my ear. Once she'd calmed down, I told her I'd be back home in a little while.

I changed back into the previous night's clothes. I told Derek, "Well, I guess I should go prepare for the onslaught." It felt like my life had become one big press conference.

"Wear your hat at all times," he said, putting it on my head and kissing my temple. I felt the warmth of his hand on my forearm. "And don't go anywhere on Sunset Strip—it's tourist hell. Now get out of here. I've got to de-Aden the place. Oh, by the way, take the robe. Throw it out the window on the 101 or burn it. Do something with it."

I laughed as he threw it over my head.

"I'll use it to wipe my ass," I said.

"Jackson Poole. I did not hear that." He pretended to be shocked, then said, "Okay, fine. Wipe away."

Later that afternoon Jess and I celebrated a little, and when she went to meet with her label I called Kane, but got sent to voice mail. It was the first time I'd ever known her not to pick up on the first ring. I left an annoyingly long message telling her I wanted her to try to find Jess's mother and giving her a list of all the details I'd been able to scavenge from Jess's prized scrapbook.

I took a bath and called Brian.

"Oh my god—I want royalties for my airport spectacle."

"Don't worry, it will all be in my memoirs."

"Okay, you can just pay me now."

I dried off, sat on my couch, and said the words to myself: I am a Grammy-nominated artist.

# 71

I said it again the minute I woke up the next day: I'm a Grammy-nominated artist! I started laughing out loud in my bed, kicking my feet and twisting around. If someone was eavesdropping on the scene, they'd probably think I was insane.

There was a note in my kitchen from Jess saying she was going to the studio to record for a couple of hours. I looked out my window and saw Emilio's cinnamon arms digging in the neighbor's garden. He noticed me looking and raised an eyebrow. I flashed to the feeling of warmth from Derek's lips on my temple, his soft touch on my arm. I waved hello to Emilio, then stepped back from the window.

As I was getting out of the shower there was a knock on my door. Jess had a key, so my heart stopped briefly. Were there reporters here? I looked through the peephole, still in my towel, and was very happy to see Neil—except his face was sad.

He walked in and handed me yet another *National Enquirer* article.

"At least I'm keeping them in business," I said.

The picture of Jess and me that Jed had taken at the Crescent Hotel was on the cover, and inside there were photos from my tour. One of them was a grainy, poor-quality shot of Neil and me holding hands in the fog from the second time I saw the paparazzo/stalker.

Neil said, "Maybe he was so pissed because he followed you everywhere and could never get a good shot."

There was a photo of me lying on the stage in Hong Kong captioned, "Collapsed from stress about hiding his true identity!" I felt sick. I once heard Susan Sarandon say she never read anything that was written about her. Well, definitely not in a sham of a magazine like this. Go, Susan.

I saw Derek's old BMW pull up. I threw the *Enquirer* on the table. He walked in to Neil and me sitting silently, with only the buzz of the fridge. Was this what happens to someone who has just been nominated for a Grammy?

"Listen," Derek said, sitting down next to me, "I saw it. You know what? They find something that smells just a little and they feed on it like vultures. I think the *Access Live* and now the *Oprah* thing are going to fend off Peter for now. Just forget about it. This is your time to—"

"Throw in the towel?" I said, realizing I still had one on.

Neil chuckled.

"Listen, I'm gonna go put on some pants and find some, I don't know, arsenic comes to mind."

"Drama queen," Neil said.

"Make yourselves at home, gentlemen," I said, then went into my bathroom and sat on the cold floor tiles. I needed to be close to the ground. Why was this happening? Because I accidentally lit that girl's hair on fire in fourth grade? Because I used to steal batteries and candy from the corner store? What the hell! The shot of me on the stage, that moment of complete vulnerability, was now shown to the masses, making it almost grotesque. My stomach growled and I felt a wave of nausea. I crawled over to the toilet and threw up. Then I rinsed with mouthwash and felt better enough to rejoin Derek and Neil.

When I came back to the living room, Liam and Jess had also arrived.

"I didn't say I was having a party," I said upon seeing them all.

Jess had just noticed the magazine.

"Oh my god, my hair looks so frizzed, and that dress is not very becoming."

"If hear any more comments like that out of you, I'm telling Liam to get your cute little ass out of LA immediately," I said. "I'm telling you, the place is a germ."

The phone rang. I put it on speakerphone because I couldn't find the cordless. It was Kane.

"I am so sorry for the delay, my dear boy—my former yoga teacher finally came through for me on the sperm! Ooh, the limbs on that man...time for a pretzel baby, I guess. Anyway, he called right when I'm usually ovulating, so I had to fly out to Chicago for a *Big Chill* moment. I'd dug up a bunch of stuff on your case before I had to leave, but there were some loose ends I just tied up today."

Jess was drawing circles with her finger near her temple, and Liam looked perplexed. Neil and Derek were trying not to laugh.

"Regarding, you know, the stalker thing," She continued.

"Yes, I know. What have you got?"

Everyone inched a little closer.

"Fuck, I broke a nail. Do you know what it's going to be like giving up scotch for nine months? Nightmare."

"Kane, about the stalker," I said.

"At least I can eat large quantities of chocolate."

Jess giggled.

"Is someone there with you?" Kane asked.

"No, go on."

"Why the hell do you have me on speaker?"

"Kane, I can't find the phone, please!"

"Well, I see we've had our latte and the *Enquirer* this morning."

Everyone moved a little farther away from the speaker, and I moved closer to go for a sincere approach.

"Kane, I love you, you're great, but can you tell us—me the news?"

"Okay, I'm starting the clock and you'll need that Grammy 'cause you may have to hock it to pay my bill. Babies aren't cheap and prices just went up."

I fell back and lay on the floor, exasperated.

"Okay, it turns out your paparazzo freak is ex-military, which would explain how he could get into your hotel room. There is also some white supremacist history in his youth—lovely guy, huh?—but no history of violence."

I sat up, renewed.

"I tracked the flower box to a florist in Torrance. I had to bribe the guy fifty bucks, but he finally showed me the credit card slip for the order. Guess who it was?"

No one stirred. We just waited for what seemed like eternity.

"Timothy Meyer."

"What!? Hang on a second; I'm putting you on hold."

I got up and walked to the window.

"The one from the pool?" Liam asked.

"Yes," Neil said, shushing him up.

I looked out the window and anger blurred my vision. I almost wished it had been the paparazzo. But someone I was intimate with?

"Creepy," was all I could say. I turned around. Everyone looked scared of what I was going to do. I took a deep breath and walked back over to the phone.

"Okay, Kane, back."

"So, I have a feeling Timothy Meyer wants you to know it was him. He is now, get this, the editor-in-chief of the *National Enquirer*."

All of our mouths opened.

"You're not serious."

"Yeah, only place that would take him after he got out of jail, I suppose. And of course he'd already showed them he was their kind of people by giving them that nude photo of you with the rose petals. That was very hot, by the way."

Liam had found the staff credits page in the *Enquirer* and was pointing out Timothy's name to Neil.

Kane continued, "I found out that Timothy's start date at the *Enquirer* was just a couple days before your first sighting of the charming orange-visor guy in London. You'll probably never be able to prove that Timothy got him to do all the creepy scare tactics, but I'd be shocked if that wasn't the case."

"Great. Well now I'm royally screwed. Oh wait, did you hear that? I think it was my career spiraling down the drain."

"Dear, chin up now. Just 'cause enquiring minds want to know, it doesn't mean they want to know the truth."

"He's never going to stop. I'm fucked."

"There's more, dear. That last bit of digging I was talking about? I think you'll really like it." She paused for effect.

Neil rolled his eyes.

"What?" I asked.

"It seems Timothy's wife's fancy family is not pleased about his new career choice, and there's talk of cutting him loose. They're sending him ten thousand a month right now just to be a good boy, and they've been paying off his back taxes and bad debt. If they decide to cut the cord, he not only loses the money, there's a good chance he could still end up in jail."

My little gathering could not keep quiet for that one. After the outpouring of sighs and gasps, Kane figured it out.

"There *are* people there. Jackson! You're not recording this, are you?"

"It's just my managers...tell me though, what does that mean for me?"

"Do your managers have badges?"

"No, Kane, it's fine. Just tell me what all this means for me."

She seemed appeased. "My dear boy, how long have you lived in Hollywood? It's called blackmail! Or in Timothy's case, an ethically sound righting of the scales of justice...ooh, I have to write that down."

Liam, Neil, and Derek all did the wave on my couch, as if the mention of blackmail were the home run.

"But what do I have to blackmail him about?"

"Any scandal at this point would be enough to make his wife's family wash their hands of him. The divorce isn't final yet, and she would love nothing more than to have one of Timothy's ex-lovers on record about his affairs. Or since you can't be officially out anywhere, you could just paint him a little picture."

"She's good," Derek whispered.

"You're in LA. How hard would it be to hire an actor to go to the corporate headquarters of his wife's daddy's company and make a scene? Or better yet, to their country club. You have no idea how uptight these people are, Jackson. They basically have permanent icicles up their asses. All his ill-gotten gains are hanging by a thread."

All of a sudden I felt empowered by the thought of having ammunition.

"Do you have his contact info?"

"I had a feeling you'd be asking me that." She gave me his work and private numbers, and I wondered how she'd managed it. I'd had sex with the guy and still not been given his direct line.

"About that other job—" she said.

I cut her off before Jess or Liam could hear anything. "We can talk about that later, okay? I've got to run now. Thank you for everything, Kane. You're amazing!"

When I hung up, I heard two car doors slam at the same time. I looked out my window and immediately ducked. While I was on the phone, about twenty paparazzi with cameras had shown up, and a few more cars were pulling up.

"Derek, we may need your water pistol."

"You can stay up at my house—it's totally secure, a gate and all, and they won't know."

Jess gave me a knowing look that I didn't meet.

"Jess, you're welcome to come, too."

"Okay, well I definitely have to get out of here."

We had to think fast. Emilio was still in the neighbor's garden, so Neil went out the back and explained our predicament to him. Ten minutes later, I was lying in a wheelbarrow underneath yard clippings, with Emilio rolling me right behind the backs of all the photographers and into his truck parked on the street. Neil, Liam, and Jess walked out my front door as a distraction, and Liam was posing for the cameras as Neil dragged him into the car. Derek had put on some of my old clothes and a hat, and followed behind me and Emilio with a rake and a shovel.

My hair full of dirt, I peered out over the truck as they drove me out of there. I could hear Derek and Emilio laughing in the front seat. But I really didn't feel like laughing. Was this going to end?

# 72

We pulled up to Derek's and I shook my dirt off.

"Never a dull moment," Derek said. "Listen, Emilio, you're a lifesaver. Hang on."

Derek went in and grabbed a bottle of wine for him.

Emilio beamed.

"You rock star?" he asked me.

I nodded.

I could almost see the thoughts twirling in his head. I thanked him again sincerely for the rescue, then went inside and took a long shower.

When I came out, Derek had made me soup. He handed me the phone and said, "Bree."

"Listen, sweet cheeks, I'm sorry about the second sting. I've temporarily cancelled the local press junket for your Grammy nomination. But not to worry, we can still control this. I've got you on *Oprah* tomorrow."

"Tomorrow?" I hadn't tried the soup yet.

"That's right, *manana*. She's sending her private plane, the big O in the sky, to pick you up. You leave tonight."

"Shit!"

"She understands what bastards the tabloids are, and she loves your music. Apparently one of her nieces has a shrine to you."

Derek was looking at me from across the table like he knew all of this before.

"Kia just got out of rehab," Bree continued, "and she's agreed to appear with you as a hetero cover. We all agree it'll be good for her to get back in the spotlight. Now go eat your soup."

I set down the phone. "What was that?"

"She filled me in while you were in the shower. The *Oprah* thing is the perfect counterbalance."

We sat in silence. I was overwhelmed. A tear landed in my soup.

"Sweetheart, I've told you before, people have survived worse scandals than this."

"I know, but where will it end? Is he out to destroy me? How dare he! And for what? What did I ever do to him?"

I pulled out the info Kane had given me and reached for the phone. Derek grabbed it before I could. "Don't give him the satisfaction of seeing he's gotten to you. Wait. Finish your soup, go for a swim, and then when you call him, act cold and dispassionate."

Swimming laps underwater, I realized that Derek was right. I should just take the high road. Timothy's whole goal was probably to freak me out. I didn't want to give him the satisfaction. I dried off and we sat in the living room, Derek on another phone listening in.

Timothy answered on the first ring.

"Hi, Timothy, it's Jackson Poole. Remember me? I just wanted to call and thank you for all the lovely presents and messages you've been sending. It was great having that doll to snuggle up to in Hong Kong—you know it gets lonely on the road. And I've really been enjoying all the free publicity, too."

There was a brief pause, then Timothy said, "You won't be enjoying it when the next issue comes out."

"Well, that remains to be seen, doesn't it? You know, I'm really curious why you've seen fit to do me all these favors. What did I do to deserve such nice treatment? Did you worship my cock that much?"

"I believe in payback, Jackson. And you fucked me over royally by giving my bitch wife's detective my number."

"This is all over a *phone number?*"

I started to lose it, and Derek motioned at me to tone it down.

"A phone number that helped the feds track me down and put me in jail, yes. I was hours away from making a deal that would have gotten me completely out of debt, with plenty left over."

An image popped into my head of him in Miami making deals with Cuban drug runners. He'd always seemed like the coke type.

"It seems to me you've done pretty well in spite of everything."

"If you like being on a leash!"

"Well, it's interesting you should mention that, Timothy, because I've actually heard quite a bit about the leash you're on." I made my voice sound falsely sympathetic. "Your wife's family seems to be running out of understanding for you."

"Deborah's family can go fuck themselves." He was rattled; I could hear it in his voice. "And you can fuck yourself, too. When the next issue comes out, your career is gone."

"Oh really, why is that?"

His voice was sneering, triumphant. "Because your little friend Jed is selling me the smoking gun. Your queer ass naked and drunk, in flagrante delicto with another man."

Shit! I looked at Derek. He wrote me a note. *You're fine! Stay strong!* I took a deep breath and let it out silently.

"You know, Timothy, I think it would be really unwise of you to publish that picture, or any picture of my friends or family, ever again."

He laughed. "I can publish anything I want. I was thinking after the next issue I might work in a little statutory rape angle. That little slice you've been hanging out with, what is she, seventeen?"

A wave of acidic anger pulsed through me and Derek put his hand on my arm. I looked down and noticed my fist was balled, the knuckles white. I took another breath and shook out my hand.

"Well, Timothy, you have to do what you have to do. But I can tell you this. If I see one more photo, one more story, even one more insinuation about me or anyone I care about that can be traced back to you, I won't pause for a heartbeat before getting in touch with your wife's family."

"Go ahead."

"I might just do that. Today a friend of mine suggested that I hire someone to make a scene at your father-in-law's country club. At first I thought it was a bad idea, but then I started thinking how funny it would be to see a real fem twink walk into a country club and ask for you. Or better yet, a tricked-out leather daddy.

Can't you just picture it? Of course, he could also ask for your wife instead and announce that you sent him. Which do you think her dad would find funnier?"

There was no response. "Oh, that's right, he's rather uptight isn't he? Not the type to understand a harmless little *prank*." Maybe I had watched too many B movies on tour, but I couldn't help letting a little inflection into the last word. Derek gave me a thumbs up.

There was a long silence on the phone. I waited and waited, then found myself filling the space. "Listen, *Tim*, it's obvious you feel I wronged you, but I can assure you that was never my intention. Isn't what you've done to me so far enough? Let's be done with this and get on with our lives."

The silence continued, then he cleared his throat. He sounded different, more human. More like the Timothy I'd fallen in love with. "There's nothing I can do about the picture. My boss already knows about it because I've been trying to get approval for the fee. Jed's been holding out for more money."

"Well why not tell your boss he wants an amount you know they won't agree to?"

"I can do that, but then Jed will just sell the picture to someone else."

I sighed. "Well, I can't hold that against you, can I? I just want this vendetta to stop."

"They're not going to let me stop printing stories about you."

"I don't know what to tell you about that, except that with ten thousand a month and all the talent you have I think you're wasting yourself there anyway."

Timothy coughed. "Are we square then?"

No, we would never be square for all he'd put me through. "Yes, we're square."

I hung up the phone.

"I'm proud of you, you did great!" Derek said.

"Thanks."

I felt exhaustion hit me like a brick wall. I was asleep before Derek had finished reheating my soup.

# 73

A short while later Derek and I were stepping onto Oprah's plane, which made Barkley's seem like a rickshaw. Bree had told me she rarely flew show guests on her plane, but apparently she and Bree "went way back." The main area looked like some elaborate living room out of Cape Cod. There were long couches and low tables with huge seashells filled with gourmet jellybeans. I tried to pick up one of the shells but it didn't move. Glued down for safety in flight.

When we got to cruising altitude, Derek fell asleep and the butler in the sky dimmed the lights. After my power nap at Derek's, I was wide awake. My head was a whirlpool of thoughts: *What happens when Jed finds out the* Enquirer *isn't buying? Was it inevitable that my career was doomed? What would my dad think?*

Derek woke up as if he could sense my anxiety.

"What should I do?" I asked. "Should I buy the photo off Jed?"

"Sweetheart, it has been my experience that once blackmailers start, they never stop."

"So what do I do?"

Derek rubbed his eyes and sat up a little.

"What's important to you?"

"My family, my friends, making music."

"Is a photo in the press going to prevent you from having any of those things?"

"Yes! Well, maybe."

"No, your friends and family don't care about the press, and nothing can prevent you from making music. There's no photo or magazine or TV show on the planet that can take away what you have inside you."

I watched him drift back to sleep as the first signs of dawn lit the horizon. I sat up thinking and watching the sky change from red to orange and then yellow as we touched down in Chicago.

The green room at the *Oprah* show was all done in baby blues, with chilled Evian bottles and silver bowls brimming with ripe green apples. While Derek was talking with the producers I saw Kia, looking beautiful and healthy in a dark blue dress. We hugged.

"How are you?" I asked.

"I'm great. Happy to be clean, excited to live my own life, and I am so leaving the soap world behind. Get this, they had my character die of an overdose!"

I picked up my water to clink hers, "To the contrary!"

Oprah was extremely gregarious, telling me I was "cute as a button." It was only when we were taping the show that she became more serious.

"So tell me how you got into the biz. Your parents are singers?"

"Yes, actually, they're in a bluegrass band. I grew up in what you could call a modern-day Partridge family."

"And you're Danny as a blonde?"

The audience laughed.

"Well, I have to tell you," she said, "my niece left your CD in my car, and I can't stop listening!"

I put my hand on my heart. "I'm honored."

"Will you show us some of that mojo on our stage?"

"I'd be happy to."

I performed solo, since Leroy and Rico couldn't make it on such short notice. While I was singing, I thought about all the people watching and how many of them even read or cared about the *Enquirer.* The studio audience was quiet and attentive, and they burst out in applause before I even finished the last note.

"We'll be back with more Jackson Poole!" Oprah said.

During the break I whispered, "Your plane is the *bomb.*"

"Not too shabby, huh?"

"Not at all, thanks so much."

"Anytime. You're going to have to pose for a picture with my niece."

"I'll even sing a song for her!"

The stage manager counted down, three...two...one...

The cameras and lights came back on.

"We're here with Jackson Poole, singing sensation and rising star. Tell me, Jackson, what was it like in the early days? Did you play on the street for change?"

"Not exactly, but I did put a lot of miles on my old car. And I met a lot of interesting people along the way."

"Speaking of, we have a blast from the past here for you today. Ladies and gentleman, please welcome Autumn to the stage!"

What? This really happened on these shows? My mind raced as Oprah greeted Autumn. She was just as beautiful as I remembered. Her red bob, the funky clothes, the determined walk. It really was her! My on-air response was authentic as could be. I was embarrassed but at the same time curious. How the hell did they find her? Or did she find them?

I hugged her; she smelled the same, lavender mixed with a tad of perspiration. She bounced up and down and said, "Congratulations!"

Oprah asked Autumn how we met, and Autumn told her the story of our kiss in the police car. The audience oohed and aahed.

"So," Oprah said with a wry smile, "what are the chances of you guys getting back together?"

The studio audience egged us on.

Autumn laughed heartily and said, "I'm afraid that won't be possible."

During the break Autumn told me she'd been contacted earlier by Aden in his search to show my hetero past, then Bree had called her the day before to ask if she would appear on the show. It was all so strange, but I was glad to see her.

"Now, we have another guest, one of Jackson's Hollywood girl-friends, former soap star Kia Diamond!"

Kia sat down, and as Oprah asked her how we met, I felt more and more wrong about the whole thing. Here I was on *Oprah*, in front of millions of viewers, still being forced to live a lie. After the next break, Oprah brought up the inevitable topic, which she'd prepped me about before the show.

"There have been many rumors regarding your sexuality, Jackson, including that you allegedly dated David Gef—"

I didn't let her say it. What was this thing about David Geffen? Something resembling a flame, with the heat of the truth, built up inside me.

"Listen, Oprah," I said, "rumors are rumors, but do we really need to go there? Frankly, I'm so tired of all of this drama over my sexuality. I mean, it's the millennium, right? I'm sure you have plenty of viewers who are gay and living in fear of anyone finding out because they might lose their jobs or be harassed. And for what? Whom they choose to love? To me, it's a civil-rights issue."

"That's an excellent point," Oprah said.

The studio audience began to applaud, and I went on after they quieted down.

"The way I look at it is like this, some people like jam on their toast and some people like butter, and there are those who prefer both. What we all do behind closed doors is irrelevant."

The studio audience started cheering again, this time uncontrollably. There was another break, and I wondered, were they cheering for me or for what I was saying? One thing was certain, if Aden were still with the company, he would have been peeing his Gucci underwear.

The break ended, and there I was, on national television, spilling my guts to Oprah and not caring about record sales or Aden or being butch. The crowd ate it up.

"So you're telling us your sexuality should have no bearing on your credibility as an artist..."

"Of course not, Oprah," I said, "who cares?"

"I don't, Jackson."

So far I hadn't actually come right out and said I was gay, and I don't know what it was—the culmination of all the drama, the fear, the hiding—but I just couldn't pretend anymore. I knew it was national television and there would be consequences, but after all that had happened with Timothy and Jed, I'd realized the truth would come out one way or another. The press wouldn't stop until they had proof. If not Jed's photo, then something else. Better it come from my mouth.

"Good, then can I bring my boyfriend to your house for dinner?"

Kia gasped. Oprah stayed completely poised.

"Only if you sing to my niece."

We laughed and I almost choked. The audience roared. Autumn was beaming and Kia was now smiling, too. Oprah signaled for another break.

Kia whispered, "Good for you."

Autumn held my hand.

Oprah said, "Are you comfortable going ahead with this?"

"More comfortable than faking she's my girlfriend. No offense, Kia."

"None taken."

Oprah gave the stage manager a nod, and once again he counted down.

"So, we're back with Jackson Poole and his, unfolding, shall we say. I must ask, how has it affected you to have to stay in the closet this long?"

"Well, it hasn't been fun, let's put it that way. I had a paparazzo follow me halfway across the world just to get a picture of me, get this, kissing my brother!"

I looked for Derek in the wings but couldn't find him. I wondered if he was freaking.

"Well, they are vicious," she said." Believe me, I've had my share. How else do you think being in the closet impacted you?"

"Well, I found that all of a sudden I was extremely susceptible to people in my life who had a grudge, and a relationship I had started failed because of the pressure."

"Well, hopefully that will all be behind you."

"I hope so, too. Honestly, I think music is a universal language that doesn't pertain to whom I'm sleeping with."

"I think we can all agree that your music speaks for itself."

More applause, and the goddess of daytime gave me a kiss on the cheek.

Then Oprah turned and asked Autumn directly, "I am curious, does it bother you that your ex-lover turned out to be gay?"

Autumn contemplated the question and said, "Why would it? He was a great friend, a great lover, and I wish him well. It's not like my femininity is dependent on his sexuality. I do just fine!"

The crowd clapped and several people cheered.

After another break, a teenaged girl from the audience stood by the aisle next to Oprah and said, "I love you, Jackson. I don't care that you're gay! Gay guys rock!"

I hoped that Peter Montgomery was watching, so he could see that the exact demographic he was so worried about was now praising my gayness!

Oprah had me sing one more song to finish, then gave away iPods to the audience with my CD already downloaded on them.

After the taping I plopped on the couch in the green room, still reeling from what I'd done.

"Good job," I heard a woman say in a Latin accent. It was Ermolinda.

"Oh, hi, I didn't know you were here!"

I introduced everyone to each other, then pulled Derek aside. "Was that career suicide?"

Derek was surprisingly calm.

"It's actually not something I would have advised, but hey, with Oprah's approval you could be fine. Maybe we'll get her to start a CD club!"

I turned to everyone and asked, "Can we get out of here?"

This soap opera was leaving.

We went to a café.

Kia and Ermolinda trotted off to make documentaries and live in bliss. Me, I was headed back west to let it all settle in. I didn't know if I still had a career as a rock star, but as Derek said, at least I knew I would keep making music no matter what happened next.

# 74

Oprah's private jet took us back to LA the next day, and after eating cheeseburgers on the way home from the airport, Derek and I went to Clean Slate. Neil had scheduled the inevitable call with Universal.

"What's the worst that could happen," Derek said. "You're still a nominated artist. You're still going to the Grammy's. You'll make history!"

I couldn't believe Derek's attitude toward life after everything he'd been through with Aden, me, and Universal. I felt stronger just being around him.

Neil put Peter Montgomery on speakerphone. He was fuming.

"Jesus H. Christ. How could you betray me like that?"

Derek put his hands to his face, and Neil looked like it was made of stone.

"Well, I thought—"

"Well, you thought wrong. It's only because we've already invested so much that I'm not yanking back funding for your U.S. tour. Do you know how much money we're set to lose on tour support alone? I took a chance on you because we all saw your raw talent, but there are plenty of other artists out there who not only have talent but also the good sense not to shit on my highly expensive marketing efforts. I do not appreciate having my time and energy wasted! This isn't about your sexuality, it's about honoring what's right in our business relationship."

He was so passionate and convinced, and on some level I knew he was right. We'd all lied, knowing that if we'd told the truth, I'd never have gotten the contract. We'd tricked him. We were gambling that nothing would come out about my sexuality, but that gamble was with his company's money, not ours. And why should he spend all that money on me, if he could find someone else who

337

was not only talented but also happened to fit their generic little mold?

But I also knew he was wrong. It was about my sexuality.

"I respect the faith you've put in my music and in me, Mr. Montgomery, and I hope I can continue to demonstrate that I deserve it. I agree that my sexuality has nothing to do with my music, but I found out about another picture of me they were going to print. I thought it would better to release the information with some control, rather than let the tabloids ruin it with their bullshit."

"Oh, perfect."

"Listen, I don't consider myself a gay musician, just a musician who happens to be gay. I never would have intentionally hurt your business because I want to be successful, too. And that's why I've hidden who I am from the press and gone along with stupid deceptions to make people think I'm hetero. Not because I want to be a liar but because I believe that what I have to offer is valuable. If it wasn't, nobody would be buying my record, whether I was straight or gay."

Neil gave me a thumbs-up and Derek seemed convinced. Not Peter.

"I don't give a goddamn about whether you're gay or straight; I care about the bottom line. And the bottom line is, I've got artists breaking down my door every day for just a whiff of what this company has done for you. If you honestly think your record would have sold without the thousands and thousands of my company's dollars making all those teenage girls want it, you're not only a liar, you're a fool."

Derek suddenly got fired up and started pacing, holding a hand up to me.

"Let me tell you something, Mr. Montgomery," he said. "You may be the VP of a major label, but I've been in this industry a lot longer than you, and I can tell you this: The greats don't fit the mold, they break it. Jimi Hendrix has been dead for how many years? And your company is *still* making money off him. If you don't know enough to get out of the way and let talent make you money, the state of your bottom line is your own damn fault."

I could feel Peter's anger through the phone.

"I will not be talked to this way."

"Then you shouldn't have talked to Jackson that way. I don't mean to be offensive. Frankly, I'm a little surprised we're even having this conversation because I checked Jackson's numbers this morning and they've done nothing but climb since he was first signed. If what you care about is the money, I would assume you'd know that, too."

"Derek, you and I both know the gay thing changes it. Revenue could fall."

"Only if you don't support him. Who can say how an out artist would do with company backing if no company ever takes the chance."

I had never seen Derek take charge like this. It was sexy.

"Don't make this into some damn gay-rights issue. I'm just watching the bottom line."

"But now it is about him being gay, and everyone in this room knows it. So let's not pretend this isn't about homophobia. I'm not saying you made the rules or blaming you for them. This country is still full of bigots and we're all just here trying to do business in spite of that fact. I understand where you're coming from. But I simply don't believe Jackson's sexuality is relevant to his record sales. Because when I look at Elton John and k.d. lang and Melissa Etheridge, I don't see any one of those artists letting down their label because of who they choose to fuck. I see musicians kicking ass, inspiring people, and making lots of money for people like you.

"So please accept my personal apology," he continued in a calmer voice, "as well as the apology of Clean Slate Management for the omissions on our side of the table. What I suggest we do right now is get out of the way and let Jackson get back to doing what he does best: making music."

There was dead silence on the phone. My mouth was open. Neil was staring at the phone. Finally, Peter spoke.

"Okay, kid. Let's focus on the music."

Neil's sigh of relief was audible across the room.

There was one catch.

"But I will have you note, gentlemen, if our market research indicates a loss of interest or your sales start to fall, we pull the plug."

"That's all I've ever wanted, Mr. Montgomery," I said, "the same chance every other musician dreams of."

# 75

Neil threw me a coming-out dinner celebration at his house with a crowd of guests. I told the rapt audience about my on-air epiphany. Everyone was proud. I did clarify one thing.

"This doesn't mean I'm going to walk around with a rainbow flag tattooed to my forehead."

We toasted.

Neil made his famous turkey meatloaf and Jess showed us her Irish dancing moves.

Toward the end of the night I ended up on the porch with Derek. Though I had looked at the glittering city lights on eastern Sunset Boulevard many times, they breathed a new radiance— their gentle glow seemed to reassure.

"You know, I think you should just stay with me for a while." Derek said.

"I'd like that," I said.

He went to go inside and I stopped him.

"I'm really, really glad I know you, Derek."

Over the next few days we were all thrilled to discover that my public "outing" was having the reverse effect from what was expected: My record sales tripled. Apparently, the truth talked. Or rather, the music talked, which was how it was supposed to be. And of course, Oprah might have had a little something to do with it, too. I got a handwritten note from her in the mail shortly after the taping thanking me for one of her "most unexpected shows ever" and wishing me good luck.

On top of the burgeoning record sales, I now had several gay fan clubs. One high school even made ribbons that said JP on them. I was touched.

Derek came into the guest room one morning with a box of

letters for me.

"I asked the intern who does your mail to put some of these aside for you. You've really helped a lot of people, Jackson. I'm so proud of you."

I sat and read the letters, including horror stories about gay kids getting disowned from their parents, telling me I was their ray of hope. It was heavy. I felt as if my life had yet again begun and ended. Now I was not only a singer but also a role model? Was I going to pull all this off?

Universal put up all over LA new billboards of me, carrying a pink fuzzy guitar with a caption reading "the future of rock... Jackson Poole."

"How did they get that picture?" I asked Neil.

"It's the shot of you with the old guitar, they just photoshopped the pink one in."

"A slight change of heart, huh?"

"Hey, none of us are complaining. You're a phenomenon. Two words. Who knew? By the way, Bree Diamond needs to meet with you tomorrow about doing some more talk shows. Her phones are off the hook."

"Maybe I should do, like, a gay rock opera."

"Easy killer, one step at a time."

# 76

Kane called me the next day with an address for Isabelle King, Jess's birth mother. It turned out she was right there in Encino, twenty minutes away. How does one migrate from the southern suburbs of London to Encino? I guess we were about to find out. I was so excited for Jess to meet her.

"Listen, I pulled some strings with a friend in the LAPD, so don't tell her how you found her, okay?"

"Kane, you're the best!"

"You won't be thinking that when you see my bill."

"I'll even tip you."

"Good luck with the reunion," she said.

"Thanks."

I called Damian Blue on the sly to ask if I could steal Jess out of the studio. He said they would start on drums and could spare her for the rest of the day.

"Where are we going?" Jess said, idly fingering her beautiful curls as we pulled away from the studio.

"To meet your maker," I said.

She obviously didn't take me literally. She didn't respond. The wind danced through her ringlets as she hummed a soft, pretty melody. I decided not to tell her until we were almost there so she'd have less time to develop nerves.

It turned out that the address was for a ratty house at the end of a cul-de-sac. There was a rusty bicycle in a bush in the yard next door, and bits of trash were scattered on the dry, undernourished lawn. I parked the car a couple of houses down and tried to find the right way to ease Jess into the situation.

"Jess, do you know where we are?"

"No, but it's not Bel Air."

I laughed then said, "We've come to find your mother."

Her angelic face turned pale white within a millisecond. "Bloody hell," she said, putting her fingers over her mouth. "You found her? She's here?"

"Yes."

"Oh my lord."

"It's okay, just be yourself. You wanted this, right? Listen, we can leave anytime you want."

"No, I want to see her! God, what if she doesn't want to see me?"

In the silence that followed I thought about the things we wish for and if they're always what they seem. Like me wishing to get a record deal and to find a true love and have kids—being naive, not realizing the implications, the stipulations, the anguish, and despair. But I had come out all right so far, and somehow I knew Jess would as well.

"I have to do it," she said.

We tiptoed toward the house, which looked like a movie set that had been "dressed down" by a meticulous set decorator.

We heard music coming from inside. Jess waited a minute, then knocked.

When the door opened you could tell it was Jess's mom, her beauty shined through what looked like years of hardship. She had the same soft blue eyes as her daughter.

She stared at us blankly until Jess said, "Mom, it's me. Jessica."

The woman didn't hesitate, simply took Jess into a tight embrace and closed her eyes. It was as if she had been waiting for this moment for all the years of her absence. Then she took a look at Jess, who was overwrought with tears, and said, "You're a woman!"

"Well, physically, almost. But I've been a woman mentally for a long time. I grew up fast."

I heard Jess's song, "Tingle" coming from the radio inside.

Isabelle pointed to me and said, "Who's this chap?" Her English accent had morphed into a Brit-Cali mixture.

"This is Jackson Poole," Jess said proudly.

"It's a pleasure," I said. "I'm going to leave you two alone for a while, but before I do, I'd like to mention that that's your daughter's voice coming out of that radio." I pointed to the cheap transistor radio with an empty beer bottle on top of it on her counter. Jess's voice was starting into the chorus.

> *You make me tingle*
> *You make me spark*
> *All the way down*
> *To the bottom of my heart.*

Isabelle was stunned and thought I was joking at first. Then she stared at the radio like it was a strange beast. She picked it up and slowly pressed it against her heart, and smiled at Jess. "That's my girl!"

I walked out to the car and phoned Neil.

"How'd it go?" he asked.

"They're sitting on the porch having a heart to heart right now. I feel like I'm back on *Oprah,* but it's for real. You should have seen the look on her mother's face when I told her it was her daughter's voice coming from the little radio in her house."

"My god."

"I know."

"I don't think you're *on Oprah,* I think you *are* Oprah."

"Well, I wouldn't mind her house in Telluride!"

"Well, good news on two issues, first on the Aden front."

"Yeah?"

"Apparently he's moved to Copenhagen."

"Well, I would have preferred the Far East, but that will do."

"Derek's so happy he got the dog back today."

"Oh that's so great!"

"And the other news is that you made it on all the big shows—*Letterman,* MTV, tons."

"Oh my god! That's awesome!"

Jess came back to the car an hour later with Isabelle, who

thanked me profusely and said she hoped she would meet me again another time.

On the ride home, Jess was on fire, talking a mile a minute.

"She's like so, what do you call it, white trash? Apparently she came here to marry some big producer, who turned out, get this, gay! I'm going to get her a room at Damian's studio; she has to get out of that catastrophe of a house. Isn't it funny how the roles get reversed? I'm going to take care of *her* now."

"Well, let's not get ahead of ourselves. You can help her out, but remember Jess, she's a grown woman."

"It's weird, Jackson, but I had so much pent-up rage, so much anger, and now it's all lifted. It's like the sight of her washed it all away. She's my flesh and blood. She sang for me, Jackson, a song she used to sing to me as a child. She said she'd sing it a lot when thinking of me, hoping wherever I was, I'd hear it. Her voice is still as beautiful as ever."

I started to well up, and when I looked over, I saw that Jess had tears in her eyes, too.

I drove her back to my house, where she and Liam had taken up residency while I stayed at Derek's. When I pulled into the driveway, Jess said she was going to go for a walk, to take it all in. I drove to Derek's and told him about Isabelle and her rundown house and everything. He looked at me admiringly.

"How sweet of you to do that for both of them. Do you realize what a great thing you've just done?"

I kissed him on the cheek. "Thanks. I just feel so protective of her. I don't know, maybe it's a sign I'm finally ready to have a kid."

"I think you'd be a great father." He looked a bit sad. "I always thought I would have kids by now, but whenever I'd bring up having a family, Aden would act like I was crazy." Derek ran a hand through his hair. "It's strange, but I still miss him."

It had been a lifetime that they had been together. What was I going to say?

"Of course you miss him. He was...he meant well. Just a different personality type."

"Well, Jackson, it looks like stardom has brought out some diplomacy in you."

I smiled.

"Anyway, I think if you want kids, you should have them," he said. "There's never an ideal time to do it, so don't wait for someone else to make it happen for you."

"Well, it's not too late for you either, you know, you can still have a kid."

"Come here," he said.

He grabbed two pillows and led me outside by the pool, where we laid down and stared at the pinpoints of satellites above the Hollywood hills. My body felt hyper-aware, especially in the places where it was touching his: my forearm, the side of my thigh. I wanted to jump on top of him, but since the Aden breakup was still so fresh, I decided to prolong the mystery. I knew I couldn't last long.

After we came in from looking at the sky Derek ordered in from Mel's Drive-In and we watched *The Ring*. Derek was genuinely scared, grabbing my arm and looking away from the TV.

"Don't worry, I'll protect you. It's just a movie."

He squeezed closer. I felt an erection forming and became embarrassed. Could he tell?

After the movie, we kissed long and slowly. He slept in the guest room with me. At three in the morning I said, "Derek, are you awake?"

"No, I'm sleeping."

He was right to be sassy. That was always a weird question to ask.

"Do you mind if I get on top of you right now?"

"That would be fine."

I could see his eyes in the moonlight, which eased through a crack in the blinds. He was so handsome, so sexy, but not in an obvious, Timothy Meyer way. No, his was a beauty that shined from within. I kissed him again and cupped his face in my hands.

I traveled with my lips from his cheek to his ear, then to his neck and to the flat part of his collarbone. When my mouth engulfed his penis, he let out a little yelp.

"You okay?"

"Oh, just dandy."

I continued until his yelps turned to moans, then an audible sigh. He came rather quickly.

"I'm sorry," he said.

I used a line of Neil's.

"It's okay, baby, tonight was on your time."

It felt wonderful to give him pleasure, something long overdue. He fell asleep within minutes, and I smiled at the ceiling for a while before closing my own eyes.

# 77

In the morning Derek woke me up by returning the favor. It was extraordinarily blissful, and afterward we held each other for a long time. Derek was a keeper.

When we finally got out of bed, he made me breakfast and we worked some more on the movie song, polishing it up a bit. Although it was strange to be in what was essentially Derek and Aden's space, the weirdness was dissipated by the ease we had around each other. Even the dog Blake was getting more used to me.

We were off to New York in a couple of days for the TV spots.

"I've arranged for you to look at some places to buy," Derek said, as if asking to pass the butter.

"Really?" I said.

"You said it was your dream. I've got an agent to show us a couple of lofts in Soho and a brownstone in the West Village. Maybe I'll see something I like, too."

He'd remembered. I touched the tip of his nose.

"I think that's a stunning idea."

I decided to go home and gather some of my things, and stopped to buy some magazines on the way—*Dwell, Real Simple.* On the front page of *Star* I saw what must have been the picture Jed had tried to sell to Timothy. It was me and my first long-term boyfriend, Thomas. I was too embarrassed to look at it in the store, adding it to the bottom of my little stack of magazines. It was a first, buying a magazine that I was on the cover of. The clerk gave me a smile and flipped it to the top.

"You look hot, Jackson," he said, and threw in a *New York Times* for free.

"Hey, thanks."

It *was* quite a flattering picture—Thomas and me on a nude

beach in Mexico, his lips on my ear. You could see my tanned abs and the beginning of Thomas's cute butt.

When I got home, I went right to my photo album and sure enough, there was an empty space where the picture had been. I remembered Jed looking through the album the day we were going through my wardrobe. He had been conniving way back then? What a sad little creature. I really had to get out of this town.

The ironic thing was, Jed would have made more if he hadn't tried to extort more money from the *Enquirer*. After *Oprah*, who cared about the smoking gun? Ha. I was sure Jed would get herpes, or at least get his foot caught in the blades of an angry lawnmower.

I played my home messages. One was from Max.

"Dude, you can't kiss me in public again. At least wait until we're in our pajamas."

I laughed.

The next message was from Bree.

"My dear boy, we are defying convention! I love, love, love the picture of you and that gorgeous man, and such loving energy between you!"

On the plane to New York for the talk shows, Derek read the comics and I napped. A stewardess asked for my autograph as we were leaving the plane.

"It's for my son," she said, slightly embarrassed. "He's gay, too."

"Well, in that case I'll include my phone number."

Both she and Derek smiled.

Derek and I were staying in a room together at the Royalton, and that night I listened to his breathing and was comforted by the sound. Small, short breaths against my arms. He really was an adorable man. And I knew my mother would love him.

The talk shows went really well, and I ended up having very responsive studio audiences. I was nervous as hell performing on Letterman. This was the king of late night!

Dave did a segment in my honor on the Top Ten Stories Made Up by the Tabloid Press:

10) Meg Ryan is a postoperative transsexual
9) JFK Jr. is alive and well, and leading the first space colony on Mars
8) Connie Chung is a lesbian
7) Jessica Simpson is a NASA rocket scientist
6) Britney Spears is really fifty years old
5) Aliens came and stole the recipe for Pop-Tarts
4) Michael Jackson is black
3) Liam Neeson was breastfed until he was eighteen
2) Bea Arthur is a sex addict
1) Jackson Poole has a crush on his brother

He asked me about my rumored relationship with Jess, who he referred to as "the English Britney."

I explained that I thought the world of her and her talent, and was planning to tour again with her. "She's a great friend."

"No romance there?"

"Right now I'm just going to stick with my brother."

The audience laughed.

"Well, your sexual orientation has been the subject of a lot of attention in the tabloid press. Is it safe to say that Jackson Poole is still gay and still single?" he asked.

"Well, I'm not too sure about the single part."

The audience ooh-ed. I noticed Derek in the wings breaking into a smile.

After the show Derek and I went to a diner on Ninth Avenue.

We ate in comfortable silence, until I asked, "Derek, what are we doing?"

"What do you mean?"

"I mean, you and me."

"Whatever it is," he said, blowing at his coffee, "lets do it slowly."

"Agreed," I said.

I was getting on a red-eye back to LA to rehearse the following day. He was staying in NYC for some meetings, and I wouldn't see him before I went on my U.S. tour.

We left the diner and sat outside a bakery, basking in the smell of fresh loaves.

"Hmm," I said. "I think bread is the new lettuce."

"You know what would make someone rich? Bread without carbs."

"Impossible."

"Like us?" he asked.

"I'd say we're highly probable," I said.

A group of laughing girls ran by us, the bread smell infused with their perfume.

When it was time for me to leave New York, he grabbed my shoulders in the lobby of the hotel.

"Always pay attention to the staff at the hotels. Learn a name, pad a tip—you'll need them the next time around. Tell Rico to cut down on the ride cymbal, it's too jazzy. Keep yourself hydrated and work the crowd. See them. You are them. The force is with you. And if you find it in that wonderful, open heart of yours, sing a few for me."

"That shouldn't be too hard."

My cab driver honked.

"Oh! Don't forget all the new disguises, and avoid the front of the venues like the plague. And you might need this."

The bellboy handed him a Super Soaker just like the one he had used to save me from the fans at the junket in LA. He slipped it into the cab.

"I'm serious, they'll maul you!"

I kissed him and got in.

I could hear him through the window as we pulled away.

"Christ, I've hardly gotten to maul you yet!"

# 78

The next few months were a blur of publicity and shows all across the U.S., which I convinced Universal to let Jess open. Neil was tour managing and continued to be hot and heavy with Liam. One night in San Francisco, Jess flew her mother up to the show and they had a little family reunion backstage. Neil was a little freaked out, but Isabelle seemed to roll with it nicely. Jess had helped her find a new apartment and treated her to a complete makeover, including a new wardrobe and a haircut by one of the top stylists in Hollywood. She looked stunning, a far cry from the day we went to visit her in Encino.

Aden, of all people, happened to be visiting his family in SF and came to that show as well. He was sober and looking great—we even joked around.

"Do you like my bracelet?" I asked him.

"Perfect," he said.

Even though I was still pissed at him over the whole Derek thing, it felt right to be on speaking terms—we had been through a lot together, and it seemed the adult thing to do.

Leroy and Rico continued to bumble around chasing girls and playing every note perfectly, hungover or not.

The most important thing:

*I wasn't straight, I wasn't twenty-eight, and my hair was so Jackson Poole...*

I wasn't playing the field like my frivolous band mates—my mind was on Derek. I missed him a lot. We talked and emailed everyday, and his career was looking up—writing with all these different big names for green-lit projects—so he was in great spirits. I learned how to be more anonymous and didn't have to use the Super Soaker once. The tour bus and the hotels were plush, and everything went pretty smooth, aside from having to run offstage every five minutes in Detroit due to a bad Mexican meal.

When the tour ended, I stayed with Derek in New York at his new place. I felt thrilled to be there in that dense mecca overflowing with culture, yet also humbled. Everyone is someone in New York. Even though the press built up before the Grammy's and I was even more in the public eye, people were more respectful in New York. The screaming blondes of Southern Cal were replaced by professionals and arty kids raising an eyebrow or saying, "hey." It was pleasantly rewarding.

Derek took me to the restaurant BED for my birthday, where we were served fine food while sitting in bed. Someone shot us making out, but we didn't care. We toasted to us.

"Are we in the medium stage now?" I asked.

"It's safe to say we've moved beyond 'slowly'. Check, please!"

# 79

I was allowed a small handful of guests to the Grammy's, but only one to walk the red carpet with, so I chose my dad. I wore the most kick-ass Yves St. Laurent suit, and Dad wore a slick tux with a bright red rose on his lapel.

We rode in the limo, and I was so proud to share it with him.

"Dad, let me see your teeth."

He showed me.

"Check. Now, you'll feel like you're inside a light bulb. Stay mellow. I'll kill you if you have another heart attack."

We had to wait until U2 was through, then they signaled us to come out. I knew it was simply one moment in time, but it was a thrilling one, and I kept whispering to my dad, "This is it."

Inside, I was sitting right in front of Sting, and he gave me a cookie out of a bag he'd smuggled in. Apparently stars always snuck food into awards shows because they were so long.

Mom and Max were freaking out, and Rose was tolerating their antics with a smile. Dad kept chatting everyone up, including Sting's wife after Derek introduced them. Neil, Jess, and Liam were watching the show on TV at Derek's new place, and I wished they could have been there, too. They were going to meet us at the after-party later.

When my nomination was called I said to myself: *No matter what happens, I will always make the music I love. It's amazing just to have come this far.*

"And the winner is..."

My mom grabbed my thigh and squeezed hard.

"Jackson Poole!"

My whole career flashed through my mind, and the cheers of the crowd seemed muffled. I hugged Mom, Max, Dad, and Rose, and at the end of the aisle I grabbed Derek and planted one on him. It had been a long road, but there I was, walking up to accept the award for Best New Artist, with millions of viewers watching. I prayed that I wouldn't trip and reminded myself to keep breathing.

I was just a tiny bit nervous.

It was like giving birth—no matter how hard you prepare or go over it in your head, you can't know how it feels. Onstage, I noticed my lips were numb, and Gwyneth Paltrow's face became a strange blur when she handed me the award, as did the whole crowd. God knows how, but I pulled it off.

"Wow. It is truly incredible to be recognized in this way, and to be included in this category with such amazing artists...Hi Mom!"

I jumped up and down a little.

"How is my hair?"

I pulled out my cheat sheet.

"There are so many people that have been the architecture upon which my career was built. My wonderful family: Mom; Dad; my brother, Max, and little Tristan; my sister, Rose, and her family. Dad, I'm so glad you are here tonight. My friends, who bring me more happiness than any award...Neil, Jess, Liam, Brian...

"My amazing band: Leroy and Rico...My inspiring producer, Damian Blue...and Clean Slate Management: Derek, Aden, and Neil, I couldn't have done it without all your hard work!"

I started to get choked up.

*You're almost done,* I told myself.

I held up the Grammy.

"This is for all those people out there who have courage in the face of adversity, for all those people who have the strength to be themselves, no matter how unconventional, no matter how mainstream. If there is one thing I've learned, it's that music speaks for itself.

"And my wonderful, wonderful fans, I couldn't have done it

without you!"

A spreading roar of applause.

On the screen at that moment they showed a picture of my family in the audience, and I was so grateful seeing my dad among them, looking handsome and proud. I was so exultant that my face started to cramp from excessive smiling.

I got offstage and was taken to a small waiting room. It seemed like I was sitting down with the Grammy in my lap for only a few euphoric minutes when a stagehand told me it was time to follow him back for my performance. I was in a daze. The roar of the crowd, now for someone else, seemed distant. I clutched the Grammy as he led me to the stage. He left me in the wings, where I stared out at all the faces, many of whom were legends I had admired my whole life.

"Jackson? Are you ready?"

Without thinking, I set the Grammy down by the curtain, and walked onstage. The next thing I knew, I was doing what I loved best, caressing the microphone with my voice, singing to the back of the theater, the chandeliers, the well-dressed audience.

Even better than getting the award was seeing Jack Nicholson dancing in his seat and next to him, Annie Lennox closing her eyes and smiling.

Toward the end of the song, I scanned the rows for Derek, and for a fleeting instant, there was no one in that theater except for us.

It was once again the beginning and the ending of it all, and I knew that tomorrow life would go on.

I wouldn't be in the spotlight forever.

But it was a warm place, with a good view.

# ABOUT THE AUTHOR

Stewart Lewis is a singer songwriter who lives in New York City. His music has been featured on ABC, CBS, and MTV. *Rockstarlet* is his first novel. For more information, visit www.stewartlewis.com.